ADVANCE PRAISE FOR
THE AMERICAN

"This bracing supernatural tale easily pulls readers into its dark, disturbing mystery." —*Publishers Weekly*

"*The American* rivals Ellis and Barker in terms of sheer darkness. Thomas combines horror and thriller to merciless effect." —Laird Barron, author of *Swift to Chase*

"With his unerring eye for the disturbing and horrific, Thomas sinks us into a Vietnam few have ever seen. A haunting page-turner about the power of friendship, debts owed, and the countless wounds of war. A brutal, riveting read." —Erica Ferencik, bestselling author of *The River at Night* and *Into the Jungle*

"Peter Straub's *Koko* meets Takashi Miike's *Ichi the Killer* in this relentless plunge into darkness from Bram Stoker Award® finalist Jeffrey Thomas. Refreshingly ordinary, fallible heroes, wounded physically and spiritually, work to solve a heartbreaking mystery rooted deep in the harrowing and gruesome underworld of human trafficking. Aided by a skin-crawling manifestation of the supernatural, their efforts lead them toward a figure chillingly banal in his unrepentant cruelty, and a bittersweet ending you'll never see coming." —Mike Allen, World Fantasy Award-nominated author of *Unseaming* and *Aftermath of an Industrial Accident*

"*The American* is a deep, dark plunge into transglobal post-colonial Late Capitalism paranoia, juxtaposing moral horror with its supernatural effects in ways that crack the reader's third eye open – gradually, terribly, implacably. It's a ghost story about history, layers folding over layers of willing, knowing self-pollution, desire melding into hunger melding into horror; the slime we leave behind ourselves as we slug-trail around this awful world, finding the places where we can debase ourselves until we disappear. I started reading and couldn't stop, no matter how much I wanted to." —Gemma Files, author of *Experimental Film*

"An exquisitely-written, compulsively-readable dark thriller steeped in Vietnamese culture with eerie supernatural overtones. The characters – villains with a touch of humanity, heroes with more than a hint of darkness – are haunted by ghosts of the past, both literal and metaphorical. This is one of the best books I've read in years, and you'd be a fool to miss it." —Tim Waggoner, Bram Stoker Award®-winning author

THE
AMERICAN

JEFFREY
THOMAS

JOURNALSTONE
YOUR LINK TO ARTIST TALENT

ISBN: 978-1-950305-41-4 (sc)
ISBN: 978-1-950305-43-8 (ebook)
Library of Congress Control Number: 2020937689

First printing edition: October 30, 2020
Published by JournalStone Publishing in the United States of America.
Cover Design and Layout: Don Noble
Edited by Sean Leonard
Proofreading and Interior Layout by Scarlett R. Algee

JournalStone Publishing
3205 Sassafras Trail
Carbondale, Illinois 62901

JournalStone books may be ordered through booksellers or by contacting:
JournalStone | www.journalstone.com

THE
AMERICAN

PART 1: MONSTERS

1: LUCKY (INDONESIA, 2010)

"SELAMAT PAGI!" THE LOVELY YOUNG woman greeted the American, showing him a wide white grin that looked fully sincere. But secretly, did she fear him? The young woman, named Dewi, was accompanied by a surly-looking but silent young man who would be their driver. The American was not afraid to entrust himself to their company, even though they would be venturing into a remote area close to the jungle. Owning a gun was illegal in Indonesia, and yet an associate who had met him at the airport had slipped him a P2 9mm military sidearm made by the local company Pindad, which he would carry throughout his stay.

The American's respectably successful legitimate business was importing decorative items from such Asian countries as Nepal and Thailand. Indonesian folk art, usually from Bali, was always popular. There were figures made from ebony, and smooth abstract depictions of lovers carved from suar wood. Elongated wooden tribal masks, intricately painted with dots via the use of syringes. Ornately carved, gorgeously colored winged masks of the mythical, bird-like Garuda. Mystical creatures like mermaids, unicorns, and dragons, hanging from strings like mobiles, which were sold as "cradle guardians" to protect children from nightmares and malignant spirits.

But it was a different kind of business that had taken the American today to Palangkaraya, in the Central Kalimantan section of Indonesia. A summons from a sometimes business partner. Over the phone, this business partner had pleaded in a whining, pathetic sort of tone that he supposed she thought would wring some manly protectiveness or gallantry from him. Instead it had only irritated him, and yet he had said he would come. It was the call of money that he answered, however. After all, he was a man of business.

The American himself was originally from Vietnam, but he had been raised in the United States since arriving as one of the "boat people" at the age of ten.

Fortunately, his business partner spoke English. Her name was Sinta, which she'd told him meant "chastity." He found this quite amusing. He called her Sin.

Sinta ran a brothel, and so it was that Dewi—being one of her workers—met the American and escorted him back to Sinta's place of business. Dewi also spoke English, was charming and as striking as a model. Sinta's pleading tone might be wasted on him, but she was wise to utilize Dewi. Previously, Sinta had saved herself a lot of the American's usual fee by gifting him temporarily with this star pupil. The girl had always retained her poise and bright smile, no matter how he had used her. Dewi's name meant "goddess," and he thought this was much more apt.

Along the ride, sitting close beside him in the backseat of the car, Dewi patted his thigh and said sweetly, "It's so good to see you again, sir." He could almost believe her, though he knew any hooker's smile wasn't worth more than the bauble on the head of an angler fish. Still, it was possible she might feel attracted to him. At forty-two, he appeared young and healthy, had smooth, agreeable features, his black hair neatly cut and spiky with gel, his customary white linen suit perfectly tailored. And most attractive of all, he was a US citizen.

But she called him "sir," because she had never been told his name.

He said nothing in return, only watched the passing countryside as it grew more lushly green, but he allowed her to slide her hand along his leg, squeezing it rhythmically. "You must be tired from your long flight. Perhaps I can give you a massage tonight, sir?"

"Perhaps," he grunted.

Sinta's compound of buildings, with their rusty metal roofs, was a step up from the deep jungle brothels consisting of thatched huts and tents in which prostitutes serviced the loggers who illegally harvested palm fruit for the making of palm oil—but as in those more humble establishments, her workers still primarily ranged from thirteen to seventeen years old. At nineteen, Dewi was a longtime veteran, and the American was surprised she had retained her looks. He'd once had a whore in Vietnam, also nineteen and with a pretty face, who had undressed to reveal withered breasts and a soft belly scored with stretch marks. At eleven years old she'd been sold by her family to a Japanese businessman working in Vietnam, but he'd recently kicked her out on the street. The American had kicked her out, too, in disgust, shoving her out of his hotel room before she'd finished dressing and throwing some Vietnamese *dong* featuring Ho Chi Minh's smiling face at her sobbing back.

He supposed he thought of the Vietnamese *con di* now because he'd be returning to that country to pursue some other business matters, both legitimate and otherwise, as soon as he was done in Indonesia.

Sinta came outside to greet them as soon as their vehicle had come to a stop, holding her arms open as if to embrace him and grinning (her grin less white and less convincing than Dewi's). He waved her back before she could touch him. "I'm dying of thirst, Sin," he told her.

"Come to my office!" she said in her accomplished English, waving an arm in that direction.

The American followed her, for the moment forgetting about Dewi, though he knew she'd be part of the bargain. Soon he sat opposite Sinta, positioned behind her desk like some proud corporate executive, while a girl who looked like she hadn't yet shed her first blood brought a few cold bottles of *Bitang* beer on a tray. As the American watched her leave the room, Sinta said, "You can have her if you want. I've saved her for you! You would be her first."

He looked back at the madam. "Perhaps." He cracked open a beer and took several long unbroken swallows. Setting the bottle down at last, he asked, "Where is this Australian woman now?"

"She's most often at that place of hers, the refuge for the animals, but she threatened us that soon she will be making a documentary to call attention to the plight of her precious pets. She said she would bring her camera crew back here to shoot Lucky, so we think she might be going to Australia soon to arrange her film."

"You were able to stop her from taking Lucky before?"

"Yes, she came here with a few forestry officers, but my boys chased them off with machetes coated in poison." Sinta smiled unpleasantly. "And, of course, we have an understanding with the local police, but she threatens to bring military police, many of them, and force us to give Lucky to her."

The American snorted a cynical laugh. "You clearly have girls working for you who haven't reached puberty, but she's concerned about a pet monkey. What is it with these Jane Goodall- and Diane Fossey-types?"

"My concern is if she brings too much attention here, people will see more than Lucky—they'll be looking at my girls next, and then the police won't be able to turn the other way anymore. This country is going to sharia law—at best I'll go broke, and at worst they'll cut my head off!"

"Sharia law. When they start making monkeys wear headscarves and stoning them for adultery, then your Australian friend will really be in an uproar."

Sinta chuckled. "When she tried to take Lucky, I screamed"—and here she imitated tearful wails—"'You can't take her, you can't...she's like a daughter to me!'"

The American grinned. "Yes, I can see the resemblance."

The madam's laughter died away quickly, her expression darkening, but she knew better than to give in to her anger with this man.

The American sucked down more of his beer, smacked his lips, then said, "Show her to me. I haven't seen your daughter since I brought her here."

"She's grown," Sinta said. "You may not recognize her."

*   *   *

JEFFREY THOMAS

In a waiting room area hot as a sauna, a number of men sat in plastic chairs watching *SpongeBob SquarePants*, so poorly dubbed that he couldn't tell whether it was SpongeBob speaking or his boss, Mr. Krabs. Some of the seated men ignored him, some looked up and met his gaze—not embarrassed at all, but smiling like kids who were about to do something naughty and made no apologies for it. As the American began to follow Sinta into the next room, one of the men, a *Bitang* in hand, blurted something drunkenly in his own language. The American stopped and looked back at him. As if nervous that her guest might become angry, Sinta hurried to explain, "He said you shouldn't cut in line." She smiled and jokingly chastised the man, then resumed guiding the American into the room beyond.

He had smelled the animal even in the waiting room, and its scent in here was as thick as the heat. A young female orangutan lay on its belly on a dirty mattress in a corner of the room, chained by one ankle. The ape's long red hair had been clipped off and completely shaved away but for one tuft on the crown of its head, like a little cap. Its pale body reminded the American of a dog's patchy-colored skin after its belly has been shaved so it can be spayed. It was pimply and mosquito-bitten, red with rashes. And yet, a man in his thirties stripped down to just a sweaty T-shirt was standing behind the animal, and had begun lowering himself to his knees when Sinta brought her guest in. She said something in their native tongue, probably apologizing for interrupting, but the man grinned and made a dismissive gesture, unperturbed. The ape started to rise up a little to look around at the man, and one of Sinta's male employees—ready with a long rod in hand—struck the orangutan across the back of the neck. Giving out a high, mournful cry, the ape went flat on its belly again, but the American saw how she raised up her rear and began to sway and rotate her hips in anticipation.

Not able to contain himself, no matter how it might offend Sinta's customer, the American burst into laughter. "You taught her your own moves, Sin? What a good mother you are. Look at her... My God."

"Listen, she's very popular! Do you think I'd have called you here if I didn't have a lot of money to lose if that bitch takes her?"

"Ahh...but you don't have a lot of money to pay me, now, do you, Sin?"

The madam stroked his arm. "I have expenses, you know that... So many girls to care for. And you are always welcome to any and all of them, anytime you come here on business."

"That's what blows my mind. All the lovely little girls you have here, and your customers want this pitiful thing? What good Muslims you have in this country!"

"I'm not a Muslim," Sinta stated, without any irony. "I'm a Christian. Anyway, these men can have a pretty girl anytime they want—our country is full of them. But this is something different, a special experience. You thought I was crazy when I asked you to get me a 'man of the woods,' but I know my customers—and I had a dream that a monkey was bringing me gold in a cup."

"A Freudian cup, huh?"

"Not only that, but she picks winning lottery tickets for me and my customers. Oh, you laugh, but one time I won a nice sum from a number Lucky picked for me!"

The customer was still grinning, stroking himself hard unabashedly, and listening to them though he couldn't understand them. Sinta continued, "Bambang, here–"

"Wait." The American held up a hand. "This guy's name is Bambang?"

"Yes—it means 'knight.' Bambang is a repeat customer…Lucky has made him a lottery winner more than once! You see those bracelets she's wearing? Bambang brings her one every time he comes here."

"Don't forget to invite me to the wedding. Myself, maybe I'll be swayed when you have Dr. Zira working for you."

"Dr. Zira?"

The American didn't explain. He motioned to the customer. "Go on, sir, please don't let me interrupt your bambanging."

He and Sinta turned back toward the door to the waiting room, the American eager to leave before the primate's stench impregnated the material of his expensive white suit. He heard a funny grunting behind him and looked back, thinking it was the orangutan—but it was the customer, now kneeling behind the ape and holding onto its hips. Surely, orangutans had the saddest faces of the four kinds of great apes?

The worker stood ready with the rod. An adult orangutan had the strength of seven men. Perhaps a wild orangutan might not have tolerated this treatment, and knowing this the American—when he had acquired the ape for Sinta upon her request—had instead purchased a pet orangutan that had grown too large for its owners to keep.

He had to chuckle again and shake his head. He did not feel disgust for these men who came here to commune with nature. He did not judge men for their tastes, however extreme. His own tastes could be quite extreme. But as he had said to Sinta, with all the lovely brown human flesh waiting under the madam's rusty metal roofs, he simply could not relate.

*   *   *

Joyo was the American's contact in Indonesia, who had met him at the airport and given him the 9mm—the American's liaison for his legitimate business dealings, who assisted him in his other projects as well. Small, thin but sinewy, with a scrap of mustache and a disarming smile. The third man drinking beer with the American and Joyo, in a shabby little bar with garlands of crispy snacks hanging on the walls, was much younger than them both: just eighteen, but one of the security guards at ORANG—the Orangutan Rescue And Nurture Group. The handful of guards, the male workers, and the girls who cared for the infant orangutans orphaned by the illegal palm loggers were primarily made up of young people working for meager wages.

It had been easy for Joyo, wearing uncustomary grubby clothes and a baseball cap, to ask around about finding work with the Australian woman, Gwenda Quigley, and her ORANG center. He'd asked in bars such as this one, in the vicinity of the center, what Quigley was paying, if her employees found their compensation adequate. This line of conversation had quickly revealed that one of her workers was badly in debt from gambling and having a rough go of it. All that had remained then was for Joyo to get the young man's name. And here he was now sitting with Joyo and the American, who also wore a baseball cap and the clothes of a simple laborer.

With his lips lubricated sufficiently by his beers, the young man complained to Joyo about his scanty earnings and crushing debt, Joyo then interpreting for the American. "You think I do this for those baby monkeys?" Joyo translated. "I work to suckle myself?"

The American smirked and said, "You see, your boss has all these apes and she's squandering their talents. They could be picking winning lottery tickets and making all of you rich, and living the high life themselves."

Joyo snorted, but didn't bother translating this back for the young guard.

* * *

A high fence topped with barbed wire surrounded the ORANG compound. Though not the largest or best known of the various centers dedicated to rescuing and rehabilitating orangutans, it covered a good-sized area, and there were eight security guards (four to a shift) to watch over it. They took turns, in a daily rotation, manning their various far-spaced posts. This night, the young guard whose gambling debts had just been significantly reduced was assigned to the main gate.

Waiting just inside the open door of a supply shed, looking out at the hot tropical night, the American regretted having to utilize the guard and thus pay him from his own pocket, but it was the nature of business that one had to spend money to make money.

The American realized his heart rate had accelerated. He would not admit to nervousness. He calmed himself by thinking ahead—thinking past this little errand, as if it were all but behind him already—to the various business ventures he would be tending to in Vietnam in just a few days. Just as he would not admit to nervousness, he would not admit to any sentimental attachment to the country of his birth. But it was undeniably a place that resonated with him. He loved the food. He loved the sexy, childish, exasperating women. He loved the smells that composed its atmosphere—not so unlike the atmosphere in Indonesia, but there was certainly nothing like it anywhere he'd been in the United States.

However many orangutans might actually be housed within the enclosure of this complex, they were all presently quiet—at rest—but he could smell their combined zoo scent in the already thick stew of the air. Were any roaming free? The American guessed not, and that was good. The guard had told Joyo that some of the infants actually stayed in Gwenda Quigley's house with her during the night.

But here she came now, walking from the direction of her house, into a patch of light with the security guard beside her. She was tall, striding quickly, and the young man almost had to run to keep up with her. The American considered that she must have been striking in her youth, and she was still attractive now, her graying blond hair secured in a bun behind her head, wearing only a tank top and very short shorts that bared long, tanned legs.

The American became conscious of the sickening flutter of his heart again, and it irritated him. He didn't need to be hampered or distracted right now, least of all by himself. But he was also experiencing relief. He had been wary that, now with half of his money in hand, the guard might reveal loyalty to Quigley and let her know about the American and Joyo—who waited in a car somewhere beyond the front gate. That she and not the police had appeared was a good thing indeed.

Quigley was conversing with the guard in his own language as she approached the shed. Her voice sounded as tense and purposeful as were her movements. Well, of course she would need to be a decisive, determined person to live the life she did. It was a life the American couldn't identify with at all— mystifying, really—but that was of no concern right now. He was weighing her up, estimating her, more than he intended. Another irritating distraction.

Closer now, entering into another thrown pool of light. The American could see the woman's handsome face better, her intense furrowed brow. Inside Quigley's house, the guard would have told her what Joyo had coached him to say: He had heard movement inside the shed, things banging around, and feared it might be a robber. One of the young orangutans, even, free of its cage or what have you. The guard would know what details to add.

She was only a few steps from the open door of the storage shed when the American heard her mutter darkly, in English, "Bloody whacker, leaving the door open. If there was an orang in there it could be anywhere now..."

Quigley stepped through the threshold, the security guard a few steps behind her. Immediately, she jerked her head to the right, spotting the American standing just around the edge of the open door. With his left hand he pushed the door away from him, at the same time swinging the machete in his right hand at the woman's neck.

But she was fast, already lunging toward him with a blurted half-cry, and the blade struck her across the lower jaw instead, laying it open from the lobe of her ear to the corner of her mouth. She threw herself into the American, her crashing momentum pushing him back a few steps, seizing onto his right wrist and forearm with both hands.

Past her head the American saw that the young guard had at least had the sense to close the door the rest of the way to block any noise, and he stood with his back against it, wide-eyed, but Joyo would have been coming to his assistance by now.

The woman's grip on his arm was strong, and she was trying to shout for help with her throat rumbling with blood. In their scuffling dance, she switched one hand from his wrist to his fist and started prying at one of the fingers curled around the machete's handle. She pulled back on the finger, causing such pain that the American grunted, "Fuck!" Before she could break a bone, he dropped the machete but immediately kicked it away from them both.

He regretted now his decision not to wait for the woman to be outside her compound, such as in a public place, and shooting her from a moving motorbike. To date the American had killed eight people in three countries—all men—and not one of them had fought him like this.

She was hunched over his right arm, exposing her back to him, and he drove his left arm's elbow between her shoulder blades, and then again. Their feet shuffled in her blood. A third blow with his elbow, and her grip loosened on his arm. He slung her off him, grabbing hold of her tank top to do so. The bloody garment tore away in his hands, leaving her thudding onto her back bare-breasted, her chest heaving, eyes wild and white in a mask of blood. She was trying to scream but only gargled.

A spade leaned against the wall close at hand. The American grabbed its handle and launched straight into a long swing as if at a speeding baseball. As Quigley tried sitting up, the shovel's blade struck her in the side of the head.

Letting go of the spade's handle, the American staggered back a few paces, away from her legs as their heels dug at the storage shed's floor. Quigley lay on her back, rolling a little from side-to-side but unable to sit up. The shovel's handle followed the motions of her head, because the edge of the blade was buried in her skull, from the side of her head to the center of her forehead. Her scalp had lifted, but this went deeper than simply the flesh; surely the metal rested in her brain. Stubborn as she was, though, the Australian woman was still alive, and in a drunken-sounding voice she cried, "Take it *out*...take it *out!*" Her head lolled this way, then that way, the spade handle like the arm of a metronome.

The American had experienced a momentary pause of fascination, but he came out of it, and glanced over at the guard. The young man was also staring fixedly at the woman, at her bared and blood-smeared breasts and long legs, and was stroking his hard cock through the material of his shorts.

The American stepped closer to the woman again, planted one sandaled foot on her chest as he took hold of the spade's handle, and with all his strength—as if throwing the oar of a Viking long ship—jerked it toward him and then away from him.

The woman's head had broken half open, and she ceased her rolling, her heels no longer digging at the floor. Her eyes remained staring from her mask of blood, however.

Panting, his grubby laborer's clothes spattered with blood, he tossed the shovel aside and turned to face the guard again. The man's eyes had a glassy, drugged look of fear and longing, and the American thought of stories his father had told him, when he'd been drinking, of things he had seen—and done—in Vietnam during the war years.

"If you like that," he said to the guard, as he gestured for him to move aside from the door, "there's an orangutan I can introduce you to."

* * *

With his suitcase open on the bed of his room in Palangkaraya's upscale Aquarius Boutique Hotel, the American got a call from the front desk telling him that a young woman wished to be allowed up to his room. Warily, he asked her name. "She says she is Dewi, sir," came the response. Not much less wary, the American nevertheless gave the okay, but he had a plane to catch today and no time for further dalliance with her.

She hadn't called first, obviously, because she didn't have a number for him, but she knew his hotel room since she had been there with him only two days before.

Admitting her into his room when she knocked, the American noted that he had never seen the lovely prostitute's poise marred before this moment, even in the midst of their most strenuous activities together. But now she appeared out of breath, and anxious.

"You're lucky you caught me," he told her gruffly. "I'll be leaving the country soon. So what's this about?"

"I'm sorry, sir, but something terrible has happened."

"What is it?" he asked again, not without a twinge of dread. Trouble with the authorities over Gwenda Quigley's murder? But how would anyone have traced it back to Sinta? Illegal loggers would be the more logical suspects, and the security guard, even if implicated, did not know his or Joyo's identities or whereabouts.

"It's Lucky, sir," Dewi explained, making a wincing expression. "One of the customers had too many beers while he was waiting his turn, and he was rough with the animal. He...he entered her rectum, and he must have hurt her. She went into a frenzy."

"And?"

"She killed him. And when the man who tends Lucky tried to subdue her with his stick, she got hold of him and killed him, too, sir. Finally two other men wounded her with machetes and dragged her outside. She was still alive, so they threw gasoline on her and set her on fire."

"Well...when one plays with fire, one may be burnt," the American said philosophically. "Sinta should have been more careful about the risks. So now what does she want? Is she hoping to sue me for selling her faulty merchandise?"

Dewi looked confused, and stammered, "No, sir—I wanted to tell you that the animal attacked Madam, as well, and she's been taken to the hospital. It...it tore her jaw off."

"Tore her *jaw* off?"

"Yes. I just thought you should know, since Madam is your good friend."

The American looked into the young woman's face for a long moment...and then burst into laughter. The same laughter as when he had watched the trained orangutan sway and rotate its hips.

Dewi looked more confused, and the American caught his breath to observe, "What an ungrateful daughter!"

Her face took on another expression he had never witnessed before, subtle as it was: a repressed resentment. In a restrained voice that echoed her tight expression, the woman said, "I suppose even an animal can feel dirtied and degraded by one with a poisoned soul."

"Indeed," the American said, his laughter dying away. "Indeed." He took hold of Dewi's arm and walked her to the hotel room's door. He didn't throw money at her back as when he had evicted the used-up Vietnamese whore, but when she turned to face him in the hallway as the door closed between them, he said, "Your boss has lost half her face and her best worker. Maybe you should go into business for yourself, huh? Call me if you need anything in the future, and I'll see what I can do."

2: FURY (MASSACHUSETTS, 2010)

"ONE, TWO…HE'S COMING FOR you," Trenor overheard Peter sing to Jim through the wall that separated their cubicles. Peter kept his voice low, but surely he must know it wasn't soft enough for Trenor not to pick up. Which meant he didn't care if Trenor was offended. Trenor's scars were not a result of fire, nor as extensive as those of the character in the horror movie Peter alluded to, but pop culture references were Peter and Jim's currency.

Trenor stopped in the opening to Jim's cubicle. Jim's was the most individualized cubicle in the office, its fabric-covered walls buried as they were under photos of Jim posing with celebrities at science fiction conventions, photos of Jim in costume as a warrior at medieval recreation meetings, printouts of Jim's warrior avatar in the online game *World of Warcraft*, with a small army of toy figurines from such films as *Star Wars* defending every horizontal plane. Jim himself was in his late thirties, round in frame, with long hair and bushy beard, wearing a purple T-shirt and purple baseball cap. For reasons Trenor had no interest in learning, Jim always wore purple. Even his medieval recreation character and *World of Warcraft* character wore purple. It was his trademark, and perhaps he felt it gave him some notoriety amongst his kindred beings.

Jim was Trenor's team leader at Innovative Productivity Concepts. He swiveled in his chair upon Trenor's appearance, and in a pirate's coarsened voice asked, "Argh, and what can we be doing fer ye this fine day, matie?" The ongoing pirate jokes from Jim and Peter had to do with the black patch Trenor wore over his right eye.

"I wanted to put in my request for vacation time," Trenor explained, handing Jim a form he'd downloaded off the company's website.

"Ah," Jim said, examining the paper, "Tricky Dick wants a vacation. We been working you too hard, Richard?"

"Well, if I don't take it, I can't roll it over to next year, so…"

"Oh…the week of Christmas and New Year's," Jim noted, and wagged his shaggy head. "The week everyone always wants to take off. Course if we did that, we wouldn't have the staff to keep the doors open, right?"

"Well," Trenor said, explaining more than he'd hoped he would need to, because it sounded to his ears like begging, "my brother wants me to come up to Vancouver to spend the holidays with his family."

Jim looked up from the time-off form. "Your brother lives in Canada? Did he move there to avoid going to Nam?"

A long moment passed in which Trenor merely regarded his group leader, and then at last he replied, "You'd make a good detective, Jim."

"Not the gung-ho type like you, huh?" Jim said. "Well, I'll have to check with Evelyn about this…see if she okays it." He set the sheet aside, and it already looked lost amidst a chaos of papers.

"Thanks, Jim," Trenor said with a polite smile, rusty at the hinges.

"Dismissed, Private Cogburn," Jim said, giving him a sharp salute.

Cogburn threw Trenor for a beat or two, before he recalled John Wayne's patch-eyed character in the film *True Grit*. Combining that pop culture reference with Trenor's military service had disoriented him.

Though he was only in his late twenties, film buff Peter must have immediately caught the reference, because Trenor heard him laugh in the next cubicle. And then Peter's head jutted up above the partition wall. He folded his arms upon it, and Trenor guessed he was kneeling on his desk to accomplish this.

Peter said, "Hey, Richard, come on… I think you just wear that eye patch to look cool."

"Like Nick Fury," Jim chuckled. "Except Richard's white."

Trenor looked slowly from Peter to Jim. "Since when isn't Nick Fury white?"

"Get with the times, Richard," Peter said.

*   *   *

Trenor sat at his computer again to input his paperwork, after having ventured into the plant to do a quality control inspection on a batch of cafeteria-style metal chairs. With his approval, they were now ready to go to the warehouse to await packaging and shipment.

Innovative Productivity Concepts also manufactured the style of office chair he himself sat in now. The ergonomic design of its seat reduced pressure on the tailbone by supporting the pelvis in such a way that the back was held in the same position as when standing. Its properties were intended to make one comfortable through long stretches of productive work. Less likely, unconsciously, to get up to stretch and wander.

But during his inspection, Trenor had briefly sat on one of the metal cafeteria chairs so as to write on his clipboard, and the experience had been quite different. Its back rest and seat were made from a hard metal mesh. Ostensibly, the lack of cushions or fabric meant no staining, little wear, longtime use. In reality, the chair's uninviting design was every bit as purposeful, as scientific, as the office chair's. How many millions did US companies lose every year to lazy employees taking long breaks, lingering in the cafeteria an extra ten minutes or more? If their desire to sit a long time in a cafeteria could be reduced somehow, if only in a minor, subliminal sort of way, wasn't that a boon to productivity? Such was the philosophy of Innovative Productivity Concepts.

And their product line was diversified. Toilets intended for use by the employees of IPC's customers. Toilets with bowls so shallow—and plumbing keyed for explosive water pressure—that workers were sure to have their buttocks thoroughly soaked should they flush before standing. (Within the company, this product was jokingly referred to as "the bidet.") A worker faced with using such a toilet might well decide to wait until they got home to move their bowels. Coupled with toilet paper especially designed for workplace restrooms (though IPC didn't make this product themselves), coarse in texture or perforated in such a way that one would break off only small segments—not only an irritant but a defense against unnecessary waste—and once again productivity was bound to be slowly but cumulatively advanced.

Of course, IPC never advertised the nature of these types of product— instead, boasting of the ergonomic qualities of their office furniture, the enhanced practicality of their desks and work stations—but it was a word-of-mouth thing, whispered knowledge throughout the business sector. *Like a conspiracy,* Trenor thought.

When one of his colleagues had first told him—in fact, in a whisper—that IPC manufactured chairs, toilets, and other items with the intention that they create discomfort, he had been flabbergasted. Disgusted. It was almost enough to enrage him.

And yet, he hadn't up and quit. He'd been out of work for eight months before IPC, and his unemployment claim had run out. He felt like a coward, a hypocrite for not walking out, not walking straight to whatever newspaper might listen to his story. Felt like part of the conspiracy, a soldier advancing the agenda of people who no doubt held him in the same contempt as they did their perceived enemy, the common worker.

It was humiliating, degrading, putting on a nice shirt and slacks every morning and coming here as if he were actually doing something productive himself. Beyond being disgusted with IPC, he was disgusted with *himself* for continuing to work here. But he made a point of taking an extra fifteen minutes at lunch, sitting in one of the very chairs IPC churned out, and he would read from a paperback book while sitting for twenty minutes on the john (though he was sure to lift himself from the seat before flushing). It made him feel just a little bit better about himself. *The human spirit will not be defeated*, he would think. *Or, at least, human laziness.*

When he'd been much younger, he hadn't thought of himself as anyone's pawn. After all, he had volunteered, not been drafted. He didn't question—until it was all over and he was back home—the motives, the strategies, the *soul* of the political machine that had churned out soldiers as its own factory product. He had simply done the job he was supposed to do without any spirit of rebellion. Through the fear, through the pain.

Given what had happened to him, it was a miracle he had come back at all. Should he really be feeling so bitter now, he wondered, sitting here in this bright, open office area instead of squirming through an airless earthen tunnel with only a flashlight in one hand and a revolver in the other? He had a warm apartment to go home to, good food in his fridge; he was *safe*.

And yet it was something he'd had to remind himself of a lot. Especially when woken by a dream in the middle of the night.

You're safe. Safe a long time now.

Sitting in his exceptionally comfortable chair before his computer, Richard Trenor made a few last keystrokes, officially giving his personal okay for that batch of chairs to be introduced to unsuspecting employees out there somewhere in the country. Thus did he maintain the highest standards of discomfort.

*   *   *

Almost time to leave Innovative Productivity Concepts for the day, and Trenor took an extended bathroom break before the ride home. As he washed his hands, he glanced up at himself in the mirror. He was still trim for a man of sixty. For years following his return to the States he had worn his hair long and unruly, along with a scruffy beard, as if to curtain and cover his scars, but over the years the beard had diminished to his current neatly groomed mustache and goatee and his hair had returned to a bristling short military look, albeit these days glinting throughout with silver.

Those scars of his not masked by the eye patch included a pale seam down the center of his forehead, where the edges of skin had been sewn together after a flap had been lifted there and rotated down to reconstruct the smashed bridge of his nose…which remained misshapen, looking stitched together from differently hued patches of skin. Other faded but still noticeable scars traced their way around his right cheek.

Trenor left the restroom, crossed the now near-empty office area on his way to the exit. Along the way he spotted Peter leaning into Jim's cubicle. Jim had opened up the game *World of Warcraft*, was pointing out something to the younger worker. The men looked up to see that Trenor had noticed, and Jim rather nervously explained, "After hours, Tricky Dick… Don't go reporting me, now."

"Hey, Richard!" Peter called to him, motioning him over. Trenor complied by shuffling nearer. "You were down in those Vietnam tunnels, right?"

Trenor had never discussed that subject with these two men, but he had mentioned it once to their manager, Evelyn, and now he regretted having done so. "Yeah?" he said, trying not to sound leery.

"There's a PC game called *Tunnel Rats*, based on the movie by Uwe Boll. It's really cool, very realistic."

"Realistic, huh?"

"You ever see that movie, *Tunnel Rats*? It's no *Apocalypse Now* or *The Deer Hunter*, but it isn't bad, for a Uwe Boll flick. You should check it out. And hey, if you ever wanna try the game, I can let you borrow my copy."

Trenor blinked his one eye at the young man, just barely resisting the urge to ask, *"Why the fuck would I want to do that?"* Instead, he merely grunted and started to turn back toward the exit. "Goodnight, guys," he muttered. He had only gotten a few steps, though, before he changed his mind and came back—close to them this time. He gave a thin smile. "Hey, remember what we were talking about earlier, about my eye patch?"

"Yeah?" said Jim.

Trenor reached up and pulled the elastic cord of his eye patch off his head.

He had no glass eye. Nor even eyelids, or a hole where his right eye had once been nestled. All that remained was a shallow cup of scar tissue, where a flap of flesh from his cheek had long ago been stretched across the bone socket like the skin of a drum.

"I'm not faking," he said, and this time when he turned away he continued on toward the hallway leading to the front exit. He didn't return the eye patch to his head, stuffing it into the pocket of his jacket.

Behind him he heard Jim say to Peter, *"Jesus."*

3: MR. CRAB (VIETNAM, 2010)

WHILE SOME OF HO CHI Minh City's internet cafés used partitions to make a mini-cubicle of each computer station, the more humble café where Thanh worked did not. Its customers were crammed shoulder-to-shoulder in front of three tight rows of twelve monitors each in the café's single, long and narrow room. From the corner of his eye, Thanh saw a male US tourist—his beefy frame perched on a little plastic chair—wave a hand irritably at the thick cigarette smoke in the air. Most of the customers were teenage boys and young men playing online role-playing games or first-person shooters, and while many of them used headphones the air was just as thick with the sounds of machinegun fire. One might believe a long-distance war was being waged from this place.

Because there were no partitions, one could view the screen and activities of another quite easily. A female US tourist with wheat-colored hair sat at the computer next to the big man, and nudged him. "Honey, look," Thanh heard her say. She was motioning subtly, she thought, in his direction. Thanh supposed she didn't realize he could understand English.

Without a partition, the woman had obviously seen Thanh's hands moving across the keyboard as he installed a new webcam on one of the computers. Both of his hands possessed only two digits, like twin thumbs opposing each other. No doubt she pitied him even as she was impressed that he was able to apply his deformed appendages to the computer's keys. Had she looked under the table at which she sat, she would have seen that the twenty-year-old man's bare, tough-callused feet were identical to his hands—consisting of two long, thumb-like toes splayed wide to give him support.

Thanh didn't much care if the US woman felt pity or revulsion, but he had been far more self-conscious only a short while earlier. A pretty Vietnamese teenager with stylish auburn-dyed hair had come in to rent some time on one of the machines, and she had been all smiles with him, perhaps finding him attractive. But he had come out from behind the front desk to help set her up, and right away he had seen the change come over her face when she noticed his hands and feet. He had felt all the worse when she had taken a seat, and he had had to lean in close beside her to get her started on the computer. When he'd left her to herself, she had muttered thanks without making eye contact with him again.

Well, it wasn't the first time he had been embarrassed in this way, and he knew it wouldn't be the last. His mother's brother had been kind to give him a good job here, aware of his nephew's adeptness with computers (and English, which came in handy with tourists), and while he was still shy by nature he had come to learn how to interact with the customers. In fact, though Thanh's uncle was currently manning the front desk, much of the time he was busy managing another café elsewhere in the city and left Thanh to run the show at this one.

With the new webcam installed, Thanh set out to test its use in chatting. Earlier he had called his youngest sister and told her to be waiting for him at the family computer in their home in the city of Bien Hoa—about an hour's drive from Ho Chi Minh City—and so now Thanh signed into his messenger service and invited his sister to chat. Though Hang Ni was only eight years old, he had taught her about computers and she had taken to them as naturally as he had. Thanh believed it was an advance in evolution that the very young seemed to possess more of an affinity for such technology than their parents did.

He used the chat's "buzz" feature to alert Hang Ni several times, began to wonder if she had grown bored and wandered away, but at last she typed in a reply: *Em ne!*—"I'm here!"

Thanh smiled and invited Hang Ni to view his webcam, then requested to view hers as well. Their respective windows opened on Thanh's screen. His own face was framed in one, and he could believe his auburn-haired customer might have considered him good-looking at first, but the tiny window did not give away the pincer-like appendages at the ends of his four limbs. The other window framed the smiling, beaming face of an eight-year-old girl with long, shining blue-black hair cut in straight bangs that covered her eyebrows. Her face was the same golden brown as her brother's, but her bare shoulders and upper chest appeared a paler hue. It looked to Thanh like his sister didn't have a top on.

What are you wearing? Thanh asked her in Vietnamese, confused.

With perfect spelling, Hang Ni typed: *I was practicing my dance! Do you want to see it?* And before he could reply, Hang Ni had hopped off her chair, pushed it out of the way and moved far enough away from the camera to reveal her entire tiny body. Now Thanh understood why he had had the impression she'd been nude. His sister was wearing a long-sleeved pale pink bodysuit and white shoes. Maybe she had pushed a button on the CD player resting on a shelf above the computer, or maybe the music played in her head; without sound, Thanh couldn't tell. When she knew she had centered herself properly in the square of her camera's window, Hang Ni commenced her routine.

Thanh grinned, fond and proud, but after a few moments as he watched his sister sway her hips, flick her hair across her face, turn in profile and move her body with the fluid undulations of a snake (the bodysuit outlining the immature roundedness of her belly), pretend to crack a whip and then thrust her hips forward and back, he became uncomfortable instead. He buzzed her in the chat to get her attention, and maybe there wasn't music after all because she heard him and returned immediately to her computer chair. She was still beaming, and typed in words that looked breathless: *How did you like it?*

How did you learn to dance like that? Thanh asked her.

Tra Mi, she typed. It wasn't necessary, however. Of course it had been Tra Mi.

Thanh wanted to tell her that he thought the dance moves her older sister had taught her were too adult, but he was afraid to hurt her feelings or embarrass her when she was obviously trying so hard to impress him. Instead, he asked: *What is the music you were dancing to?*

'*Run Devil Run*' *by SNSD!* she replied. It was a Korean group of nine sexy girls, popular throughout Asia. *I wish I could be in a group like them someday!*

Where is Ba? Thanh asked about their father, deciding to change the subject.
Sleeping, I think.

And Tra Mi is at work? To an outsider's ears, the name would sound like *Cha Me.*

No, she came home for something. I think she is still here somewhere. Hang Ni looked back over her shoulder. When she faced forward again, she typed: *When are you coming home again? I MISS BIG BROTHER SO MUCH!* She wrote this last as: *EM NHO ANH HAI NHIEU QUA!*

The two digits Thanh used for typing—one on each hand, but he was still fast with them—hovered in hesitation over the keys. He missed his sister, too…but what excuse could he use this time to avoid coming back home? Thanh didn't want to say to his sister, though she no doubt already understood, that he no more wanted to see their father than their father wanted to see him.

Even as he was trying to think of what to type, a figure moved into the frame behind Hang Ni, and she was lifted under the arms out of the computer chair. In Hang Ni's place, her eighteen-year-old sister Tra Mi sat down in front of the webcam, her thin figure attired in the clingy white tank top and black miniskirt she wore as a coffee shop waitress. She immediately typed: *Sorry but I need to use my email now.*

We were still talking! Thanh protested, those two fingers racing across the keys. Let the foreign woman admire his skills now.

I don't have much time, it's my break and I have to get back to work. Goodbye.

Wait! Hang Ni showed me the dance you taught her. I don't like it, it's too sexy.

You're just jealous because you can't dance on those scary feet, Anh Cua. Tra Mi had called him Anh Cua—which in English would be "Mr. Crab"—too many times for it to hurt, but it still irritated.

She used to want to be a nurse, but thanks to you now she wants to be some dancing girl in little shorts like SNSD.

Oh, Anh Cua, I'm sure you've excited yourself watching SNSD videos. Just be careful you don't snip your bird off with your crab claw.

Even having lived with her all his life, it was unthinkable to Thanh that a sister could speak to her older brother in such a disrespectful manner. She'd been so much worse since he'd stopped sending her money and she'd had to go to work. Worse since he only sent money home to Hang Ni.

He pounded out the words *Cho cai!*—"Bitch!"—but Tra Mi had already signed out of the chat before Thanh could say goodbye to Hang Ni.

4: SNAPSHOTS (VIETNAM, 1970)

THE HOOCH AT THE LAI Khe base camp had been nicknamed Tango Romeo. A romantic name for a primitive structure of wood and canvas without one woman inside; just a group of young men in camouflaged fatigues with their sleeves rolled up past their elbows, lazy from the heat and listening to George Harrison singing a song from his new album *All Things Must Pass* on the radio.

A sign fixed to the hooch's front door bore a rough painting of a wild-eyed, Rat Fink-inspired character with a bullet whizzing through one ear, a whiskey bottle in its right hand and a pistol in the left. This same character was featured on a crude patch worn on the right breast of the young men's fatigues, except this time the rat held a flashlight instead of a bottle. Below the rat in questionable Latin was the motto: *Non Gratum Anus Rodentum*. Or, "Not Worth a Rat's Ass."

The hooch's front door was left open inadequately against the heat, and Staff Sergeant Richard Trenor stood on the wooden walkway leading to its threshold. Another soldier might have found this a good time to be smoking. The twenty-year-old Trenor didn't smoke. The enemy could smell it on your clothes, and know you were inching up on them.

In 1970, the 1st Engineer Battalion had two former Viet Cong in their Tunnel Rats team. In Vietnamese these defectors were called *Hoi Chanh Vien*— "members who have returned to the righteous side"—but the Americans called them Kit Carson Scouts. The team had dubbed ingratiating little Hieu "Baby-san," because he looked about six years younger than his eighteen years. The other man was named Quan, a good-looking eighteen-year-old of a more serious demeanor.

It was Quan who stood beside Trenor now outside the Tango Romeo hooch, opening a beat-up wallet and reverently slipping out an equally beat-up photo for the young sergeant to see. Trenor leaned in close but didn't deign to touch the holy relic.

"That's your mother, huh?" Trenor didn't know much Vietnamese and Quan didn't speak much English. "Mama-san?"

"Yes," Quan said proudly.

"Yeah, well, she's very beautiful. *Dep lam.*" He knew that expression from interacting with prostitutes, not soldiers' mothers. "Really, she could be a movie star." He considered making a joke that if Quan's mother were ever to divorce then he'd be happy to marry her, at which point he'd be Quan's father, but he thought it might be disrespectful or even unwise to joke along those lines. Despite his age and size, Quan wasn't to be underestimated, formerly being one of the men this team confronted in the anthill-like bunker complexes.

"Thanks, Rick," Quan said. Rick was what the team called Trenor, a nickname he'd never known in civilian life. Beaming as he returned the frayed and creased photo to his wallet, the Kit Carson Scout asked, "You picture?"

"Me? Of my mama-san? Nope. No picture of a girlfriend, either. Guess I'm not the sentimental type." He saw Quan wasn't getting all this and asked, "You got a picture of a girlfriend? Wife?"

"Wife? Me?" Quan grinned. "No, no wife."

"Ah, we're both young handsome dudes, right, brother? Plenty of time for that."

"Fuck, Rick," another of the squad called from inside the hooch. "Don't you two guys be showing each other pictures of the girl back home! Don't you watch those old war movies? Next thing you know one of you is going to get zapped!"

"Hey, man," Trenor replied over his shoulder, "that's not funny." He nodded at Quan's wallet, which he was just returning to a pocket in his fatigues. "No pictures of papa-san, either?"

Quan looked up and smiled, but the smile was subdued. "Father dead."

"What? Oh...oh, sorry, brother." Then a terrible possibility occurred to Trenor, and he said, "Hey, your father, he didn't... It wasn't us, was it? Us?" He tapped his own chest.

Quan lifted his eyebrows. "Hm?"

"USA? Made your father dead?"

"Oh! No, no, Rick. Father sick and die. Only sick."

"Oh, that's good. I mean, shit, that isn't good." Trenor winced. "You know what I mean."

Quan grinned. "Okay, Rick."

Trenor couldn't help but chuckle, finding it funny that here they were both amused now over the subject of Quan's father's demise. Though of course it was really their challenge communicating that had changed the conversation from grim to humorous. But he was grateful he hadn't made that joke before about marrying Quan's mother.

All humor aside, in Quan's eyes Trenor believed he saw gratitude that he had expressed concern about his father's death. Some soldiers, particularly the South's own ARVN, didn't trust the *Hoi Chanh Vien.* Trenor couldn't speak for every defector, especially since they were known to defect back again or even turn out to be spies, but he trusted his instincts about this one man. He felt Quan knew he trusted him, and appreciated it. These things transcended the limitations of language.

"Hey, you lovebirds, let me take a picture of you." The speaker was Alvarez, another man in their team of thirteen men, who had been walking toward the hooch carrying his Pentax camera.

Trenor hung his arm around Quan's shoulders and Quan stood awkwardly with his own arms by his sides, both men smiling and holding still for Alvarez to take his shot and steal this one moment from time's flow.

Many years later, Victor Alvarez would email a copy of this photograph to Trenor, who would in turn email a copy to Quan. Trenor would frame a glossy 8.5 x 11 printout of it and hang it on a wall in his living room.

Many years later, too, on one of the infrequent occasions that he found himself paging through a travel guide to contemporary Vietnam in a bookstore, Trenor would read something he'd never known before: that the Vietnamese believed a "genie" resided on one's shoulders, and to touch the shoulders was to disturb this spirit and bring bad luck.

Quan had endured Trenor's arm weighing on his shoulders without complaint, no doubt not wanting to insult him by demurring. Yet inside, was the former VC fretting that the USA soldier's touch would bring him bad luck? At the time, Trenor had thought Quan was only shy to put his arm around him in return, though after seeing the book he would think that perhaps Quan had only been trying to spare him from bad luck of his own.

But in the here and now, another of the team—their commanding lieutenant, who was always nicknamed "Rat Six" no matter who currently held that position—came toward the three men at a jog, calling ahead, "Grab your gear, guys; 1st infantry have found themselves a hole."

There wasn't much gear to grab. Their floppy bush hats, a flashlight, knife, and each man's preferred make of pistol. The Tunnel Rats traveled light.

5: HOME LIFE (VIETNAM, 2010)

STANDING BEHIND TRA MI AS she signed out of her email account, still wearing her pink bodysuit, a pouting Hang Ni stamped a foot and said, "You cut me and my brother! I don't see him often—I miss him!"

"It's better that you don't see him often," replied Tra Mi coolly, standing again and smoothing her skirt. "It isn't lucky if you look at him too long, or someday you'll have babies with hands and feet like his. But maybe it's in our family genes and your babies will look like that anyway."

"Your babies too, then!" Hang Ni blurted, close to tears.

"I don't want babies…I'm afraid to have a spoiled brat like you. Why are you getting so upset? If our brother missed you like you miss him, then he never would have left you to go live in Saigon, would he?"

"Shut your mouth!"

"You think he cares about you? Who takes care of you? I do. Who is it that brought you to Dai Nam Van Hien, huh?" Tra Mi referred to the fairly new theme park in Binh Duong Province.

"Father made you take me! He paid the money for it, not you! You were mean to me the whole time! And my brother *does* take care of me… He sends me money every month. You're just jealous because he doesn't send money to *you.*"

"*Du ma may,*" Tra Mi said, raising a hand as if to slap Hang Ni's upturned face.

"Hey hey hey!" a male voice exclaimed.

Behind Tra Mi, Hang Ni had seen her father throw back the curtain that hung over the doorway separating this room from the next, where a steep metal staircase more like a ladder led to the upper level. He had been napping up there, on a mattress on the floor under a tent-like mosquito net. He wore only wrinkled khaki shorts, his wiry little body dark brown from the sun, and his hair—just shot through with gray though he was fifty-eight—mussed across his forehead.

His eyes were flinty in a hard-lined face. His snarling mouth revealed that he was missing a number of teeth.

Tra Mi heard her father pounding barefoot across the living room's ceramic tiled floor and began spinning to one side, but he still managed to whip out a hand and catch her with a hard slap across the face. He was always unerring with his blows, even when drunk. When only half-drunk his hands were still clever at repairing motorbikes.

"Ba! Ba!" Hang Ni cried, throwing herself between them and encircling her father's waist before he could advance on Tra Mi again. "Please don't!"

"If you ever put a hand on your sister, I'll throw you out on the street!" their father growled, pointing a finger at his oldest daughter.

With a hand to her stinging cheek, Tra Mi barked a laugh. "Throw me out? You're lucky I haven't left already! If I leave, who will take care of your precious daughter? Your son? You already chased him out...now you want me out, too?"

"*Con di!*" her father spat. "You're a whore, like your mother!"

"Ba," Hang Ni wailed, hugging him tighter, "don't say that!"

"At least I work!" Tra Mi shouted. "I'm not a lazy drunk like you. You hardly work anymore—how will Hang Ni eat if I go? I should take her with me someplace where you'll never find us."

"You'll take her nowhere!" their father snapped back at her. "You can go away anytime you like, I don't care, but you won't bring her with you!"

"Fine, as soon as I have enough money I'll go, and I won't have to listen to a crazy old drunk anymore." Tra Mi turned away sharply, but spun back again and cried, "You say my mother is a whore? Maybe that's true...because I'm sure Hang Ni isn't your daughter!"

"*Con di!*" their father shouted, half lunging toward her, but Hang Ni held tight despite her sudden attack of hard sobs.

Tra Mi left the living room for the kitchen, and from there she stepped outside. Through the living room's closed glass doors they could see Tra Mi adjust her helmet, straddle her Honda—her short skirt riding up even higher in the process—then start the bike and rumble away.

Hang Ni still clung to her father, and now he held his sobbing daughter, too, and rubbed her back.

"I *am* your daughter, Ba!" Hang Ni moaned.

"Of course you're my daughter," he told her.

Quan stared blankly across the room, where a gaudy little Buddhist shrine with flashing rows of inset Christmas lights rested on the floor. From the look of his eyes, one might have thought the flickering lights had hypnotized him. "You're the only good one in our family," he muttered. He held her tighter, almost enough to hurt her, and his own voice sounded close to sobs. "The only person who loves me."

6: ICED COFFEE

"WHERE YOU FROM?" THE GIRL asked the American in English, lowering herself into a chair beside him at his table after having brought him his *ca phe sua da*—iced coffee with sweetened condensed milk as thick as the heat in the air. He hadn't invited her to join him, but of course she was a *ca phe om* and it was her job to entertain the customers, just as a *bia om* would do in a bar, or a *karaoke om* in a karaoke joint. A *xe om* would be a man, a taxi driver on a motorbike, but "*om*" meant the same thing anyway: hug. One hugged close behind a *xe om*, and one could hug—or grope—a coffee or beer *om* whilst they kept you company. And of course there were rooms upstairs, if hugging didn't suffice.

"I come from Vietnam," he told her.

"Oh, I know you Vietnamese," she said, "but you come from USA, huh?"

He ignored her question to ask one of his own. "You're new here, right? I haven't seen you before."

"Yeah, I here three month. So you know all the other girl, huh?"

He did. There were a half-dozen waitresses, all identically dressed in white tank tops and black miniskirts—a few already sitting with customers—and he'd ignored the rest to address this girl, his choice thus made clear. She'd said her name was Kate. He hadn't asked for her real name. She was older than the other girls, her grin a little tight, her eyes a little too hard and sad. He found this a refreshing change from the fresh, sunny smiles most of the other girls wore like their tight-fitting outfits. Her unhappiness was a kind of honesty. There was one teenager here so damn perky and sweet that he almost hated her, though hatred of course was part of his hunger. He'd had her before, and once made her cry. That had been refreshing, too.

The American had sat at a table toward the rear of the long, narrow room, away from the coffee shop's open front and the loud, constant buzzing of motorbikes in the streets of Bien Hoa. This café was dark but clean and artfully decorated, more upscale than most. There were also partitioned booths along one wall for greater privacy, almost made into duck blinds by tactfully positioned pots of plants. From one of them the American heard a single moan; some customer being stimulated by hand or mouth while he waited for the slow drip of his hot coffee through its little tin filter.

"What your name?" Kate asked him. He wouldn't have told her, would maybe have given her a fake name as she had done, but just then the American spotted the man he'd come to meet with, stepping inside from the glaring sunlight. Long Dien—whose name sounded like *Lum Dean*—craned his neck, gazing toward the back of the room until his eyes adapted to the gloom. When he spotted the American, his thin brown face split into an exaggerated grin and he approached him swiftly, snapping at Kate to get up and adjust a nearby fan to blow on the American more directly. She complied, then made herself busy elsewhere while Long Dien occupied her seat.

"How are you, my friend?" he asked in Vietnamese. "How was your flight?"

"From the US to Indonesia, long. From there to here, not too bad. New girl, huh?" The American nodded toward Kate. "Very nice. She has a broken elegance I like."

"Broken elegance! Oh, such a poet, such a romantic!" Long Dien exclaimed.

The American cracked an amused smile. He'd never thought of himself as romantic. "Now *her* on the other hand," he said, motioning toward a girl who was wiping down a table at the front of the room, "I don't understand why you hired her."

The girl in question looked up at the American, maybe having noticed his gesture peripherally, but after meeting his eyes she averted her gaze again quickly, resuming her cleaning.

Long Dien had glanced over his shoulder, momentarily confused. "Huh? Tra Mi?"

"She's ugly. No chin, terrible overbite, front teeth like a horse, one droopy eyelid, and that long plastic nose of hers—horrible. Plus, she's so thin she looks diseased."

"Oh ho, poor Tra Mi!" Long Dien chuckled, facing the American again. "But her young sister who comes here sometimes will be a beauty to break men's hearts, I can tell you. And I have to say, Tra Mi can suck your liver out through your dick. You've never tried her?"

"No, I have no interest, and all of your girls can suck your liver out through your dick. Suck your money out through your dick, at least."

"But always free for you, my friend, always free for you! And what else can I do for you this time?" Long Dien spread his hands wide magnanimously.

The American flicked his eyes about to ensure that no one was near enough to overhear, but the coffee shop was barely occupied, and he said, "One of my contacts has introduced me to a new client who wants to entertain a visiting friend. We'll only be dealing with the client, not the friend. In fact, though normally I wouldn't ask you to meet with my clients yourself, this time I'm going to be busy with some import concerns in Hanoi, so I'll be giving this man your contact information. You can see to his needs yourself, all right?"

Long Dien looked a bit thrown at having to take part in the American's affairs in such a direct fashion, but he maintained his grin and said, "Of course, of course. So, what are their needs, then? Two girls? Two each?"

"Just one girl, for just my client's friend. But there's a challenge. She obviously can't be one of your *ca phe oms*, here. He wants a virgin…maybe between twelve and fourteen. Something very fresh."

Long Dien grimaced now; couldn't help it. "Are you sure this client of yours is safe? Not setting us up for the police?"

The American compacted hours of staring at Long Dien into one moment before he said, in an even lower voice than he'd been using, "Do you think I'm stupid?"

"No…no, of course not! Forgive me, my friend! Naturally I will do my best not to disappoint your client."

The American sipped his iced coffee and considerately glanced away—at Kate wiping down another table—to give Long Dien a few moments in which to regain his composure, lest his fear embarrass him. The dour way Kate's mouth was set made the waitress look like she was sucking on a lemon, which made him wish she was sucking on him. He found many Vietnamese women had deeply sad eyes, like a genetic suffering, as if they had personally experienced all of their country's long history of occupation and war. Maybe feeling the weight of his own eyes, Kate looked up at the American and awarded him one of her secretly wounded smiles. She'd remained far from a new customer who'd come in, saving herself for *him*.

When the American faced Long Dien again, he saw that the coffee shop's owner was watching another of his waitresses as she gravitated toward the new customer. In a musing tone, Long Dien asked, "Could the girl be younger than twelve, by a few years?"

"Younger would be better, it seems to me. But as you say, it would have to be a safe situation."

"I believe it could be arranged. And faster and easier than you might have thought."

The American twisted around to look behind him again, in the direction Long Dien was staring, and saw his least favorite *ca phe om* Tra Mi in conversation with the new customer, showing the man her prominent front teeth in a big inviting smile that in its own way was as covetous as the customer's.

7: PILLOW TALK

THE AMERICAN FOUND IT AMUSING that after he had lain on his back with her ass in his face only a short time earlier, his nose burrowed in its furrow, the *ca phe om* who called herself Kate had pranced toward the shower demurely, hiding her small bottom self-consciously with a cheap white hotel towel. He sat up from the bed, swung his feet to the floor and reached for his pack of Vinataba cigarettes. Though it was not unpleasant to shower with a woman and be scrubbed clean by her attentive hands, it was also a tad too romantic a scenario for his tastes and he'd cleanse himself of their drying juices when he was ready.

He had moved to a window of his Bien Hoa hotel room and was gazing down at the flat rooftops of pastel-colored buildings, interspersed with rusted roofs of corrugated metal, when Kate reemerged dressed again in her *ca phe om* outfit. She sat on the edge of the bed with apparent uncertainty and expectancy, watching him as he turned naked from the window to smile at her, as if he had rehearsed some amorous lines while she had been in the other room.

"My father fought against the Viet Cong," he told her in Vietnamese, "and later we escaped from here on one of those miserable little boats. In the USA, he was walking down a city street one day when a body thudded to the pavement only a few feet from him. It was a man who had thrown himself to his death from a high building, and he almost killed my father along with him. Wouldn't that have been ironic, to survive a war and sailing on the ocean braving the elements and Thai pirates, only to be squashed accidentally by some suicidal American?"

"Mm," Kate grunted, sounding more noncommittal than philosophical. Her expression was bored and nervous, which again he found more attractive than cute and sweet affectations, and though she didn't quite have Dewi's anomalous grace he already preferred her to the Indonesian prostitute.

"My father told me there wasn't much damage to be seen on the body, and it's that way sometimes. After all, there have been parachutists who survived their chutes not opening. But other times…well. I once saw a man who dropped from the twenty-fifth floor of his hotel in Pattaya, Thailand, and hit a balcony on the way down. He reached the sidewalk split in two." The American made a horizontal slashing motion across his own chest. "He was Irish—a seventy-two-year-old former businessman, who 'may have fallen accidentally or committed suicide,' according to Thai police and the man's grieving, twenty-eight-year-old beautiful Thai wife."

In Vietnamese, Kate asked, "You saw his body on the street?"

"No…actually, I saw it from a balcony on the twenty-fifth floor."

The American waited for horrified realization to manifest itself in the woman's large dark eyes, and when he was satisfied continued.

"In the Thai papers and news sites you can read about a shocking number of tourists and expats who meet their end in Thailand, especially in Pattaya. Some Lieutenant Colonel Something-or-other will preside over the scene, and he'll say findings are inconclusive but of course the investigation will continue. An article might read that the *farang* in question passed away in bed while watching porn—that will actually be in the headline—and a photo of him as he was in life will be thoughtfully provided. He'll be described in death right down to the color of the clothes he was wearing. Brits, Americans, Australians, Germans, and Swedes. Japanese, Finnish, Norwegian. Supposed hangings, supposed falls, supposed heart attacks, occasionally a plain assault but with no known perpetrator. I don't know why so many alleged suicides. What's to get depressed about when you're in exciting Pattaya, unless you realize you just drank away your life savings or possibly caught AIDS from that ladyboy you took to bed last night?" He tamped out the stub of his cigarette in an ashtray. "Naturally there are people who benefit from such rashes of bad luck. Those enchanting ladyboys, who figure they can make more money killing their john and emptying his wallet than by having the sweaty old pig fold them up like a bendable sex doll. Pretty little wives on vacation to the home country, who've earned their citizenship back in the States and don't need fat old hubby anymore. Husbands who've taken generous insurance policies out on their wives, and know a police investigation in Thailand will be less competent than one in their own country. But sometimes these people who have something to gain are not capable of the deed themselves—in which case, arrangements can be made even before their plane takes flight, just like any travel reservation, and a friend of a friend or even someone with the hotel will put them in touch with an individual who can take care of the matter for them."

Kate's eyes tracked him as he retrieved his indigenous cigarettes to light a fresh one, and as he did so he frowned thoughtfully. "I'm sure there was something behind the alleged accidental death of David Carradine in Bangkok, but I'm hardly responsible for all these incidents and I wouldn't have accepted that job anyway. I always admired the man's movies and TV show."

Kate's gaze shifted from the man to the window and back again, as if she wondered if all this were a prelude to her own suicidal flight from a hotel window. Had she done something to anger Long Dien?

The American went on, "I don't know what you'd want to call me. An entrepreneur. A renaissance man." His tone was sounding affected even to his own ears, but he was enjoying himself. "Because I'm adaptable, because my services are diverse, I think of myself simply as a supplier. That's all some people know me as. The Supplier. But here and in the other countries I deal in, most people who know of me just call me the American."

At last Kate spoke up. "Why are you telling me all this?" she was bold or terrified enough to ask.

"I prefer working alone, but of course it's impossible all the time. No matter where I go, I need to be able to trust certain people to assist me in my various endeavors."

"But how do you know you can trust them?"

The American took a deliberately long drag on his cigarette, his eyes unblinking behind a caul of blue smoke, before exhaling and replying with a smile and a shrug, "If any of them think to betray me, then I'll simply kill them, of course."

8: THE NEST (VIETNAM, 1970)

THE HUEY HELICOPTERS THAT HAD airlifted the team to the discovered tunnel entrance had already ascended and turned away, their heavy pulse receding to a jungle insect trill. Staff Sergeant Richard Trenor removed his camouflage fatigue top, preferring just his military green undershirt. Not for the first time, in a routine that was born as much from nervous compulsion as caution, he checked the batteries in his green anglehead flashlight, then swung out the cylinder of his revolver to be assured that every chamber was loaded. Standard issue .45s were deafening in the tunnels, so the Tunnel Rats opted for other choices of weapon. Trenor's handgun was a five-shot, snub-nosed Airweight Bodyguard .38, its hammer enclosed so it wouldn't catch on clothing when drawn. Trenor's father had bought it and shipped it to him, at his request.

"Time to earn that fifty dollars," Trenor said, smiling at the man who would take point in the tunnel, Castillo, a lean little Mexican. Every month, a Tunnel Rat received an extra fifty dollars in hazard pay. In addition, each Rat could only serve a six-month stint in this hazardous occupation. Trenor was four months into his.

"Don't forget," Castillo said, jabbing a finger at him. "Beware of darkness." He'd heard tracks from the new George Harrison album, too.

Trenor would come second after Castillo. The Kit Carson Scout Quan, standing beside Trenor, spoke up that he would go third, holding up three fingers to supplement his English. Though the Kits didn't go down as often as the Americans did, and by policy were never trusted to go in first, the commanding Rat Six assented. Quan grinned at Trenor and said, "I watch your ass, Rick."

"Enjoy the view, brother."

"You want the caboose?" said the Rat Six. "Then you can carry the heavy artillery." The young lieutenant handed Quan a 12-gauge pump-action shotgun with a green shoulder strap. It was bulky for the tunnels, and punishingly loud, but sometimes the last man in line might carry a more formidable weapon to pass up front if the need was there.

"Don't let that go off by accident, little man," the Tunnel Rat named Alvarez growled in mock threat, shaking his fist at Quan.

"Okay, motherfucker," Quan said, saluting.

In the past, the reaction to finding a tunnel had been to destroy it immediately, but the logic had since turned to determining first whether the tunnel was hot—still in use—or cold and abandoned. Further, there might be documents, weapons, and other items of importance discovered within. And so the team prepared to descend into the darkness, with Castillo first checking around the entrance, gingerly probing with his combat knife to be sure there were no mines or booby traps.

Castillo had opted to go completely bare-chested, and was already sheened with perspiration. Trenor didn't like the heat any better, but he liked the sensation of animal life crawling across him even less. Snakes and scorpions were sometimes used in booby traps but were also to be found naturally, not to mention rats and spiders, and Trenor sometimes wondered if he was more wary of the spiders to be found in the tunnels than he was a potential enemy. Maybe not logical, but a primitive reaction.

At last Castillo was lowered in, legs first. For Trenor this was the most terrifying point, like the shocking submersion into a cold lake before the body acclimated. Once fully inside, he would click into adaptive mode, just as his eyes would adjust as best they could to the darkness. Trenor knew he and the others above were tensed up inside just as much as Castillo must be at this vulnerable moment. The entrance to a tunnel often held any variety of nasty surprises. But the Mexican didn't cry out; no bamboo spear had been thrust into him through a false wall, no tripwire had released a poisonous viper from inside a bamboo tube. Above, however, they did hear three shots fired off from Castillo's own revolver. The others weren't unduly alarmed; this firing ahead, down each new branch and around each sharp bend, was standard procedure. It might give the exploration team away, yet it would also hopefully drive the enemy back, dissuade them from engaging, maybe to flee out another opening further along in the system. But Castillo would already be replacing the spent cartridges in his .38, because the strict rule was to never fire more than three shots in succession without reloading, to keep the enemy confused about how many shots the soldier held in his gun.

Trenor was lowered down next.

At the bottom of the vertical tunnel, he awkwardly repositioned himself to crawl forward. Already it was near-impossible to draw a breath, the narrow tunnel packed solid with heat as if it had been flooded with boiling water. In his nostrils, the smell of the concrete-hard clay through which the tunnels had been painstakingly bored. The ragged ends of tree roots protruded from the curved walls here and there, catching his flashlight beam and glowing white, looking like veins or nerves, as if this were some organic passage through the body of a vast beast. A great dragon.

Trenor inched forward on elbows and knees, pistol in his right hand, his left holding the flashlight out away from his body, in case its beacon should make him a target. He could see Castillo about five yards ahead of him, and heard Quan reach the tunnel's floor behind him. Though they would remain in view of each other, the trio wouldn't group too close; if a grenade were thrown or a booby trapped mine triggered, this way it might not engulf all three of them.

His breath came back to him, close in his ears, as if he were wearing an enclosing helmet. He smelled sour sweat, human body odor, but it wasn't from him or his companions. His heart was punching fast and heavy, and he could almost hear that, too. He could almost hear the hearts of Castillo and Quan. Their heartbeats were linked, intimately—maybe even with the heartbeats of others down here. For Trenor felt it as a trained intuition, as a primal instinct like that of a prehistoric hunter, that this was not a cold tunnel.

Trenor saw that Castillo had arrived at a left bend, so radical that when he negotiated the turn he briefly disappeared from view. He wondered why the Mexican had not blasted off the customary three shots, but thought that it might be because this was not a fork or tributary in the system; there was no other way to proceed. It had been instilled in the men not to let each other stray from view, so Trenor hastened his crawl just a little, and thrust his head around the same tight turn.

Perhaps this was what the enemy had been waiting for—an additional target—for that was when the distinctive sound of AK-47 fire thundered from the darkness ahead of them. A sustained, fully automatic barrage.

Castillo took the brunt of the attack, blocking Trenor, though some shots went wild and dug into the tunnel walls. Struck in his uncovered head and bared torso, the wiry young Mexican never even had the chance to cry out, let alone return fire.

Maybe the shooter never actually saw Trenor behind Castillo, after all; perhaps the point man not only blocked him from the bullets, but from the enemy's sight as well. It might only have been a stray, lucky 7.62 mm round that hammered Trenor on the bridge of his nose, and continued on into his right eye socket, carrying bits of broken bone with it. Trenor didn't return fire, either, though he did let out a single grunt of surprise and stunning pain.

Quan was five yards behind Trenor. He saw his friend roll loosely over onto his back, still gripping his pistol and flashlight. The Kit Carson Scout looped the shotgun's strap over his shoulder, freeing his hands to scrabble forward that much quicker. With his hands free, he was able to grab hold of Trenor by both ankles when he came to him. He yanked the larger man toward him, seized hold of his fatigue pants and tugged at him with a second surge of strength, hauling him back safely around the sharp bend in the path.

Quan had not seen Castillo, and though his instincts told him the point man was dead—no, that full AK-47 magazine was what told him—he still resisted the impulse to take a grenade from Trenor and hurl it around the corner, down the tunnel. Instead, he slipped the shotgun off his shoulder again, then flung himself over Trenor's body, onto his belly, his head and shoulders and the shotgun's short barrel clearing the earthen corner. Immediately, he pumped the shotgun's slide and fired blindly down the length of the tunnel, into the blackness, at a slightly elevated angle to avoid as best he could the body that must be lying between him and his target. Sure enough, in the brief flare of gas erupting from the shotgun, he caught a lightning flash image of Castillo's crumpled, punctured form.

The unseen enemy did not fire again. In his own desperation to bring down the lead American, had he truly exhausted his ammunition, now preoccupied with changing the depleted magazine? Or might the shooter have already retreated, to escape from the tunnel system further down the line? Not taking any chances, Quan fired the shotgun a second, third, and fourth time down the tunnel. The concussions of the blasts were like awls driven into his eardrums. His hearing went muffled and fizzing.

Edging backwards, Quan turned his attention to Trenor. He had dropped his own flashlight, but took Trenor's from his hand and shifted its beam to his friend's head. A deep pain like another stray bullet plowed through his chest when he saw the American's face lost in blood, overflowing the shattered cup of one eye. But then Quan saw Trenor's mouth working, heard him gurgle as he fought to breathe against the blood running down the back of his throat.

Quan acted quickly, his thoughts clear and sharp. He drew his knife and cut the green shoulder strap free from his shotgun, the fastest means he knew of removing it. He then used the strap to bind Trenor's wrists together, as if taking him prisoner. All the while he dreaded the enemy making their way down the tunnel toward him, not realizing he hadn't yet pulled out.

He would leave the shotgun until they could come back for it, and Castillo's body, later. Only then would the team find a single enemy soldier, killed by shotgun pellets in the neck and chest. For now, Quan took Trenor's .38 and tucked it in the front of his own waistband. Then, having repositioned himself to retreat the way they had come, he looped Trenor's linked wrists around his neck, and hoisted the American onto his back.

Ahead, he heard someone shouting, "Rick! Castillo!"

As Quan crawled toward the voice, he could only hope that he and Trenor would not both be shot in the back. Could only hope that his friend would survive even if they did make it to the sunlight.

Lying heavily across the back of the smaller man, through a white noise of pain Trenor noted that even while exerting himself under these conditions Quan did not allow himself to grunt or pant loudly, and in a detached way Trenor found himself admiring that discipline even more than he did the man's efforts to rescue him. Through the buzzing static of pain he noted that blood from his lolling head was soaking Quan's back, and he felt apologetic for it. Almost idly, he watched the erratic movement of Quan's flashlight beam ahead of them. And with a distant sense of concern he too wondered if they'd be shot in the back before they could reach their friends. With that muted concern in mind, against the pain he raised his head and twisted his shoulders around a little to look over his shoulder behind them.

There was a little backwash of light from Quan's flashlight, but somehow Trenor felt he could see more clearly than he should be seeing. Not clearly enough, to be sure, but he could still make out movement across the low ceiling just above their heads, in their wake. Not isolated movement, but a solid seething mass of movement.

Had the ceiling been like this before, upon their entrance into the tunnel, and he had been so focused on what lay ahead that he had overlooked what lay above? It wasn't like him to overlook anything, but it was possible he had mistaken the great congregation of spiders for pure darkness.

For that was what these countless, boiling little bodies appeared to be: small spiders. Or else, large ants. Again, in a detached and analytical kind of way—detached because he was fatalistically accepting of the fact that he was close to death—he recalled that there was a type of spider in Vietnam that for some inscrutable reason mimicked the form of an ant.

Trenor could only look back over his shoulder, only hold himself up a little, a few seconds more before he blacked out and slumped upon his friend's crawling body...so the last thing he saw was that solid mass of tiny black bodies spread above him...and the last feverish thought through his broken and leaking head was: *It's a door made of spiders.*

PART 2: LOST SOULS

1: CHECK OUT (VIETNAM, 2010)

NGOC HADN'T SEEN THE FOREIGNER herself, which she regretted. She was twenty-one and very pretty, and might have attracted the foreigner's eye. But her aunt, who along with her husband owned and managed the hotel, had told her this morning that the guest had come yesterday afternoon just after Ngoc had finished her cleaning rounds, with the intention of staying but a single night, and had paid for his room up-front so that he might set out today before dawn for wherever it was he was headed. Maybe he had to travel to Ho Chi Minh City to catch an early plane at Tan Son Nhat International Airport?

Her aunt had told her the man was attractive enough for his age—whatever that was—and it was obvious he had money, but Ngoc dismissed her frivolous regrets. Anyway, he wasn't the first foreign tourist to have stayed at the hotel, and he wouldn't be the last.

The hotel was a narrow structure of seven floors, but in her experience it had never seen an abundance of guests at any one time—even during holidays like Christmas or Tet—and so she began on the fourth floor in no time, skipping all the rooms that had seen no tenants. Yesterday, the only guests had been a large family on the second floor, who had left in a clamorous bustle in the morning; a couple on the sixth who were staying on and would need a change of sheets and towels today; and the foreigner on the fourth floor. Ngoc's aunt liked to spread her guests out so as to give them more privacy—or perhaps this allowed her the illusion that the hotel wasn't so vacant.

The foreign guest had left his key at the unmanned front desk, and Ngoc's aunt had passed it on to her. Ngoc used it now to let herself into the room, pulling after her the cart she had tilted and dragged up the stairs one glossy granite step at a time, for lack of an elevator.

The rooms were small, and that was why they were only the equivalent of seven US dollars per night. This one had no windows, except a very small curtained panel that inexplicably looked down only into the stairwell. The room was gloomy inside, so Ngoc pressed the light switch.

The guest had left the air conditioner running, mounted on the wall near the low ceiling. Maybe it was to dispel the room's smell, which was unpleasant. Ngoc sneered as soon as she encountered it. The guest must have had food of some kind in here, but it wasn't durian; as strong as that infamous fruit was, its stench was of another quality. To Ngoc, the room stank partly of the musk of sex—the trapped, concentrated stink of animals in rut. Maybe the foreigner had brought a girl up here during the evening? By night, masseuses on bicycles patrolled these streets, crammed as they were with hotels, announcing their presence by shaking rattles made from strung together, flattened beer bottle caps. A hotel guest would call down for one of these mobile masseuses to come up to his room, and some of them were willing to go beyond a mere back rub.

The bed sheets and blanket were in heaped, crumpled disarray, and Ngoc snicked her tongue, but her mood brightened instantly when she spotted a bill resting on top of the mini refrigerator, weighted down with an ashtray filled with stubbed out butts. She all but pounced on the bill, which was ten US dollars, the equivalent of 195,000 Vietnamese *dong*. The Vietnamese didn't believe in tipping, but this—more even than the cost of the room—was generous even for a foreigner. Ngoc folded the bill and slipped it into a pocket. Of course she wouldn't mention this to her aunt.

Her sunny mood persisting, she moved first into the tiny bathroom to clean. A better hotel would probably have a bathtub, but most Vietnamese homes did not and this room lacked one also. There was not even a shower stall; a person simply stood on the floor of dark red tiles to shower and the water ran into a drain. No more towels were on the rack, every one of them having been used. One damp white bath towel was draped more or less neatly across the closed toilet seat cover. The rest were balled up on the floor. They were wet, as if they'd been soaked under running water, but they were still all stained red. Had the guest cut himself? If so, the cut had been a bad one. Ngoc was reminded of the time a drunken guest had fallen in another room's shower, struck his head and required a few stitches. They'd been thankful his injury hadn't been more serious; who needed that kind of trouble?

Ngoc retrieved a face cloth from the floor, wrung it out, and wrinkled her nose in disgust at the amount of reddened water than ran over her hands. Much more of the same was wrung from the larger towels. "*Troi oi*," Ngoc muttered— "oh heavens!"—exasperated and perplexed. No wonder he'd left such a big tip.

Before hanging two new sets of towels on the rack, Ngoc took up the shower hose and sprayed the floor. The water that swirled into the drain took a long time to turn clear.

Before stepping back into the bedroom itself, Ngoc rearranged the two pairs of blue plastic courtesy sandals guests used when showering, both, she knew, much too small for a foreigner. Out of the bathroom, she sighed and turned to the bed with its rumpled mound of bedding. She took hold of the whole mass and jerked it toward her, so she might wad it up into her laundry sack. In so doing, she uncovered a nude person sleeping on their side in a near fetal position.

Ngoc cried out, *"Troi oi! Troi oi! Troi oi!"* She backed away from the bed several steps, as if afraid the sleeping person would rise up and turn toward her, and reveal a face she really didn't want to see. But the curled figure did not rise up, and never would. Her original impression that the tiny person had been sleeping had lasted only a fraction of a second, as the dark-haired back of the head was revealed. When the bedding was swept fully away and she saw the rest, she comprehended the true situation.

The small unclothed body lay on its side facing the far wall. Its flesh was imprinted all over with what looked like the circular marks from the tentacles of a titanic octopus.

The corpse rested in a great irregular patch of stiffening blood, with smears and spatters around its edges, but the body itself was not bloodied. Its hair was damp, plastered across the face that lay in profile, turned away from Ngoc. The damp hair and clean body furthered the impression that this person had been dragged down into the depths by some ravenous creature, before washing ashore again.

But at odds with this image was a cigarette, dry and unlit, extending from the lips of the obscured face.

Unconsciously holding the bedding close to the front of her body as if to hide behind it, but with her tearing eyes locked on the diminutive corpse, Ngoc understood then that the ten-dollar tip had not been a real gratuity, but—like that cigarette—a little touch of whimsy.

2: TIME OFF (MASSACHUSETTS, 2010)

VRISHNI WAS ANOTHER OF THE quality control inspectors for Innovative Productivity Concepts, his cubicle next to Trenor's. Trenor found Vrishni polite and respectful, so he liked the younger man and took breaks with him sometimes, though he preferred sitting alone, shielding himself from other coworkers behind the book he brought with him. Vrishni's computer desktop image was always some voluptuous and exotically attired Bollywood actress baring her fleshy midriff, and he would address the current actress every day with a greeting such as, "Good morning, Asin… Would you like me to lick your dark, sweaty armpits?" But he changed his comments as he changed his images, and the greeting to today's actress was, "Good morning, Anushka… I know you want my cock in your big sexy ass."

Trenor smiled as he settled into his own chair. He figured Vrishni's comments were for his benefit. His own desktop image was of a harbor in Rockport, Massachusetts. Somehow he had always pictured himself retiring early and refurbishing boats in such a setting; Zen and the art of boat repair. Something down-to-earth, romantic for its simplicity. At the very least, some honest-to-God factory job with grease on his hands. Something, dare he think, more manly—or at least more respectable—than this office drone existence, giving the thumbs up to the products of Innovative Productivity Concepts. He'd done those greasy jobs in the past, but most work of that kind had immigrated to Mexico or overseas, and it seemed the best a man could hope for was toner ink on his hands. That was one reason he had been drawn to this company initially, though he himself would be doing less manual work—because they actually manufactured products here. He was bitterly amused now by his naiveté. His own cubicle was sparsely decorated, but he had tacked up a printout of a flag encircled by the words MADE IN THE USA WITH PRIDE. No doubt his superiors didn't realize the sarcasm behind it.

He heard a swish of pant legs advancing along the row of cubicles, recognized by sound the particular shambling walk of his immediate supervisor, Jim. As ever wearing purple T-shirt and matching baseball cap, Jim leaned into Trenor's cubicle and said, "Hey, Richard, when you have a chance Evelyn wants to talk to you."

When Jim had moved on, in the next cubicle Trenor heard Vrishni mutter, "What Evelyn wants is my cock in her ass."

Jim had obviously just come from their manager's office. Trenor felt it was best to go see her now and not keep her waiting. He left the report he'd been entering into his computer, got up and walked back down the aisle the way Jim had come, turned a few corners in the rat maze of cubicle rows, and came to a glass-walled office in which Evelyn was housed behind her desk like a museum specimen representing her species. Though she could see him, she waited for him to rap on the door before gesturing for him to come in. As he took a seat opposite her, she asked him how he was, then moved quickly to the matter at hand.

"Richard, I'm sorry, but I'm afraid I'm going to have to deny your vacation request for the week you submitted. You probably already know Vrishni will be in India at that time, and Jim has the week off, which just leaves us too shorthanded in QC."

"Jim has that week off? He didn't tell me that when I turned in my form."

"Well, he only just put in for it, but we also have to take into consideration his years of service, Richard."

"I see."

"Jim mentioned you wanted to visit your brother in Canada. You know, Christmas itself is on a Saturday this year; would it be possible to get up there Friday night and be back by Monday?"

"It's not really practical. So if not the week after Christmas, how about the week before?"

"Richard, as I say, we have to bear in mind that Vrishni is out for the last three weeks of December. It's just not good timing." She made a pained expression. "We still have time between now and then that you could use your vacation in, but of course you do have to use it before the year runs out because we can't roll over vacation time, as you probably know." Evelyn smiled, tried to make her tone brighter and optimistic on his behalf. "You know, you could break that week up and make some three-day weekends out of it—take off some Mondays or Fridays. That's not a bad idea, huh?"

"I guess I might do that," Trenor said quietly.

"Again, I'm sorry, Richard, but it's just such a popular time for people to take off."

"I understand," Trenor said.

"Thanks for understanding," she said.

Trenor was about to rise from his chair when he found himself distracted by the sight of one of Evelyn's false eyelashes coming half off, and wondered why a woman of her age would even wear such things. But then he saw the eyelash crawl around the corner of her right eye, scurry down to her doughy cheek and poise there, and that was when he realized what he was seeing. A spider. Or an ant. Or something like both a spider and an ant—something familiar despite this vagueness—and he immediately looked away so he wouldn't see it, rose from his chair and moved to the door more quickly than might otherwise have seemed polite.

He saw them sometimes. He couldn't tell when those times would come, so even to this day the creatures could still take him by surprise.

Trenor bypassed his own cubicle on his way back, and stopped outside Jim's instead. He reached in and clapped his supervisor on the shoulder. "Hey there, mighty warrior, congratulations on getting the big holiday week off."

Jim swiveled around in his chair, looking startled and then wary. He hadn't heard Trenor approach. "Yeah, thanks."

What he wanted was to tell Jim he had once worked alongside men who risked their lives for each other, not purple-caped role-players who fucked you behind your back. But instead he asked, "So, what do you think you'll be doing that week to celebrate? Maybe having a few virtual flagons of ale with your fellow avatars in your online game world?"

"Well, we've talked about that, yeah, probably."

Trenor couldn't even laugh at that. He just nodded, turned, and sought out his own work station.

*   *   *

When he'd caught up on his work, Trenor stole some time to check his email. Promises of more money and a larger penis and other American dreams. He sent an email to his brother in Vancouver, explaining why he wouldn't be able to make it this year. Thoughts of email and Christmas made him think that this year, as in the past couple years, he'd just send virtual Christmas cards to the people on his contact list. And his contact list made him think of Quan. He'd still send Quan an email greeting this Christmas, even though his friend hadn't replied to any of his emails for a few years now. At one time the two of them had even exchanged packages through the mail. Well, their friendship had gone the way of all things, Trenor thought.

It was not a coincidence that he should think of Quan at this particular time. Quan was often in his thoughts. In his memories.

3: LOST (VIETNAM, 2010)

THANH WAS IN THE INTERNET café when his father called him. At first he thought he was mistaken about the caller, for all the noise around him, and poked one of the two digits of his left hand into his other ear, squinted as if that might help too, and asked the caller to repeat himself.

"Your sisters aren't home!" the voice repeated, louder with impatience, and now he recognized its slurred gruffness. "Two days! No…three days!"

"What do you mean, they're not home? Did Tra Mi take Hang Ni somewhere? She probably told you but you forgot."

"The bitch threatened me she'd take Hang Ni away! Three days now they aren't home! You need to find them and bring Hang Ni home!"

"Did you try calling Tra Mi?"

"Of course—am I stupid? I've tried a hundred times!"

Thanh sighed, but he heard the worry under his father's anger. He must indeed be worried to be speaking to his son right now. And so Thanh said, "All right, all right, I'll be there."

*   *   *

Despite his deformity Thanh could ride a motorbike capably, and rather than take the bus or rent a taxi he rode all the way from Ho Chi Minh City to his family home in Quyet Thang Ward, just one row of houses away from the edge of the wide green river that snaked through Bien Hoa. Thanh slowed his Honda and turned it into the little unpaved courtyard that his home faced onto. He found his father and a snowy-haired older neighbor sitting outside the house on a cement bench, drinking coffee and smoking cigarettes. His father looked like he'd sobered considerably from when he'd phoned.

Thanh dismounted and walked his bike up beside them, slung off his helmet and immediately asked, "Tra Mi didn't tell you where she might be bringing Hang Ni to?"

Quan glared up at him, and growled, "You better not have taken her yourself, and be trying to trick me."

"I didn't take her!"

"You've threatened to take her in the past, too."

"I didn't take her. I ask you, did Tra Mi say where she might take her?"

"Far away from me, she said."

"I can't believe Tra Mi would really want to look after her. Are you sure you don't forget ordering Tra Mi to take Hang Ni to Dai Nam theme park again, or some other place?"

"No!" Quan snapped.

Again Thanh sighed, as if with a great weariness that even moving to Ho Chi Minh City hadn't relieved, and said simply, "I'll look for them." Then he donned his helmet again, rolled his Honda backwards into the courtyard and mounted it.

Despite the disgust he felt, his father had infected him with his worry.

*　　*　　*

Thanh had been in the coffee house before, though he was sure he had embarrassed Tra Mi in front of her coworkers, and had been embarrassed, himself, to be in the presence of its attractive *ca phe oms*. So it was that one of these young women, whose name Thanh remembered was Hoa, recognized him (he knew he was hard to forget) and turned toward him as he stepped into the cave-like interior through the café's open face. One of the customers paused from his conversation with his own *ca phe om* to gawk at Thanh openly.

As he approached, Hoa smiled pleasantly and called, "*Anh oi*—where is your sister Tra Mi?"

"I was about to ask you the same thing," he said, stopping in front of the girl. She was too pretty, much prettier than his sister. "My father says she hasn't been home in three days."

"She hasn't been to work in three days, either. We haven't seen her, so we were wondering."

"Where is your boss, Long Dien?" Thanh said the name with distaste as he craned his neck to look past the girl toward the back of the café.

"He isn't here now. I think he may be at the Angel Spa, in Saigon."

Thanh had heard that Long Dien owned an uncertain number of other establishments—anything from massage parlors to discos to karaoke joints, in assorted cities—and even managed a casino for foreign tourists in one of Vung Tau's four-star hotels, but Thanh was only sure of the beauty salon in Ho Chi Minh City that Hoa referred to. He hated having to ride all the way back to that city to question Tra Mi's boss if the man couldn't be of help. "Can you give me his number?"

"Okay, but he doesn't know anything—he's confused about Tra Mi not coming in, too."

Thanh took a seat at a table toward the rear of the room. He had requested no *ca phe om* to sit with him, and none had volunteered. He held his cell phone to his ear, and after several rings Long Dien answered in English as many Vietnamese did: "Hello?" In the background, the thump of the Angel Spa's loud club-style music.

"This is Thanh," he said in Vietnamese, without wasting time on a more polite greeting, "Tra Mi's brother. My father says she hasn't been home in three days. Do you know where she is?"

"Ah, Thanh, I remember meeting you once or twice. No, no, I'm sorry—I haven't seen Tra Mi for several days myself, and I was starting to worry."

"Did you try calling her?"

"Yes, but she hasn't returned my calls."

"Hm," Thanh grunted.

"If you see her, please let me know; it isn't like her to miss work like this."

"All right," Thanh said. "And you can call me, too, if you hear from her. She has our younger sister Hang Ni with her."

"Oh! Well, then I'm sure they must simply be away visiting a relative or a friend."

"Maybe," Thanh said. "Okay…thanks." Then he hung up, before they had to exchange any further pleasantries.

*   *   *

At dusk, when Thanh returned to his family home, he found his father's Honda gone. He sat outside on the cement bench, talking on his cell phone, until his father returned. He was completely sober now, and Thanh couldn't recall the last time he had seen that.

"Has she answered your calls?" Quan asked, nodding at Thanh's phone.

"No—you?"

"No."

"I called around to some of my aunts and cousins," Thanh reported. "No one has seen them."

"Did you call your whore mother?"

"Don't say that!" Thanh snarled.

"Did you call her?"

"Yes," he admitted reluctantly.

"And what did she say?"

"She said she hasn't seen Tra Mi and Hang Ni. Now she's concerned."

"Concerned? If she was concerned she never would have left her children behind to go off with her boyfriend!"

"She wanted to take us—you wouldn't let her!"

"If she cared she wouldn't have left!" his father insisted. "I want you to go to Cu Chi tomorrow and see for yourself. I'm sure she's lying, and they're with her."

That did actually seem to Thanh to be the most likely situation at this point. He knew his mother's boyfriend would not be happy to see her two daughters show up on their doorstep, but he also knew that wouldn't necessarily stop Tra Mi.

Thanh offered to make his father some dinner, but he grumbled that he'd already eaten, so Thanh cooked something for himself. As the darkness of evening settled, Quan remained sitting outside smoking—waiting, watching—and Thanh retired upstairs to sleep in Hang Ni's little room, with its green tiled wainscoting and pastel blue plaster walls. The sight of her cheap stuffed animals and stacks of school workbooks gave him a deep pang. He turned on her TV, then prepared to stretch out on the thin mattress that lay on the floor in the corner. As he was straightening out a quilted blanket, he found a dry shriveled object in its folds. It was the tiny dead body of one of the geckos that often clung to the walls of the house, inside and out. Usually they kept out of harm's way, but Hang Ni must have unknowingly crushed this one. He dropped it into a trash basket.

As he considered Hang Ni's belongings a thought occurred to him and he scanned the room, then went to a wardrobe and peered inside. It seemed full enough with Hang Ni's clothing. He left her room, turned into Tra Mi's room, which was only a little larger but featured a curtained glass door that led out onto the second-floor balcony. Thanh probably hadn't set foot in here for a year or more, but his immediate impression was that things were missing. He didn't spot any of Tra Mi's various makeup kits, and when he opened her cheap wardrobe it was clear that much of her clothing wasn't present. Mostly what was left were some older outfits and a couple of *ao dais*. His sister had always said she didn't like to wear the traditional *ao dai*, as she was too thin to look good in one.

Thanh grew hot thinking how Tra Mi had selfishly seen to it that wherever she had gone, she would have her best clothing and personal articles with her, while apparently not bringing along much of anything for Hang Ni. He still couldn't believe she would have wanted the responsibility of taking Hang Ni with her, at all.

He returned to Hang Ni's room and lay on the mattress, taking up the TV's remote. This TV didn't receive the US programming that the one in the living room did—such as the Discovery Channel, which he liked, and HBO Asia—so he searched through a limited selection of local channels. After watching a little of this and that he finally settled on a news program to listen to a story about the flooding in the central part of the country, which had claimed nineteen lives and forced forty-thousand people to evacuate.

The story concluded and the camera switched back to a practically unblinking female newscaster dressed in an *ao dai*. In a voice as stiff as her expression she reported, "Today in Vung Tau the body of a murdered young girl was discovered in a hotel room by cleaning staff…"

Holding the remote in one claw-like hand, one digit resting on the channel advance key, Thanh had been ready to change to another station after the flood story but stopped himself. The reporter went on to name the hotel, and relate other details. "…The hotel's owner claims that the guest who rented the room was a foreigner, but did not see the man's passport or learn his name. When he rented the room he was alone, and hotel staff insists they never saw the young girl enter the building. The girl also remains unidentified, but was not a foreigner herself. Police experts estimate that she was between seven and ten years of age…"

"*Troi oi,*" Thanh whispered. Oddly, just then he felt like a person does before they slip and fall—painfully, disastrously fall—and in that suspended bubble of time understands fatalistically that the impact is approaching.

"…In order to help identify the girl, police have released this photograph…"

The image they cut to, the photograph that filled the screen, was of a child's face. A sheet covered her to the chin. Her hair seemed to be damp, her bangs stuck to her forehead.

Despite his presentiment, Thanh sat up sharply on the mattress. His heart had tried to cannonball its way out of his chest, but had struck a wall.

"…if you have any information…"

The lovely face was unmarked. With her closed eyes and slightly parted lips, she looked only asleep under that sheet. But they'd said she was dead.

They'd said she was dead.

When Thanh came out of the house, already wearing his helmet and wheeling the motorbike he had earlier rolled into the living room to prevent theft during the night, his father looked up at him from where he sat alone on the cement bench and asked, "What was all that noise inside?"

"TV…I was watching TV," Thanh choked, keeping his face down so his father wouldn't see his burned-red eyes.

"Where are you going?" Quan demanded.

"To see if Hang Ni is with my mother in Cu Chi," Thanh lied. As he threw one leg over the saddle, he added, "I can't sleep."

That much was true, at least.

4: FOUND

BY CAR, IT MIGHT HAVE taken Thanh over two hours to drive from Bien Hoa to the seaside resort city of Vung Tau, but on a motorbike it was even longer, and it took longer still to locate the provincial police station he sought. By then it was deep into the night, and hours of inhaling bike and car exhaust—and hours of being propelled by an anxiety close to panic—had left him with a headache like a bullet plowed through his sinuses. When he climbed off his bike in front of the *Cong an Tinh Ba Ria Vung Tau* his legs were shaking so badly he had to steady himself with a hand on the seat before he moved toward the entrance. It was as though he had never walked on his bare, malformed feet before, despite the hard calluses that belied this.

Immediately inside behind a large desk sat a police officer in a green, short-sleeved uniform with red epaulettes. On his head, a green military cap with the national emblem on the front. The man appeared unsettled by Thanh's appearance at this late hour—and by his physical appearance. The officer might have intended to ask what he could do for Thanh, but instead blurted, "What do you want?"

"The girl you showed on TV," Thanh said breathlessly, sounding to himself like a drunk or deranged person, "the murdered girl...I want to see her."

"Why?"

"I think it's my sister."

*   *   *

Two policemen on motorbikes rode side-by-side ahead of him toward the Le Loi Hospital, just a short drive north from the police station. Thanh experienced every sensation along the way with supernatural vividness: the flapping of the cool wind in his face, the sight of the scrolling city half darkened and half twinkling. The black abyss of the sky sucking at him, and the nearby abyss of the ocean presently unseen but somehow exerting its weight against him from behind. The sensations were bittersweet, and he understood that after tonight he would never experience them again in his life with an untroubled soul.

To the left now a steep hill loomed above a greyhound racetrack. Directly opposite was the *Benh Vien Le Loi*. They brought their trio of bikes to a stop in front of a metal gate in a stained yellow plaster wall with a red cross painted on it.

They waited beside their bikes for what seemed to Thanh an excruciating eternity, though the police had phoned the individual they waited for in advance. At last the man who had told them to meet him at this point arrived on his own Honda. He was tall for a Vietnamese, balding, with a pleasant smile but eyes that appeared somewhat crossed. When he saw Thanh he looked him up and down in a way that suggested he had just discovered an interesting specimen.

The man guided them inside, and along the way to their destination stopped in a small office to retrieve a lab coat and collection of keys, coming finally to a room he unlocked with one of these. He reached in to switch on overhead fluorescents before they entered.

The air was very cool within, but Thanh had begun shivering violently before they even crossed the threshold. He took in the rows of labeled metal hatches. The man in the lab coat went to one of them and unlatched it; the unlatching sound made Thanh flinch. He felt nauseous, and his gorge yawed at the sound of the drawer being rolled out. Upon its surface lay a small form covered by a sheet. Without any sign from Thanh or the two police officers to prompt him, and without preamble, the man in the lab coat folded back the sheet from the face beneath it.

A drawn-out animal sound, rising in pitch, issued from Thanh and he dropped to his knees. As he emitted this cry it felt as if all his entrails were being pulled out of his mouth in a continuous chain. Then he was emptied. His head sagged and he sobbed, and the younger of the two policemen leaned over to speak gently, a hand on Thanh's back. "Please…please get up now."

"It's his sister," the man in the lab coat confirmed needlessly. Perhaps it was a little joke.

With the younger policeman holding one elbow, Thanh rose. He returned his eyes to his sister's face slowly. When he did, his sobbing strengthened again but he remained standing. "Hang Ni," he moaned.

"I'm sorry," said the older of the two policemen stiffly. "We'll need to ask you some questions about your sister."

Thanh could only blurt a question of his own. "How did she die?"

"She was murdered."

"I know she was murdered!" he shouted. "I need to know how! I need to know everything! Show me!"

Again, the man in the lab coat did not wait for the assent of the policemen. He drew back the sheet from the tiny cadaver fully.

Thanh retched, whirled away and doubled over and pressed the palms of his misshapen hands into the sockets of his eyes, as if they had been sprayed with acid. "Ohhh," he said. "Ohhh."

"The Y cut is of course from her autopsy," the man in the lab coat hastened to explain, lest his stitched handiwork be mistaken for the killer's by this layman. "The other wounds you see across her body are bite marks. Most of them are only bruises but others break the skin, like this one around her nipple here." He pointed, though Thanh didn't look. "Most of these markings—the most severe bite marks—are concentrated on her buttocks, but her upper arms and legs were repeatedly bitten as well. There are even markings on the soles of her feet."

"What did he do to her throat?" the younger policeman croaked, staring down at the body with an aghast expression while his partner only scowled.

"It appears the perpetrator actually bit into her throat rather than cut it," the man in the lab coat explained, with the same interest in his voice that his eyes had shown upon meeting Thanh. Again he pointed. "You see the tearing, or chewing? The jugular vein was opened, though whether the perpetrator drank any of her blood as a result, in a fantasy of vampirism, I can't say."

"Ohhh!" Thanh wailed. "Hang Ni, *Hang Ni!*"

"That should be enough," advised the senior police officer.

"Was her virginity taken?" Thanh managed to get out.

"Yes," the man in the lab coat replied freely, "she was raped. Of course. But I found no marks of resistance or signs that she had been violently subdued, that would indicate a struggle had occurred during the rape or the biting of her throat. No apparent blows to the head, signs of strangulation, ligature marks to indicate she might have been bound at any time, bruising or scratching around her female parts. I thought perhaps all the biting and even her violation had come *after* death, but my true suspicions were confirmed when I ran my various tests."

"What did you find?" the older policeman demanded.

"In her blood I detected traces of the drug flunitrazepam. In the USA they call it a 'date rape' drug."

"The killer is said to be a foreigner," the younger policeman reminded them.

"Flunitrazepam is used throughout the world," the man in the lab coat advised. "In the USA it's illegal, but it's prescribed legally in numerous other countries. It has legitimate uses, but rapists utilize the drug not only to sedate their victims, but to create amnesia after the attack." His pleasant smile widened. "You're lucky I was able to detect the drug; it can be difficult to do."

The younger policeman turned to Thanh, who still covered his eyes, and placing a hand on his shoulder intoned solemnly, "Don't worry; we'll find this foreigner, whoever he is, and he'll be shot for this."

"If he hasn't already left the country," the man in the lab coat said. "That's what I would do if I were him."

Thanh lowered his hands to glare at the man, then turned to the older policeman and asked, "So where is my other sister, Tra Mi?"

The two policemen exchanged looks, even looked to the man in the lab coat before turning to Thanh again.

The older policeman said, "*Other* sister?"

5: LINES OF COMMUNICATION (MASSACHUSETTS, 2010)

IN THE WARM MONTHS, ON weekends, Trenor often slept on a futon in the glassed-in front porch of his small two-story house on the periphery of the town center, bought on the GI Bill and fully paid for. After his mother's death, he had taken in his father and given him the second floor, but within the past ten years he'd lost both parents. In that same period, he had also lost his longest relationship, which had lasted three years. Lost his longest-lasting job, which had been fifteen years. Had even lost his twelve-year-old dog. His brother had told him he should try to see past these losses, however traumatic, and take on the outlook that he was free to start life anew. In publicity interviews Trenor read, actors frequently said they felt life was just beginning for them at forty, or fifty, or sixty, but to him that was just bullshit to deceive their fans and themselves. Life didn't begin with facelifts, and it didn't begin with the pains he felt in his knees. The only freedom he felt he was up for, at the age of sixty, was sleeping on his front porch in the warmer months of the year.

But it was early December, and Trenor had fallen asleep on his sofa watching TV—a winter months weekend habit that during eight months of being laid off, prior to his employment at Innovative Productivity Concepts, had encroached into weekdays as well. When his phone rang, he lifted his head from the sofa, looked at the time display on his TV's cable box, and saw that it was 2:46 AM. "What the fuck?" he muttered, but he swung himself into a sitting position quickly, rose and crossed the room to the phone. His immediate concern was that the caller was his brother in Vancouver. Had something serious happened to one of his children, his wife or himself?

Trenor didn't recognize the number on the caller ID, and it originated from an "Unknown Caller." He reluctantly lifted the handset before his answering machine could kick in, thumbed the TALK button and grumbled, "Hello?"

"Is this Mr. Richard Trenor?" asked an unfamiliar, accented voice.

"Yes." Trenor's wariness was mounting, as was his irritation; tomorrow was a workday. "Who is this?"

"I'm Thanh. My father is Nguyen Van Quan." The caller pronounced *Nguyen* as *Win*, but Trenor knew how it was spelled.

"Quan? Who did you say you are...his son?"

"Yes, I'm Thanh."

"Thanh, right, of course." Trenor felt relief, followed swiftly by concern again. Why would Quan's son be calling him after he hadn't heard anything from Quan himself in several years? Had he been ill, then, and now his son was calling to report that he'd just passed away? "What's going on, Thanh?" he asked, dreading the answer.

"Do you have a computer, Mr. Richard?"

"Yes...why?"

"I'm calling you with a phone card. It will be easier for me to talk with you in a chat. Do you know how to chat, Mr. Richard?"

"I chat with my brother, yes. Thanh, just tell me what it is."

"Please, Mr. Richard, it isn't easy for me to tell you in a few words."

"Okay, Thanh," Trenor sighed. "But you do know there's a twelve-hour time difference between Vietnam and Massachusetts, don't you?"

"Oh...yes...yes, sorry, I forgot about that! I'm so sorry, Mr. Richard, but please..."

"Okay, okay, just hurry and tell me what I need to do."

Several minutes later, Trenor was sitting in front of his computer, having signed in to his chat program and sipping a tall can of coffee-flavored energy drink while he waited for Thanh to make an appearance. His gaze drifted from the computer screen to another of the living room's walls. Hanging there in an 8.5 x 11 printout, beside a Bronze Star and Purple Heart mounted in a frame and several certificates of achievement from martial arts schools, two young soldiers posed for a friend's camera. A young Caucasian man, still with two good eyes, with an arm slung carelessly around the neck of a small Asian man.

A chime alerted Trenor and brought his attention back to his computer. Thanh had sent a message that asked Trenor to accept him into his contacts list. Trenor did so, and immediately Thanh was there with his first typed message.

Thanh: *Hello, Mr. Richard?*

Trenor: *Yes, I'm here.*

Trenor was invited to view Thanh's webcam. He clicked to open the broadcast, dragged the window to one corner of his screen, and took in the face framed within it. A young man of—how old would he be now, twenty?—with a pleasant if serious face. Didn't look like his father; his mother, Trenor supposed. Quan had mailed or emailed a few photos of his family in years past, and Trenor remembered his wife as very attractive, ten years younger than her husband. He couldn't recall ever having seen a photo of Thanh before, however, even as a child.

Thanh requested to view Trenor's webcam. He hesitated, considering whether to lie that he didn't own one, but then he figured the boy had surely heard the story of how he had been wounded before his father came to his aid. So Trenor left his chair for a moment to find his patch and cover the fleshy bomb crater of his right eye socket before positioning himself in front of his computer again. He assented to Thanh's request, and permitted him to view his webcam.

Thanh: *I see you.*

Trenor: *I see you, too. So what's up, Thanh? Is something wrong?*

Behind Thanh, Trenor could see the backs of people hunched in front of other computers. An internet café, then. The young man sucked at his lips, then leaned forward to type: *Do you know I have two sisters?*

Trenor: *I remember that, yes.*

Thanh: *One week ago, my sister Hang Ni was killed in a hotel room in Vung Tau.*

"What?" Trenor hissed aloud. "God damn." He typed: *Killed how?*

Thanh: *Someone killed her.*

Trenor groaned. He wagged his head for Thanh to see, and typed: *Oh my God, Thanh, I'm so sorry. Do the police know who did it? Why they did it?*

Thanh: *No. They say they are looking. I don't know how much those hookers are looking.*

Trenor: *Hookers?*

Thanh: *That is what I call the police. You can buy them like hookers. If I paid them something maybe they would look more carefully.*

Over the years Trenor had tried avoiding reading about Vietnam, not caring to know how the country might have healed or changed since he'd left there, but sometimes his curiosity got the better of him, and in one travel guide he'd once thumbed through in a bookstore he'd read that Vietnam's police were "the best money can buy."

He typed: *Where is your father right now? Did he ask you to contact me?*

Thanh typed rapidly, and Trenor was impressed with his written English; he seemed even more adept with the language than his father had become over the course of their correspondence. He wrote: *My father is in Bien Hoa. I'm in Saigon. My father is very sad, but I can't stay in the house with him anymore. He is drinking too much, drinking all day and night. He can't work. He only wants to fight with me. He blames me for Hang Ni. He says if I never moved away to Saigon, and I stayed in Bien Hoa to care for Hang Ni, she would still be alive.*

Trenor shook his head. *That's unfair of him. What about your mom?*

Thanh: *She came for the funeral, but she went back home already.*

Trenor: *Back home?*

Thanh: *My mother left my father. She lives with a man in Cu Chi.*

The name Cu Chi made Trenor wince inside. He had a bizarre mental flash of Thanh's mother hiding from Quan down in the famous Cu Chi tunnels with her lover. He replied: *Poor Quan. No wonder he's a wreck. Does he know you're contacting me?*

Thanh: *No, I did it on my own. I can get into his email so I found your email address there. I saw my father never opened the most recent emails from you. In one older email I found your phone number.*

"Jeez, smart kid," Trenor muttered. He typed: *I forget…is Hang Ni the big sister or the little one?*

Thanh: *My little sister. She was eight years old. My sister Tra Mi is missing.*

Trenor: *What? Missing?*

Thanh: *She must have taken Hang Ni to Vung Tau, and someone kidnapped them. We don't know where Tra Mi is. Maybe she is dead, too.*

Trenor: *Oh my God, Thanh. Jesus Christ.*

Thanh: *I want to ask you for your help, Mr. Richard.*

Trenor: *Sure, Thanh, what can I do? You need some money to light a fire under the cops' asses? Or you want me to talk with your dad, see if I can get him to stop drowning himself in the booze?*

Thanh: *I want to ask you to come to Vietnam, Mr. Richard.*

Trenor almost laughed aloud, though in some way Thanh's simple words horrified him. He typed: *Thanh, what do you want me to do in Vietnam? I can send some money through Western Union, or talk with your dad on the phone. I can call him, so he doesn't have to worry about the charges.*

Thanh: *We need help to find the man who killed my sister. My father used to brag to us that you were not afraid of anything.*

Now Trenor did laugh; couldn't help it. *Kid, I'm no superhero Rambo or vigilante Travis Bickle. I'm 60 years old! A lot of guys have fought in this or that war, including your dad. I really don't know what I could do for you.*

Thanh: *My father told us you were a crazy badass.* For the first time Trenor saw Thanh smile in the little square on his screen.

Trenor: *That's half right. You had to be, to be a Tunnel Rat. Like most young guys I thought I was immortal. But that doesn't mean I wasn't afraid.*

Looking grim again, Thanh wrote: *The people at the hotel told the police the man who rented the room was a foreigner. A foreigner killed my sister. I'm sorry, but maybe he was an American. Maybe you could help us find him because you are an American.*

Trenor: *If it was a tourist, from the US or anywhere, he might not even be in Vietnam anymore. In fact, I can bet on that, Thanh.*

Thanh: *If he returned to the USA you could find out about him here and follow him back to your country.*

Trenor: *And do what if I found him? Blow him away?*

Thanh didn't type a response, just stared at Trenor from that window.

Trenor blew out a long exhalation and wrote: *Again, he might not be an American anyway. I know this sounds terrible, but is there a chance Tra Mi killed her accidentally and ran away in fear? Or maybe even Hang Ni slipped and fell or something and her death was an accident, but Tra Mi still ran away?*

Thanh typed: *The man who killed my sister bit into her neck and she bled to death.*

"Holy fuck," Trenor said. "Holy fucking Christ." Collecting himself again, he replied: *Thanh, I know this is all a horrible nightmare for you, I know you're feeling distraught and desperate and you're grabbing at straws, but I truly can't see how I could do any more than the police could do. I don't even know your country anymore. And I have a job.* He regretted typing that last comment, but had already sent the message into their dialogue box.

Thanh: *I understand, Mr. Richard. Forgive me for asking you. I was foolish.*

Trenor: *No, you're not foolish, and don't apologize. I apologize to you. If there's any other way I can help you, help you from here, you've got it. I think it's important for your dad to talk with me. Could you try to get through to him to call or email me?*

Thanh: *I will try.*

Trenor knew the Vietnamese were by nature polite and reserved, and in his webcam broadcast Thanh's solemn expression hadn't turned to one of anger or open resentment, and yet Trenor still felt he could sense the bitter disappointment the boy must be experiencing. He almost resented himself at that moment, wished he was that crazy twenty-year-old soldier again, who had volunteered to go to Vietnam and once there had volunteered to become a Tunnel Rat. They only took volunteers to be Tunnel Rats.

When he'd lost his eye, he had been the age that Thanh was now.

And it was Thanh's father, only eighteen years old in 1970, who had pulled Trenor out of that tunnel.

He wouldn't have made it home if not for Quan. But made it home for what? To be living in a house alone? To be working for Innovative Productivity Concepts? And what had Quan won for his service in the war? Imprisonment for six grueling years, Trenor knew, for "reeducation." A wife who'd left him, one daughter dead and the other maybe dead. Quan had saved Trenor, but couldn't save himself from what lay down his own booby trapped path.

Thanh: *I'm sorry I woke you at this time, Mr. Richard. Please go back to bed. I'm sure you have to work in the morning.*

Trenor: *I am so very sorry, Thanh, for all you're going through. I'm bleeding for you inside, believe me.*

Thanh: *I see I need to take care of this myself. My father is right, it is all my fault. I should not have moved far away and left my little sister.*

Trenor: *Hey, look, kid, you can't be saying that.*

Thanh: *Thank you, Mr. Richard. Goodbye.*

Trenor: *Hold on.*

But a little box rose up for a moment in the bottom corner of Trenor's screen to let him know that Thanh had already signed off.

6: LEAVE OF ABSENCE

IN THE PLANT, TRENOR HAD just inspected and released for shipping a batch of the toilets the workers called the "bidet," and he returned to his cubicle to enter his report. But for the moment, he laid his clipboard aside and poked around a bit on the internet instead, doing a number of keyword searches.

He looked into the time it would take to arrange a visa to Vietnam. About five days once the embassy had the application in hand. He found the processing could be expedited to one or two days, for an additional charge.

His house and car were paid for. He had no wife or children. He had a substantial amount of savings in the bank. Additional fees were not daunting.

He did a search into tours geared for Vietnam veterans, found one organization that even helped vets pay for such trips if they couldn't afford it. But again, that wasn't really a concern to him. Would there be any such tours, though, during the Christmas season? Anyway, if he were to go, he would need to move freely, not be tied to a group and making new buddies. Still, except for Canada he had never traveled alone outside the country. Even the first time over there he hadn't been alone.

He went on to do a search for local travel agencies, discovered several that catered to the Vietnamese community right in the nearby city of Worcester. He called one of these and asked how soon a person might be able to arrange a flight to Vietnam.

The male agent replied, "Oh, sir, this is a very busy time of year. Many people go to Vietnam to be with their families for the holidays. It would be very difficult to find a seat right now."

"Yes, I'm very much aware this is a busy time of year," Trenor said. "So...difficult, or impossible?"

"Not impossible, but expensive, I'm afraid."

Trenor didn't doubt this was all true, but also didn't doubt that the agent wouldn't want to make it look easy when there was extra money to be made. "How expensive?"

"*If* I could find you a seat somewhere, it could possibly be in the area of eighteen hundred dollars, sir."

"I see. And can you arrange visas, too, or do I have to take care of that part?"

"Oh, we can handle all that for you, sir. Do you have a passport?"

He did, for his occasional trips to Vancouver. "Yes."

"Very good. Would you like to come into the office and see what we can find for you?"

"I'm, ah...I'm interested in that, yes. You're on Green Street, right?"

Before Trenor hung up, he got the agency's full address and hours of operation. Having done this, he promptly rose from his desk and left his cubicle, headed for the office of his manager, Evelyn.

"Maybe I should have got more sleep," Trenor conversed with himself in a mumble on the way. "I'd be more clear-headed. Less likely to do something stupid, here." But he didn't turn back.

Maybe if he hadn't had to inspect those bidet toilets first thing in the morning, he reflected.

He knocked on the glass wall of Evelyn's office, and waited until she was off the phone and had gestured for him to come in and sit down.

"Evelyn," he said, his voice comfortable and unhesitant, even good-natured, "I need to take a leave of absence from work."

"Oh?" She raised her eyebrows. "Is something wrong?"

"A death in the family, overseas."

"Overseas?"

"Vietnam."

"You have family in Vietnam?"

"Well, it's not exactly my family. A friend's family. His daughter."

"I see. I'm sorry to hear that. But you know, Richard, a leave of absence should pertain to a member of your immediate family."

"Wouldn't that just be funeral leave? Shouldn't leave of absence be a little broader in scope than that?"

"Well, I'm just thinking of our company's policies, and our production needs. When would you need this leave of absence, and for how long?"

"Immediately. And, I guess a month." He'd read that a standard tourist visa to Vietnam was good for thirty days, though one could get an extension once in the country.

"Immediately, huh? So, all of December, then?" Evelyn shifted her weight in her chair and sighed. "Richard, I realize how important it was for you to take a week off to visit your brother in Canada..."

"This is Vietnam, Evelyn. Not Canada."

"But the timing is a little coincidental, isn't it?"

"Life is full of intriguing coincidences, Evelyn."

She stared at him, obviously not quite sure how to digest this statement. During that long unblinking moment, he saw the spider push its head out of the duct of her eye. This time it didn't surprise him. "Richard, I'm very sorry, but I'm going to have to deny your request for the same reasons I couldn't accept your vacation request for the last week in December. Jim and Vrishni will both be out...you know that."

"You won't even discuss my request with Human Resources?"

"They would defer to me, and our department's needs," she said, as the insect-like creature fully emerged to perch upon the rim of her skull socket, like a butterfly fresh from the chrysalis drying its wings before it can take flight.

"Okay, well." Trenor sighed, too, and sat back in his chair. "Then I'm going to have to give you a one-week notice, Evelyn."

"Notice? Richard, come on now..."

"Sorry. I have to do this."

"If you think this will change my mind, I'm sorry but I just can't."

"I understand you can't lose me for a month. But, well, now you'll be losing me anyway. That's where you're at, and that's where I'm at, isn't it?"

"Richard, I can't have employees threatening me to get their way."

Trenor grinned, and leaned far forward in his chair. He said in a low voice, "Threatening you? Evelyn, if I were threatening you, you'd know it."

His manager broke eye contact to adjust the position of her computer's keyboard. The slight movement seemed to nudge the spider-thing, and it scrambled lower to pause again beside one nostril, as if to peer into another region of dark interior. "Well," was all she said.

"Look," Trenor went on, "maybe I'll just leave right now. I think that would be better for both of us. I have a lot of things to do before my trip, anyway." He rose from his chair.

Evelyn looked up at him, appearing more nervous now than firm. "I'm sorry, Richard... Please don't be angry."

At her door, Trenor glanced back and said, "Don't be afraid, Evelyn, I'm not going to come back to work with a shotgun and blow everybody away or anything." He enjoyed that her face seemed at a loss for finding an expression, that it remained utterly slack even when the spider disappeared up her nose. He let himself out of her glass terrarium.

He was gathering his few personal belongings from his cubicle when barrel-bellied and bushy-bearded Jim stepped into its opening, garbed in purple T-shirt and purple baseball cap. "Richard, Evelyn says you're leaving us?"

"Yep." Trenor rose from his chair, a plastic shopping bag in one hand. "Nice working with ya, mighty warrior." He brushed past Jim on his way from the cubicle, turned back and said, "And Jim, for God's sake, will you change your color scheme? You look like Barney the fucking dinosaur."

On the other side of the row of cubicles, Jim's friend Peter had poked his head up to listen in. Trenor faced him and said, "What do you want, numb nuts?"

Peter sank down quickly out of view like a gopher into its hole, and Trenor marched for the exit to the parking lot.

* * *

That evening, once he'd arrived home from his excursion to Worcester, Trenor opened his chat program and invited Thanh to chat. He sent a few messages, but the automated responses told him that Thanh was offline and would receive them when he signed in. Of course, Trenor remembered, it was only seven o'clock in the morning over there.

But not even an hour later, a chime sounded on Trenor's computer and he dropped down the screen he'd been looking at (a web site about modern day Vietnam) to view the chat screen. There in the dialogue box was a return message that read: *Mr. Richard?*

Trenor typed: *All I can say is you'd better be waiting for me at the airport when I get there, kid. Book a hotel room for me in Saigon, because my plane arrives at night and I'll be too tired to go to Bien Hoa till the next day. Don't worry, I'll pay you back for the hotel and the taxi if we need one.*

Thanh: *Mr. Richard, are you coming?*

Trenor: *Didn't your dad tell you I was crazy?*

PART 3: CONVERGENCE

1: BUYING BEAUTY (VIETNAM, 2010)

WHEN ONE STEPPED INTO THE Angel Spa, it was to be immediately greeted with the sight of a dozen young women loitering about up front, leaning against support columns or just ranked in a fidgety line, all wearing an identical uniform of tube top and tight miniskirt, white with a matching flowered pattern. Long Dien might have gotten away with a less than beautiful girl or two in his Bien Hoa coffee shop, but not at his Ho Chi Minh City beauty salon. Especially not here in the tourist-heavy area called Walking Street, where competition was tough. Each young woman had been selected for her long legs and light skin. Any one of them could have been a model. Or, at least, a mannequin.

They greeted the American with familiarity and winning smiles, praised him for his smart attire, called him, *"Dẹp trai quá"*—very handsome. Did he want his hair washed? A massage? He grunted a few brusque hellos but didn't indulge in pleasantries. He had no time for it. While tending to business in Hanoi he hadn't distracted himself with women, either…though he had found himself thinking of the somber beauty who called herself Kate, had found himself anxious to see her again. He'd surprised himself in this; maybe disturbed himself a little, too.

Foregoing further interaction with the cloned lovelies, he waited for the older and more conservatively dressed hostess to approach him. "Where's Long Dien?" he asked in Vietnamese.

"Upstairs, sir. I'll take you."

They moved toward the back of the establishment, past men and women having their hair shampooed and lathered scalps massaged in front of mirrored walls. In the past the American had enjoyed the same treatment here—plus haircuts and manicures, while sipping an iced coffee or orange juice—but he was not in the mood for pampering today. He followed the hostess up narrow flights of stairs to the more subdued third floor, the Angel Spa's club music booming below them. The hostess knocked on a door and waited to be cleared before she stuck her head in. Then she held the door open for the American, and retreated.

Long Dien lay on his belly on a massage table, the only one presently occupied in the dimly lit room, his rear covered by a towel. One of the salon girls had removed the platform heels that made her legs even longer and was walking on her manager's back, one hand holding onto a metal rail bolted into the ceiling as if riding on a rocking subway train. Long Dien lifted his head and said, "Hello, my friend. How was Hanoi?"

"Never mind that. Send the girl out."

Long Dien did so, and the young woman climbed down from the table and retrieved her shoes, but scurried from the room barefoot with her eyes averted. Long Dien sat up slowly and discreetly adjusted his towel around his middle.

"So have you seen the news?" the American asked him. "The little girl in Vung Tau?"

"Yes, I have." Long Dien wagged his head as if at some national disaster...in some other nation.

"It's a big story."

"I know...yes, I know."

"When you arranged it, did my client say anything to you about *his* client intending to kill the girl?"

"No, no! My understanding was that she would be drugged, then returned to her sister later, unharmed. Without remembering a thing."

"Maybe he wanted to be certain she didn't remember a thing." The American began pacing. "I'm not happy about this at all. Not one fucking bit. In the newspapers, on TV. All the more attention because he's not Vietnamese."

"I swear to you I didn't have any knowledge the girl would be hurt. I'm sure your contact and I didn't misunderstand each other. But remember, I never met his friend."

"I never met him, either." The American still paced, like an agitated tiger in its cage.

"Have you talked to your client yet?"

"I want to see him in person." The American glanced over at Long Dien. "What about the sister...your waitress? Did he kill her, too?"

"Maybe; I haven't seen her since. Maybe the police haven't found her body yet."

"Or maybe she's still alive out there. Surprised about this like we are. But she'll be more than surprised...she could hurt us. And it isn't just you she knows. She may not know my name, but she knows my face."

"Her brother called me." Long Dien's tone was hesitant.

The American quit his pacing. "Brother? What did he say?"

Long Dien managed to avoid meeting his friend's scalpel gaze, fussing with his towel again instead. "He asked if I had seen Tra Mi. I said no, and I told him I was concerned about her. I was good...I told him to have her call me if he heard from her."

"You see? You see how dangerous this is for us now? Because my client didn't make it clear to us what his customer wanted, or didn't make his customer aware of what was permitted."

"I'm sorry, but I handled it very clearly myself."

"All my professional relationships are based upon trust. With mutual trust and honesty, the risks can be managed. So I don't appreciate having myself made vulnerable like this. It isn't professional of my client to put me in a threatening position."

"I understand."

"I should hope so, because you're under threat now, too."

"So what are you going to do?"

"Like I said, I plan on meeting with him. I want him to account for himself." The American took a step closer to Long Dien, lowering his head as if the tiger were free now and stealing up on its prey through tall grass. "If the sister is alive, and contacts you about this, get her to tell you where she is."

"I will…immediately, my friend. I will."

"Same thing with the brother. You let me know if he calls you again, too."

2: FLIGHT (MASSACHUSETTS—
VIETNAM, 2010)

SITTING AT HIS GATE AT Boston's Logan Airport, Trenor realized he was just as tense now as when he had first left home for basic training, over forty years ago.

His United Airlines flight left Boston shortly before eight AM, and three hours later touched down at Chicago's O'Hare Airport. He had an hour and a half to kill before his plane left Chicago for Hong Kong. He made sure he located his gate before allowing himself to wander the concourse a bit, pulling his rattling carry-on bag behind him. He resisted eating because he knew he'd eat on the flight, but despite his nervousness bought himself a coffee just as he had at Logan. After all, he'd barely been able to sleep last night and already felt burnt-out, everything unreal and fizzy at the edges. He told himself he'd sleep on the next—the longest—leg of the journey.

He looked around at the primarily Asian travelers waiting to board with him. How many were headed to Hong Kong, and how many would continue on with him to Vietnam?

The flight from O'Hare to Hong Kong was over fifteen and a half hours of straight flying. They passed through numerous time zones. Vietnam was in the UTC+07 time zone, twelve hours ahead of Eastern Standard Time; they were already living tomorrow. The plane was like a time machine, cutting into the future. Or, for him, from the remembered Vietnam of four decades past to modern day Vietnam.

Regardless of his weariness he found he was unable to sleep on the plane, only dozing in fragments. He resented those passengers he saw who covered themselves with a blanket and slept for hours, but also knew better than to try to sedate himself with alcohol; the last thing he needed was one of his headaches. His knees hurt enough already, jammed as he was into a tiny seat. He was sure he felt more claustrophobic than he had in the tunnels, ready to burst out of his skin. He ate his meals with his elbows pressed to his sides. At least he had a window seat.

He alternated between reading from his new travel guide and watching movies on one of the overhead monitor screens. He would doze off toward the end of one movie, wake to find himself in the midst of another, as if they were all one continuous exercise in Hollywood filmmaking as prefabricated, prepackaged, and bland as the airplane food.

But there were breaks between the films, during which the monitors and the main screen toward the front of the economy class cabin showed the plane's progress. His heart sank every time he saw how much farther, how many hours, yet remained.

It had gone from night to day, as the plane plowed along diligently to catch up with the sun. At last, outside his little window—through an intervening migration of small clouds—Trenor could see dense clusters of tall buildings strung along a broken shoreline, white-outlined islands afloat in a gleaming silver sea, and rumpled green mountains. The plane descended to the great flat island that was Hong Kong International Airport.

He passed through customs, where his bag was X-rayed, and felt as edgy as if he were smuggling dope. The stern-faced agents motioned him through, and he was free to explore his terminal. The first thing he explored, with much relief, was the men's room.

Again, he established immediately—and triple-checked like an obsessive-compulsive—that he had the correct gate for his flight before setting out to wander the vast airport. He had three hours to experience this one bit of Hong Kong before his flight departed for Vietnam.

The airport was modern, polished and immaculate, already beautifully decorated for Christmas. Pretty shop girls wore red Santa hats. Disregarding the long, automated walkways, he pulled his carry-on bag past duty-free liquor stores, shops selling trendy clothing, electronic gadgets, magazines and books. He stepped into one shop to admire the designs on a series of T-shirts and considered buying one for his brother's son, but decided not to chip into his money or start filling up his luggage so soon into his trip. He did give in, though, when he encountered a Starbucks. He paid for his coffee with US currency but the change he received was a heavy coin representing five Hong Kong dollars. Maybe he'd give that to his nephew instead.

Sipping his coffee, he watched the bustle of travelers but tried not to admire excessively the many, to his mind, exotic women. Because of his maiming, over the years he had endeavored to maintain a monk-like peace of mind in the presence of the opposite sex. But he was idly fantasizing about remaining in Hong Kong and not even going on to Vietnam at all (would he need a visa in Hong Kong?), knowing all the time that he couldn't do that to Quan's son, when an attractive Chinese woman in a smart business outfit approached his table, smiled, and asked in perfect English, "Excuse me, is it all right if I sit here?"

"Ah, yeah, sure," Trenor stammered, sitting up straighter as the woman took a seat at the table he sat at, placing her own coffee before her.

Were the tables beside the coffee shop that full, or was she trying to flirt with a foreign man? If that were the case, Trenor thought, then she must not see too many foreign men. Maybe coming toward his table from a distance, at an angle, she hadn't noticed his eye patch or at least the ruin of his nose? From a distance he might have appeared clean-cut and distinguished. He would sometimes contemplate his actions as he shaved, clipped his nose hairs, trimmed his eyebrows. Why even bother with such details when his disfigurements would eclipse all else? But they were human routines, and for him perhaps a resonance of military routines. He wondered now if, up close to him, the woman regretted joining him. As she arranged her pocketbook and carry-on bag beside her, before she could open any conversation, Trenor made a show of checking his watch as if the flight of his plane were imminent, gathered up his own coffee and carry-on, and walked away.

He hoped he hadn't offended her, but maybe he had saved them both from embarrassment.

He spent the remainder of his time waiting at his gate, reading from his travel guide and occasionally glancing up at his fellow travelers—the Vietnamese now sifted from the Chinese that had debarked here. He overheard their conversations but understood little of the language; most of what he'd learned years ago was slang and mutilations. Finally, it was announced in several languages that the plane was ready to be boarded. Trenor's heartbeat quickened, though he had already monitored the time on his wristwatch, and he sat stiffly while he waited for his seating section to be called. This was it—the last leg of his journey.

This plane was smaller than the last, but they didn't have too much farther to go. After that last ungodly stretch, a mere two and a half hours of flight time. It would be 10:10 PM when they got there. He had read his travel agenda over and over.

Trenor couldn't make out much of what Ho Chi Minh City looked like these days when the plane was making its descent. Twinkling lights, earthbound constellations; he might have been anywhere. And yet he had been here before, when the city had worn another name. He tried to joke with himself, imagined Martin Sheen starting off his narration of *Apocalypse Now* with the rueful words, "Ho Chi Minh City…shit…I'm still only in Ho Chi Minh City."

The plane touched down on its runway at Tan Son Nhat airport, and it was still taxiing along when passengers started popping up from their seats and digging into the overhead bins. The stewardesses tried to discourage them. Trenor sat tight, knowing he would want to be among the last to file out to avoid the crush.

When he did follow the last straggling passengers into the exit chute, he was immediately struck by the change of the air—from cool air conditioning to humid and hot, and there was already a peculiar, singular underlying scent to it. Maybe not exactly the same brew he recalled, but it still made his stomach gurgle with recognition.

Once more he hung back to avoid the more aggressive travelers as they claimed their baggage from the rotating belt, then followed other foreign tourists into the correct check-in line. His heart hammered again as a grimly pretty agent in a green uniform looked from his passport up at his face, down at the passport then up at his face again. Trenor wanted to ask her if she thought he might be a different disfigured man with an eye patch from the one in the photo.

But his visa was stamped (why had he feared it wouldn't be…as if his older and transfigured face might still be recognized from his service years ago, his name on some kind of list of former enemies?) and his passport was pushed back to him. He thanked the young woman, gathered his bags, and officially entered Vietnam.

He stepped out into a sea of faces—came up short against a dense wall of faces—dark-haired brown faces, and each one of them seemed to be staring directly at him as he dragged his bags behind him. His thoughts became breathless at this scrutiny, real or imagined: *he was a foreigner, he was disfigured, maybe they knew from these things that he had killed their people, perhaps killed their own family members.* The faces disoriented him; his mind skipped and stuttered and blanked. How was he to find his way here? How was he supposed to pick out the face of a young man he had only seen as a webcam image? Why hadn't Thanh coached him better on how they were to meet? As he continued moving forward past the bodies pressed up against the dividing barrier, he could only trust that the boy would spot him and call out.

Then he noticed that groups of people held up cardboard signs with travelers' names handwritten on them. One of these signs stood out and became a sudden beacon. The sign bore the words: MR. RICHARD TRENOR.

Trenor cracked a big grin of relief. Above his sign, Quan's son—recognizable now from their online chats—was smiling more reservedly, but Trenor could understand that under the circumstances. When Trenor reached him, he let go of his luggage to extend his right hand. "Hey, Thanh… It's great to meet you."

Thanh didn't take Trenor's hand, turned instead to a man standing beside him and handed him the sign. When Trenor saw the boy's hands, he understood why Thanh hadn't wanted them to shake. While Thanh was turned away, Trenor's gaze flicked down to the youth's bare feet, almost identical in formation to the claw hands.

Thanh turned back to Trenor as he and the other man each took hold of one of the visitor's bags. "This is the taxi driver," Thanh explained. "He'll take us to your hotel."

The cab waited at the curb and the driver slung the luggage into the trunk while Trenor and Thanh let themselves into the back. Once he was seated, Thanh pressed his hands together between his thighs, glanced out the window with obvious discomfort then back at Trenor. "You didn't know about my hands and feet before, Mr. Richard."

"No, Thanh, I'm sorry—I didn't." Trenor had thought Thanh hadn't caught him looking, but he was sure the boy was too familiar with people's reactions to miss them. Awkwardly, he said, "You weren't in any of the pictures your dad sent me."

"My father never took many pictures of me, so I'm not surprised he never sent one to you." Watching out the window again, Thanh added bluntly, "My father is ashamed of me."

"Oh, come on, Thanh, that can't be it. I always got the impression your dad was proud of his kids."

"He liked you to believe that. He wanted you to believe he was always happy. But because I'm like this, he thinks I'm not lucky. In Vietnam, luck is everything. Bad luck is a curse. He blames me for my mother going away…and my sister dying."

The driver slammed his door closed and got them moving. Trenor looked forward, frowning, and said, "Well, I'll have to straighten out that old son of a bitch."

3: ACCOMMODATIONS

TRENOR WAS EXHAUSTED FROM A full day spent above the Earth, and had cultivated a fine headache, so he couldn't take in much of nighttime Ho Chi Minh City. Motorbikes still buzzed about even at this hour, and he observed, "When I saw Saigon it was more bicycles in the streets than motorcycles."

"There are more than three million motorbikes in Saigon," Thanh stated. "And yes, we in the south still like to call it Saigon."

Trenor smiled at his companion. "You're a very bright kid. Do all young Vietnamese speak English as well as you?"

"We study it in school, but of course some people learn languages better than others. Maybe I was given a good brain to make up for my hands and feet."

"So it would seem."

"I liked to study English because I always dreamed of coming to live in the USA. Huh—me and every other Vietnamese. But it isn't so easy to get a visa to leave our country."

"Yeah, you got that communist government of yours. Your dad and I tried to lick those guys, but..." Trenor remembered the taxi driver and checked him in the rearview mirror, but if he understood English he didn't seem fazed. "Tell your countrymen the US isn't all it's cracked up to be. You might even say it's a fucking train wreck. Once upon a time, immigrants set down roots and wanted their descendants to do the same. Now what I see, from all kinds of immigrants I've worked with, is they just want to make money in the USA and send it home, and save up enough so they can retire to their home countries when they get old. Can't say that I blame them, either."

"But you make a lot of money in the USA."

"And a cup of coffee can cost you four dollars in the USA, too."

"Oh...I'm so sorry, that reminds me—are you hungry or thirsty, Mr. Richard?"

"I ate well enough on the plane, but I could use a cold drink when we get to the hotel."

"It's not far now. After we check you in, I'll go home, and I'll come back early tomorrow morning. Okay, Mr. Richard? I live here in Saigon with my uncle—my mother's brother. My father hates him, too."

"Does your father know I'm coming?"

"No. I'm sorry, I didn't tell him."

"Well is he in for a surprise," Trenor said.

* * *

At the hotel's reception desk he was asked to hand over his passport, apparently lest he think of running off without paying his bill. Trenor was not comfortable about this, but when Thanh whispered that it was a common practice in reputable hotels he relented. His room was on the second floor, and he looked it over with approval. "Thanks for taking care of this for me, Thanh. How much do I owe you for it, and the taxi? I've only got US dollars at the moment."

"Many people in Vietnam will accept US dollars. Tomorrow we can stop at a jewelry store to exchange for Vietnamese money; that's where you go for that. This room is thirty dollars a night. I'm sorry if that's too much."

Trenor passed Thanh some bills, saying, "Are you kidding? It's triple that at least for a halfway decent motel room in the States."

"You have a bathtub, cable TV, a mini-bar." Thanh knelt down to open a small refrigerator and it proved full of various beers both local and familiar to Trenor, plus soft drinks. Thanh offered a can of Heineken. "You said you were thirsty, Mr. Richard?"

"How about a Coke? With this headache I can't do alcohol."

Thanh handed over a Coke in a can with Vietnamese writing. "The hotel will count what you leave and only charge you for what you drink." He rose. "And now I'll go, Mr. Richard. I hope you'll be comfortable here tonight. I'll see you in the morning and take you to eat before we go to Bien Hoa."

Before Thanh could protest, Trenor reached out and took his deformed right hand firmly in his own two hands and shook it. "It's a pleasure to know you, Thanh. I admire what you're trying to do for your family."

Thanh averted his eyes. "My family has been troubled a long time."

"Welcome to the human race." Trenor released his hand. "I know your dad started drinking before you were even born, but you gotta remember he went through hell in those prison camps. Six years—and he was lucky it was only six. Some people did a lot longer, for less: teachers, doctors, poets. Everybody told me, come on, no Kit Carson Scouts would've been left alive, not after they were sent back to their old regiments to be dealt with. And after the war, all the records of who defected through the *Chieu Hoi* program ended up in the government's hands. But I still kept trying to find your dad; it was a pet project of mine, or an obsession, I don't know what you'd call it. A debt. Anyway, you can't imagine how fucking happy I was to find out he was alive. That was in 1983." Trenor sipped from his can of soda, and, staring past Thanh, went on, "So we began our correspondence. I tried to talk him into coming to the USA, but he wouldn't. He was too devoted to his mom. He was her only surviving child, and his father—your grandfather—died years before."

"Yes. I'm afraid he was more devoted to his mother than to our family. My grandmother died only a few years ago. My father got worse after that. It was one of the things that have broken him."

"But he straightened out for a while there, back before he met your mom. He was repairing motorbikes, doing well for himself, bought a house. Met your mom a little late in life; thirty-six, I think?"

"Yes. And she was ten years younger—twenty-six. She was very beautiful; he was crazy about her. But he was still handsome back then, too, and making okay money, so she didn't care about their difference in age."

"So, if you're twenty you would have been born in, ah, 1990?"

"Yes. My father was thirty-eight, and my mother twenty-eight. Two years later, Tra Mi was born. And Hang Ni came much later, in 2002. My mother was forty then. Late for another baby." He shrugged.

"Like I say, I hadn't known your mom left your dad."

"Yes. After that, he fell apart. It was even worse for him than losing his mother. But I don't blame my mother for doing it…she isn't a bad woman. With all his drinking and fighting, he drove her to it."

"Thanh, your sisters—I know I've seen both of them in photos, at least. Were they born with any…you know, problems?"

"You mean, like this?" Thanh raised the hand that Trenor had just gripped. "No, only me. Of course it must be from Agent Orange. People here in Bien Hoa still have high levels of dioxin. It's in the food we eat. Chicken, ducks, fish…"

"I know there was a big spill of Agent Orange at Bien Hoa Air Base back in the sixties," Trenor said. "Thousands of gallons. Probably seeped into the water." He shook his head. "I'm sorry, Thanh."

"It's okay, Mr. Richard. There are people from the USA in Vietnam right now, to prepare for a big cleanup in Bien Hoa next year. From 2007 to now your country has already spent nine million dollars to help with our Agent Orange problems."

"Well, that's the USA for ya," Trenor said. "When we aren't raining bombs and toxins, we're raining money."

Maybe Thanh was feeling self-conscious about the turn in their discussion, or was simply concerned for Trenor's well-being; in either case, he moved toward the door. Far enough away to avoid a second round of handshaking. "I must go now, and you must sleep. I hope your headache is gone in the morning."

"I've got some ibuprofen. I'll pop a couple, take a nice shower and hit the sack. I'll be fine, kid."

Thanh opened the door. "Good night, Mr. Richard."

"Good night, Thanh. And Thanh? This 'Mr. Richard' stuff has gotta stop. Your dad always called me Rick. Sound good?"

"I must treat you with respect."

"You'll be respecting my shoe in your ass if you don't knock it off."

Thanh smiled. "Okay…okay, Rick. Good night. And thank you again for coming."

Trenor nodded, watched the boy slip out and close the door after him. After which Trenor shook his head sadly, as if he felt guilty for perpetrating a ruse. Lying to the young man that he might actually be of some help in Vietnam. He didn't feel he had really done any good here forty years ago, with all the resources of the most powerful country on Earth behind him. So what could he possibly do now, alone?

4: SELLING LOVE

TREE-LINED LE DUAN BOULEVARD, in Ho Chi Minh City's District 1, boasted the looming Sofitel Saigon Plaza Hotel. The distinctive green bulk of the Diamond Plaza shopping center. The 19th Century Notre-Dame Basilica cathedral with its twin bell towers. Behind its pale yellow wall, the US Consulate General, where on a number of trips the American had gone to have his month-long visa extended.

On a whim he had entered the Diamond Department Store and on its third level purchased an expensive watch for Long Dien's *ca phe om*, Kate. Thinking of how he'd surprise her with it, he ate lunch in the Kentucky Fried Chicken contained within the same complex. Having grown up in the USA, he had a taste for Western junk food. But out in the street again he treated himself to a Vietnamese favorite: sugar cane juice pressed right on the spot, something like a ship's wheel on one side of the mobile cart, flattened husks piling up in the gutter. Over ice, it helped quench his thirst in the drowning heat. As he sucked at his straw, ignoring the flirtations of the cart's attendant, who recognized him as a foreign *Viet Kieu*, his eyes sought out his true destination this afternoon.

The Taiwanese marriage broker had his offices in another of the impressive modern buildings on Le Duan Boulevard.

*   *   *

When the elevator deposited him on the second floor, the American found himself in a large reception area. On one of the small sofas arranged about the room, four pretty young women were pressed shoulder-to-shoulder like new chicks in a crate. A more polished beauty in an *ao dai* was introducing them to a Taiwanese man in a bad suit who smiled with a kind of bashful lechery. On another sofa, another woman in an *ao dai* sat close beside another plain-looking little man, a binder open across his legs as she pointed out cheap, photoshopped glamour shots of more women. Elsewhere, a man was bowing deeply to show respect to the parents of the coltishly thin, long-haired, and quite younger future bride who stood beside him. One might have easily thought he was adopting her.

In a number of individual glassed-in rooms off the reception area, broker agents sat with clients at small round tables, or clients spoke for the first time— no doubt with difficulty—to their prospective mates as if interviewing them for a job.

While the receptionist behind her counter spoke on the phone, the American glanced at the room's walls, almost completely lost behind framed photos of blissful couples. Framed newspaper and magazine articles testifying to the matrimonial service's successes. But the American knew there were always many more articles, and TV news segments, that had a much less approving view of services such as this. They used words like "human trafficking." He found this attitude a bit much. He was certain plenty of women eager to live in a foreign country and send money home to their families ended up as bored servants to these homely and often ill-educated older men, who couldn't find a wife (or at least a sexy young wife) in their own country. That there were plenty of women who became baby machines, maybe not only bored and lonely but also beaten. And sometimes, were even tricked into a vulnerable situation whereby they could be made into prostitutes. But he had heard, too, especially in his own country— the US—of many an immigrant bride who broke free of her hulking and horny foster father of a husband at the earliest opportunity. Usually right after she'd won her green card (and after his bank account was suitably depleted), though a woman didn't even need to wait a few years for that. All it took was a 911 call and some sobbing lies that overweight old hubby had slapped her around, and the woman was suddenly living in a shelter, getting a little free money in her pocket, going to school for English and nails while the government now took care of her permanent resident status, instead. The American saw victims on both sides of the border. The border between hopes and greed, loneliness and desperation, love and deceit. It seemed to him like the eternal, mystifying, hostile, and disillusioning struggle between male and female, but cast in the distorting light of caricature.

This was why he preferred interacting with hookers. No facades or illusions; the cards were all right there on the table. Hookers were honest, and so was the animal hunger of their johns.

Finished with her call, the receptionist beamed up at him and said, "*Ni hao!*" Obviously mistaking him for Taiwanese, come to select a bride or meet one he had already chosen online as if ordering a book or CD. He was insulted. Did he really look like one of their usual clients? Like he needed their service?

In Vietnamese, in a cool and professional tone, he said to her, "I'd like to see your boss, Chen Ti-sai."

"Do you have an appointment, sir?"

"No, I don't."

"Can you tell me your name?"

"Just tell him that his new American friend is here to see him. I'm sure he'll understand."

The woman picked up her phone again. While she spoke into it in Mandarin, he read a plaque on the wall behind her, written in Chinese, Vietnamese, Korean, and English. It listed four guarantees, which in their English translation were: *"(1) Virgin. (2) Marry in three months. (3) No extra fee. (4) If she escaped in one year, another one will be indemnified to you."* The price for matchmaking services was also given in various currencies. In US dollars: $8,000.

The woman replaced her handset and said, "Mr. Chen will see you now, sir. Down that hallway"—she pointed—"to the door at the end."

"Cam on, em," he thanked her, turning toward the carpeted hallway she had indicated.

The American knocked; a voice on the other side of the door invited him to enter. When he did, the man behind the desk within had already risen to his feet. He was in his late forties, with thinning hair and glasses, wearing a suit as expensive as the American's and a smile so perfect he might have taught it to all his workers in the outer room. "Hello, my friend," he said in Vietnamese. "I wish you had let me know you were coming, so we could have met somewhere other than here, like we did the first time."

"Did you know?"

"Know?" The American had not taken a seat, so his host didn't return to his, either.

"That your friend would kill the girl?"

"Ah. That."

"Of course, that. Why didn't you tell me or my partner what your sick friend intended?"

"Hm. You seem so morally outraged. Excuse me saying so, but when you were recommended to me, I didn't think you'd be so squeamish about a death."

"Squeamish? I'm not squeamish about people being killed. I'm not squeamish about killing people myself. Under other circumstances I could have done away with this same girl, if it served a logical purpose. But what makes me so unhappy, Mr. Chen, is being kept in the dark. It's the same as lying, and I don't like being lied to."

"My friend," Chen Ti-sai said, tired of standing and sinking back into his chair at last, "you asked me in the beginning if I knew. Do not assume that I did. I did not. But now that it's done, where is the problem?"

"Where is the problem? You don't watch TV or read the newspapers?"

"No one will connect either of us to this."

"Do you really feel as confident as you sound? I'm not so confident. My understanding was that the older sister would bring the little one to Vung Tau. The little one would be drugged beforehand, never see your friend, never know a thing of what had happened. But it didn't go that way, did it?"

"What happened in that hotel room was out of my control."

JEFFREY THOMAS

"Did he kill the older sister, too?"

"I couldn't tell you; we haven't spoken since then."

"I really hope he killed her, too, because she didn't expect her sister to die any more than I did. She could betray her boss, the man you dealt with. And if the police take him, do you think he won't betray the both of us? That doesn't concern you at all?"

Chen Ti-sai dropped his gaze, nibbled at his lower lip, swiveled side-to-side in his chair. "I'm not saying it's a good situation."

"Your psychotic friend—is he still in the country?"

"I believe so."

"You believe so? Where would he be now?"

"I honestly don't know."

"I don't think you are being entirely honest, Mr. Chen."

"The damage is done. What would you do—kill him? I thought you were a man of business, not a man so full of pride he kills for vengeance. Vengeance can be expensive."

"There is no price on honor, and I believe in mutual respect. To not respect me, to put me in a dangerous situation I hadn't adequately shielded myself from, is to dishonor me. If I get tied to a pole because of this, face a firing squad of Vietnamese policemen and take a final *coup de grace* in the temple, I will feel greatly dishonored indeed."

"You speak very passionately of honor and respect." Chen Ti-sai had thoroughly lost his cheery smile. "But you barge in here speaking disrespectfully to me. Accusing me, berating me…"

"I haven't begun to accuse and berate you. That you're a pimp behind your romantic screen, I don't care at all. That you would supply children to your extra-special clients doesn't morally outrage me. But even a pimp like you has to know when he isn't conducting business with the proper caution!"

Chen Ti-sai drew in a long whistling breath through his nostrils, his lips sealed in a heavy scowl. Unbeknownst to the American, his given name Ti-sai meant "pig manure." It was an old tradition in Taiwan, even in Vietnam, to change a child's name to something ugly or give it an unpleasant nickname, to discourage evil spirits from trying to steal the child's life. Chen Ti-sai had been a premature baby and sickly child, and hence his own name.

"And I thought you truly were a man of honor," Chen said. "A calm and sturdy professional, who wouldn't panic at a little blood. I thought you were smart. But the way you talk to me isn't smart."

"Really?"

"Have you ever heard of the Bamboo Union?"

The American absorbed that, gave a small nod. "Yes. They're the most powerful Triad in Taiwan. So you're telling me you're a member of the United Bamboo Gang?"

"I'm just saying, I have friends. Friends who wouldn't appreciate your treatment of me."

"Maybe you should have asked your friends to find a little girl for you, instead of me."

"Maybe I should have. But what's done is done, and I won't listen to your recriminations any longer. I ask you to leave, and don't come back. Don't worry—we'll never do business again, you and I."

"I'll ask you one more time. Do you know where your crazy friend is?"

"Leave. Now."

The American stepped close to the desk, leaning his hands on it and grinning icily. "If there weren't people in these other rooms," he purred, "I don't think you'd be speaking like this to me right now."

From behind the desk, Chen Ti-sai lifted a Type 54 Chinese pistol, a knockoff of the Soviet TT-33 Tokarev. "If there were no people in the other rooms, I too think things might be different."

The American straightened, but kept his outward composure, despite the fury that percolated inside him. He shook his head. "You really believe I'm so insignificant?"

"And you only see me as some pimp? I told you, it's time to go. Let's consider our business concluded and go about our lives. This thing will blow away. The child was nothing. She'll be forgotten. If you regain the proper respect, I'll forget you, too."

Afraid to speak more, lest uncorking what was inside him trigger an explosion that would consume them both, the American turned toward the door, but Chen called for him to look back.

The gun was gone and the smile had returned. "If you're so afraid of facing a Vietnamese firing squad, might I suggest you return to your own country? Return to the USA, and never come back to Vietnam."

5: LONG JOURNEY HOME

TRENOR SLEPT SOLIDLY FOR SEVEN hours, woke to find his headache gone. He was grateful Thanh hadn't come too early, drank another Coke until he could get a coffee in him. He put on the TV; *The Terminator* was playing on HBO Asia. "I'll be back," he muttered, turning to the window with his soda can. Under the sun's full blaze, the street was alive with the sound of an enraged hornet's nest. From here he could see the flow of tightly packed motorbikes like corpuscles in a bloodstream. "Goooood morning, Vietnam," he said.

Restless, he moved to his hotel room's door with the thought of venturing into the lobby, perhaps, or the adjacent restaurant for a coffee if he could get away with ordering one, or standing out on the sidewalk to watch the street's churning activity closer up. As soon as the door was open he was met with a solid wall of heat, realized how much his room's air-conditioning had kept it at bay. As if that wall prevented him from leaving, he shut the door again. But inside, he knew the real reason he'd decided not to venture outside the room without Thanh was the timidness he felt. Once he'd been able—been *eager*—to crawl into a tunnel in this country and fight a war in the most intimate possible arena. How things had changed; not only this city.

He didn't have to reproach himself long. Raps on the door, and Trenor opened it to find Thanh there, smiling. "Good morning, Rick. Did you sleep well?"

"Like a baby, my friend. Like a big, one-eyed cyclops of a baby."

The young man held up a bag of pastries, some with meat inside, from a bakery next door. "Some breakfast for you; I hope this is okay."

"Everything will be okay if you can get me a coffee to go with it."

*   *   *

After the brief stop for coffee, the little white and green taxi bore them along again. Trenor's iced coffee was contained in a plastic bag with a straw through the top, rather than a cup, but it was strong, sweet, and cold, so he wasn't complaining. He glanced over at the little metal can Thanh drank from. "What's that you got?"

"Bird nest drink. The birds make their nests from their spit. Very good if you're hot! Want to try it?"

"Well, hm." Trenor accepted the can, took a little sip, nodded and handed it back. "That's not bad. I guess I've been baptized now, huh?" He looked out his window again. "Who am I kidding? The baptism has only begun."

He was in that swarming bloodstream himself now, swept along as part of it. But shouldn't a bloodstream, even, have order? This was a chaos that nature and even civilization should both shrink from; motorbikes filling the street from one bank to the other in a solid mass, riders almost rubbing elbows where the bloodstream looked as though it might clot. Automobiles were in the minority; cars, trucks, and Mercedes vans conveying tourists kept up a constant beeping of their horns to carve a way for themselves. But this was sedate compared to the intersections. Here, bikes came hurtling from every direction, just in time angling out of each other's way. Trenor tensed up inside several times for a crash that never came. To add to the tension, often the riders carried passengers: a lover or friend seated behind them, or worse, a mother behind her husband with a child or two sandwiched between them. The parents wore helmets, but the children didn't.

When Trenor remarked on this, Thanh related, "Only three years ago Vietnam ordered people to wear helmets. My cousin died in a bike crash in 2006. I don't know if a helmet would have saved him. Maybe. He was drunk, so…" He shrugged fatalistically.

Trenor couldn't tell when they'd left Ho Chi Minh City, nor when they entered its suburb of Bien Hoa, an hour's drive away—outside there seemed only to be endless rows of box-like concrete buildings, sometimes looking mildew-stained and moldering but often neatly painted in pastel hues such as sea green, sky blue, coral, peach, aqua, many with balconies in an echo of French Colonialism. Green growth was integrated everywhere, in an amicable balance of life, but there was no real open country; even the broad stretches of highway were hemmed by civilization. Trenor didn't mind. He hadn't come here wanting to venture into any jungles again.

The driver had considerately put on a cassette of Western songs for his fare. From Leo Sayer's *More Than I Can Say*—possibly the most popular Western song in Vietnam—to those more holiday-themed favorites, Abba's *Happy New Year* and *Feliz Navidad* (sung in Vietnamese). When the theme song for the movie *Titanic* came on, and the driver cranked up the volume for the American with a smile in the rearview mirror, Trenor wanted to thank the man by slapping him across the back of the head.

Trenor stared out his window at the long teardrop-shaped back of a young woman hunched over a bicycle, pedaling furiously, a straw *non la* shading her head and flesh-colored gloves extending up her forearms to protect her from the sun, aristocratic pale skin being the height of beauty in Vietnam. Two girls riding double on a Honda wore masks over their lower faces to protect them from fumes, both dressed in the white *ao dais* of students. The tight-fitting *ao dais* made their backs look long and willowy as well.

Despite his usual psychological defenses, Trenor couldn't help but remember golden-brown bodies, skin preternaturally smooth and unflawed, surprising wild bursts of secret hair, straight and coarse. Long hair streaming from small round heads he held in his hands. Held at his groin. Midnight hair flowing between his fingers and across his legs like ink.

Back then he wouldn't have guessed that he would have more sex partners in his brief time as a soldier in Vietnam than he would in the following forty years of his life.

He looked across at Thanh, hesitated for a beat or two, then said, "Kid, I hate to be so personal, but since we're buddies now and all...have you, ah, ever been to bed with a woman?"

Thanh looked aghast, then hugely embarrassed, dropping his gaze to the claw hands resting on his knees. Significantly, to the claw hands resting on his knees. "No. I don't think I ever will."

"You can't say that. I'm sure it's just you holding yourself back. You're too self-conscious to allow the opportunity. Trust me, I know—I'm the same. So...I shouldn't even be giving you advice about it."

Thanh looked back up at him. "You never had a wife, Rick?"

"No. Longest relationship I had was three years. I met her in the VFW back when I used to warm a bar stool there, till I got sick of it. Sick of drinking, mostly. But she never got sick of drinking. Never got sick of other guys, too. So those three years were probably more unpleasant than they were rewarding. I missed her when she left, but mostly I felt relieved."

"Was she beautiful?"

"No. She was okay, but very thin, practically anorexic. But Thanh, you and I can't afford to be that vain, can we? Beauty doesn't guarantee happiness for the person who beholds it, or the person who has it, either."

"I used to think about becoming a monk, but my sister Tra Mi told me that even a monk must be able to put his hands together to pray."

Trenor frowned. "That's kind of a shitty thing to say."

"Tra Mi and I don't get along any better than my father and me."

"Well," Trenor sighed, reaching over to slap Thanh's thigh, "I just had the inspiration that you and I might go visit some ladies who won't mind at all how we look, so long as we blind them sufficiently with money. My treat."

Thanh blinked, confused. "Hookers?"

"Yeah, Boom-Boom Girls or whatever you call them around here these days."

"Rick," Thanh said grimly, "my sister Tra Mi...Tra Mi is a hooker."

"*What?*"

"She works in a coffee house in Bien Hoa. The waitresses there are all hookers."

"Oh fuck," Trenor said. "I'm sorry, Thanh. Another thing I didn't know. Man. I can see where that would impact your feelings about hookers."

"Yes."

Trenor sighed again, watching more female riders pass alongside the cab, their long glossy hair snapping behind them from under their helmets. "Well...there goes my vacation."

They rode for a little while in silence, silence except for the cassette playing again from the beginning. Trenor switched from watching the landscape—which reminded him a bit of the Vietnam he'd known, a bit of the US, and a lot of another planet—to checking on Thanh, who seemed to have lapsed into solemn introspection. He was sorry for whatever part he had played in bringing about that mood, but he had also been doing some heavy thinking of his own. When he spoke, the young man lifted his head as if roused from a waking dream.

"If Tra Mi is or was a prostitute," Trenor said, "that could be significant, Thanh. That could be very significant."

*   *   *

The cab deposited them in the little dirt courtyard off Cach Mang Thang Tam Street, in Hamlet 2 of Bien Hoa's Quyet Thang Ward. The driver helped remove Trenor's luggage from the trunk and carry it closer to Thanh's family home. Trenor paid the man, and as the driver returned to his cab and Trenor bent to pick up his bags, he heard a gruff, marred voice come from beyond the open double doors at the front of the house, calling out in Vietnamese as it approached.

Trenor set his bags down again and turned slowly to face the man who stepped through the open glass doors. His hair was in disarray from sleep and he wore only a dirty pair of shorts. Sun-darkened skin stretched across the jutting cheekbones of his gaunt, scowling face. No longer the handsome youth Trenor recalled. He didn't even resemble the last photos he had sent in the mail and through email. Trenor wondered if he would have recognized the man had he not known where he was.

"Hey, you little bastard," Trenor said, his voice catching. "Do you remember this ugly face?"

Hard-eyed and confused, Quan stared at Trenor for a moment, and a moment more. Then he blurted something unintelligible, even to Thanh, and looked as though he would collapse to his knees. Trenor rushed to him, scooped him upright and held onto him. Shaking hard with sobs like the sound of some trapped and slowly dying animal, Nguyen Van Quan held onto Trenor, too.

PART 4: RECONNAISSANCE

1: CATCHING UP

THE FIRST THING QUAN DID when he had sufficiently composed himself, having sufficiently absorbed the reality that a forty-years-older version of Staff Sergeant Rick Trenor stood in his house, was to excitedly shuffle to the fridge in his small, oddly shaped kitchen with its grimy green-painted walls to get them both a can of Tiger beer. Trenor reached out and held the refrigerator door shut before Quan could get it open. "No, Quan, listen—you've had enough beer for the time being, and I'm not much of a drinker these days. Maybe later."

"No, no, Rick, please, we need to toast! Toast old times!" Quan's deeply lined grin revealed the gaps in his once winning smile.

"Brother, I didn't come halfway around the world to talk to a drunken man. Okay? I came to talk to you about your family."

Quan's expression, at least, sobered. "Okay, Rick. Okay. But, you hungry?"

"Well…"

Quan leaned around Trenor and barked to his son, who stood uncertainly in the threshold. Thanh offered, for Trenor's benefit in English, to cook something up himself but Quan commanded him to get some dishes from a local restaurant instead. Thanh left on his father's Honda, and Quan set about making Trenor an iced coffee. He held a large chunk of ice in his palm, over a bowl, and hammered it with a metal pestle that was probably a piece off one of the motorbikes he repaired.

They sat at the kitchen table on mismatched chairs. Trenor drank his coffee, and Quan had begun cleansing himself with a bottle of La Vie water.

"My son talk to you about my daughter?" Quan asked him.

"Yes. That's why I'm here. He contacted me about it."

Quan wagged his head, muttered something that was maybe in Vietnamese, then looked at Trenor again and said, "Why he bother you to come here?"

"Don't be hard on the kid; it isn't bothering me to help an old friend."

Quan reached across the table and gripped Trenor's hand, almost upsetting his bottle of water and Trenor's glass of *ca phe sua da* in the process. "You always my good friend, Rick."

"I tried. So why'd you stop writing back when your wife left you? Your Tiger beer became a better friend than me?"

Quan sighed, drawing back his arm for another swig of water. "Sorry, Rick. Sorry, brother."

"Tell me what's going on now about your daughters, Quan. Thanh doesn't seem to think the police have done enough."

Quan spread his hands. "They think a man from other country kill my baby. I'm sure the man go home to his country so soon! Police do what now?"

"But what about the older girl? They don't know anything about what might have happened to her?"

Quan held up empty palms again. "Tra Mi is a bad girl, Rick. I think Tra Mi take away my baby to give me pain. She talk to me before, get my Hang Ni go away. So maybe Tra Mi talk to a boyfriend kill my Hang Ni, so she and boyfriend run away."

"Quan, you don't really believe that, do you?"

The former Kit Carson Scout watched his thumb rub at smears of water left from the condensation of his bottle on the glass table top. "Tra Mi is a hooker, Rick. My daughter, *con di* hooker! Bad…bad like her mother!"

"I'm sorry your wife left you. I didn't know until Thanh told me about that, too. But you gotta admit, brother, your drinking hasn't made it easy on your family. I'm not trying to blame you for all this, but it's time to quit. Quit before you lose everything."

Quan snapped hard, wet eyes up to meet Trenor's. "Lose what more? I lose everything already!"

"Tra Mi might still be alive. Whatever problems you've had with her, she's still your daughter. And you have a fine son."

Quan made a dismissive sound and rough gesture.

"Hey, what is it with you, man? When did that brave little fuck I knew turn into such a self-pitying asshole? Yeah, you had it bad in those camps, I know. I can't even imagine. But it wasn't your kid who did that to you. All that shit happened before he was even born. So I don't know where you get this idea about him giving you bad luck."

"My mother is dead, Rick! Then my wife go away with boyfriend! Now my baby is dead! You see bad luck enough, Rick?"

"I don't see your boy having anything to do with that. My mom's dead, too. And I never even had a wife. I don't have a son to blame for that stuff."

Quan broke eye contact again. As he slowly sobered, as the water purged him, long submerged truths came dislodged and floating to the surface. "Rick, some things I can't talk about in letters. I'm afraid police see; they always wait put us in jail again. I'm shy, too, and sad. I can't tell you about my wife. My daughter hooker. My daughter die. But I can't tell you everything before, too. I can't tell you about how bad in the jail."

"I understand that. But I read about the reeducation camps. People tied to a post standing up for weeks at a time. People with their thumbs tied together behind their back, or with their thumbs tied to their toes, for *months* at a time. People catching millipedes and grasshoppers because they had no protein to eat. I know it was hell, brother. People were driven insane; you're lucky you got out as intact as you did."

"You know why I don't die in jail, Rick? You know why I'm out only six years, and other people get more time?"

"No. I figured maybe they still respected your past service, before you switched sides. Maybe an old friend or two pulled some strings."

Quan shook his head. "My mother get money from her family. She pay big police let me out before I get more years sentence."

"She bribed an official."

"Yes. You always ask me to come USA; you will help me. The USA invite soldiers who fight Viet Cong before. But how I can leave my mother, Rick? My mother have only me."

"I understand, brother."

"Now she dead. Wife gone. Only I have my baby. Only Hang Ni." His voice quavered. "And something more, it hurt me to say, Rick."

"What's that?"

"Hang Ni…Hang Ni not my daughter. I know that. My wife get her with boyfriend. This boyfriend or boyfriend before, I don't know. But I understand about that. About my Hang Ni."

Trenor nodded, looking like a serene father confessor, but he felt his own lone eye welling up. "I see. But you loved her all the same."

"Yes. I love her because she have no sin. She is not wrong to me anything. She don't understand about that. She only love me. Love me more than *anybody*. I have only Hang Ni, and now—gone."

Trenor reached between their drinks to squeeze Quan's hand again, but he shook it with stern emphasis as he spoke. "Listen. Whatever might have happened to Tra Mi, you have a very fine son. And why do you think he called me, man? Thanh isn't looking for revenge; he's looking for a father to help him deal with this. Because somewhere along the line you stopped being a father to him…if you ever were one." He looked up at two geckos clinging to the wall just below the ceiling, but his gaze passed through and beyond them. "When I was a teenager, I saw a guy with hands like Thanh at the Brockton Fair, in Massachusetts. His little baby was with him, and it had the same deformity. Except this guy's legs were very stunted and he couldn't walk good like your kid. Later on I read a book about this guy, and he was a mean son of a bitch…killed his daughter's boyfriend with a shotgun and got away with it, but his own wife and stepson ended up murdering him. Can you imagine what their life was like, that they would do that? Sometimes one person can suck his whole family into all the pain and shit he's feeling, and pull them down with him until all they want to do is escape. Your wife escaped. Maybe Tra Mi escaped, and in so doing got your little one killed. And maybe Thanh escaped to Saigon to get away from you, too. But he's here now, isn't he? I think you need to respect that. The friend I knew back in the day—the friend who dragged my sorry ass out of that hole— would respect that kind of strength and commitment. I think if you were in that same hole right now, facing a bullet yourself, your son would go in there after you, fucked-up hands and all. He might hate you for having to do it. But he'd go."

Quan held onto Trenor's hand, lowered his head, and openly wept. Trenor glanced toward the fridge, for lack of any better medicine tempted to break out two beers for them after all, but he restrained himself. He just kept quiet a little while, gripping Quan's hand as if to slowly, slowly ease him out of a very deep tunnel. A tunnel through time and suffering, where in one way or another every human soul had to face combat.

2: RESERVATIONS

THANH HAD SPENT ANOTHER NIGHT in Hang Ni's closet of a bedroom, with Trenor sleeping on the mattress on the floor of Tra Mi's room. Trenor had poked around in the room a bit when he was alone, before turning in early for the night (still feeling jetlagged, though the heat wasn't helping to invigorate him, either), but he noted nothing unusual beyond the missing clothes and other belongings that Thanh had already filled him in on.

His sleep was uneven, despite his weariness. He woke to use the bathroom twice, tossed and turned a bit, and suffered a bad dream.

He dreamed he woke to see a sickly thin naked girl with a stream of inky hair running down her back, standing in the corner of the room facing the wall. He wondered if this girl with fragile limbs, a small slit dividing her bottom, and pallid yellowish skin was the child Hang Ni, because he felt this was not a living being, but decided she was too tall for that. In the dream, he said, "Tra Mi."

The nude girl heard him. He saw her head turn just a fraction. Then a moment later her entire body began to shuffle around slowly, jerkily, to face him.

He couldn't be sure if the face he saw corresponded with photos he had seen of Quan's older daughter, sent to him over the years—particularly because this girl's eyes glowed red with living fire, and her jaw was stretched to its limits, her mouth packed solid with a clod of earth.

Trenor woke to the sound of his own moaning, and lay there expecting Quan or Thanh to burst in to see what was wrong, but after some moments he decided he hadn't moaned loudly enough for anyone else to hear…and in the morning he said nothing of his dream.

*   *   *

A sober Quan was prepared to enlist his son's help in preparing their guest a breakfast feast of innumerable dishes, but Trenor succeeded in talking him down to just fried egg sandwiches. While they ate, Trenor asked Thanh for more on what he knew about Tra Mi's alleged work as a prostitute. He felt awkward broaching the topic, especially in front of her father, but this was what he was here for, wasn't it? Thus did Trenor learn about the Bien Hoa café where Tra Mi worked. And thus, too, her boss, Long Dien.

"I should kill him already, before," Quan grumbled ominously, listening in as he drank coffee. "He disgrace me, get my daughter work like that."

"Hold off, tiger," Trenor told him.

"If I'm not drunk so much, I kill him before already!" Quan thumped a fist on the glass table top.

Trenor motioned for his friend to calm down. "You just stay here today, brother. Work on those bikes, make some money, and keep away from the beer. If you're a good boy, maybe you and I will have one or two when I come back later."

"Okay...okay." Quan closed his eyes and nodded, making an effort to control himself. He gave a brave smile and saluted. "Okay, Sergeant."

Trenor turned back to Thanh. "I want to meet this guy, Long Dien, for myself. You said you have his number?"

"Yes—one of his girls at the coffee shop gave it to me." Thanh remembered the pretty *ca phe om*, Hoa.

"Good. Call him. Tell him you want to see him. If he's reluctant, tell him about me. Say you've got a visiting friend of the family who's concerned about your sisters. Did you ever talk to him again after they found Hang Ni?"

"No."

"Well, call him. Be politely insistent. If he doesn't agree, then we'll just have to find a way to surprise him without an appointment."

So Thanh did call, half-expecting Long Dien wouldn't answer or call back, but he surprised Thanh by picking up right away. Trenor listened to Thanh speaking in Vietnamese. After only a few minutes, the conversation ended and Thanh explained, "I thought he wouldn't want to talk about this again, but he said he would be happy to help us." He snorted. "Like you suggested, I told him I have an American friend of the family who is here to help us look for Tra Mi."

"Good. When can we see him?"

"He's in Saigon, but he said he will come out here to meet us in the coffee shop. He said he's not sure when he will be free today, so he will call me back as soon as he can. I hope he means it."

Trenor grunted and glanced over at Quan. "Huh. I kind of expected a pimp to be uncooperative, too."

*   *   *

The American had changed his accommodations, upgrading to a room in the five-star Sofitel Saigon Plaza Hotel, on tree-lined Le Duan Boulevard in Ho Chi Minh City's District 1.

Kate seemed impressed to spend time with him in such surroundings. She appeared grateful for the watch he'd bought for her several days ago in the nearby Diamond Department Store. Yesterday he had stolen her away from Long Dien's café in Bien Hoa, assuring her the boss would never complain.

She had given the American a long expert massage this morning, which of course had turned into long vigorous sex. In his fervor he had wanted to penetrate her in the rectum, at the very least probe her with a finger, but had contented himself with tonguing her anus. After his efforts to win more smiles from her, he didn't want to tramp on his own garden of carefully planted flowers. Still, he wondered why—if it was her haunted, unhappy beauty that had first attracted him—he should be so keen on winning prosaic smiles from her.

Returning from showering alone, he found her still in bed, still naked, hair oily with sweat, watching TV with a glassy stare. He felt both fondness and mild disgust. Most women in this country or anywhere were driven to prostitution by poverty, but in his opinion some were simply too lazy to work conventionally, and he was beginning to feel this was the case with Kate. She was languid to the point of sluggishness, as uninteresting as a blank wall; or at least, not willing to share whatever qualities of herself that he might find interesting. Beyond her beauty, he couldn't much account for his oddly intense attraction to her. Unless her very simplicity struck him as a kind of sullied innocence?

It was actually comforting that he could feel *some* disgust for her. If the fondness were too great, he would be more confounded with himself than he already was.

His cell phone rang, and he picked it up, found Long Dien on the other end. "Yes?" he answered. "Are you looking for your girl?"

"My girl?"

"Kate."

She looked over at the sound of her name.

"No, no," Long Dien replied. "You told me to let you know if Tra Mi's brother ever called me again."

The American immediately padded barefoot across the room to put more distance between himself and Kate, and lowered his voice. "He's asking if you know something again?"

"He wants to meet me. And he says he has an American friend visiting, who is helping him look for Tra Mi."

"An *American* friend?"

"Yes. They both want to meet me. I said I would. Was that okay? I should find out what they want to ask, don't you think?"

"Who is this American friend? A *Viet Kieu*, or white?"

"I don't know!" Long Dien sounded more nervous by the second. "I'm sorry, my friend! Oh, why did my girl Hoa ever give this freak my number? Stupid bitch! I should kill her!"

"Listen, get control of yourself! Where do they want to meet you?"

"I said I'd come to see them at the café in Bien Hoa. They're waiting for me to call back and give them a time."

The American drew in long, deep breaths like one practicing meditation. Finding his core of calm. He stood at a large window, holding back the drape and gazing toward the building that housed Chen Ti-sai's matrimonial service. It might not seem prudent to, on a heated whim, move into a hotel close to Chen's place of business, but it did provide the American the opportunity to watch out the window for what times the man came and went.

After a protracted, thoughtful delay, he finally said to Long Dien, "Tell them you'll meet them two hours from now. That will give me time to come out there for this little meeting, too."

3: COFFEE KLATSCH

WHEN THANH LED TRENOR INTO the café, right away he saw the *ca phe om* Hoa clearing a table of emptied glasses of coffee and complimentary jasmine tea. Since she had greeted him so brightly the last time he'd come here, he smiled at her and opened his mouth to speak, but when she lifted her head and saw him she gave him a hard look, turned her back and hurried off with her laden tray. In the brief moment that she'd faced him, he'd seen that her eyes were red from crying and her upper lip puffy, already turning blue/black in one spot. Thanh looked to Trenor. He'd noticed the young woman's face, too.

"She's the one who gave me Long Dien's number," Thanh explained in a low voice.

"Is that him back there?" Trenor asked, motioning with his head. Toward the rear of the murky coffee house, Long Dien sat alone at a table, his thin brown face split into an exaggerated grin. He waved them over.

"Yes," Thanh said with distaste.

"Be cool, brother." Together they started moving toward the man. "Does he speak English?"

"No. I can translate for you."

Thanh greeted Long Dien much less enthusiastically than Long Dien greeted him. Thanh introduced Trenor, after which he explained in English, "I told him you're a friend I met online, in a forum about Vietnam. I mentioned you're a war veteran, but I didn't mention my father; he doesn't like people to know he was in the *Chieu Hoi* program, fighting with the Americans."

"I understand. But I hope this guy doesn't think I'm your internet boyfriend."

Thanh winced. "Oh, Rick."

They seated themselves, and after another exchange in which Long Dien made sweeping courtly gestures, Thanh interpreted, "He invites us to order anything we like, on him."

"Tell him thanks. An iced coffee would be good." Trenor nodded at Long Dien, smiling faintly. He was happy they hadn't shared a Western handshake...especially when he noticed a spider—or was it an ant?—resting upon one of the man's knuckles like a black-jeweled ring.

After Long Dien had conveyed their orders to one of the waitresses, he and Thanh commenced speaking in Vietnamese more at length, with Thanh repeatedly breaking from their discourse to fill Trenor in on both the questions and answers.

Thanh said to their host, "I was hoping you had heard something about where my sister Tra Mi is."

Long Dien's grinning theatrical mask turned to its overstated grimacing opposite. "Thanh, my friend, if I had heard something don't you think I would have called you, as you requested? I wish I had heard something! And I was so shocked to learn about your poor little sister...what was her name?"

Thanh couldn't answer for several beats. In a tight voice: "Hang Ni."

"Yes. Dear child! I saw the story on TV. A terrible tragedy! Are the police keeping you informed of their progress?"

"I haven't heard from them. There is no progress. I'm sure Hang Ni was with Tra Mi, at least in the beginning. I want to know if someone killed Tra Mi, too."

Long Dien shook his head as if to dispel such an ungodly possibility. The movement seemed to rouse another creature, which scurried out of the man's ear. Trenor felt a sympathetic tickle in his own ear, but Thanh didn't notice, nor did Long Dien as he replied, "Oh, I hope that isn't true!"

"If she isn't dead, why wouldn't I have heard from her?"

"She may be afraid you'll blame her for not protecting her little sister. Or she may be afraid of the police blaming her for the same."

"Or she may be afraid the killer will come after her next," Trenor cut in, when Thanh had interpreted the last remark.

"But I can't imagine why anyone would want to hurt those poor girls," Long Dien moaned. A third spider slipped between his teeth to sit upon his brown bottom lip. Trenor felt like they were lies coated in chitin.

"Well," Trenor said, through Thanh, "Hang Ni's murderer abused her sexually, and sexual abuse often leads to greater violence. Even willing sexual partners, like prostitutes for instance, can be attacked violently. Prostitutes are often murdered."

Long Dien nodded thoughtfully at Trenor's point, holding his gaze. "Well, of course this little girl wouldn't have been a willing partner, so we aren't talking about prostitution in this instance, but obviously just some madman."

Their coffee and accompanying tea arrived. Trenor glanced up at the *ca phe om*. She was exceedingly beautiful, though in a haunted kind of way, her striking eyes hiding unnamable tragedies. If not her own, perhaps those of her country, or of her gender.

Kate took her tray and left them.

Trenor shifted his attention to the tin filter atop his glass. The first dripping bead of coffee dropped onto the thick layer of sweetened condensed milk at the bottom of the glass; an initial dark dot like virgin's blood. He said, "If Tra Mi was a prostitute, it could be that one of her clients got violent with her. And if Hang Ni happened to be with Tra Mi, he may have decided to hurt her, too."

Long Dien looked uncomprehending, stunned and appalled. The spider fled down his chin, then his neck, to vanish under his shirt collar. "Tra Mi...a prostitute?"

An icy grin carved Trenor's face. Thanh translated, "Come on, we don't have to pretend here, do we?" Trenor waved his hand around the room. "These lovely girls of yours...if I wanted to take one of them to bed, well, that's what they're here for, right?"

Long Dien sat up straight in his chair as if hugely insulted by such an insinuation. A scattering of spiders hid at the edges of his forehead, at the roots of his hair, like beads of perspiration. "My friend, this is a coffee shop! Nothing more! My girls are not for sale! Of course, their lives are their own, and they can go with any man they choose. But that's their business, not mine!"

"Really? And you don't make any profit, should one of your girls—on her own—decide to go to bed with one of the patrons of your coffee shop?" Trenor hooked his thumb toward a staircase at the very back of the room. "Go to a room upstairs, for example?"

Long Dien glanced past Trenor, looking nervous and angry and barely in check. Thanh followed his gaze. There were partitioned booths along one wall for greater privacy, almost made into duck blinds by tactfully positioned potted plants. In the nearest of these booths, through the foliage, Thanh could make out—in bits and pieces, like a partly assembled jigsaw puzzle—a man apparently sitting alone, wearing a baseball cap and, odd for this cavern-like gloom, dark glasses. A goon or bodyguard, he had no doubt.

"I don't want to be rude to your friend," Long Dien told Thanh, no longer looking at Trenor at all, "but he is being rude to me, after I was so kind to offer you my help. I must return to Saigon now, if you'll excuse me. If I hear from Tra Mi I will call you, as I promised you before. I truly hope that she is still alive somewhere."

"I know the work my sister did for you, Long Dien," Thanh told the man.

Long Dien rose from the table, still not acknowledging Trenor's presence. Less shy now, a dozen spiders came trickling down his cheeks like tears, and one circled his right eye around and around in an agitated frenzy. "She served coffee, Thanh. Enjoy yours." He started to turn toward the open front of the room.

"Can I ask one more question, before you go?" Trenor spoke up. "If you haven't got anything to hide, why did you hit that girl who gave Thanh your phone number?"

Now Long Dien did look at Trenor. His face was a busy ant farm of movement, but what work the bustling spiders had in mind Trenor couldn't glean. After a pause in which Long Dien sought composure, he managed, "I have nothing to hide, and I didn't hit Hoa. Her boyfriend struck her; it's none of my affair. It's none of your affair, either." This time he did turn away and stride across the room, with spiders running up and down in columns across the back of his neck.

Thanh and Trenor met each other's gaze. "Now what?" Thanh asked.

"I'm not sure, kid; I'm totally lost here. But I don't like this sleazebag." Trenor couldn't tell the boy about the spider-things. He'd think he was mad—shell-shocked. He himself had long thought he might be mad, or shell-shocked. But he did permit himself to say, "He's evil. I can tell."

Thanh glanced toward the booth where he had glimpsed the man in the baseball cap and shades. Either he had shifted further behind the potted plants or he had left the booth—maybe gone upstairs?—without Thanh noticing. Either way, he seemed to have disappeared.

*　　*　　*

"Do you want a ride back to Saigon with us?" Long Dien said into his cell phone. He sat in the back seat of his Lifan 520, a Chinese sedan, currently parked at the curb down the street a bit from his café. Behind the wheel sat a cousin's young son, Hiep, tallish and athletic, with an electrified haircut like a character from a Japanese video game, a long handsome face, and a fast smile: huge, white, and cruel.

On the other end, the American replied, "No. I'll take care of myself. Did you find out who this friend is?"

"Just his name." Long Dien attempted to remember and pronounce it.

"That doesn't help," the American growled, only getting "Richard." From where he had been sitting he hadn't heard their conversation well, and hadn't caught the man's name himself.

"The USA wouldn't send police to investigate this, would they?"

"Not the girl, no. But the man who killed the girl is an American; maybe they're onto him. Or maybe they don't know, but they're just sniffing around a little because they heard the killer was a foreigner in general. This old guy could be with the US embassy. He could even be from Interpol. But some friend the kid met online? Come on."

"Did you see his face?" Long Dien said. "Whatever he is, he's been in some kind of fight before."

"Whatever he is, he's trouble. You see, this is exactly what I was talking about. *Fuck* Chen. Fuck him and *his* American friend!"

"I wish we knew if Chen's friend killed Tra Mi," Long Dien said. "This one-eyed man has Tra Mi's brother at his side like a guide dog. If she isn't dead, and decides to contact her brother…"

"I need to find out if she's alive," the American muttered in Long Dien's ear, "before that happens."

Long Dien related more of what had been discussed at his table. When he complained that the stranger had brought up Hoa's fat lip, the American cut him off. "You hit that girl?"

"Yes, I sure did—you didn't see her? She shouldn't have given Tra Mi's brother my phone number in the first place!"

"Are you that stupid? If she hadn't given him the number he could have found you in person easily enough, so what does it matter that she did? Of course this man made the connection between the girl giving the brother your phone number, and you beating the girl."

"Maybe we should get rid of her in case this man decides to question her."

"*Do ngu!*" the American snarled, calling Long Dien an idiot. "Did you just hear what I said? What could she know? And if the girl disappears you could make this man even more suspicious than you already have! The girl isn't what worries me...it's you. You'd better pull yourself together and think clearly."

"*Xin loi*," Long Dien apologized. "Sorry, my friend...you're right, of course."

"Let me know if this American contacts you again."

"What are you going to do now?"

"I'm going to look for Tra Mi in the last place we're sure she visited—Vung Tau. But there's one bit of business I want to finish in Saigon, first."

The American disconnected. Long Dien wanted to curse him aloud, but even though he could plainly see from his cell phone's screen that the call had ended, he was still irrationally too afraid to do so, as if somehow his American friend might still hear him. Hiep might betray him, too, being more afraid of the American than he was of his father's cousin. And, looking furtively out his window, Long Dien realized he didn't know where the American was at this moment—still inside the café or out here on the street somewhere?

"Take me back to Saigon," he told Hiep, and he felt better when their car started back into motion.

4: THIRD EYE

TRENOR AND THANH PLANNED ON going to Vung Tau, too.

"Until I think of how we can push this Long Dien asshole some more," Trenor told Thanh and Quan back at the house, the three of them sitting on the cement bench out front eating chunks of grapefruit dipped in a mixture of salt and red pepper, "I'd like to go to the hotel where they found Hang Ni."

"Sure," Thanh said. "The police told us the owner said the man in that room was a foreigner."

"I want to talk to them, then. Have you?"

"No, Rick. I haven't, myself."

"Who's in charge of the investigation—the Vung Tau police?"

"Yes," Quan spat, as if tasting poison. *"Thuong Ta* Luong Van Tien."

"Huh?"

Thanh explained, "His name is Luong Van Tien. *Thuong Ta* means, uh…Senior Lieutenant Colonel. I'm sure he isn't happy that Hang Ni was killed, but I'm also sure he is much less happy about the shadow it cast on Vung Tau. It's a major tourist city."

"Yeah—I went swimming there on R&R, back in the day." Trenor left out the prostitutes he had slept with in Vung Tau. Under the circumstances, witnessing a father's shame and pain, he felt guilty for his past indulgences. But then, he had never murdered a prostitute…assuming, as he tried not to, that Tra Mi had suffered that fate. He returned to the subject at hand. "I wonder if this Senior Lieutenant Colonel has tried to determine how many foreign tourists were in Vietnam on the day Hang Ni was killed."

"Rick," Thanh said, out of politeness trying not to laugh, "Vietnam is very popular with tourists! Not only Americans, but people from Australia, the UK, Germany, all over the world. And there are more than a thousand Russians living in Vung Tau—oil workers. Maybe the killer was a Russian. So you see how difficult it is?"

"Wow...yeah, I guess I do." Trenor sighed, then shrugged. "Well, it doesn't hurt to talk to these hotel people anyway. Before we go, though, I'd like to check my email...let my brother know I got here okay. Now I regret I don't have a laptop I could've brought with me. Mind if I use your PC here?"

"Of course not...I'll get you set up." Thanh smiled. "That's my job."

At that moment a reed-thin young man scuffed past the house in dusty sandals. He was badly scarred on the right side of his face and down the length of his right arm, with gauze patches taped to his neck and forearm. He didn't look happy with his condition. When he'd passed, Trenor nodded after him and said quietly, "What's his story?"

"Oh," Thanh said, "about two years ago he got a new girlfriend behind his girlfriend's back, so his old girlfriend threw acid on him."

"Holy fuck. Two years ago, and he still needs to dress the wounds? Jesus." Trenor watched the man turn the bend in the little alley leading out to the busy street. *Brother monster*, he thought, *I feel your pain.*

Quan gathered the remnants of their snack and rose from the bench to carry the plate inside. On his way he gave Thanh a single pat on the shoulder— brusque, maybe self-conscious, but a pat on the shoulder all the same. Thanh turned and watched his father disappear into the house, flatly surprised.

"I haven't seen my father stay sober this long in more years than I can remember," he said. "He's afraid to disappoint you, Rick."

"That's the only thing your old man is afraid of. I hope he's remembering just who the hell he is. He's a fucking Tunnel Rat."

Thanh nodded thoughtfully, but was distracted by another person passing by them in slapping flip-flops, a neighbor girl named Thuy—twenty, like himself—wearing a faded blue-flowered pajama suit. She was taller than him, as thin as hope, with long limbs like flower stems, and a delicate beauty; heavy-lidded eyes and crooked front teeth Thanh found endearing. Sometimes she spoke with him, however briefly and shyly, and when he had lived here he had ever been on the lookout for her to walk past the family home, but when she glanced over now and noticed the foreign stranger she averted her eyes quickly.

Trenor noticed her, too; her bared, bony upper back was covered in a pattern of shocking red marks. "God," he said as she went on her way, with the fast, awkward steps Thanh had never told anyone he found achingly adorable, "did someone throw acid on her, too?"

"Oh, no...she must have a backache. Her mom must have rubbed green oil on her. You rub it into the skin with something metal, like a spoon."

"Ouch," Trenor said. Then, he finally picked up on how Thanh had followed the girl with his eyes. "She's cute, huh?"

Thanh shrugged and switched from watching Thuy's receding form to watching a gorgeously colored rooster chase after a small drab hen directly in front of them.

"You should ask her out."

"Rick, I thought you said you shouldn't give me advice about women."

"Listen…remember you told me you wanted to be a monk? Well, for years I hid away in hobbies or disciplines I could lose myself in. When I was younger it was martial arts, which phased into meditating to find my inner serenity. Or my inner abstinence—take your pick. Did a lot of reading…and I lost myself in drinking for a while there, too. Luckily, I never got into drugs; we Tunnel Rats were never the druggie type. Mostly I lost myself in my work—back when I had jobs that were *worth* losing myself in, at least. But I imposed a kind of monk-like life on myself, Thanh, and now I'm old. I've missed whatever chances at deep and lasting relationships I might've had." Sometimes Trenor felt his last truly intense human interaction had been with his enemy down in that final tunnel. He went on, "But you're young, and you're a good-looking kid. Don't do the same thing I did. Don't dig yourself down in a hole." He squeezed Thanh's knee. "Listen to your Uncle Rick."

Thanh said, "Thank you, Uncle Rick," in a lighthearted way meant to dismiss the uncomfortable subject. Then to flat-out change the subject, he said, "You studied martial arts?"

"A couple. Mostly aikido."

"I wish I could do that. Children used to start fights with me in school."

"I could still teach you a few moves; you don't have to fly around like fucking Bruce Lee."

"Were you ever in a fight?"

"Nope. Eh, a couple almost-fights, in a bar or two. But I haven't had to fight anybody since I was last here."

"Do you remember how to fight people?"

"You mean, with martial arts?"

"No, I mean…in a war."

"I don't know. I haven't had to know."

"My father never told us too much about what he did, either for the Viet Cong or for the other side when he became *Hoi Chanh Vien*. But, Rick, how many guys did you kill?"

"Oh man." Trenor shifted his weight. "Well, six, for sure."

"Oh…only six?"

"What do you mean, *only* six?"

Thanh smiled. "Hey, in the movie *Hard Boiled*, Chow Yun-Fat kills seventy-seven guys! I love that movie."

"Shit—'only six' guys. If I wasted six guys in my country, I'd be a very respectable serial killer."

"Did you do terrible things?"

Trenor's manner grew darker. "What do you mean, like kill women and children? Some guys did. I'm sure you know about My Lai. Guys raping women and then shooting them. Shooting them in the vagina. Cutting little girls' vaginas open with their knives because they were too small to fuck."

Thanh muttered something in Vietnamese, wagging his head as he held Trenor's one-eyed gaze.

"Some guys went crazy. Evil ran wild. No other way to describe it—their evil poured out. But no…not me. I just killed men." He snorted. "Heh—*just* men. Killing one man is like killing a whole bunch of people, because he can be a father, and a son, a husband, a brother, a friend. And you're killing part of everybody who loved him, too."

"I understand," Thanh said, equally grave. "Because of Hang Ni. Because part of me has died."

Trenor rubbed Thanh's back. "I'm sure you do understand."

A few heavy moments passed silently between them, and then Trenor sighed, "Well." He slapped his palms on his legs, about to rise and ask Thanh if they could look into the matter of his email now, when a motorbike came rumbling along, a kind of cooler fitted behind the seat…set up, from what Trenor could determine, to sell snow cones or some other frozen treat. Under his helmet the rider's hair was uncommonly long. He stopped his bike directly in front of the two men, grinned at Trenor and gestured behind him at his wares.

"Uh, no thanks," Trenor said, smiling and shaking his head.

The man nodded, looked to Thanh and said a few friendly words, which Thanh responded to politely, then started his bike back into motion again. Trenor watched after him as he continued on his way, and then said, "There's something that guy is hiding. I think he's a drug dealer."

"My father calls him 007," Thanh said. "He's a policeman, Rick, or maybe just an informant. He drives around spying on people, and if he sees something funny, like people gambling, he calls in the police."

"Baretta disguised as an ice cream man, huh?"

"How did you guess he's not what he seems? It was his bike, right? It's too good for a man driving around selling ice cream."

"That was probably it," Trenor lied. In truth, it had been the spider or ant positioned exactly in the center of the man's forehead like a third eye. Others had circled around his wrists like living bracelets. Not meaning to, he added in a kind of faraway voice, "He has a black soul."

"A black soul? I can believe it…but how can you tell?"

Trenor looked at the young man and said, "I just have a special insight into these things, I guess."

"Is it a skill you developed during the war, Rick?"

For several seconds he couldn't respond, but at last said, "I guess that's the only explanation."

5: BEHELD

AFTER TRENOR HAD WRITTEN HIS brother, he asked Thanh why the window the computer desk was positioned in front of had been completely covered over with old calendar and magazine pages.

"Oh, there's a little alley outside and rainwater runs through it, so a lot of mosquitoes would be out there and get in through the window. But I used to tease my mother that she wanted it covered because of the ghost."

"What ghost?"

"A number of times when she was younger, my mother said she saw a person moving out there in the alley."

"A neighbor?"

"The person had white clothes and long black hair."

"Okay…sounds like an Asian ghost to me."

"But our next-door neighbor saw something more, looking into the same alley. One night she thought she saw someone out there and she was afraid they were trying to steal something, so she snuck up to the window and put her face close to it. At the same time, the person on the other side put their face close to the window, too, and stared right into my neighbor's face. She said it was a woman with red eyes."

"Bloodshot eyes?"

"No…eyes like fire."

"Fire," Trenor echoed.

"Yes."

"Huh," Trenor said. He tried to swallow, found his throat was almost seized up, and took a sip of the iced tea Quan had brought him.

"Do you believe in ghosts, Rick?"

"I'm…not sure. How about you?"

"Yes, I do," he said earnestly. "My mother told me other ghost stories. She has an uncle out in Tri An—a very rural area. A man lived right next-door to her uncle's house, and one day he saw a beautiful woman with long black hair walking over a bridge across the river."

"Was she in white clothes?"

Thanh smiled. "Yes, Rick, she was. White is a funeral color...the color of death. Not black like in your culture. Anyway, the neighbor said she was beautiful and so he called to her, 'Hey, where are you going?' Like to flirt with her, you know? But she didn't hear him, and walked down to the river's edge. She walked right into it, and disappeared down in the water."

"Yikes."

"The neighbor was almost crazy with fear, and not long after he saw that woman he grew sick and died."

"Like she was an omen of his death, huh?"

"Yes. Or unlucky for him to see. And there was another story my mother told me about Tri An—something that happened to a man just a little more down the road. In the old times there weren't as many TVs as now, especially out in a place like Tri An, so a lot of neighbors would gather at one family's house to watch TV. Well, one night after people finished watching they all walked back to their homes, but one man didn't return home. His family grew worried about him, so they started searching. They finally found him standing in a, uh, thicket of bamboo." Thanh made sprouting gestures with his misshapen hands. "But the bamboo grew so close together they couldn't understand how he could have got into the middle of it. They had to chop it down with machetes to get to him. And when they reached him, they saw that he looked crazy, and his mouth was completely filled with dirt."

"His mouth...filled with dirt."

"Yes. He was never the same again. He couldn't tell anyone what he'd seen, and he was simple-minded after that, like a little child."

Trenor blew out the air he found he had been clutching tightly in his chest, like a submerged swimmer. "Wow. Yeah. I guess when we see things that are beyond our understanding...beyond our world..." He let the words fall away. He sipped his iced tea and changed the subject. "Do you have any photos of Hang Ni and Tra Mi?"

"Of course...why?"

"We'll be needing to show them to people in Vung Tau, especially at that hotel."

"Right... Okay, let me go find some."

Trenor played with the computer a bit, but his thoughts were in a formless state, and Thanh came back with a couple of good pictures of both girls, though in none did they appear together. Hang Ni's sunny face gave him a pang, so he could only imagine how Thanh felt seeing the photos again. A small ID-style photo of Tra Mi showed her as sullen as a person in a mug shot, but another was a studio portrait of her in a tank top and jeans. This photo had been so touched up with digital enhancement that she was like a corpse after a mortician was through with it. Both photos were unlike the face Trenor had seen in his dream, but he couldn't say they weren't the same person, either.

*   *   *

Thanh called a taxi to come and drive them to Vung Tau, so Trenor emptied his bladder before the trip. As he stood before the toilet he noticed movement directly in front of his face, and was startled to see a stream of tiny lifeforms racing along a narrow channel of grout between ceramic tiles, like cars or motorbikes navigating a street seen from the window of an airplane. These flea-sized ants were too small to be his spiders, but they still put him in mind of them.

He shuddered and tried not to think of it as an omen.

6: AN APPOINTED TIME AND PLACE

WHEN THE ELEVATOR HAD DESCENDED from the second to the ground floor of Chen Ti-sai's place of business on Le Duan Boulevard, its door slid back to reveal an attractively dressed woman seemingly waiting to board. Her gaze met Chen's as if her eyes had locked on his own before the door had even opened. Her lips parted ever-so-slightly, as if in hesitation to speak. Carrying his laptop case, Chen stepped over the threshold and she took a corresponding step back, eyes still on his, lips still parted. Vietnam was full to the brim with beautiful women—who knew better than Chen, who made his livelihood off that beauty in all its hunger and desperation?—but this woman's beauty was transcendent in a way that was hard to put a finger on. She emanated a deep, unarticulated misery that spoke of classical drama, beyond the scope of one person's paltry life; a misery of the whole of human existence, no doubt beyond her own capacity for understanding. She was a mute and uncomprehending vessel of that suffering, like a small child with terminal cancer.

Chen smiled, and unmindful of the people getting off or boarding the elevator around them, asked in Vietnamese, "Are you lost? Can I help you?" The elevator's door closed again behind him. The woman hadn't stepped past him to enter it.

"I'm sorry," she replied. "I…I was going to go upstairs, but…I'm not sure."

"Upstairs where? To the marriage broker?"

"Yes. But…"

"But you're undecided."

"Yes."

"May I ask why you're undecided?"

"So many reasons. Money…"

"Various reasonable arrangements can be made."

"…and I'm afraid to go to some far place like Taiwan if my husband doesn't truly love me. He may give me to his father or another man, or only want me as a servant. I heard one Korean man killed his Vietnamese bride only a week after she came to Korea."

"Oh, an isolated case—one crazy man my company would have weeded out quickly."

"Your company? You work with the marriage broker?"

"*Em*," Chen said gently, "I am the company's owner."

The beautiful woman flashed a nervous smile, and gave a quick little bow. "I'm so sorry, uncle," she said respectfully. "I had no idea."

Chen winced. "Uncle? Please call me Ti-sai." He took her hand and squeezed it. "It's a Taiwanese name."

"I think I need to consider everything more," she said. "Do you think you could discuss my situation with me? But I don't want to trouble you…"

"Of course!" Chen said, straightening up, full of gallantry. "Of course! This is what I do! I frequently consult with clients personally. But I'm afraid the office has closed for the day. If you'd prefer not to have to return tomorrow, perhaps you and I could go have some coffee and discuss your story in a less formal setting. If you feel that's comfortable for you."

"I was about to suggest the same thing," the woman said.

*   *   *

Out on the street, the woman had pointed toward the Sofitel Saigon Plaza Hotel, towering against the orange banners of evening sky, and said, "I hear there are very beautiful bars and restaurants in that hotel."

Chen had chuckled. Clever little girl! So she was going to milk him, eh? Then she had better be prepared to milk him in another way, he thought. "Yes," he replied, "I've entertained clients there before."

He had driven her across the street to the hotel, because he had wanted to impress her with his vehicle and because Chen Ti-sai didn't walk the street like some rubbernecked tourist. The TV he had in place of a rearview mirror played the cockfighting tournament called the World Slasher Cup, held in the Philippines.

That had been some hours ago. The two of them had spent little time in the L'Elysee Bar, little time discussing the woman's typically sordid little tale of poverty and discontent, before Chen had suggested they take a room upstairs so that they could converse in even greater privacy. He had been holding her hand for a while by the time he made this suggestion, and her palm was almost dripping with sweat. He found that detail oddly agreeable. So she wasn't such a calculating creature, after all? More nervous and uncertain than that?

Whatever her uncertainties, she had gone down on him with a too-easy skill and he had climaxed in her mouth, which surprised him. Though he had no shortage of women—this was hardly his first private consultation with a woman concerned about money—he hadn't been able to climax from oral pleasure alone in years. They had then showered together, and he was once more surprised...this time at how quickly he became aroused again. This woman did indeed possess a singular magic. She was liable to take ten years off him at this rate. Back to bed, and they made love vigorously, until he rolled onto his back heaving and sweating, instantly withered. He fell asleep that way.

When he woke, it was to the distant sounds of night's street traffic as heard through an open window, and when he recalled his whereabouts it was with a flash of alarm that he would find his wallet, laptop, and the woman missing...but no, there she sat at a desk, fully dressed yet still here, though he wasn't pleased to see she had opened and activated his laptop. He sat up, reining in his displeasure. He didn't want to frighten her off, didn't want this to be their last private consultation.

She smiled at him. "I'm sorry...I was bored."

"You should have awakened me."

"You were sleeping so comfortably."

Chen glanced at the time, groaned inwardly. He'd slept *too* comfortably. His own wife—who was of course Vietnamese, and still beautiful—would be waiting for him. Well, apparently she hadn't tried calling him yet, as it was not uncommon for him to go out with friends and clients after work, though he expected a call would be imminent. He wasn't afraid for this woman to discover he had a wife; she couldn't be that naïve.

"I can speak a little Chinese," she told him, "but I can't read Chinese characters." She indicated the screen of his laptop. She had opened his word processing program. "Can you show me how you write some things?"

He pulled on his underwear, smiling with patient indulgence, and seated himself close to her. "What would you want me to teach you?"

"Something romantic." She pressed the side of her body more tightly against his. "Write *I love this woman with all my soul.*"

"Hm," he said, leaning over to kiss her at the base of the neck, "that *is* romantic." He typed out the phrase in the traditional Chinese characters used in Taiwan, and then explained the various logograms to her, pointing at the screen, its blue light washing over their faces intimately like a spectral fire.

"I love how the words sound when you say them," the woman said, squeezing his bare thigh. "Write *I would rather die than live without her.*"

Chen chuckled. "Are these song lyrics, or words from your heart?"

"Perhaps I'll tell you soon."

Chen stared into her face, those eyes that seemed to ache and made him ache in a way he couldn't articulate himself. So, was it going to be love, then? The thought made him wary of the headaches love would bring, and yet it had been more years since he had experienced love than since the last time he had climaxed in a girl's mouth, and he felt the flutter of exhilaration. It was like an ailment of the heart.

He turned to his laptop and typed out the logograms that expressed the phrase, "*I would rather die than live without her.*"

While he had slept, Kate had done more than open his laptop. She had unlocked the expensive hotel room's door.

Behind them, the American stepped out of the bathroom. Chen didn't hear nor see him, but he did see Kate suddenly turn her face to look away, a moment before the American swung the cover of the toilet tank and struck him across the back of the skull with its edge.

Chen grunted softly, and folded over into his own lap. Kate couldn't stop herself from glancing at him, and let out a retch though no blood had been spilled.

"Get a hold of yourself," the American snapped, starting back toward the bathroom to wipe down and replace the tank cover, having determined a second blow wouldn't be necessary. "And turn out the lights."

When he returned, the only light was the city's ambient illumination through the large window, and that spectral glow from the laptop, intensified. He stepped around in front of Chen and took hold of him under the armpits, hoisting him to his feet. Chen mumbled something like a drunken friend, slumping heavily against the American, his mouth mashed open against the younger man's shoulder. The American dragged him toward the window.

"You should have shot yourself with your gun right there and then," he said close to the unconscious man's ear, "instead of pointing it at me."

The window's large central section couldn't be opened, but there were two narrow side panels flanking it that could be unlatched. Kate had already swiveled open the one on the right. "A tight squeeze," the American grunted, pressing Chen's slack, heavy body into the gap, "but a man committing suicide can be determined." He was having trouble, however, and glanced back at Kate, who stood transfixed in the middle of the room. "Give me a hand here!" he huffed.

"No," she said.

"What do you mean, 'no'?"

"I can't. Don't ask me…I can't."

"The outcome will be the same either way, but you might spare me a hernia."

She didn't respond, nor take a step closer to lend him aid. Cursing under his breath, the American doubled his efforts, getting an arm around the other man's legs and tipping his upper weight outward. In so doing, Chen aided his murderer himself. Like a baby squeezing his way into the world, one moment he was wedged and the next slipped cleanly through…and then he was gone.

But a second later, they heard a tremendous crash, and screams from down at street level.

The American didn't pause to look out to survey the scene. He strode quickly away from the window, seized Kate by the hand, and pulled her toward the hotel room's door.

Only the next day, in a newspaper, would he learn that the ironically heartbroken marriage broker—after leaving a suicide note on his laptop, and having leapt from the window of his twelfth-floor "Superior Room"—had plunged to his death through the glass roof of the carport out in front of the hotel. In the process, one of his legs had been torn off at the hip and his skull had been split down the middle, all the way to his lower jaw. His brain had been deposited a short distance away.

The American peeked out into the hallway, saw no one about, then he and Kate walked briskly to the nearest elevator. They rode it down to the tenth floor, where the American had taken his own room. Once inside, he locked them in safely for the night. He had a wig for Kate, inexpensive but made of real human hair, chin-length and of a reddish hue, for her to wear when they checked out tomorrow before noon, lest anyone recognize Kate as the woman who had accompanied Chen up to his room.

"Try it on," the American instructed her. She did. He nodded approval. "I like it," he murmured, coming toward her. Her eyes widened, as if she feared he might put his hands around her throat to eliminate his only witness, but instead he roughly undressed her. She moved her body minimally to assist him, and stepped out of her panties. He pushed her back onto the bed, and stared down at her body—as slack as Chen's had been—as he stripped away his own clothing. He was almost trembling with the intensity of his lust. It was a strange delirium, making his heartbeat stutter.

He lay atop her, pressed himself into her steadily though she was dry and let out a tiny moan of discomfort. She stared up at him blankly at first, but couldn't face his fierce eyes so close to her own so she closed her lids and tilted her head back as if in pleasure, as he took one of her legs and lifted it in the crook of his arm. Her foot made circles in the air with the rhythm of his driving thrusts.

"Poor lovesick fool," he muttered in English, not knowing fully whether he spoke of Chen or himself.

PART 5: VUNG TAU

1: THE KEY

THE TAXI WAS A KIA New Morning, bright green. When it pulled up in front of the house Trenor remarked, "I can't get over the taxis here. When I was a kid, I had toy cars bigger than this."

Buddha perched on the dashboard, all imitation gold; beauty and tackiness walked hand-in-hand here. As was customary, the driver drove with one hand on his horn to alert the motorbikes ahead of them. Trenor dreaded the idea of driving in Vietnam himself.

Some time later, as they drew close to their destination, Thanh said, "Near Vung Tau there's a tunnel complex called the Long Phuoc Tunnels. Have you heard of it?"

"Yes," Trenor said. His voice sounded tight and wary to his own ears. "But I never fought in that system."

"I know—my father told us. But I wondered if you might like to see it, since we'll be close."

Trenor was reminded of his coworker Peter asking him if he wanted to borrow his PC game *Tunnel Rats*, but he controlled his tone when he asked, "Has your father ever gone to see them?"

"No. As far as I know he hasn't been to Cu Chi to look at those tunnels since they've been open to tourists, either."

"Well, I'd rather not, too."

Thanh finally read the older man's mood. "I'm sorry, Rick," he said, becoming nervous about having discomforted his companion. In a flurry he said, "I went to Long Phuoc with some friends—you wouldn't like it. Stupid dusty mannequins posed around, pointing guns through spy holes, like a haunted house in an amusement park...and the tunnels have been made taller for Westerners, so they're no longer authentic."

"I'll say. If they were authentic, those wouldn't be mannequins aiming guns through spy holes."

Thanh repeated, "I'm sorry, Rick. It wasn't a good suggestion."

Trenor elbowed him in the arm. "Forget it. No biggie. Anyway, we have more important stuff to be spending our time on."

"Right, Rick. Yes, of course."

The green-gray ocean was out there on their left, the South China Sea, and facing it on the other side of the street was a small rounded mountain. Trenor noticed a white figure at its peak, with arms outspread as if to summon the sun into rising from the horizon each day, or to bring down rains to feed the water. The statue was tiny from here, but he knew it must be sizable. "What's that?" he asked.

Thanh leaned past him to look up. "Jesus."

"Are you surprised, or is that who it is?"

"It's Jesus. There are many Catholics in Vietnam, Rick. It's very tall...like the one in Brazil."

"Huh. Maybe I'm naive but I guess I'm just surprised in a communist country it isn't Ho Chi Minh instead. It sure wasn't here the last time I was in Vung Tau." He nudged Thanh with his elbow. "Guess I'm not the only white savior here, huh?" But Thanh didn't appear to get the joke.

Across from the shoreline at street level now was a continuous string of hotels and cafés. The taxi eventually turned off the highway onto a side street, festooned here and there with red flags sporting a yellow star or else a yellow hammer and sickle. These and other seemingly outmoded accoutrements of communism, such as billboards Trenor had seen since arriving in the country—done in classic propaganda style right down to stalwart soldiers posing with AK-47s—put him in a rather surreal state of mind. His enemy of long ago had definitely won. White-bearded Uncle Ho, grinning and crinkly eyed, was as omnipresent as Big Brother, but against his red background reminded Trenor more of Colonel Sanders.

The little green taxi pulled up in front of the address the driver had been given: a tall, skinny hotel with tiers of balconies, wedged in a row of similar structures—differing superficially in their facades, and give or take a level or two—facing more of the same on the opposite side of this shadowy chasm. At the end of the street, the ocean could still be seen as a silvery line under a silvery sky.

"So you haven't been here before?" Trenor said to Thanh, watching his face as the young man surveyed the building.

"No," he said.

"Do you want to maybe stay in the car?"

"You need an interpreter, Rick. But even if you didn't...no, I want to go inside."

Trenor nodded. "Okay, then. Let's do this." Somehow, he felt as he had years ago, when he and this man's father had readied themselves to descend into a tunnel. Into *that* tunnel.

The driver left his taxi at the curb to enter the lobby with them. Trenor was learning that when one rented a cab, one gained a new close friend for whatever the duration, who often ate with his fare and stayed in the same hotel—at the fare's expense, of course. Not that it was expensive. But the man hung back unobtrusively to let Thanh do the talking.

The thickset, middle-aged woman behind the lobby's counter watched the approach of this odd trio distrustfully, and when Thanh introduced himself as the brother of the murdered girl who had been found in a room on the fourth floor of this establishment, her meaty face looked even more on guard. Thanh extended a photo of Hang Ni, and asked the hotel's owner, "Did you see my sister at any time in your hotel?"

"No, never," the woman said curtly, though her eyes were more focused on Thanh's malformed hand than the photograph.

"She wasn't with your customer when he rented his room?"

"No—he was alone."

"No other person who works here saw the man leave and come back later with my sister?"

"No."

"No other worker saw her come in here with anyone else...like this person?" This time he extended the ID photo of Tra Mi, which had put Trenor in mind of a scowling mug shot.

"No one here saw the little girl alive at all. I never even saw her body; my niece is the one who found her. How she got in that room, I don't know. The foreigner must have brought her up there at a time when he saw no one was at the counter."

"No one is accusing you of wrongdoing," Thanh said patiently, though his heart was thudding. The reality that his sister's life had ended in this building, in a room a few floors above his head, was settling in and his breathing was becoming shallow, a nauseating vibration like internalized trembling running through him.

"Good, because we did nothing wrong."

"Can you describe this foreigner?"

"I've described him for the police."

"Please describe him for *me*. Was he an American? How old was he?"

The woman gestured brusquely, exasperated to repeat herself. "I don't know how old...maybe in his forties. Older? Who can say? Not too tall, not too fat. He looked nice. Nice clothing. He was very polite. Maybe he was an American—he said some English words, like 'thank you'—but I don't know accents. He might have been Australian for all I know. We get a lot of Australians...they speak English, too."

Thanh faced Trenor and related all this. He only nodded, absorbing the information, then Thanh addressed the owner again. "You never learned his name? Why didn't you ask to hold onto his passport during his stay, like hotels usually do?" This time he couldn't help but betray a hint of anger in his voice. The internal trembling was threatening to become external.

The owner heard the anger, and became yet more defensive. "I asked him for it, but he said he needed to leave very early in the morning, so he couldn't wait for me to return it. He said he didn't want to wake any of us up. That's why he left his key here on the counter when he left. I don't know what time that was."

"Did he give you some extra money to overlook his passport?" Thanh snapped.

Trenor didn't know what was being said, but he laid a hand on Thanh's shoulder and whispered, "Easy, kid."

"Yes!" the owner answered defiantly.

Thanh wanted to curse her then, but felt the weight of Trenor's hand and refrained. It wasn't easy. His eyes had gone moist now as he clung to the last thread of self-control, feeling as if he might shake to pieces like a disassembled mannequin at his friend's feet.

He still held the small photo of Tra Mi, his wrist braced across the counter, and something caused Trenor to snap his attention to it. An insect had just alighted on the image of Tra Mi's face. A wasp? No...it had no wings...it had dropped from above, and Trenor threw back his head.

A half dozen more of the same sort of creature crawled aimlessly on the ceiling, directly overhead.

"It's getting toward evening," Trenor said, still staring at the ceiling, "and we're going to need a hotel to stay in anyway. Do you want to do this one, kid?"

Thanh turned toward him as if Trenor had just suggested they should go skinny-dipping in the South China Sea. "I can't sleep in this hotel, Rick. Not where my sister died."

"Yeah...I understand. I couldn't stay in this place with all these bugs, anyway."

Putting away the photograph of Tra Mi, Thanh followed Trenor's gaze to the ceiling and said, "Bugs?"

"Never mind." Trenor met his companion's eyes and said, "I need to see the room."

"The room she died in?"

"Yes. That room."

Thanh addressed the owner again, and she grew exasperated once more. "This isn't a museum!" she snapped. "You aren't policemen! If you want to go in that room then you'll have to rent it."

"Bitch," Thanh spat in English. He translated for Trenor, who then told Thanh to pay the fee from the Vietnamese currency they'd exchanged from Trenor's US dollars, and which Trenor had instructed him to carry on his behalf.

This time it was Trenor who extended his hand across the counter, smiling amicably at the owner as he said in English, "Give me the fucking key, you butt-ugly troll."

2: THE SIGN

THE TAXI DRIVER HAD LISTENED to the conversation at the check-in counter, and so he prudently remained downstairs in the lobby to smoke, seated in an ornately carved and heavily lacquered wooden chair, while Trenor and Thanh climbed the granite stairs to the fourth floor.

Trenor slipped the key into the door, and the click of its turning felt like a gun hammer being cocked. He pushed the door open, reached inside and found the wall switch for the lights.

And then he flinched back so violently that he stepped on one of Thanh's bare, two-toed feet, causing the young man to ask, "What is it, Rick?"

Thanh's fear, not seeing clearly around Trenor's body, was that the room hadn't been cleaned since Hang Ni had been found here, used and discarded...chewed up and spat out and left with a mocking cigarette in her mouth, the most contemptuous detail of all. He dreaded Trenor moving out of his way to reveal a bed still painted in blood. As if that blood might still be wet, an eye-stabbing brightness of red.

But it wasn't blood that had made Trenor recoil. Recoil even though he had expected something of this kind. But not to *this* extreme.

The room had in fact been cleaned, the sheets and even the mattress replaced, though the owner had not rented it to a customer since the discovery. The hotel was never so full that she had had to do so...and she might never do so.

What Trenor saw was the spiders, of course, but more than he had seen in the forty years since he had first witnessed the manifestation in the tunnel. They infested the room as if he had stumbled upon their very nest. Dotted the walls in shifting constellations. Scampered across the bed, the pillows. Skittered across the floor, making him instinctively afraid they would crawl over his feet, climb up his body...even though not one of them had ever attempted to touch him in four decades. He had experimentally tried to touch *them* in the past, however. He had thought he experienced a whispery itch in his nerve endings when he made these attempts, but had that only been his imagination, prompted by his revulsion?

The spiders in the hotel room were as silent as always, even in these numbers. Most of all, they covered the ceiling, made it almost a solid blackness of small bodies scrambling over each other. Living shadow, sentient darkness. Massed individual creatures like a dense collection of cancerous cells seen under a microscope. Were they, then, collectively the cells of a vast single entity that could never be viewed in its entirety?

"Rick? What's wrong?" Thanh had squeezed around Trenor a little to peer into the room, and had seen that it was innocuously clean, but when he looked to Trenor he found his friend's expression dazed...even stunned.

The ceiling was a door made of spiders, and she must have come through that door. But how was it that Trenor hadn't noticed her at first? Yet there she was now, standing in one corner of the small room on the other side of the bed. She faced into the corner, back turned to him...this sickly-thin naked girl with a stream of inky hair running down her back...this girl with fragile limbs, a small slit dividing her bottom, and pallid yellowish skin.

"*Rick?*" Thanh usually felt too self-conscious to touch people, but he gripped Trenor's arm in one claw hand.

The nude girl seemed to hear Thanh. Trenor saw her head turn just a fraction. Then a moment later her entire body began to shuffle around slowly, jerkily, to face him.

Unlike his dream, the girl's eyes didn't glow red with living fire, and her jaw was not stretched to its limits, her mouth packed solid with a clod of earth. Maybe for that reason, this time he recognized her clearly from the photos he had seen as Tra Mi. But although her mouth was not stuffed with dirt, from her slightly parted pale lips a spider emerged, and then another, and more, a column of them marching down her chin, scattering across her chest and circling her small breasts with their prominent brown nipples. There was such an infestation of spiders in her long hair that it seemed fully composed of their bodies...shifting restlessly as if in a breeze only she was experiencing.

Her eyes were obsidian black, and fixed on Trenor's one eye. Were the spiders flowing from her mouth an attempt to speak...their bodies all she had in place of words? They swirled around her navel in a slow vortex. Some had strayed down to her thick pubic hair and blended into its darkness...had maybe even ventured back inside the shelter of her body.

"Rick!" Thanh shook him. "What did you see?"

He was still seeing it.

Tra Mi kept her unblinking gaze fixed on his, but she lifted her left arm with unnatural jerky slowness and pointed to the wall behind her, near the corner where she had been facing. Trenor had to wrench himself free of her eyes in order to follow her finger.

A group of the insect-things was congregated in that area of the wall, and their formation grew more concentrated as he watched. He realized quickly what he was seeing. They were assembling themselves into three letters...to form a word.

Trenor read the word, but didn't understand it, and when he switched his focus back to the girl she was no longer there. And then he noticed that he couldn't see the spiders as distinctly as he had at first; now they were grayish-translucent, mere phantoms, like spots burnt on one's eyes from staring too long into the sun, or floaters one can see under certain conditions of light swimming on the surface of one's own eyes. Another few seconds and even these last ghostly traces of the spiders faded, and by then Thanh was forcibly dragging Trenor back from the threshold of the room.

* * *

Out in the hallway, and with the spider-things and Tra Mi having vanished, Trenor seemed to come to like a man awakening from a deep sleep—looking a little groggy and disoriented, but back in the waking world. He saw the concern in Thanh's face, and motioned for his friend to follow him further down the hallway. Here they stepped out onto the fourth floor's open balcony, and Trenor leaned against its shiny metal railing for support. Behind him, a red Vietnam flag hung limply over the street in the motionless air, and the sun had slipped below the high roofs of the neighborhood of oblong hotels, looking like a profusion of giant coffins standing on their ends.

"Rick, what happened to you?" Thanh asked.

"Thanh," Trenor sighed, "your sister is dead."

The younger man was only further confused by this statement. "I know she's dead, Rick."

"I don't mean Hang Ni. I mean Tra Mi."

"Tra Mi? How do you know?"

So Trenor sucked in a long breath, and told him about the spiders.

He had never told anyone about them before. He had considered it. Telling his brother. Telling some psychiatrist, therapist, some fellow drunken vet at the VFW. But in forty years, not another soul—until this boy, on this balcony, in this country where the door of spiders had first opened.

Trenor was saying, "I can't claim these things are any kind of real animal, from some other place. Some other dimension, or some spirit plane. I think I'm *interpreting* what I see as spiders or ant-things, because it's just how I process what I'm seeing. It's like...when you and I are riding in a taxi, I see all these signs for stores and cafés and such from a distance, and I swear I'm seeing words in English. I even start to think I'm putting them together into a meaningful phrase. But when we get a little closer I see they aren't English words, but

Vietnamese. I was only interpreting what I was seeing based on my own frame of reference. Does that make any sense?"

"I…I'm sorry, but I'm not sure I understand that."

Trenor smiled and wagged his head. "I'm not sure I understand it myself. For all I know it could just be hallucination…illusion. How many times have I wondered if my brain just got a little too shook up from the force of that bullet smacking my skull? I must sound crazy to you…"

"No, I don't think that."

"…but I can tell you, Thanh. No matter how many times I wonder if my brain is fucked up, or my one good eye isn't so good after all, or if I'm just imagining this stuff…deep inside, it feels real to me. Even if you can't see it. Even if I've never found anything on the web or in a book about anyone else ever seeing quite what I see. Despite all that, deep inside I *know* it's real."

"I would never call you crazy. I believe you about Tra Mi; I believe you saw her ghost. We very much believe in ghosts in Vietnam, Rick…I told you that."

"I'm sorry. Sorry about Tra Mi."

Thanh lowered his eyes. "Yes. I'm sorry, too. Tra Mi was my sister. My sister."

Silent, thoughtful minutes drifted past like debris on a river. Trenor knew Thanh was weighing his resentment for Tra Mi—resentment that she had taken Hang Ni from her home only to die, resentment that he and Tra Mi had apparently never much gotten along—against his grief for having lost a sibling, nonetheless. Giving his friend privacy in which to grieve in his own way, Trenor turned away to lean his weight against the railing and survey the street below. On the corner, where there was a vacant lot, a group of people had pulled up little plastic chairs and started a bonfire. Fun, he thought, wishing he sat down there himself with a beer in hand. This would be a good time to lose oneself staring into a snapping fire. Almost subliminally, he was aware of a forlorn dog whimpering somewhere. Then, in the gloom of deepening evening, he realized that a crude spit had been erected over the bonfire, and a carcass positioned above the flames.

"Hey," he said to Thanh, "check it out…they're going to roast a pig right down there in the street."

Thanh shuffled closer and looked down from the balcony himself. "That isn't a pig, Rick…it's a dog."

"What?" Trenor looked harder, and despite the murkiness he thought he could indeed make out the shape of a dog in that dangling carcass. Now the whimpering he'd been hearing came to the fore. It couldn't possibly be coming from the animal on the spit…let it not be that. Another dog, caged somewhere nearby, waiting to become the second course? The mourning friend of this sacrificed creature? Or was it only a coincidence, unrelated? Please let it be that.

He had thought it was a pig, until he realized it was a dog…interpretation, based on his own frame of reference.

"There was a word on the wall," he said suddenly. "Back in the room, the spiders spelled out a word—Tra Mi was pointing to it. She wanted me to read it. I forgot about it when I told you all that about the spiders. I guess I forgot it because it didn't make sense to me. But of course it didn't make sense…it was in Vietnamese."

"What did it say?"

"I hope I remember it right…" Trenor began.

*   *   *

Thanh watched his father's friend as he worked at remembering the letters he claimed he had seen spelled out on the hotel room's wall. Thanh kept his expression neutral, though inwardly he felt a great sadness.

He had asked this man to come here from across the world to help them, and help them Trenor was obviously keen on doing, despite his initial reluctance. But Thanh had never suspected that Trenor might be profoundly wounded psychologically. Then again, knowing his own father's demons, should it surprise him? Shouldn't he have anticipated it?

Yes, they did believe in *ma*—ghosts—in Vietnam. He himself believed in ghosts, believed the ghost stories his mother had told him. He might even believe that Trenor had seen his sister's spirit. But creatures like otherworldly spiders or ants, crawling out of people's faces—an externalization or embodiment of the blackness in their souls? Spectral insects spelling out messages on walls?

He had told Trenor he didn't think he was crazy. He had lied. What else was he to say? He cared for this man. He was deeply moved by Trenor's loyalty to his father, to their whole family. Anything but an avowal of belief would be disrespectful. But it made him sad now, disillusioned, looking into this man's face and waiting for him to recall his delusion. Once again, Thanh felt terribly alone in his quest to find Hang Ni's killer.

Then Trenor said, "I'm pretty sure the letters were Q-U-Y."

"Hm. Well, depending on accents, which can change a word's meaning, that might mean…uh, something valuable, of high esteem."

Trenor smiled. "If the bugs made any accents, I didn't notice that part."

What Thanh hadn't suggested, but which came to mind under the circumstances, was that *con quy* or *ma quy* were names for a demon or devil. Inexplicably, he shuddered, as though someone had run the cold surface of a beer can along his bare back.

No…it wasn't because he was thinking of demons or devils that he shuddered, he suddenly realized. It was because he had thought of another possibility.

"Quy is also a name," he said. "For women or men."

"Do you know anyone named Quy?"

Thanh was staring out into the infinite darkness beyond the city's rooftops, which blended together under that blackness like frail, frightened things, corralled and cowering, whimpering as they waited their turn on the spit. With the smell of roasting flesh wafting to him, he said, "Tra Mi knew someone named Quy. Hang Ni told me. She said Tra Mi met a boy named Quy at Dai Nam theme park, when my father ordered Tra Mi to take Hang Ni there some time back. When we chatted about it, Hang Ni said Tra Mi liked this boy named Quy a lot."

"Well, that's the word Tra Mi was pointing to."

Slowly Thanh turned fresh eyes on the man from America. A great sense of relief flooded into him, as his confidence in Trenor was restored. But the icy sensation along his spine remained.

3: FOLLOWING LEADS

THE AMERICAN HAD BEEN HESITANT to talk with the hotel manager himself, lest she remember his face and describe him later to any investigators still on the case—had at first thought to have Kate do it for him and report back—but then he'd decided that he would be the more authoritative figure for the job. He had considered masquerading as a policeman himself, but without a typical green uniform and cap, pretending to be some plainclothes detective like in the US, that was problematic. At last, he'd decided on telling the woman he worked for a newspaper, following up on the tragic story. Her frown was quickly alleviated by the new 100,000 *dong* note he slipped to her across the counter, after which her face became as warm and crinkly as that of Ho Chi Minh on the waxy green note.

He asked the manager if anyone else had come in with the foreign man when he rented the room, such as a young Vietnamese woman. No, she replied—no one at all had accompanied the guest when he rented the room. She saw no one else in his presence during his stay…only saw him when he first checked in, in fact.

Had a young Vietnamese woman rented a different room that night, then? In the company of a child, or a young man who might be a boyfriend, or even alone? No, was again the answer—besides the foreigner, at that time the only other guests in the hotel had been a large family on the second floor and a couple, probably about thirty, on the sixth. No one as young as the American suggested—in her late teens or early twenties. "Why?" she asked.

"Just following up on a possible tip," the American said vaguely. But he could see that Tra Mi had probably only delivered Hang Ni to the john—either accidentally or by design, at a time when the front desk was untended—instead of lingering around herself, expecting to pick the child up again when it was all said and done.

But she hadn't picked her sister up—the police had. And so the American was no closer to answering the question of whether Tra Mi was alive or not...and where she was now, in either state.

"When they questioned you, did the police mention any theories," he asked, "about where the killer might be now, or whether he had any accomplices? Anything that hasn't appeared in the news? Maybe in an offhand remark, or suggested in the line of their questioning, or in something you just overheard discussed amongst them?"

The woman looked confused by all this, and stammered, "I...I don't understand. No, they only asked questions. Why should they tell me what they think?"

He knew he was just grabbing at straws, but that was all he had to grab at right now. "You told the police this man said he had to leave early the next morning, but did he specifically say he was leaving the country, or just leaving the city? Did he say anything to suggest a precise destination?"

Her confusion wasn't lessening. "He didn't really say where he was going, but I thought...maybe the airport...I really don't know. We didn't chitchat; I don't speak English, and he only knew a little Vietnamese. I didn't even get his name. He rented his room for one night, said thank you, and that was it. If he left the building at any time before he checked out, or if anyone came up to see him during his stay, I never saw it."

"I understand."

Perhaps in an effort to be helpful in some way, lest the journalist ask for his money back, the manager related, "The little girl's brother was here yesterday, and he was asking about a young woman, like you. He had pictures of her. An American was with him...at least I think he was an American; I can't tell these things. They asked about my customer, too."

"They did, did they?"

"Yes. What a pair they were! Terrible, like demons out of Hell. The American had only one eye, and the boy had hands and feet like a crab." She demonstrated with her own hands, nipping at the air as if the boy had tried that on her.

"I see," the American said quietly, turning to look over his shoulder at the narrow side street outside, as if he might see the strange pair standing just behind him even now. But there was only the car he'd rented, parked at the curb, with Kate in the passenger's seat watching him through the closed window. He wondered if she fantasized about scooting over behind the wheel and driving off without him, hoping to hide somewhere safely far away from him. But he figured she probably didn't know how to drive a car, just a motorbike, like most people here.

"They even went up to look at the room the girl died in," the manager offered. "I don't know what they expected to find. The police went over it thoroughly, and then we cleaned it up beautifully. But an awful thing to have happen at our hotel; I hope it's forgotten quickly so it doesn't hurt our business." There was a hint of accusation in her voice at her last words, as she finally realized that a newspaper man asking questions of her was not likely to help people forget about the unfortunate event anytime soon.

The American faced her again, and asked, "Do you have any idea where the two of them went, after they were through here?" He really didn't expect an answer in the affirmative, the question more or less obligatory, so he was surprised when the woman nodded.

"Yes...while the man and the boy were upstairs, their taxi driver stayed down here to smoke. When they came down, the boy told the driver they'd be staying in another hotel—not mine." She gave an insulted grimace. "Then the boy asked the driver if tomorrow—today, I mean—he could take them to Dai Nam Van Hien."

"Dai Nam Van Hien," the American echoed. "Did they mention why that place?"

"How should I know? A lot of tourists go there, don't they?"

"Of course," he said. "Thank you." Smiling handsomely, he placed a second 100,000 *dong* note on the counter between them, as if to stamp a seal on their contract.

PART 6: AMUSEMENTS

1: HEAVEN

THE GREAT WALL HOTEL APPEARED to emulate China's Great Wall in form. On the other side of the crenulated and seemingly endless fortress barrier was the sprawling amusement park called, for short, Dai Nam. Thanh told Trenor the hotel that composed the wall offered over a hundred rooms, and yet the enormous parking lot facing it was all but empty. Trenor remarked on this fact, as a bellhop in a maroon uniform and matching cap carried his single suitcase, packed with clothes for both of them, up a flight of stairs to the lobby. "You sure this place is open?"

Thanh said, "It was like this the one time I came here with some friends. I guess it depends on the time of day and the day of the week. It must be busier on the weekend." Their taxi drove off behind them, and they reached the top of the stairs, where the bellhop waited with their suitcase. Thanh smiled at him and said in Vietnamese, "Hey, is your name Quy?"

"No...I'm Minh," the young man replied.

"Sorry. My sister has a friend who works here, named Quy. She said he works the door at the hotel, and also drives the guests around." Thanh gestured behind him at a green-painted shuttle parked at the curb. However novel, the attenuated form of the hotel made walking its length a chore.

"Ohh," the bellhop said, "yes, I know Quy. He did this job before me, but he's on the evening shift now... He looks after the karaoke rooms. I think he works someplace else during the day."

"Ahh, I see." Thanh turned and explained to Trenor. He added, "The karaoke rooms are above the food court. The park closes at five, but karaoke will still be open."

"Then we wait. Let's get a room." Trenor surveyed the handsome lobby, where life-sized gold soldiers stood about at attention, clutching spears. "Do you want to tell the desk you're my adopted son, or my boyfriend?"

"Oh, Rick, not that again."

*　　*　　*

"It was very important to my father that Hang Ni have a good time in Dai Nam," Thanh explained, as the bellhop drove them in the little shuttle from the hotel to the entrance of the theme park itself. They had left their suitcase in the room they'd rented. "Thirty-five dollars for one night in the hotel might not seem much to you, but it was a lot for my father. Of course, it isn't expensive to get into the park itself."

The bellhop left them at the entrance to the food court, a short walk from the entrance to the park, and turned the shuttle back toward the lobby. As they walked on, Trenor glanced into the building housing the food court, which was really just one counter, a cashier's desk, and a scattering of tables…though adjacent to this was a sizable restaurant, for which he had been given coupons for a free breakfast in the morning when he'd checked in.

"Food court, huh?" Trenor said. "Huh. You hungry yet?"

"Not really, Rick, but please tell me when you are. There are also places to buy food all through the park."

"No hurry…just checking with you."

Thanh nodded, glancing up at the man's face as they continued walking. With a little time having passed since the episode in the Vung Tau hotel room, Thanh was once again experiencing uneasy doubts about what Trenor had claimed to witness. That word he'd cited, QUY, could have multiple meanings…or none at all. But Thanh tried to remain optimistic, tried to believe they weren't both wasting their time.

They passed through a great archway into the park grounds. Immediately, Trenor was struck by the vision of a mystical-looking mountain range on the horizon. Thanh explained that the five dramatic mountains, a green foam of vegetation splashing up their bases, were man-made. Trenor gazed on them in wonder; to him they were a personification of Vietnam: beautiful and tacky in the extreme.

Close to the extreme end of beauty was a great golden temple the two of them proceeded toward, reached by traversing a broad, arched bridge supported by artificial tree trunks. "Wow," Trenor said, marveling at the ornate, green-roofed temple's size and grandeur as they crossed the bridge.

"Do you want to go inside?"

"Why not?"

"Are you Christian, Rick?"

"Are Christians not allowed?"

"Oh no, anyone can go inside; I was only curious."

"Let's just say 'curious' is my only real religion."

They were required to don black booties before being admitted inside. The security guard looked down at Thanh's feet for a baffled moment, but then handed him the largest sized booties, and Thanh was able to pull them over his two long, bird-like toes.

They crossed the threshold into a darkened but spacious interior, and Trenor experienced as much a sense of religious awe as he was capable of. He felt it was a good thing he was agnostic regarding all faiths, or he might be overwhelmed. He could easily believe a devout Buddhist might feel that they had stepped into a court of the afterworld itself. The high ceiling was a painted blue circle of heavenly sky through which soared white cranes. Religious and/or historical personages, all of them alien to Trenor, sat arrayed in tiers on the gold-paneled walls, gently spotlighted in the gloom; several of them with eerie greenish faces. The atmosphere was of incense, and from somewhere played soft but reverberant, unearthly chanting.

The two of them circled the periphery of the room toward the great central figure, which was of course Buddha himself. Thanh stopped to pray before one figure—Trenor didn't know why this particular person—pressing together the strange prongs of his hands, causing Trenor to remember Tra Mi's taunt that, "even a monk must be able to put his hands together to pray."

While Trenor respectfully waited for Thanh to finish—perhaps praying for the success of their quest—he realized that a gold-plated figure sitting to Buddha's right was none other than Ho Chi Minh. Trenor wagged his head and muttered, "Good God."

* * *

Beyond the golden temple, they wandered close to that eerily beautiful faux mountain range, and as they skirted its edge Trenor realized there were points of entry into it. He urged Thanh to follow him into one of these cave-like openings, and Thanh hesitated a moment before doing so. Trenor soon realized why; it was unlit inside, and at first he assumed the fake rocky tunnel was still in its construction phase, but they turned a corner and emerged into an open spot where the sun streamed in. Continuing on, however, they were soon in near darkness once more. Meanwhile, to their left, just on the other side of the imitation cavern wall, a mad cacophony raged. It was an impossible chorus of birds chirping and chattering, and at last Trenor stopped to ask Thanh, "What the hell is that?"

"They keep a lot of birds in Dai Nam…the kind they make that bird nest drink from. Remember you tried a little? They let the birds make their nests here, then they collect them. Each nest is worth a lot of money. I don't know the name of the bird in English…but at night here the sky is full of them. It sounds like a lot of them are close by."

"I'll say." To Trenor, it was as though he were leading the boy into the labyrinths of Hell—or was the boy leading him there?—and these were the overlapping and incoherent cries of the uncountable damned.

They continued on toward the far side of the mountain range in this way, weaving in and out of darkness, but when they turned one corner Trenor froze

143

in his tracks and so did his heart. At first he thought it was a huge black snake coiled directly in front of him, until he realized it was only a garden hose. His hand had wanted to reach for a gun that wasn't there.

They had booby trapped the tunnels with snakes.

*   *   *

Thanh explained that there was an impressive zoo on the grounds, and Hang Ni had told him she'd most enjoyed the sun bears that rose on their hind legs like people, gesturing for their keepers to throw them bananas and moaning forlornly, but closer to the pair right now was the amusement park area of Dai Nam, with its rollercoaster and numerous other attractions. They stopped for drinks, and as they continued along Trenor pointed his cup of iced coffee and said, "Jesus Christ, what's that?"

A row of crouching titanic dragons, golden except for their feral red eyes and the huge red orbs clutched in their gold-fanged maws. Standing as sentries in front were a golden minotaur and another gold demon with an apparent horse head, both with tridents. Over a loudspeaker a grim narrator was going on incomprehensibly, though his commentary was interspersed with distressed cries, made disturbing by the wavering, muffled sound quality.

"It's like a haunted house ride," Thanh told him. "It's supposed to show the different punishments for sinners in Hell. This is the ride where Hang Ni got so upset."

"Why...it scared her?"

"Yes, because Tra Mi made her go in alone. Tra Mi was supposedly busy on her cell phone, talking to that boy Quy after she'd asked him for his number, but I think she was actually afraid to go inside herself." Thanh paused, then reluctantly added, "But I hate to think there was an even more terrible reason she didn't go in with Hang Ni."

"What's that?"

"I think maybe Tra Mi made Hang Ni go in alone because she *wanted* Hang Ni to get upset. Maybe she found that funny." Thanh turned solemnly from Trenor to stare at the imposing monsters. "It was a quiet weekday like this. No one else went in with Hang Ni. She and I went into a very similar ride at Suoi Tien once—that's a smaller amusement park in Ho Chi Minh City—so she should have known what to expect. She really shouldn't have gone inside...but maybe because she and I went into that other place together and had fun, laughing and grabbing each other, she thought it would be fun again. But she went in alone. Alone."

"That wasn't very cool of Tra Mi."

"Maybe it was her revenge for my father pushing her to take Hang Ni. Hang Ni said she was crying hysterically when she came out, and Tra Mi was laughing at her. Laughing and laughing."

Trenor wagged his head and looked back toward the towering dragons himself. They reminded him of the mountain range: merely an edifice one could pass inside, hollow and full of trickery, and yet somehow hardwired to something primal...and vulnerable. Mostly, a fear of darkness, and the unexpected.

As he regarded the fanged mouths, cradling those red spheres like new, unformed molten worlds—or doomed worlds turned to seas of blood—he experienced an odd sensation...like a whispery itch in his nerve endings. It was familiar. It was the way he had felt when he'd made attempts to touch the spiders.

Without making a conscious decision to do so, he said, "I need to go inside."

Thanh looked up at him. "Why?"

Trenor tore his gaze from the mouth of the central, largest dragon. The entrance to the attraction was directly below its bottom jaw.

"You coming with me, or do I have to go in alone?"

2: HELL

IT WAS A WEEKDAY, AND because they had left Vung Tau so early they had entered the park just as it opened for the day: 9 AM. Thus, it had seemed to them that they had the entire place to themselves. Aside from the workers about, at concession stands and tending to the various attractions, the whole immense park appeared desolate, abandoned, occupied only by stubborn ghosts. So it was that Trenor and Thanh mounted the steps of the haunted house attraction to enter it alone, like a ragtag Dante and Virgil.

At the top of the stairs they were met with a courtroom scene. Demonic figures in conical hats stood with their hands upon the heads of kneeling sinners, with long black hair and dressed in white robes, as they awaited their judgment. Thanh led Trenor past the scene to a set of stairs leading downward, into the underworld unjudged, countless skulls set into the walls above them. Through the darkness—which at the bottom of the steps became almost absolute—they followed glowing discs set into the uneven floor of bogus rock.

Somehow Thanh had moved just behind Trenor, with one hand lightly on his back. Trenor might have smiled, were it not for the anxiousness that had come over him as quickly as the blackness had swallowed them like the closing maw of a dragon. Trenor felt like a child again, in "dark rides" like the Kooky Kastle at Paragon Park, in Hull, Massachusetts. It had been his favorite attraction at the amusement park, and yet on one or two occasions even after much anticipation he had frustrated himself by not being able to venture inside, missing out on the opportunity until next summer. Kooky Kastle was in the past now, long gone and no doubt torn down…and yet for all that, he might have just been transported back in time, back into its bowels. At midnight, with the doors locked behind him.

Don't be crazy, he chided himself. This was only so much papier-mâché and plaster, painted with fluorescent colors, but even as he thought this he and Thanh jumped—as though through their contact they shared an electric shock—

when a loud pop burst near their feet (a firecracker?). Air blasted them as they shuffled along like blind men, afraid to trip, and a skeletal ghoul flung itself at them only to crash into a wire barrier across a lighted scene of torture. They didn't linger to study its finer details; one scene after another was more or less the same. Demons—somehow all the more disturbing for being so poorly rendered—punishing sinners, apparently in a manner that complemented their particular crimes. It was all a blur to Trenor, one briefly glimpsed horror blending into the next, but a few details registered: one white-garbed sinner suspended upside down, legs wide, while demons used a huge saw to cut him in half. Another damned soul having his face pressed down toward a bubbling cauldron.

All this might have been less disconcerting had they been seated in a moving car, as in the Kooky Kastle—at least partly shielded—instead of blundering through the dark...and if things weren't *touching* them. Logically, Trenor thought that brushes or such were being thrust at their feet, but it felt like actual human hands groping for their ankles. The first time he had thought it was only Thanh stumbling into him, until he realized that wasn't it. He was angered for being unnerved, felt a kind of outrage. In dark rides in the USA, they surely wouldn't be allowed to actually touch a person's *body*.

Another "animatronic" figure swooped down over them, trailing its ragged shroud. Trenor tucked his head into his shoulders, biting back a curse. He found he was flicking his gaze from side-to-side, above and behind. Oddly, he found he wanted to drop to hands and knees so as to more safely feel his way along. He wanted his flashlight. Where was his flashlight?

Gradually Trenor had become aware that the spiders were here.

They *abounded* here, all around him, on the walls and ceiling and floor, but camouflaged by the darkness—an unseen but overwhelming presence like all those shrieking cave swifts beyond the wall of the mountain tunnel. This was a bad place. Not because of plaster skulls and sheeted mannequins in and of themselves, but because of the place's intentions, which were not merely to entertain...but to intimidate. To bully. To threaten people with damnation. To instill fear in their minds, as they fretted for their souls. All Hells were designed that way, whether on paper or papier-mâché.

Disoriented, his senses pummeled, wanting *out* of these tunnels (why was Quan behind him pushing him along instead of dragging him back toward the entrance?), Trenor turned a corner and saw a damned soul that was not caged behind wire in a lighted alcove. This figure stood only paces away from him. Like many of the others, long black hair curtained its face, but instead of being dressed all in white it was entirely nude, its too-thin body glowing softly as if with some deep-sea fish's bioluminescence.

It raised its head, looked into his face, opened its mouth to speak...but a great ball of spiders was disgorged like vomit, cascading down its front, across its delicate breasts in a crawling wave.

But Thanh pushed him past the figure…as if he had seen it, too, though Trenor knew he hadn't, unless deep in his unconscious he had felt his sister's presence.

They stumbled into a tunnel that revolved around them, as though they plummeted down a swirling vortex, while they crossed a rickety bridge. Then suddenly they were staggering into the sunlight…coughed up by one of the lesser dragons, as if evicted for having trespassed in the netherworld.

Just ahead of them walked one of the park's young workers in a maroon uniform shirt. Trenor realized he must have been operating some of the assaults on their senses, now vacating the ride again for want of customers. He was the most mundane and bored demon Trenor had ever seen.

3: HUNTERS

THE AMERICAN DISLIKED TURNING OVER his passport in a hotel like this, or the Sofitel, revealing his identity in a place where he might need to kill someone, but there were some hotels where it wouldn't do to try to bribe the desk clerk. At least the clerk didn't ask for Kate's ID, as she stood quietly behind the American with her hand on their suitcase. It was an unspoken understanding that she was either his wife or a hooker. She wore her chin-length reddish wig and oversized sunglasses.

As he paid for their room—wearing a baseball cap, polo shirt, and shorts, like any good tourist—he said in a good-humored tone, "Your parking lot looks empty... Where are all the tourists? I thought this place would be crawling with them. I'm starting to get lonely for other Americans!"

"You're from the USA, sir?" the clerk asked politely.

"Yes—California." He did in fact have an apartment in California, in Orange County's Little Saigon, but it wasn't giving away much to say so; he liked to joke that California was the Nirvana all Vietnamese people dreamed of. His address was in his passport, in any case.

"The park is much busier on the weekend, sir," the clerk reassured him a little stiffly, as if restraining his defensiveness. "And, in fact, there is another American staying at the hotel right now."

"Oh, really?" He sounded delighted, as if he might make a new friend. "What room?"

"Just a few doors down from you," the man replied readily. He didn't cross the line of professionalism by revealing the exact room number, but it made sense that with so few guests in the hotel they should not be spread far along the wall's great length.

"Wonderful," the American said, handing over 700,000 *dong*. "*Viet Kieu*, like me?"

"No," the clerk replied, accepting the bills. "White."

"Oh...I see. What's his name, in case I should run into him?"

"Ah..." The clerk hesitated a moment, but then looked down at the guest registry and said, awkwardly, "Richard Tren...Tren-or." Uncertain of his pronunciation, he spelled it out. "T-R-E-N-O-R."

"Mm-hm." The American nodded a little, as if he wasn't really all that interested, after all—lest the clerk spot this Richard Trenor and try to introduce them to each other. If they were to meet, it would be at a time of the American's choosing.

*　　*　　*

There was a variety of great cats in Dai Nam's zoo: lions and a number of types of tiger, including white tigers. The American and Kate stood at a clear barrier looking in at a pair of Indochinese tigers, one of them cooling itself in a pool. Kate had asked him if they could go into the park, and it was logical to do so. Even if Thanh and this mysterious friend of his, Trenor, were here on the trail of Tra Mi, it made sense that no one came to Dai Nam not to go into the park. But it was a huge place, and the unlikely duo could be anywhere within it. Still, he'd been lingering at the great cats. Who would pass up the chance to see them?

The park had finally become busy, with hordes of uniformed school children having been shipped in. They pushed in around him and Kate to get a better look at the tigers, to thump the barrier and making growling sounds. He entertained himself with the image of scooping one of them up and tossing him over the barrier.

Kate sighed, maybe signaling him that she'd had enough of the cats now, or at least this pair of Indochinese tigers that he seemed particularly fascinated with. He ignored her, except to encircle her waist with his arm and draw her closer; not so much romantically, but to remind her who was in control...that this was a mission, not a honeymoon.

In a low voice, she asked him, "Why do you want to find this man so much?"

"The man with one eye? It's not him I want, but he may lead us to your coworker, Tra Mi."

"I mean the man who killed Tra Mi's sister. Do you want to kill him because he did that? Because he's evil?"

The American faced her, amused and surprised that she would ask him this. Was it her only way of interpreting his intentions, seeing him as some kind of avenger? How simple she was. The only person he would ever care to avenge was himself.

"Evil? He's not evil—he just has different needs, different limitations. He doesn't deny the hungers the rest of the sheep have had bred out of them. I can understand that. But he crossed me, and that can't be forgiven." Through his own dark glasses, he tried to penetrate hers to perceive her mood, gauge her thoughts. He found her moroseness strangely sexy, but he didn't want her morose toward *him*. "We don't need morals, but we need principles, or there would be chaos. I might not have killed Chen if he hadn't pointed a gun at me. No one would know my shame if I didn't punish him for that, but he would know it…and *I* would know it."

He gestured toward the bathing tiger on the other side of the wall, and asked, "Did you know that a while back, one of the park's Indochinese tigers leapt over an electrified fence, from its pen into the white tiger pen, and attacked two workers? One of the men died from his wounds."

Kate stared at him rather than into the tiger pen, her lips parted, and after a few seconds said, "I didn't know that."

"But a tiger is not evil, my dear. A tiger is only following its nature."

Slowly, the American realized it wasn't him she was staring at; she was looking over his shoulder. He turned to glance behind him, and saw two familiar figures at the barrier of the white tiger enclosure, only a short distance away. A white man with a patch covering one eye, and a young man with deformed hands and feet whom the American thought should be in a pen here himself, on display for an additional charge. He turned back to Kate and said, "When were you going to tell me you saw them?"

"You're the hunter," she said in a flat voice, "not me."

PART 7: RUN DEVIL RUN

0: BEDFORD

HE HADN'T PLANNED TO KILL the girl, and now he wasn't sure how he was going to deal with the situation, so he sat at the foot of the bed upon which her body lay and watched *First Men in the Moon* on the hotel room's TV.

The movie took his mind off any troubling concerns. He hadn't seen it since his youth, and it remained visually fascinating, though it changed tone oddly from whimsical to grim once the moon was reached. The protagonist's fiancée only wanted him to marry her, tried to discourage her man from something so trivial as journeying to the moon. *Of course*, he thought, thinking of his own perpetually disapproving wife, who had complained at length about his journey to the alien world of Vietnam, even though he had convinced her the trip was business related. In fact, the tall Earth men among the smaller, insect-like moon race reminded him of himself among the Vietnamese. It was funny, though; years ago he had simply seen the hero as a rugged good guy fighting monsters (against the protests of his mad scientist partner), but now he was struck by how ignorant the hero was (the inventor actually being a voice of reason), killing the moon people the moment he encountered them—these "Selenites" only wanting to study the invaders and then later, rightfully, to prevent more of them from coming to the moon once they discovered the Earthlings' potential for violence.

He had loved to read as a boy, still did, and as a result of enjoying the film had borrowed the novel by H. G. Wells from the town library. Even at such a young age, one sequence of the novel—not portrayed in the film—had resonated strangely with him. Traveling home from the moon, the protagonist, named Bedford, entered an odd state of mind in which he questioned his very identity. The lines that had particularly struck him were: *"'It is not you that is reading, it is Bedford, but you are not Bedford, you know. That's just where the mistake comes in.'*

'Confound it!' I cried; 'and if I am not Bedford, what am I?'

But in that direction no light was forthcoming, though the strangest fancies came drifting into my brain, queer remote suspicions, like shadows seen from away. Do you know, I had a sort of idea that really I was something quite outside not only the world, but all worlds, and out of space and time, and that this poor Bedford was just a peephole through which I looked at life?"

He had felt this way often in his life, even before he had read that novel as a boy. It had excited and rather reassured him to find such ideas articulated by another. He had felt like less of an aberration, then…less alone.

The movie had been released in 1964. He reflected that the USA had already been involved in Vietnam for some time, back then.

Taking his eyes from the TV screen, he glanced around behind him a little and saw the young woman's feet were almost touching his back. They were small and brown, with tough soles. When she had entered the hotel room, she had immediately removed her shoes, just as one did in Vietnamese homes. Even now, her small high-heeled shoes stood beside his own big black shoes against the wall near the locked door. What a quaint domestic composition.

Her name had been An, and An was the most beautiful woman he had ever had successful intercourse with. She reminded him of the movie actress Q'orianka Kilcher, but with a shorter and flatter nose. He had watched that actress in a film called *The New World*, another movie about foreign intruders amongst an indigenous people—though much more dull than *First Men in the Moon*—because he had heard the actress was fourteen at the time she played Pocahontas. Ah, teenage girls, he thought—they were wasted on teenage boys.

An had told him she was eighteen. The man who'd introduced them had said she was twenty. She could pass for eighteen, though, and if the man had spoken correctly then he supposed she had lied to further excite him with her youth. Still, as tiny and fresh-faced as she was, he would have preferred someone even younger…but without Chen's help he hadn't known how to pursue that. He had been afraid to entrust his new contact with his true desires lest he be linked to that other girl—whom he had not planned to kill, either.

Though perhaps some other, deeper "Bedford" had in fact planned such a thing all along—maybe even before he'd left the States—but hadn't wanted him to be frightened off, or interfere.

After the little girl, he couldn't contact Chen again. He only hoped Chen protected his identity, not out of loyalty but to preserve his own hide by association. Before the hunger that had overwhelmed him in that Vung Tau hotel and changed everything, he had been in contact with Chen even prior to coming to Vietnam. Behind the legitimate business of his matrimony service, Chen was part of a network that arranged "sex tours" for Americans, Europeans, and Australians throughout Southeast Asia…Thailand, Cambodia, the Philippines, and Chen's own territory was Vietnam. These tours could be above the board, involving only adult women and ladyboys, or as under the board as one's client had the yearning, and stomach, for.

But murder was not on that menu, and now he was on his own. It was a rather frightening but oddly exhilarating sensation. Fortunately, though he had lied to his wife about the nature of this trip (it helped that he never got into too many details about his actual work), he had been called upon by his company to travel abroad a number of times before, including to Vietnam. Enough Vietnamese knew English sufficiently to help him get what he required, whether that be a hotel room or a cab ride or the fulfillment of his body's needs.

His wife had complained the most that he would be away for Christmas and New Year's Eve. He hadn't told her that was one of the reasons why he had decided to take this journey. All those mask-like smiles for her family, for his family, all that disingenuous "on earth peace, good will to men." Aside from communicating with the Vietnamese to satisfy his needs, he was glad to be in a country where most of the populace didn't speak his language. He liked being alone among them...an outsider. He felt like Scrooge visiting his past life, standing outside it as an observer. Except, of course, when his desire upon observing all these Vietnamese beauties built to too great an intensity and interaction was called for, at that point to the Nth degree.

He'd read that the American journalist William Prochnau, who had reported during the war, had called Vietnamese women "tiny porcelain images of ephemeral feminine grace." Ha, yes...who gambled, swore like truckers, sold their bodies. Well, at least An had been ephemeral.

He picked up his pack of cigarettes, one of his other needs. It was a brand called Craven A. As he lit one, not for the first time he almost sniggered at the name. What kind of name was Craven for any product? Before setting the pack on the mattress again, he twisted around to look more squarely at An. He extended the pack and muttered, "You want one?"

He almost sniggered again. But in fact, though he had never seen a Vietnamese woman smoking before—the men were another story, avid smokers—An had definitely been a smoker. He had found that out to his dismay. It had been the first element of his dissatisfaction.

He had no tolerance for women who did not tend to their hygiene, who did not strive to smell inoffensive. His wife was okay in this regard, or he wouldn't have been able to marry her and remain with her all these years, but then again, he hadn't found her aesthetically pleasing in a long time. He understood he was immersed in another culture here, amongst people who were not affluent, so he was forgiving in casual circumstances. For instance, yesterday he had gone to a barber for a haircut. A man had cut his hair and trimmed his eyebrows, but then a cute young woman with shortish hair had taken over. First she had cleaned his ears, a rather alarming sensation, hovering over him with a bright lamp and metal probe. Each time she dug out a nugget of wax she had smeared it onto his forearm, as if he might want to keep them for souvenirs. She had finished up with long cotton swabs, inspiring a sensation that was like the worst tickling itch and the most relieving scratch to that itch, at the same time. It made him feel like a dog getting a belly rub, kicking one leg at the air.

Then she had shaved him with a straight razor. She had not only shaved his faint beard stubble, however, but around his nose and his forehead. Scraping away dead skin cells, he supposed. He didn't question it; he was enjoying her ministrations—except for one thing. When she leaned close enough to breathe on him, he smelled her tooth decay. Such a young woman, too.

But An had been even younger, and his brief whiffs of her breath had been even more strongly tainted with tooth decay. When she smiled, it was with her lips pressed together. If she knew her breath wasn't good, why didn't she take better care of her teeth? He was very disappointed, however pretty her little sealed smiles; he had wanted to kiss her deeply. Kissing helped arouse him, and he was nervous about not becoming fully aroused. When he was unsettled or distracted, even when in bed with his wife (not that they had had sex for over a year, now), he would either have trouble becoming erect, or else he would wither inside before he could find release. He was keenly aware that he'd never been popular with the opposite sex, but of those sexual encounters he had experienced, probably half of them had ended in embarrassment, unfulfillment, and resentment due to this sensitivity on his part.

An had gone down on him, though, and that had helped get him going. However, in bending over him, kneeling naked on the bed, more offensive odors had come to him in addition to the dry cigarette stink that had permeated her clothing and still tainted her hair. He became aware of the unwashed smell of her ass, and fishy reek from between her legs. It was all too much, almost like an insult to him…that she wouldn't have thought him important enough to shower before meeting him here at his hotel.

Still, she'd aroused him enough that he pushed her off him and onto her back, lay upon her and successfully entered her. Thankfully she'd turned her face to one side, and he'd held his breath besides, but he did that anyway even with his wife, as holding his breath helped him build toward climax. And to his surprise, he'd been able to climax fairly quickly despite the repulsive distractions. She was, after all, still adorably cute, at least visually. Golden skin smooth as that of a plastic doll…in that sense, very nearly flawless except for those two irritating tattoos of hers; self-imposed defects.

Up close, while still moving on top of her—his bulky body almost entirely covering hers—he'd stared at the tiny blue dot of a tattoo on her forehead, between her full eyebrows, like a bindi. Before she'd undressed, he'd tried asking her what it meant, pointing to it, but the girl had only smiled and shrugged. She didn't speak English. While she'd gone down on him, he'd also seen that she had a tattoo on the nape of her neck: a Roman Catholic cross. So she was a Christian. Maybe the dot on her forehead, though, was some secret code identifying her as a prostitute…or a pimp or possessive boyfriend had forced her to wear it to identify her as his property.

Her expressions had helped bring him to release, too; her grimaces of pleasure, her moaning. (Though thank God she hadn't opened her eyes to look up at him…having her watch him would probably have made it impossible to reach climax.) He believed she had truly experienced pleasure, because he had felt eager pulses inside her, drawing him in, when he'd first begun entering, as if her body at least wanted him. How surprising that had been.

She had apparently been too polite, or shy, or afraid, to ask why he didn't wear a condom...was no doubt relieved when he pulled out of her just in time. He was willing to risk disease, but not planting his seed in her. He had no children at home; the last thing he wanted was one gestating in this creature.

After he had rolled off her they had lain together, An cuddling up against his side. With a finger she traced around his pink nipple, and gave him a thumbs up. Then she pointed to the flat brown nipple that tipped one of her dainty breasts and gave a thumbs down.

"Oh no...I like yours more," he'd told her.

She had then pointed to the skin of his chest, once more made a thumbs up, and rubbed her own thigh and made another thumbs down. He understood: Vietnamese women desired white skin, even used dangerous products to bleach their faces, because traditionally white skin meant one wasn't a common laborer toiling in the sun.

"No, no," he assured her, "your skin is beautiful. *Dep.*" She shook her head, smiling with her lips closed, and he insisted, "*Dep! Dep qua!*" He knew a bit of Vietnamese, and knowing how to compliment a woman could be very useful.

"Baby?" she asked. So she knew a little English, after all. She was pointing to his hairy belly, still smiling.

"Har har," he said. "That's funny! Am I really that hideously pot-bellied?" He looked down at himself. "I suppose, compared to your men. It's all those hamburgers and pizzas we eat, what can I say? All our cheese and butter and french fries." He grinned at her. It was okay to look in her eyes now that they weren't in the act.

She pointed to herself and said, "Honey?"

"Honey? You have honey-colored skin, I know that, foul as it is." He felt the fishy smell was more prevalent now, almost enough to make him gag, and part of him was growing enraged by that; at the same time, he was charmed by her sweet manner, however insincere.

She tapped her sternum again. "Your honey?"

"Huh? You want to be my honey? Ahh...I see. You want to be my girlfriend, huh? Divorce my wife and marry you and take you back to the USA with me? Where a beautiful girl like you, if she was born there, wouldn't even say hello to me? And then you can dump me as soon as you get your green card...right?"

An nodded brightly, and said, "Your honey, okay?"

"Sure, honey. Sure, my honey."

She held out a pinky, and he linked his with hers. "Okay?" she repeated.

"The rite of marriage is all but complete. But... First, I need you to take a shower now before my baby-faced bride asphyxiates me, okay? Shower?" He pointed toward the bathroom.

She pointed at him and then at herself. "Shower?"

"Both of us shower, together? Not a bad idea…I need to get your slime off me."

"Shower, okay?"

"Let's do that," he said, having come to his decision; he couldn't reverse this train now. He needed her flesh to be more fragrant if he was going to experience it with his teeth.

And so he had scrubbed her thoroughly himself, soaped her up and rinsed her off and soaped her up again, and shampooed her hair besides. Like a wife…like a young daughter.

She hadn't tasted too bad, after that. But she wasn't drugged like the younger girl had been, so he'd first instructed An to lie on her belly on the bed, and he'd begun to massage her, working his hands from her shoulders to her neck. Her moans of approval then turned to desperate struggles, but he leaned his elbows on her back and pinned her down with his much greater weight until she finally stopped struggling, her face mashed deeply into the pillow.

At least, he considered, he had controlled himself enough not to tear into the meat of her throat, or anywhere else, thus avoiding the mess he had left at that other hotel. But then, that girl had been more to his taste. So perfect.

He looked around at An's body again. It had only been a bit more than an hour. Rigor mortis had not yet set in, and livor mortis was not yet discernible. He put a hand on a plump, hard calf, which bore multiple rings of teeth marks, and found her warm to the touch.

He stood up from the bed, gazed down at her, came to another decision…but first he needed to empty his bladder. In the bathroom, he found her lacy purple panties dangling from a towel rack. He leaned in to smell them, knowing he would find that they stank, but he wanted to feel a renewal of his disgust, of his revulsion and frustrated anger, these things driving his arousal.

Was there a more hateful, more desirable thing, than a woman? They were, to his mind, like this country—full of great beauty and crude ugliness. Well, just like all the rest of the world.

0: THE MONSTER FROM THE ID

SOME TIME AFTER *FIRST MEN in the Moon* ended, and he had sat for a long while just flipping through channels, night came. Already small, the room felt like it was steadily, insidiously shrinking—felt too crowded because he wasn't quite alone—and he knew if it had smelled bad with An alive it would soon begin to smell even worse with her dead, even though by now he had covered her entirely with the one thin blanket. Was she growing hard under it, like the smooth plastic doll he had compared her to in his mind?

In Vung Tau, he had paid up front for the room where the child would be brought to him by her older sister, and he had told the manager he'd be leaving in the small hours. Thankfully, no one had been in the lobby when he'd left with the one bag he'd brought, though he'd heard snoring from a curtained room behind the counter. He'd already called a cab and it was waiting outside his hotel for him, to take him to his *real* hotel in Ho Chi Minh City.

After the cab had left him there, he had gathered the rest of his luggage and checked out, called another cab, and checked into his current hotel—a good distance away in this sprawling city from the other—where he had been staying ever since.

Though he had made an excuse about not wanting to hand over his passport for the manager to hold onto during his stay, and had given her a healthy bribe, if he wanted to flee this time and take all his luggage with him it would be obvious he was checking out. He'd have to settle his bill, and they might even send someone upstairs to count the beer and soda in the mini fridge to see what extra he might owe. And he knew from venturing out at night that in this particular hotel someone always manned the front desk, around the clock, even if the desk person on the overnight shift had to nap in a chair, so sneaking off in the small hours wasn't an option.

Thus, sneaking a body out of the hotel in the small hours wasn't an option, either. And anyway…sneaking it where?

On top of all this, though he hadn't let them hold his passport he'd still given them his real name. Even if he could slip away unseen, they'd still know who it was who had stiffed them on the bill. *And left that stiff,* he allowed himself to joke.

No, he hadn't been as careful this time. But then, he hadn't thought this older girl would drive him to the same act that the little girl had. His hunger toward An had been partly fueled by revulsion, and his hunger toward the child had been all about appreciation.

Not being able to check out just now, then, and needing more time to contemplate his course of action, he decided to go out on the town to seek some distraction…to escape from his suffocating room if only for a while. He took the cramped elevator down to the ground floor, and entered the lobby. Pretended to look at texts on his phone until a family checking in at the counter had the desk person sufficiently distracted that he wouldn't have to turn his room key over to them as he was normally required to do, and he slipped outside and down a flight of steps to the street.

This was De Tham Street, in District 1, and thus only a short walk over to Bui Vien Walking Street, the pulsing and strobing heart—at least for tourists—of the city formerly known as Saigon.

Oh, and what a lurid and carnal heaven on Earth it was. *Streetwalking Street would be more accurate,* he thought. Women who to his mind could be models in the USA—or at least car show girls—abounded here in their tight, revealing clothing, balanced on stilt-like high heels, asking passing foreigners if they wanted to come into an establishment for a massage. Too bad he hadn't met a girl here and taken her back to his room…too bad he'd gone through a contact he'd made. A contact who tomorrow might be wondering about An's whereabouts. Thank God he had paid for An to spend the whole night, upon seeing how cute she was and thinking he might want her more than once.

Well, he *had* had her twice already, but he didn't think a third go would be prudent. The delirious thought made him snigger to himself as he walked.

On top of the already dazzling lights and signs, Walking Street also wore the accoutrements of Christmas. Even those in Vietnam who were not Catholics found excitement in that holiday, just as atheists embraced it back home as readily as devout Christians. Not that the celebration would be anything like Tet, he knew, when that came in February. All of Ho Chi Minh City, not just this gaudy nest of decadence, wore the glitter and garland of Christmas. Elsewhere in the city, right now intricate lights in colored patterns would be flickering across the face of the Notre-Dame Cathedral, stately by day but at night resembling some theme park attraction.

Throbbing disco music from countless bars, where more of the tables were outside on the sidewalk than inside. The mingling scents of cooking food, both local and geared toward foreign bellies. Children aggressively selling lottery tickets, adults selling cigarettes or knickknacks from trays that hung from straps around their necks. He saw a boy maybe not even in his teens yet, breathing blossoms of fire into the air for tips from the sidewalk sitters.

After walking the length of the street and turning back again, Bedford—for this was the name by which he now thought of himself, transfigured or remade as he was in this alien place—settled on a bar dominating a street corner, where he had stopped for drinks on a few nights previously. He sat at a wobbly little sidewalk table and scanned the menu he was given by one of the handsome young waiters, who when not serving drinks and food tried to coax tall, sweaty Australian backpackers and portly middle-aged Brits as they passed to come sit or play billiards inside.

Last time here he'd had mai tai after mai tai, sweating them away so fast that he had barely felt drunk by the time he'd wound his way back to his hotel—walking in the gutter, bikes buzzing close alongside him, to avoid the gorgeous displays of fruit that had overtaken the sidewalks—but this time he decided to return to his go-to drink: gin on the rocks with a slice of lime. Except that when Bedford's drink came, along with a dish of peanuts to keep him thirsty, it was a slice of lemon instead. It irritated him but he decided not to complain. Lost in translation. He must be tolerant of another culture.

A woman stopped in front of his table, carrying a sleeping baby that she had probably been lugging around for hours out here in the heat and bike exhaust, and probably did every day. She held up an empty baby bottle to show him, her expression partly sorrowful and partly hostile. Bedford slipped out his wallet and gave her a few small greasy bills, which she almost looked surprised to have successfully won from him. He said to her, knowing she couldn't understand, "Now go away, before I give you some more money to come back to my hotel with me…the both of you."

As the woman rushed away, lest he change his mind about the money, Bedford's phone rang, and he pulled it from his pocket to look at its screen, not surprised it was his wife. It would be 9:35 AM there. She'd be at work, on break. It *was* a weekday, wasn't it? He'd forgotten what day of the week it was. He declined the call, shut his phone off, and returned it to his pocket.

There is no going back, he thought, and it was a calm thought. He even smiled, thinking it. There was no returning from this.

As a boy, another old science fiction film he had loved, more so than *First Men in the Moon*, had been 1956's *Forbidden Planet*. That wonderful flying saucer like a precursor of the starship Enterprise, Robby the Robot improbably producing a mountain of bourbon bottles for the ship's cook, and of course the Monster from the Id…invisible until it came into contact with the ship's force field and blaster streams. He had found the monster deliciously terrifying as a kid. Years later he was surprised to read that the plot had been inspired by Shakespeare's play *The Tempest*, with Walter Pidgeon's character meant to be Prospero, and the Monster from the Id being Caliban.

One thing that tested his patience here was that waiters and waitresses didn't check back to see if everything was okay, if another drink was required.

163

JEFFREY THOMAS

Bedford finally caught a waiter's attention, held up his empty glass, and the boy
came over. "Same thing," he said. But he waggled the lemon slice and wagged
his head. "No...I want lime this time, okay? Green? Lime?"

The boy smiled in a way that gave Bedford doubts that he understood, but
off he went to fetch him gin-with-something. While he waited, he turned his
attention back to the scintillating chaos of the street and, with a smile, recited
aloud to himself a passage he had memorized from *The Tempest*:

"...this thing of darkness I
Acknowledge mine."

PART 8: MESSAGES

1: Q-U-Y

BACK IN THEIR HOTEL ROOM, waiting for evening and that young worker named Quy to come in and tend the karaoke rooms, Thanh took a nap on his bed while Trenor sat at the foot of his own, idly flipping through TV channels. He found one that played music videos of Western artists, watched Adam Lambert perform *For Your Entertainment* and Norah Jones sing wistfully of *Chasing Pirates*. Before he knew it, still circulating through available channels, watching snippets of movies on HBO Asia and programs on the Discovery Channel—one involving the hunting of the elusive Sasquatch—he returned to find the same music videos playing again, on rotation. He glanced toward Thanh, who was softly snoring, then rewatched those videos. Time loop. That was where he was at these days anyway, right?

At least, Norah Jones was very cute.

Unable to nap himself, Trenor restlessly got up, used a pitcher-like water heater to make coffee from a packet of G7 instant, and carried it to the room's window, which looked out into the theme park, closed for the evening. This window offered a view of a tennis court upon which no one played. Dai Nam "Wonderland" was beginning to take on, for him, the aspect of a post-apocalyptic wasteland. An ambitious dream that just hadn't worked out. Well, that was pretty much a metaphor for everything ever, wasn't it?

Standing there sipping his G7 "3-in-1" coffee, gazing back at the TV, Trenor muttered, "I do believe there's a squatch in these woods."

Thanh moaned, rolled from one side to the other.

Trenor looked down at him, considered the reddening of the sky outside the window, decided to let the boy sleep a little more.

*   *   *

Thanh roused on his own, before Trenor could wake him, sat up and glanced toward the darkened window.

"Yeah," Trenor said. "Let's go."

Outside the hotel entrance they were able to catch a ride in one of those golf cart-like shuttles, which saved them a considerable walk to the food court building.

The previously empty adjacent restaurant now had some customers, and the smells of food were enticing, but Trenor and Thanh had had a bite in the park that afternoon. They veered to the side and approached a young man standing behind the food court's counter.

"Is that him?" Trenor muttered to Thanh.

"I don't know, Rick."

Hiding his misshapen hands in the pockets of his baggy shorts, when Thanh reached the cashier he spoke to him in Vietnamese. The man shook his head, and made a gesture toward the ceiling.

Turning to Trenor, Thanh explained, "He's not Quy. Quy's upstairs, cleaning up after a party. I told him I'm a friend of Quy. He said we could go up and see him, but if we want a karaoke room we have to pay."

"Pay him. Tell him we'll have Quy set us up."

The second level looked even more lonely than the park had today; a shadowy area of columns, with the silhouetted figures of musicians and singers along one wall like the shadows of vaporized victims, imprinted there by an atomic blast. None of the rooms thumped with music, none of them being occupied. One door was open, though, and they went to it. Thanh passed inside first, Trenor looming behind and to the side of him.

An attractive young man with a stylish haircut, dressed in a uniform of white shirt and black vest and pants, was leaning over a low central table, gathering up numerous Heineken bottles and unfinished plates of cubed fruit. He straightened when he saw the pair come in.

"Quy?" Thanh said. "Do you know who I am?"

The young man looked down at Thanh's exposed hands. He said, "Anh Cua?"

"*Du ma!*" Thanh swore, starting toward him. Mr. Crab, huh?

"Sorry," Quy stammered in imperfect English, perhaps for Trenor's benefit, "sorry! It what your sister call you! I don't know your name!"

Trenor put a hand on Thanh's shoulder to hold him back, but through clenched teeth Thanh demanded, "Where is Tra Mi?"

Trenor saw the man glance nervously at a small knife on a plate of fruit in front of him. He himself took note of a heavy microphone on his own side of the table. Swinging it by its cord, it would make an adequate weapon, if it came to that.

Quy evidently decided against lunging for the knife, and said, "She told me she coming here and meet me, but she never show up."

Thanh asked him, in Vietnamese, if he had had contact with her since a certain date. It was the day of Hang Ni's murder.

In Vietnamese, Quy answered, "No, not since then. No phone call, nothing."

"But she said she would come here to meet you? Did she say she would have my younger sister Hang Ni with her?"

"No...no, she said she would come here alone. She wanted to come be with me...to be my girl. She told me she had all her clothes with her, and wanted us to live together. I had to tell her the truth, then...I told her I already have a girl. I'm sorry!"

"Don't tell me you're sorry," Thanh snapped. "Maybe if you hadn't toyed with her and got her hopes up, she wouldn't have thrown Hang Ni away to be murdered!"

"Hang Ni? Murdered?"

"She's dead!" Thanh shouted, still tensed up as if he might pounce across the table.

"I'm sorry! I didn't know!" The boy truly looked stricken.

"No spiders," Trenor said.

Thanh looked around. "What?"

"There're no spiders on him. He didn't have anything to do with Hang Ni's death, or Tra Mi's disappearance."

Thanh related what Quy had told him, then said, "Maybe he didn't help Tra Mi run away somewhere, but he played around with her and made her believe she could move away from home and be with him. Maybe she *wanted* someone to kill Hang Ni, so she could be free to do that!"

Quy went on in Vietnamese, and they listened. "Tra Mi was very sad...I'm sorry. She cried a lot when I told her about my girlfriend. Crying like she was *crazy*. She said she still wanted to come out and talk with me here...I guess she wanted to plead with me in person. But she never came. I haven't heard from her since, I swear!"

"Oh God," Trenor hissed softly.

Thanh looked at him again. "Rick?" He saw Trenor gazing toward a corner of the low-lit, poorly soundproofed room.

He saw her there in the corner, nude and dimly luminous, this time not facing into the wall but toward Quy—only a few paces from him. Her arms were stretched out toward him, at their limits, but it was as if she couldn't move her feet those few steps to reach and touch him. What would Quy feel, if anything, if she did?

The spider-things belched out of her mouth in place of a forlorn cry, spilling down her chest and belly.

"You see her," Thanh said.

As though she had heard Thanh, she jerked her head to look toward them with her dead black eyes. She thrust her left arm toward the wall and flattened her palm there. The insect-like creatures raced down her arm, began to spread upon the wall.

"Yes," Trenor whispered, not daring to blink, as if afraid she would vanish if he did.

More spider-things flowed down her arm and onto the wall, like a speeded-up film of diligent ants at work.

"They're writing a word again," Trenor said.

Quy looked from Trenor to the empty corner, confused. "What going on?" he said in English.

"It's Tra Mi's ghost," Thanh told him. "She's dead, you idiot!"

"Jesus," Trenor said.

"What does the word say, Rick?" Thanh asked.

Tra Mi was gone in a blink, though Trenor hadn't done so. The word on the wall was already turning a translucent gray as it quickly faded.

"Jesus," he repeated. "It said *Giesu*. That's Jesus, right?"

"Yes."

Trenor addressed Quy. "When you last spoke with Tra Mi, was she in Vung Tau?"

"Yes," Quy said. "Yes, Tra Mi was stay in Vung Tau when she call me."

Thanh watched Trenor. "What are you thinking, Rick?"

"I'm thinking of that big-ass statue of Jesus, up on that cliff in Vung Tau." He nodded at Thanh, going with the intuition. "I think we need to go back there. Coming here was a waste. She didn't have anything to show us here…she just missed her man. She told him she'd come, and she did. To say goodbye." He furrowed his brow, thoughtful. "But maybe…maybe she wanted us to know that after Quy rejected her, she didn't have anything left to hope for."

They soon left Quy, visibly shaken and no less confused, to resume cleaning up after his last customers. As they crossed the second floor to descend to the food court area, they didn't spot a man in a baseball cap hanging back in the shadows, watching them from behind one of the support columns.

2: KATE

THE AMERICAN RETURNED TO THE Great Wall Hotel, following in the wake of this man Richard Trenor and Tra Mi's freak brother, Thanh. He too called to summon one of those open golf cart-like vehicles, having previously got the cell number of the driver who had taken him to the food court, as the others had no doubt done with their own driver.

Riding in the little shuttle, he thought about the odd conversation he had listened in on through the karaoke room's open door, heard clearly in the otherwise unoccupied level above the food court. He had considered questioning that boy Quy himself after the others had left, either paying or threatening him for further information. Still, it had sounded like he wouldn't know much. He had sounded sincere in claiming he hadn't heard from Tra Mi after the child's murder, and honestly surprised to hear of that death. The American doubted Tra Mi had revealed to Quy that she would be delivering her drugged sister to Chen Ti-sai's client. Therefore, she wouldn't have mentioned the involvement of her boss Long Dien to him. And of course she didn't know *his* name, did she? So why step into the light in this case if it wasn't really necessary?

But what to make of other things he had overheard? Had he heard the conversation so clearly after all? The white man had seemed to see something that the other two didn't. The freak had then explained to Quy that what Trenor was witnessing was his sister's ghost. Then Trenor had claimed to see this ghost writing on the wall…the word *Giesu*. And so now this vision, this delusion or hallucination, was enough to make them return to Vung Tau?

This Richard Trenor had to be disturbed. Maybe broken by drugs. But why did the boy believe him? Was he *that* desperate to find his sisters? Or was the boy only humoring the older man?

And anyway, how did they even know each other? Was Trenor like Chen's elusive client, a sex tourist hungry for a youthful foreign body, this boy his lover…and Trenor was getting what he wanted from him by promising he would find his missing sister?

It was too much for the American to wrap his head around just yet. The main thing was, the pair intended to go back to Vung Tau. And if they thought they'd find something there, he had to keep following them to see what that thing was. Their quest had become his quest. He had to admit to himself, his curiosity had now become the equal of his concern for being dangerously compromised by them, or by the missing Tra Mi.

The *dead* Tra Mi?

From a distance, as his shuttle was approaching the hotel entrance, he saw the pair climbing out of their own and then disappearing into the building. When his cart pulled up, he paid his driver and hurried inside after them.

Their head start on him was shortened because they had to stop in the lobby to regain their room key. The American could skip this, because Kate had remained in their room. He had clarified this with the receptionist when he'd set out earlier this evening.

He hung back, watched the pair leave the lobby and enter into the long white corridor that would deliver them to their room. Again, he stole forward to follow. He saw their door shut, took note of its number. Indeed, only three doors down from his own. He hung back once more, beside his own room, until he heard the clack of their door locking.

He turned toward his room's door and was reaching out to let himself in when it cracked inward on its own. He didn't hear the handle's tongue withdraw, so it seemed that the door hadn't been entirely closed to begin with.

Kate began to slip out into the hallway. She was facing away from the American…down the corridor toward the room Trenor and the boy stayed in. Only when she had put one foot over the threshold did she sense the American, or glimpse him peripherally, and whip her head toward him with a gasp.

He smiled at her. "Sorry to startle you," he whispered in Vietnamese. "Going somewhere?"

"I…was wondering where you were," she said. "I was looking for you."

"Oh? Go back inside."

She hesitated there, poised half in and half out, her eyes wide and agitated. The American was reminded of something he had experienced in the USA. Driving on a rural back road in Connecticut, past midnight, on his way to the Foxwoods Casino, where so many fellow *Viet Kieu* liked to gamble away their life's savings—on some errand there that he no longer remembered—he had slammed on his brakes to avoid striking a deer that stood just at the periphery of the road. Its eyes had eerily reflected his headlights. Kate's eyes almost seemed to glow like that now.

She turned back inside. With her back to him, he looked her up and down. She wasn't wearing her reddish wig, and she was barefoot. How far had she intended to go in search of him, without her shoes or even the hotel's blue complimentary sandals? He saw she clutched a folded square of paper in her right hand, and held that hand close to the curve of her hip. Hiding it but trying not to be too obvious about it.

She sat on the bed and faced him. In seating herself, she had slipped the square of paper under her thigh. The American kept his eyes away from there, so as not to give away that he'd noticed.

"So you missed me?" he asked.

"I was bored," she stammered. "I got lonely." Like a young lover wounded by her man's neglect, she added a petulant tone. "Why did you make me wait here for you?"

"You could have been sleeping."

"I didn't want to sleep without you."

"Ohh! That's *sweet!* I'm learning new things about you all the time, my dear."

"What did you find out?"

"I listened to them talk to Tra Mi's boyfriend. We're going back to Vung Tau."

"Is she there?"

"Sounds like it. In one form or another."

"Hm?"

"Is that for me?"

"Is what for you?"

"The note in your hand." He pointed at her leg, bared by her short shorts. "Is that a love letter for me?"

"What? It's nothing. A piece of trash."

"I'll throw it away for you." He held out his hand, palm up.

"No need!"

"Give it to me." His lips were still smiling. His eyes weren't.

"Wait!" Kate said, holding up her free hand. Her voice had the quality of a rope from which a mountain climber dangled off a sheer cliff, quickly fraying…strands unraveling. "I was trying to help you!"

"Really? I appreciate that."

"I was going to try to trick the boy and the old man to trust me, and tell me what they know!"

"A clever but ill-advised plan. You really should let me handle this, you know. Now…give me that note."

Kate hesitated again, but he could see in her eyes that she knew it was futile to conceal it any longer. She slipped the folded paper out from under her thigh and extended it to him. "Please," she said, cocking her head to the side, tears coming to her eyes. "I thought you would be proud of me—for helping you! *I love you*, you know?"

Oh, but wasn't that the worst part of this? The American almost winced at her last statement. He couldn't bring himself to reply with another quip; instead, only unfolded the note and began to read it. Handwritten in Vietnamese, obviously meant to be read by the boy Thanh. In translation, it basically said:

"A man is following you. This man is afraid you will find Tra Mi. He is afraid Tra Mi will tell you about how he and Tra Mi's boss Long Dien arranged to have your little sister sold to an American man for sex. The man following you is dangerous and evil. I think he is insane. I saw him kill a man in Saigon simply for crossing him. He will kill both of you, too, if he thinks you are a threat to him. He is a Vietnamese man, living in the USA, but he comes here on business. I don't know his real name. I'm sorry about your sisters, but I'm afraid to go to the police. All I can tell you is, you must be very careful."

"Hm," the American said, reading it over again. "This is pretty eloquent. Again, you're full of surprises." He looked up. "Were you going to knock on their door and hand this to them? Introduce yourself by name? Invite them to our room for some coffee?"

"No…I was going to slide it under their door. I meant to do it before they got back, but I waited too long."

"Lucky for *me* you waited too long, don't you think?" He chuckled. "I'm disappointed in this part." He read it aloud. "*I think he is insane.*" He looked up again. "Do you really think that? After how I explained to you the principles, the code of integrity, I follow? I know that might be a bit much for you to take in, but…*insane?*"

"I'm sorry," Kate blubbered, openly weeping now. "I told you…I was trying to trick them into trusting me!"

"If, after giving them this, they discovered us following them and we were caught as a result, weren't you concerned that you'd be apprehended by the police as my accomplice? Ah, but I suppose this note would help make the case that you were my prisoner, right? A poor innocent hostage?"

"I *told* you, honey…" she whined, face crumpling further.

"*Don't call me that!*" he bellowed in English. He saw her flinch back, as if a bullet had struck her square in the chest. He clamped down on his breathing, closed his eyes, dropped his chin to his breastbone. After a moment he lifted his head again, his voice once more under control. "All right," he sighed. "All right. I'm glad I saw this note. It tells me we have a lot to talk about." He folded it again, stuffed it into a pocket of his touristy shorts, then sat down beside her on the edge of their bed.

"I see your conscience has been stirred by all this. I understand. My conscience is stirred right now, too, because of the unpleasant things I've exposed you to. I realize that was unfair of me, and I'm sorry for that. I'll be quite frank about why I wanted you with me through all this mess, and I'm sure you can guess it isn't only because I occasionally need your assistance with this or that."

He pulled in a deep breath. "I realize this sounds foolish, but…I've been thinking about it more and more. In the USA, I could really use someone to assist me with…you know, my various projects. Someone who could help care for my day-to-day concerns, too…to free my time for more important matters. For a while now I've actually entertained the idea of marrying someone…taking them back there with me. Someone loyal. Someone I could trust." He grinned;

this grin stretched in an unnatural way, like a painful contortion, but it was the best he could do right now. "Someone beautiful, of course. Well, forgive me…I'm only a man." He spread his arms. "Someone beautiful like you."

"Me? Marry *me?*"

"Would you be willing to do that? To become my wife? So I could sponsor you to live in the USA with me?"

"Really?" Though her face was still flushed red, cheeks still slick with tears, she quivered a timid smile. "You would take me to the USA?"

"Do you realize, now, how important you are to me? Not that I fault you for not understanding before. I should have let you know sooner that I was thinking this way. Then again…ha…it kind of took me by surprise, myself. But yes, honestly. I'd like you to come to the USA with me. *If…*"—he held up a finger like a stern but loving father—"…I can trust you, from now on, to trust *me.*"

"Yes!" she blurted. "Oh yes, honey!" She looked honestly happy about his suggestion—his proposal—though whether she was happy about the idea of living in the United States, or because he wasn't strangling her at this moment, he couldn't say. Both, he supposed.

"No more notes? No more *anything*, without my approval?"

"I promise you, honey!" she cried. She put her hand on his leg. "I promise you!"

"That's my girl." And he leaned close, enfolded her in an embrace, stroked her hair soothingly as she sobbed gratefully, wetly, against his shoulder.

Their tight embrace, the smell of her hair, even the intimate sensation of her tears of gratitude and fear soaking through to his skin, were causing him to become aroused. As he caressed her, his gaze fell on a low table bearing an urn that heated water for instant coffee, packets of G7 and a metal spoon resting beside it. He envisioned himself slipping out of their embrace, leaning past her, picking up that spoon and driving the end of it like a blade all the way into her eye socket.

But he couldn't, could he? They had checked into this hotel together, using his actual passport and her photo ID. They had to check out together. Both of them. Both alive.

That was why he couldn't kill her, despite his urge to do just that right now. *That's the reason why*, he insisted to himself.

So instead he gave himself over to his arousal, and he pushed her back gently onto the mattress, and pulled her shorts and then her panties down her legs, and he fucked her fiercely and they both cried out like souls in Hell, frustrated by their very damnation.

Afterwards, immediately she slept, and that was how he knew she trusted him. This storm, for now, had passed.

He got up, naked, dug her note out of his own discarded shorts and read it again. Lowering the paper, he whispered to himself in English, "What am I doing? What am I even doing?"

PART 9: MARTYR

1: STEPS

"I WILL FUCKING DIE BEFORE I get to the top," Trenor huffed to Thanh, beside him as they mounted this latest flight of rough-carved stone steps. "Either my poor knees are going to give out, and I'm going to roll all the way back down, or my heart's going to explode. If I don't make it, man, you've got to keep going without me."

"We're doing this together, Rick," Thanh insisted, facing his own challenge as he climbed with his bare, cleft feet. "We can stop to rest whenever you want."

"If this is something your people set up," Trenor gasped, as he continued trudging up the steps, "to test our faith, then fuck them."

"I think it's something *your* people set up, Rick," Thanh said. "To test *our* faith."

"Fuck you, Thanh," Trenor said.

Thanh laughed. "Rick...did I tell you? I remember hearing there are about eight hundred and fifty steps to reach the statue."

"Did I happen to say fuck you?"

The statue—more a monument in the shape of Jesus Christ—loomed above the coastline city of Vung Tau atop rugged Nho Mountain. He looked out over the platinum-colored ocean, today being overcast but no less scorching for that. Every so often along the arduous climb, there was a level area where visitors might stop to catch their breath, admire lesser statues that looked cheaply cast in plaster, or buy a cold drink or souvenir. Truly afraid his heart might give out, when they reached the next level area Trenor did indeed stop to rest. Here, a Vietnamese woman asked him in perfect English—apparently a *Viet Kieu*—if he'd take a photo of her group. Maybe she didn't trust her former countrymen not to run away with her digital camera. Trenor complied, and she thanked him cheerily. Not everyone was here investigating a murder.

Palm trees here had their trunks wrapped in red and green banners in anticipation of Christmas. The pair drifted to a pool choked with lily pads, alongside which stood a trio of white statues of women dressed in *ao dais*, with angel wings. Trenor got close to one of them to look at the pages of an open book she held in her hands, as if he might find some revelation waiting for him there. He found only decaying plaster.

He shaded his good eye and gazed up at Christ, glowing white against the oyster-gray sky. Arms outstretched, but rather than appearing crucified, He held His hands palms upward as if inviting these tiny mortals not only to ascend inside His majestic body, but to continue on to heaven beyond that. He was crowned with a halo with three spokes, three groups of rods or spikes emanating like rays from that. Solidified radiance, as if from an immense fossilized spirit.

"He is thirty-two meters tall," Thanh said, watching Trenor stare at the monument. "With, I think, over a hundred more steps inside him, to get to the top."

"Ohh, Christ. Pardon the pun. Do you go up inside His head?"

"No…you come out at His shoulders. See?" He pointed a claw hand.

Ah…sure enough, Trenor saw small clusters of human heads at either of Christ's shoulders.

"Well," he sighed, shaking his head. "Let's keep moving."

"Rick?"

Trenor had started forward, but looked back. "Yeah?"

"So, we need to go inside? To the top?"

"I think we do."

"What are we looking for in there?"

"You know who we're looking for in there," he said. Then he started toward the next long section of steps.

During his climb, more exhausting than any jungle trek recalled from his youth, Trenor stopped when he spied an odd shape tucked inside a broken gap in one of the steps. He leaned in close and peered into the shadowy nook. He made out the hindquarters of a huge brown toad, covered in small dark bumps, lurking like some witch's familiar. He couldn't see its head.

Further up, on another step: a large millipede coiled in a spiral—dead with its head either accidentally or intentionally squashed under a tourist's shoe. Why did these innocent creatures seem to him like ominous portents? That was surely only something in his own mind, superimposing itself over the natural world.

They finally reached the base of the statue, with Trenor almost woozy from their ordeal. He had to sit for a few minutes on a bench in its shadow, massaging his aching knees while he waited for his heart to remember its normal pace. Besides the climb and the heat, he hadn't slept well last night in their room at Dai Nam. They had roused early this morning, arranged a ride here to Vung Tau, secured a new hotel, and then continued on to this site before it could close for the day. Like devoted pilgrims, hoping for some enlightenment, and willing to suffer for it along the way.

A flotsam of shoes fanned out in front of the entrance to the monument. Shoes were not allowed, nor was revealing clothing permitted inside this sacred structure. Oddly, though, Trenor didn't feel a sense of spiritual awe—at least not yet—as he had experienced at that golden temple at Dai Nam. Despite there being many Catholics in Vietnam, this site just seemed less...sincere to him. It didn't help that here and there amongst the trees at the summit of this mountain were huge cannons dating from the French occupation, trained out toward the sea, incongruous in the presence of the Prince of Peace.

It was free to enter the Jesus statue, but donations were expected and Thanh paid this on their behalf before leading Trenor inside. Within, tilting back their heads, above them they saw the stairs that corkscrewed up through Christ's body. This was either an opportunity to integrate oneself body and soul with the so-called son of God, or a hollow edifice. For his part, Thanh felt unmoved.

Thanh paused before heading for the stone stairs and waited for Trenor, watched him as he looked around at the walls. Was he studying the framed historical photos hung there, or looking for clues in the spaces between them...the words he claimed to see, spelled out in those bug-things he had described? Thanh idly thought about the worst of Buddhist hells, Avici hell, and the hundreds of thousands of lesser hells. If a reality, such a number of demons they must all contain! He wondered if those creatures Trenor saw, if they truly did exist, might actually be infinitesimal demons from those hells, overflowing into the mortal realm.

If so, was his friend gifted or cursed that he had the ability to perceive them?

Trenor finally looked around and nodded at Thanh. Thanh waited for a break in ascending tourists, then fell in after them, with Trenor following right behind.

They worked their way up slowly, sliding their hands along the discolored marble banister smudged by thousands of hands before their own. They would often have to press themselves to one side to permit the passage of those returning from having visited the top, there being only the one staircase. At one point, as they neared the top, Trenor leaned forward to gaze down at the spiral of stairs and groaned. He said to Thanh, "Geez...it's giving me vertigo."

"Are you going to be all right, Rick?"

"The ultimate question," Trenor said, and resumed climbing.

They had to scrunch up against the white-tiled wall to allow another party to descend. Trenor poised there, pretending to be a statue, holding his arms out from his sides with palms turned out like a martyr. The group, composed entirely of Vietnamese women, laughed and one of them indicated that she wanted her picture taken with the foreigner. Trenor humored them, striking his pose again as this woman gave the V sign with one hand. She thanked him, her friends giggled again, and they continued their descent while Trenor and Thanh resumed their ascent.

At last, they reached the top of the stairs. To either side, in the open air, extended the great arms of Christ. Trenor was surprised to see that on both His shoulders there was a bed of tall nails, to discourage people from climbing out onto those arms, as if the fall wasn't incentive enough to refrain from such action.

They couldn't venture out to the root of Christ's right arm. There, hogging the dizzying, panoramic view of Vung Tau and the sea, was an amorous young couple, the wind whipping their black hair. Instead, they waited until two others had turned away from the left-hand side and squeezed past them before edging out into the open.

Here, the exaggerated sharp planes of Christ's Anglo-styled face, in profile, jutted out into the air. He looked vigilant, expectant.

"Whoa," Trenor said to Thanh, who hung back behind him. The wind flailed at his face, as if it meant to rip his patch away and reveal the damage that lay hidden beneath. "What an amazing view."

Then, suddenly, Thanh was no longer hanging back, but rushing forward, slipping past Trenor on his right. Trenor didn't feel the youth's body pass but he saw him peripherally, and began to turn to speak to him. He understood that Thanh wanted to experience the dazzling view, too, but why the sudden urgency?

When he looked, he saw that it wasn't Thanh who was streaking past him but a young woman with long inky hair. Because she sped past him, he didn't get a good look at her face. Without breaking momentum, she boosted herself up onto Christ's shoulder, on hands and knees crawled out toward that bristling bed of nails.

"No, no, no!" Trenor bellowed, lurching forward to grasp at her slim ankles.

In her frantic effort to scamper out onto Christ's shoulder, the girl misplaced her left hand and skewered it all the way through with one of those spikes. It popped out the top of her hand. She screamed, but her scream was unheard except to Trenor. Then, she toppled either accidentally or intentionally to one side. In a blink, she was gone...to plummet.

"Rick! *Rick!*" Trenor vaguely heard Thanh cry.

Heedless, Trenor levered his upper body out over the edge of Christ's shoulder to look far below.

He expected to see a body down there, smashed by the great fall. He saw nothing, though, but the tiny, ant-like bodies of more tourists, faces turned up toward him, having heard the commotion even at that distance.

"Oh God," Trenor murmured, sinking down against Thanh's body as the young man got an arm around him.

"Is he okay?" a man behind Thanh asked in Vietnamese.

"Please," Thanh implored the man, "help me get him downstairs."

"Quan," Trenor muttered. "Get me out of here, man. Get me out of here, Quan."

"I have you, Rick."

As big as he was, compared to Thanh and even the other Vietnamese man who had positioned himself on the opposite side, Trenor staggered repeatedly, dangerously, on the way down the spiral of steps. "Is he drunk?" someone asked in Vietnamese, and Thanh answered tersely that he wasn't; it was the heat, the climb.

Along the way, other men and women reached out a number of times to help steady Trenor, as if to help pass him down the line. One of these times, as he almost lapsed into unconsciousness, a strong hand snapped out to grip his shoulder to prevent him from toppling forward. Something about this contact caused Trenor to look up sharply, where previously he had been nearly unaware of the hands on his body.

He looked into the face of the man who had taken hold of his shoulder. A man wearing a baseball cap. Trenor actually gasped, his posture flinching more upright. The man quickly withdrew his hand and stepped back against the tiled wall of the stairwell. Thanh and the other man kept him moving downward, with other people squashing themselves out of his way, and Trenor looked back over his shoulder to get another look at the man in the baseball cap, but already he was blocked from view.

2: RETURN TO HELL

"YOU ALREADY CAME HERE BEFORE," said the young policeman in his crisp green uniform and military cap. "I remember you." Intentionally or not, he gestured down at Thanh's pincer-like hands, his feet. "You didn't say your other sister was dead."

"I didn't know anything about what might have happened to her!" Thanh blurted. "I told you she was missing."

"You said nothing about the girl who committed suicide."

"How was I to know about that girl?"

Having rented them a taxi, Thanh had taken Trenor to Vung Tau's Le Loi Hospital. It was here that Thanh had been shown Hang Ni's violated body. How could he have known, then, that in this very same room...at that very same time...

"Does this fucker need some 'coffee money' or something?" Trenor growled, going for his wallet. He knew now how things went here with the police, and the innocent term that was used for their bribes.

"Wait," Thanh hushed him.

The same tall man as before, in his same lab coat, unlatched one of the metal wall hatches and rolled out a narrow platform upon which a body lay enshrouded. With it seemed to come a gust of extra cold air in the already chilly room. In Vietnamese, the tall man said to Thanh, "You're lucky she's still here. But she's a curious case, and still unclaimed. Quite a dramatic ending. Usually with young people it's bike accidents, or a drowning. We've had seven drowned people recently. Just last night a twenty-four-year-old woman was drowned. They had to dive for her...her body got caught under a rock."

In Vung Tau was the Dinh Co Temple, built almost two hundred years ago after the body of a sixteen-year-old girl had washed up on Long Hai Beach. Every February there was a festival in her memory, at the "temple for the drowned." Who did those ghosts haunt?

The man in the lab coat unveiled the face of the body on the slab, and instantaneously Thanh jerked away to double over and vomit onto the floor, between his splayed two-toed feet.

Trenor had to resist joining in with him. It had been many a year since he had seen a ruin of a human body like this. Let alone smelled such a ruin. And yet, it put him back into the *then*, immediately. And he acclimated, as he had then. Not that he didn't have to cover his nose and mouth with one hand.

In addition to the distortions of decay that had occurred since this person's death, the head of the body on the slab was riven down to the nose. Its leathery eyes veered off radically in different directions. Bulging from the V-shaped gulf between them was a mass of brain tissue, which for all its exposure still withheld all that it had once contained. Every memory, every hope and desire, was just another kinked coil in this spilled blob on the cold, clinical slab.

"Can you identify her?" the man in the lab coat pressed.

"Ohhh…God!" Thanh groaned.

"Is that your other sister?" the man in the lab coat persisted.

"It's her," Trenor stated.

"Did you know the deceased?" the man in the lab coat asked, turning to Trenor, dubious but intrigued. His eyes shone, his mouth in a little smile. Death, for him, was too seldom more than mundane. Perhaps he relished that this death had been something exceptional.

"It's her," Thanh echoed, between sobs. Though he himself couldn't recognize this horror of burst and rotting flesh on the slab, he trusted Trenor in this matter. Absolutely…no more doubts. "It's her. It's my sister…Tra Mi."

"There was no identification on her body," the policeman said, no doubt feeling defensive. "We didn't know there was a connection with the little girl."

"Ask him," Trenor said, "when Tra Mi died."

Thanh managed to do so, and the policeman replied. Thanh turned to Trenor and said, "It was on the same day that Hang Ni's body was discovered. Before five o'clock, when the statue would be closed to the public."

Trenor grunted in acknowledgement. He said, "Ask him to show me her left hand." He didn't know why he felt the need to see it; he was already convinced who this was.

Thanh passed his request along. He himself turned away, but Trenor looked down and the man in the lab coat and the policeman both watched him with interest.

Sure enough, a wound like stigmata pierced the young woman's swollen, discolored hand, all the way through. Not that he had had any doubts, but the wound was almost like a punctuation mark for the matter.

He put a hand on Thanh's shoulder. "Come on, buddy. We have to tell your father about this, now."

Thanh nodded, eyes squeezed shut. "He has to plan another funeral. I'm all he has now, Rick, whether he likes it or not."

JEFFREY THOMAS

"Thanh," Trenor said, with a hiss of urgency. He was staring past the open drawer on which lay the shattered body. Staring toward an open surface of wall. "What does *dia nguc* mean?" He struggled with the pronunciation.

"What, Rick?" Thanh opened his eyes.

Trenor spelled it out. Listening with fascination, the man in the lab coat pronounced it before Thanh could do so.

Thanh whirled to look where Trenor was staring, but of course he saw nothing. Still, he did not doubt what his friend was seeing. He said, "Um... 'Back to hell.'"

"I don't think I'll be seeing Tra Mi again," Trenor said. "I think she's shown us what she needed to show us. And I know you might not believe this, but I think she's sorry."

*   *   *

They were back on the street in front of the hospital, grateful for the heat after the chill of the morgue, gulping in the evening's fresh air, though it hadn't yet rinsed the taint of death from inside their nostrils and mouths. Here, the young policeman questioned Thanh as to why he had believed he would find his older sister in the hospital's drawers when he hadn't thought of looking before. Having regained his composure, Thanh said since that time he had heard rumors of a young woman who had committed suicide by leaping from the top of the Jesus statue, and having learned this had happened later on the same day his younger sister had been discovered dead in that hotel, he had wondered if the suicide might be Tra Mi.

"Why would she do it?" the policeman asked.

"I'm sure she felt guilty. She was supposed to be taking care of Hang Ni."

"She blamed herself for the little girl being kidnapped?"

"Yes...something like that," Thanh choked.

When the policeman had driven off on his motorbike, Thanh and Trenor remained standing there, not yet having hailed a taxi, staring into the gathering darkness.

Thanh said, "She gave Hang Ni to the man who killed her. She didn't expect her to be killed. She came back the next day to get her. She saw the police at the hotel...she heard from bystanders what happened..."

"She called her boyfriend at Dai Nam," Trenor continued. "He said she was a mess when she talked to him. She thought they could run away together, but he admitted he already had a girlfriend..."

"So she went to the statue," Thanh said. He shook his head. "I should hate her, Rick. I should hate her."

"She hated herself at the end."

"I hope so."

Trenor turned to Thanh, his mouth hanging open as he remembered something. "At the statue, when we were coming downstairs…a man touched me. I looked in his face."

"Yes?"

"He was wearing a baseball cap. He had no eyes."

"What do you mean? He was blind?"

"No…I mean, instead of eyes he had two bunches of those spider-things I see. Hundreds of them, filling both eye sockets. They were pouring down his cheeks…like streams of ink."

"And what does that mean?"

Trenor wagged his head. "It means that guy was a very, very bad man."

3: STAKEOUT

A FEW HOURS EARLIER, THE American had instructed his taxi driver to follow the taxi that the one-eyed white man and his young companion had hailed in the street at the foot of Nho Mountain, upon which towered the statue of *Giesu*. In Vietnamese he had told the driver, "Don't lose them. There's a nice tip in this for you."

Now, though the odd pair's taxi had driven off and left them in front of *Benh Vien Le Loi*, the American and Kate still sat in their own taxi, which had pulled up against the curb a discreet distance away. The American had ordered the driver to kill the engine and his lights. The man could keep track of the time, in regard to what he was owed, on his watch if he wanted. The driver had shrugged. Why not? This would be easy work. He even slumped in his seat and pulled down the bill of his own baseball cap.

Beside the American, in Vietnamese Kate asked, "Why did they go to the hospital? Is Tra Mi in there?"

"Why don't you take a nap, too, my dear?" he said to her.

She grunted sulkily, "Okay, honey." She slouched down in her seat beside him.

Trenor and the boy had gone on into the hospital. Evening was beginning to discolor the street a bruise-like shade.

Why indeed? the American wondered. He recalled the one-eyed man's odd behavior and statements in the karaoke room. Then, the incident inside the statue of Jesus. He no longer suspected the man was faking these...visions?...so as to manipulate Tra Mi's brother. Which only meant that he was not only deluding the boy, but himself.

Then again... What was it they were going into the hospital to see?

"*It's Tra Mi's ghost,*" the boy had shouted to his sister's lover in the karaoke room. "*She's dead, you idiot!*"

The American hardly considered himself superstitious, but the belief in ghosts was as much a part of his people's DNA as their belief in luck. He'd heard his share of secondhand, even firsthand ghostly encounters from his parents and from other Vietnamese. He'd even had one unnerving experience of his own, as a young boy. He'd woken in the night to see a dark figure standing at the foot of his bed, shining a flashlight on him. The silhouetted figure held something else in its other hand, but he couldn't be sure what it was. Thinking this might be his father looking in on him, he'd finally worked up the strength to get out, "Ba? Ba?" But even as he cried out, the figure and its light faded away…and moments later, his father was there in his bedroom's doorway, drunk and groggy, gruffly asking him what was wrong.

As an adult, he'd reflected that it had just been an episode of hypnagogic hallucination, but as a boy he suspected he had been visited by a ghost. And now, unexpectedly, he wondered again if that had been the truth after all. But the ghost of a person from the past, or from the future?

And he wondered, too—though he tried to resist this line of thought, because it conflicted with the clinical outlook, the uncompromising mindset, he demanded of himself—how much truth there might be to what this Richard Trenor was experiencing.

Ghosts. He surely hoped not. For if there were ghosts, then he himself had made a fair number of them. And they would be watching him, wouldn't they? Wishing ill upon him?

Not long after the pair had disappeared inside, a policeman pulled up in front of the hospital on his motorbike. "What's this?" the American whispered to himself. Neither the driver nor Kate sat up to look; both had drifted to sleep, the driver snoring like a man breathing through a slashed throat, while air whistled softly in and out of Kate's nose in a way he had come to know.

The policeman went on into the hospital.

The American watched, waited. You could delude a grief-stricken boy. You could delude yourself. You couldn't delude a hard little Vietnamese cop.

The street grew more deeply blue-black, like a decomposing corpse. Maybe out of bored lust, or maybe out of some need beyond sex he didn't want to confront even here in the sheltering dark, the American rested his right hand on the thigh of the woman who called herself Kate. He could smell her human though not entirely unpleasant breath. She wore short shorts, as so many women did in this tropical climate, and her hot, sticky skin under his palm was the most primal and mindlessly satisfying of sensations. If only it could be enough. Beyond this sensation, this awkward closeness, he wasn't sure what might satisfy him. He supposed he never had.

Either through accident or artifice, her head had slumped against his shoulder.

Honey, he thought, her voice echoing back to him. Was she so stupid as to think that insincere words, her head against him, would have some potent effect on him? Now, after that note? He didn't *want* to like her less…less and less…with each moment. Less *like* would become more *dislike*. He was stretched painfully between his desire and disgust. He'd read of a tug of war contest in 1997, in Taipei, that had resulted in two men having their arms ripped off. He remembered seeing pictures accompanying articles, strong limbs detached and lying in grass. Arms like severed dicks. Men torn, emasculated. What an embarrassing display. How pathetic.

"You've never loved me, am I right, sweetheart?" he cooed, kissing her temple where her dark hair was rooted in soft swirls. He sniff-kissed her, a Vietnamese habit ingrained in him. Her scalp smelled a little like shampoo, a little oily. "Not for a fraction of a second."

"Mm," she replied groggily.

"Of *course*," he whispered. "Well…I knew that, didn't I?"

"Mm," Kate said again, from out of her dream.

"But I could have loved you," he said—and immediately he wanted to gulp back the words and swallow them and burn them in his guts like grotesque origami figures, the moment he heard himself say them. What madness to utter, even unheard by anyone but himself.

While Kate slept against him like a daughter on a road trip, and drooled a little bit against his shirt, the American's thoughts drifted from that grisly tug of war in Taiwan to stories his father had told him while drunk. Could they have been real? Were they only exaggerations, if not outright fantasies? Either way, as a boy, these stories had become *his* fantasies. One in particular. Fueled by alcohol, his father had told him how—during the war that the Americans called the Vietnam War, and the Vietnamese called the American War—he and a white soldier from the US had tightly lashed the legs of a naked captive woman to two young trees, bent low toward each other and secured with cords. When the white man had cut the cords, his father had told him in a thick slur, the trees had sprung upright and the woman had been torn into two pieces.

Had it really happened? Was it even physically possible? In any case, as a boy lying in bed later that night and envisioning this scenario, the American had experienced his first orgasm.

Since those delirious fantasies, those mental images—the drawings he had made as he tried to work out the mechanics of such an act, using as his models photographs from his father's adult magazines—how could commonplace fantasy or desire compete? Let alone prosaic notions such as relationships? But…there were times he had hoped. Hoped something would come to change him, from within or without.

"They've been in there a long time," the American muttered to himself. The policeman, too. *He wouldn't stay if there was nothing,* he thought. If Tra Mi wasn't in there—in a bed, in a drawer—this information would have been quickly conveyed and the strange pair turned back onto the street in no time. In fact, the policeman would never have been asked to join them in the first place.

But eventually the three of them emerged onto the street—together, as if there could have been any doubt the policeman had arrived here specifically to meet with them. They spoke briefly, then the cop departed on his bike, going in the opposite direction so that the American didn't feel the need to lower his head to hide his face.

He watched Trenor and Thanh converse a bit on the sidewalk in front of the hospital. Then, finally, he saw them glance around...and look directly at the parked taxi. He heard Thanh cry out, "*Anh oi! Anh oi!*"

"Hey." The American thumped the back of the driver's seat. "Wake up, now... Let's get going."

"*Anh oi!*"

The driver sat up and blinked, hearing the voice. Through the windshield, he no doubt saw Thanh waving a deformed limb.

"Never mind him," the American said in Vietnamese. "Take me to Ho Chi Minh City."

"Ho Chi Minh City?" the driver groaned, wagging his head, but he started his car. "*Troi oi.*"

"What is it, honey?" Kate slurred.

"I'm not sure how they did it, but they found Tra Mi," the American told her, as the car started forward. "And I don't know how she died—whether she did it to herself, or the guy who killed the child did it—but there's no way she's in there only injured."

"Are you sure? Should we go in and talk to someone?"

"Why risk it? I trust my intuition. Well, anyway, this is good news. She can't tell them anything now, can she? Except, just by the fact of being dead."

"Where are we going, then?"

"To tell your boss, of course!" the American said brightly. "Tra Mi's boss. I'm sure Long Dien will want to hear about this. My good friend, Long Dien. *He's* not dead, at least. He can still talk with us. And with anyone else who might listen."

He averted his face from the sidewalk as the taxi drove past the two figures standing in front of Le Loi Hospital.

"You've all failed me, haven't you?" he said in English. "That bastard Chen...stupid Long Dien...you. No one with a sense of honor. No one who can be trusted." He sighed. "But then, I don't know if I can even trust myself anymore."

PART 10: KILLER APE

0: WEAPON OF CHOICE

NOT FOR THE FIRST TIME, and as always unaccompanied, Bedford leisurely explored Ho Chi Minh City's famous Ben Thanh Market, stopping to eat lunch at one of its many food stalls. He liked much of Vietnamese cuisine, and had found his favorite dish to be *bun thit nuong cha gio*, which was rice noodles with grilled pork and eggrolls. Along with this, a nice cold *ca phe sua da*, though these were always more ice than iced coffee. Oh well, such was Vietnam: delight and deceit.

He sat at a shallow counter, and a boy just into his teens gave Bedford his food and drink, and Bedford idly wondered what *that* would be like...a boy. Smooth, not too hairy or masculine, because that wouldn't do. Yes...he could imagine this, though as yet he'd never experienced it. A young cock, thrust outward, bobbing like some divining rod that might show him the way to...where? Didn't such a thing, a cock, transcend the masculine, after all? An object of such essentialness, such consequence, was beyond the limits of mere gender. A cock was the staff of God. The very emblem of Creation.

While Bedford ate—proudly having become pretty accomplished of late with chopsticks—he read a text from his wife:

"Jesus Christ, do you realize today is Christmas? Just let me know if you're okay!"

Oh! Today was Christmas? Well, imagine that! With a packet of pork in the side of his mouth like a wad of chewing tobacco, Bedford read the text again and muttered aloud, "Jesus Christ...Christmas." He snorted a laugh. "Oh, *yeah!* Jesus Christ...Christmas!"

The boy brought him his bill. Bedford asked him, "Would you like to come back to my hotel room with me? I'll move the girl onto the floor. Then I'll sodomize you and kill you...for a nice tip, of course. Hm?"

The boy smiled, showing bad teeth, and said, "Okay...okay." He nodded/bowed repeatedly and backed off to let Bedford work out the bill.

On this Christmas day, Bedford went on to wander the crowded maze of Ben Thanh's sprawling indoor market. Souvenirs in frames: preserved animals like giant black scorpions, prehistoric millipedes, bats with veiny translucent wings, moths as large as the bats. Figurines fashioned from scrap metal, like the hammer-headed monster from the movie *Alien*. Jewelry, flip flops, and so much clothing. T-shirts that bore English phrases that seemed generated randomly by some computer program. *You Deserve The Cvery Best Because of Your Kindness. Verything Has Beauty 1980. Femibist. Niggas Love Kids.*

A hand reached out, touched his wrist, and Bedford flinched back with the flashing urge to lash out and shatter a skull, and he looked down to see a seated woman who sought to sell him some blue jeans. She said something to him in either Vietnamese or bad English, and he replied without comprehension, "No, thank you."

Around and around, weaving through the labyrinth, maybe never to exit it, until he eventually found a stall that sold kitchen wares. Pots, pans, cutlery. Cleavers to chop through chicken bones, pork bones. Knives...scary, crude knives, like they'd been hammered and cooled only yesterday.

Bedford weighed some of these implements in his hand, tested their feel, ultimately selecting two items. He motioned to the proprietor, asked for a price.

And though he was certain he was being exploited, being a foreigner, he paid the price that he was quoted.

Carrying his plastic shopping bag, he continued on through the maze. He spied on couples. Women of extreme attractiveness leaning close to bony, leather-skinned males, often missing teeth and with sharp cheekbones that to his mind presented a much less desirable effect than in the females. How was this fair and balanced? Except for the tourists these women encountered, especially in a Westernized city like this, they knew no better. Still, while understanding these women's ignorance, their shortsightedness, it exasperated him.

He went out beyond the walls of Ben Thanh Market, aimlessly, walked and walked, as though dazed, shell shocked. He came upon another coffee shop in which to drink his next iced coffee in the shadows.

Here, still watching females bustle around him—coffee shop waitresses, coffee shop patrons, people passing in the street—Bedford reflected that this was a time of evolution, and these common humans didn't share the perspective he did.

Bedford had read somewhere that 4% of the population (in the US...or was it worldwide?) were sociopaths. That 1% were psychopaths. He wasn't clear on the difference, but it was food for thought. It wasn't an anomaly, he thought. It was a trend.

In the past, human beings had relied on close groups to ensure their survival against the rigors of nature. Of nature's harsh elements, of nature's predatory—or at least, competitive—animals. Nature had required that humans bond together, create tribes, societies, cities and nations (and of course, the resultant aberrations of religions and political parties).

But…wasn't humanity beyond all that now? Survival was more assured, taken for granted. And hence: the evolution of a superior human. No longer inhibited by the bond to a tribe. A human freed of fearful loyalties, except the loyalty to oneself. To one's own needs and urges.

He thought of another favorite science fiction movie from his youth: *2001: A Space Odyssey.* The killer ape, forced to evolve by its need to stand upright so as to wield a bone weapon in its hand.

Violence was the very spark of evolution.

That one bold ape had reached out to touch the black monolith that had manifested. Bedford had given himself to that blackness, now…and was ready for wherever his evolution, his transformation, would take him.

In his crinkly shopping bag—hanging in his hand like some new, external organ—in lieu of a bone club, he had one good kitchen knife and one meat cleaver.

0: THE SMALL HOURS

"EXCUSE ME. HEY… EXCUSE ME."

Bedford gently prodded the shoulder of the young man who sat in a tiny plastic chair—his back propped against the wall—asleep behind the hotel's front counter. The man jolted awake, panicked for a moment, before blinking up into Bedford's face.

Before awakening this youth, at only a few hours past midnight, Bedford had first taken it upon himself to examine the logbook spread open upon the receptionist's counter. Okay…there he was: his real name. His obsolete name. He could only hope the hotel stuck to old school methods, that his name wasn't keyed in, somewhere, in some computer.

"Yes? Yes, sir?" the groggy young man got out. He scrambled awkwardly to his feet. "Yes, mister…"

"Bedford," he lied. The boy wouldn't remember his actual Anglo name. "Hey…I've got a problem, my friend."

"A… You have a problem, sir?"

"Yes!" Bedford said, though for a man with a problem he grinned widely. He had already torn away and pocketed the page from the logbook on the hotel's reception desk. "I saw a rat in my room, my friend. God, the thing was huge!"

"A… What did you see, sir?"

"A *raaat!*" Bedford cried. "Um, a *chuot? Con chuot?*"

"A mouse? A mouse, sir?"

"No…listen to me, man. A *rat*. Understand?" He spread his hands apart. "A rat…a big-ass diseased rat…in my room! Can you come look for this thing for me?"

"Oh! Oh…yes, sir!" babbled the groggy young man. He stood up behind the counter. "Can you show me, sir?"

"Of course!" Bedford cried, grinning, eyes agleam. "Of *cooourse!*"

They rode up together in the tiny elevator cabin. It was like a crate packed full to bursting with hot humid air. As they did so, Bedford kept his head down, stared at the young man's legs, bared by his creased shorts. Ugh. The hair, the too-tanned skin's lack of smoothness. No...no, he could never. Not even in desperation. But that was okay; his disgust fueled him.

They disembarked, advanced down a gloomy mint-green hallway, and Bedford let the counter man into his room. The plastic tag of his room key, inserted into its wall slot, allowed the lights to be switched on.

"Look!" Bedford said, pointing, as if in accusation. "Will you look at that?" He was gesturing toward the broad mattress.

"What...what is that, sir?" the young man said nervously, taking a few steps toward the room's only bed...toward the sheeted figure lying motionless upon it, like something from a morgue slab.

Bedford reached down to a plastic bag he'd left at the foot of the bed, withdrew a pleasingly heavy implement, rose up and raised the recently purchased meat cleaver behind the young man as he leaned slightly over the form on the bed.

"Who...who is this, sir?" the young man asked in a wary voice, reaching out to the edge of the cloaking blanket, but twisting around to look up, behind him, at his foreign guest.

Bedford brought the cleaver down with all his might.

Thunk. Deeply into the forehead, cleaving one eyebrow in two.

The boy let out a garbled cry, but Bedford reached down and grasped his shoulder in his left hand as, with his right, he tugged the cleaver free. The boy grasped his left wrist, and tried to make his cry louder, but Bedford swung the cleaver down again. *Thunk*. This blow split the boy's nose in half, diagonally.

He yanked the cleaver free. Swung again. *Thunk*. Again. *Thunk*.

Blood sprayed not only upon the bed's petite sheeted figure, but upon the walls, even upon the ceiling, in long artistic slashes. A calligraphy that, despite its stark boldness, might never be deciphered.

The young man had fallen backwards across the bed, overlapping the body already there. In the force of his attack, at one point Bedford missed and struck this sheeted little body instead. Maybe in her shoulder? He felt sorry for defiling her, though he couldn't see her through her makeshift winding sheet. The young man slumped from the bed down to the floor. Bedford went to his knees and continued chopping with all the weight of his heavy Western body.

"Ohh, *God*," he cried aloud, both repulsed and ecstatic as he acted out his most extreme fantasies. The killer ape wielding its new, liberating weapon. Smashing more than just tapir skulls.

Anyone overhearing this noisiness in another room might have just assumed he was fucking. Standard tourist procedure.

When the young man no longer squirmed, lying there in his thick coating of blood upon blood, Bedford kneeled over him and stared intently, like a student over his first dissected frog. The young man's head had lost its integrity, but his right eye—such surprisingly stubborn structures, eyes—remained all too intact, and glared up at him in reproach. Well, that wasn't true. Without the lids, without the face, to frame and give it context, that object was just an orb, like a ball of plastic or one small part dislodged from a smashed machine. There was, really, no reproach or any other emotion. That unwelcome impression was all in his head.

Bedford rose, tossed the cleaver onto the bed. "Wow," he said. "Oh…*wow*. Look at me, huh?" He snorted a laugh, shaking his head. He looked down at his round-bellied body. He'd need a shower before he went anywhere. "Who'd have thought?" He imagined he was talking to his wife on the phone resting in his pocket. "Hey…honey? Who'd have thought, huh?"

Merry Christmas, Happy New Year, and no going back. No ever going back. He had gone through the monolith, through the star gate, into the great unfathomable void beyond.

He packed his belongings into his one suitcase and one carry-on bag. From his wallet he pulled one of the business cards he'd collected, phoned a cab. He took the elevator down to the now-unmanned lobby, dragged his rolling suitcase out into the thickly humid street. Hoping for a nice tip, the driver who eventually pulled up insisted on squeezing into his trunk, without assistance, the foreigner's single heavy suitcase.

Bedford directed the man to take him to another hotel. And there, on the sidewalk in front of this establishment, Bedford called yet another driver, whose card he had also previously saved. He had this man take him to *another* hotel in the city of Saigon. Such an amorphous, monstrous city…as great cities of the modern age tended to be.

PART 11: BEWARE OF DARKNESS

1: GLASS TABLE

THIS TIME, TRENOR DIDN'T TRY to stop Quan from drinking. With the two of them seated at the kitchen table of Thanh's home in Bien Hoa, Quan had dug out a half-empty bottle of Hennessy from somewhere and poured them both a drink. Trenor disliked cognac, but he accepted. Apparently it was popular here. He sipped it, winced. Horrid.

"*Bitch*," Quan growled, after having shot back his drink in one gulp. He started refilling his glass. "I don't want make a funeral for her, Rick, you understand me? If Tra Mi sell my Hang Ni for some man to kill her, you think I want do that? My son should get her body and throw in the ocean in Vung Tau! I don't like see her ugly face *again!*" He swung around to glare at Thanh, who sat quietly at the glass table. "Why you don't throw away that bitch in the ocean?"

"Quan, man, stop it," Trenor snapped. "I don't want to see you blame this kid for anything ever again. You're lucky to have him, and if you still can't see that then I don't know how I could be so bad at choosing my friends."

Quan dropped his head, staring down into his second drink. "I'm sorry, Rick. I'm..." He shook his head. "Stupid girl. Long time ago...when she a baby...I love her, too." He looked up, his deeply creased brown face wet with tears. "What happen, Rick? What happen to Tra Mi? *I* do that? Her mom do that?"

"Maybe the world did it," Trenor said. "Who understands these things?"

"I told you before, Rick," Quan said grimly, wagging a finger. "Tra Mi work for that fucking Long Dien. She *cong di* hooker for that fucker! I want to *kill* him, Rick."

"I agree that we didn't lean on that pimp bastard enough," Trenor said. "I know...it comes back to him. Me and Thanh are going to revisit him. But you stay out of it, you hear me?"

"You can't hurt him, Rick. You hurt him, you in trouble...you can't go back USA okay. *I* go talk to Long Dien!"

"No. *No*, man. You stay out of it. You just handle Tra Mi's funeral, now. You keep busy with that. Thanh and I have got this. We'll figure out how to come at Long Dien."

Quan bolted back his second cognac, then blurted, "You can't kill him, Rick!"

"I ain't killing nobody, brother. I keep telling you…let me handle this."

"You don't care your life anymore, Rick?" Quan started pouring a third glass of cognac.

"*Fuck.*" Trenor grabbed the bottle of Hennessy and reached down to place it on the floor under the table. "Brother…I don't even know what my life is about, anymore. Except that I'm here to find out what happened to your little girl. That's all that matters to me now. And no one is going to stand in the way of that. Not even you."

Cowed by these words, Quan said only, "Thank you, Rick."

Trenor said, "So you just fuck off and let me do this."

Quan nodded. "Okay. Okay, Rick." He switched his tortured eyes to his son.

"Okay, ba?" Thanh said.

"Okay, son," Quan answered, his lips quivering. In Vietnamese he said, "You told your mother about Hang Ni. I'll tell her about Tra Mi."

Replying in their language, Thanh said, "Are you sure, ba?"

"Yes. She was our child together. I should have been the one to tell her about Hang Ni, too… I shouldn't have left that to you." He reached across the table, and laid his hand on one of Thanh's claw-like appendages. He tightly clutched one of the two opposing thumb-like digits. In English again, Quan said, "Rick is right. You all I have now."

Awkwardly, Thanh squeezed his father's hand in return. They had never gripped each other's hands before this moment.

2: BLACK STAR

LATE ON THE SAME NIGHT that they had sat in the taxi outside Vung Tau's Le Loi Hospital, the American directed his weary driver to pull up in front of a two-floored house compacted amongst others on a Saigon back street barely wide enough to accommodate the vehicle, red paper lanterns strung down the alley's center. Sitting up awake now and looking out, Kate said, "I thought we were going to see Long Dien?"

"Not tonight; it's too late."

"What is this place?" she asked dubiously.

He got out, retrieved their luggage, started counting bills for the driver, who suddenly looked less resentful about his long night. "You never mind about that right now, my dear."

The American stepped into a dimly lit front room, open to the street with its metal gate folded back, and called out, "Hello?" Moments later a curtain parted and toward them came scuffing a sun-baked old man in an unbuttoned shirt and pair of shorts that looked many years unwashed.

"Oh," croaked the old man, "it's you!"

The American went to him and handed over some more bills he had fished out of his wallet when he'd paid the taxi driver. "For you," he said. "I need my room tonight."

"Thank you! Thank you!" the elderly man said in Vietnamese, nodding his head enthusiastically. He patted the American on the arm, then grinned toothlessly at Kate, but he obviously knew better than to ask if she was some other man's wife; if that was the reason they'd come here.

"We're going to sleep *here*?" Kate asked, following the American up a steep set of metal stairs, more like a ladder, to the second floor.

"Don't be so snobby. You've been spoiled by the nice hotels we've been staying in. What is your family's home like?"

"Worse than this," she admitted. "So, is he your father?"

The American now stood outside a door secured with a padlock. He had taken a single key from a zippered pocket in his wallet's lining. He turned slowly to look at her. "My father is dead," he said. "This man is my maternal uncle."

"Oh. Okay. Don't worry, I won't tell anyone."

He smiled. "I know you won't, my dear."

Inside, with overhead fluorescents having reluctantly fluttered to life, Kate looked down at the bare mattress resting on the linoleum-tiled floor and muttered, "*Troi oi.*"

"Here." From a wardrobe the American retrieved a folded sheet, folded blanket, pillowcases. "Make the bed, would you?"

She turned away to do this. With her back to him, the American knelt and used the tip of the padlock key he still gripped to work out a piece of trim that ran along the bottom of the wardrobe. He peeked in the space that was revealed, saw that the Type 54 still rested in there, and quickly wedged the strip of trim back into place.

When Kate was finished and turned to him, he told her what he wanted her to do next. "Then we can sleep," he promised.

A PC rested on a desk in a corner. He used it for his work, whatever that work might be, whenever he needed to utilize this room. He sat before the computer now, awakened it and got onto the internet with only a modicum of mumbled swears. He found the web site he wanted, and thereby a telephone number.

He watched Kate as she began entering the number for Le Loi Hospital on her cell phone. As she did this she remarked, "I thought you said we didn't need to check with them."

"It doesn't hurt to confirm," he said. Intuition was a valuable asset, certainly, but that didn't mean rashness or carelessness were to be embraced. They had the time now to double-check, to gather details.

Someone answered. Kate's eyes were on his as she gave Tra Mi's full name and introduced herself as a friend, without actually giving her own name. "Her brother Thanh and his American friend came to your hospital tonight, looking for her. I was supposed to come with them, but I couldn't make it…and now I can't get through to Thanh. Can you tell me, is it true? Did something happen to my friend? Is she a patient there?"

"Yes, they were here, but I don't know what happened. Hold on and I'll speak to the person they met with."

"*Cam on,*" Kate said. A minute passed, in which she and the American never broke eye contact, until the receptionist finally came back on.

"I'm sorry, but your friend is here in our mortuary. She committed suicide. She was positively identified by her brother."

"Oh! Oh no… Oh, poor Tra Mi!"

"How?" the American whispered. "When?"

Kate asked, and the receptionist replied, "She threw herself from the top of the statue of *Giesu* on Nho Mountain. She was that girl. It was in the news."

"Oh no...how terrible!" Kate said, without having to feign her reaction.

"I'm sorry," the receptionist said tersely, no doubt hoping to end the call now and get back to some TV program.

"Okay," mouthed the American.

"Thank you for telling me," Kate said, and disconnected.

"Wow," the American said. "How dramatic! Well...no shadow of a doubt, now. We can sleep easy tonight."

"I'm very tired," Kate told him, looking shaken.

"No worries...I won't bother you tonight." He smiled, knowing she knew what he meant. And he truly had no intention of pursuing sex with her this night. It was not so much that he was tired, himself; he simply had no desire for her right now. He wondered if resting his hand on her leg in the dark this evening would have been the last time he would feel a craving for her flesh.

He told her to go ahead and sleep without him; he was going downstairs for a smoke. He found his uncle in the front room sitting before an obsolete little TV, with torturously ill-adjusted colors, and they both had a Vinataba cigarette. The American asked his uncle how he had been doing. The uncle knew better than to ask too much about his nephew's doings. Pulling on his second cigarette, the American looked out toward the street and caught a glimpse of a large rat scampering past on the sidewalk. He shuddered, as if a chilly breeze had just blown over his nape. Funny.

When he finally returned upstairs, it was to unsurprisingly find Kate asleep on the thin mattress, her body covered under a quilt but her hair spilled blackly in rivulets across her pillow. He knelt in front of the wardrobe again, pried loose the strip of trim, reached into the space there and drew out the handgun.

He rose, turned its pleasing weight over in his hands, examined it. Guns were strictly forbidden in Vietnam; even crude "rifles" fashioned from plastic tubes, powered by compressed air and used to shoot marbles at rats and birds that threatened crops, would be confiscated. But how could every single weapon of the thousands upon thousands that had shed blood in this long-embattled land have been found and collected? Here was one that hadn't. Called a *sung ngan* K-54 during the war, it was actually a Chinese Type 54 semiautomatic. On its black checkered grips was the star insignia that had inspired some to call the gun the "Black Star" pistol.

Huh, he thought, bitterly. His gun was the exact same type as the pistol Chen Ti-sai had threatened him with in his office.

He slid out and checked the loaded eight-round magazine, though he didn't really need to; it was just part of the masturbatory act of handling this satisfying weapon. He slid it back in. He looked down again at Kate, deep in sleep, then he reached to his jacket hanging in the wardrobe and tucked the handgun into a pocket in the jacket's lining.

He undressed to just his boxer shorts, got down onto the creaking plastic-coated mattress beside the woman. This motion caused her to roll toward him with a dreamy murmur, and she hooked one bare leg over one of his. She breathed warmly in his face.

"Hm," he said, looking at the dark shape of her head, though he couldn't discern her features. He briefly reached out, stroked the hair that lay along the contour of her face. "Goodnight, my dear," he whispered.

Soon, he himself was dreaming. He dreamed he was a boy of eleven, only recently come to live in the United States as a "boat person," lying in his seemingly safe bed, and he opened his eyes to see a figure standing at the foot of it. A silhouette, shining a flashlight on him. In its other hand, he could see this figure held an iconic shape that he recognized as a .38 snub-nosed revolver.

"Ba?" he cried out, terrified. "Ba?"

The American awoke with a sharp intake of breath. He lay gasping in utter darkness. His first instinct was to jump to his feet, lunge to the wardrobe, grab at his jacket and rip free his handgun.

Then he remembered where he was, remembered he'd only been sleeping.

The problem was, though, that he also recalled his earlier thoughts of the night...his rumination on the matter of ghosts. Of ghosts past and future.

He again reflected on this Richard Trenor's strange episode inside the colossal statue of Jesus. Though he hadn't heard their every word with perfect clarity, back at Dai Nam, it had seemed that Trenor witnessed an apparition of Tra Mi, spelling out the word *Giesu*—which Trenor took as a sign that they must return to Vung Tau. What Kate had learned from her call to the hospital tonight supported Trenor's claims and subsequent actions. The American didn't believe that Trenor had secretly already known that Tra Mi had cast herself from the top of that monument, so then what explanation could there be for what the one-eyed man had asserted he'd seen?

"*It's Tra Mi's ghost. She's dead, you idiot!*"

No...all his steely confidence and clinical thinking aside, the American could not profess to understand all the workings of the universe.

For now, though, it came back to earthly concerns. Even with Tra Mi dead, this matter wasn't over. Somewhere out there was the man who had killed the little girl. They would still be looking for him. Talking to anyone who might help them find him. Probably talking again to people they had already talked to.

"They think they have to end this," the American whispered into the room's black void. "But I'm the one who has to end this."

3: THE MIRROR, PART 1

AS HE HAD BEFORE, TRENOR would spend the night on the mattress laid without benefit of a box-spring on the floor of what had been Tra Mi's bedroom, in the home of his friend Nguyen Van Quan.

Back in Vung Tau, he'd had the sense that Tra Mi was making her presence known to him for the last time. Lying here in complete darkness, though, he was less convinced of that. Did she stand over him even now, watching him? Wanting to reveal more to him, or maybe apologize, but unable to do so in words…and unable to show him with her spider-things, due to this pitch black?

Eventually, though, he slid into dream, as if slipping over the side of his mattress raft into an inky and infinite ocean.

He dreamed that he awoke to find Tra Mi's bedroom bathed in an unearthly light with no discernible source, an ambient greenish glow, like that within a neglected swimming pool scummed with algae. Trenor rolled his head on his pillow to see a figure in the room, but it wasn't that of a slim young woman with streams of black hair. Rather, quite differently, it was a man with his back to Trenor. Though the man stood before a full-length mirror nailed to one wall, from this angle Trenor couldn't see his reflection. The man wasn't really overweight, yet he appeared heavier than one would expect from many a local man. Trenor saw only the back of his head, his apparently jet-black hair. His slice of profile in this weird greenish murk was too shadowy to make out.

"My visa's expired," this male figure said in a dreamy voice, in unaccented English. Was he saying this to Trenor, having noticed he'd awakened? Or was he simply talking to himself—to his reflection? "It's only good for thirty days. You can get an extension, at the embassy. But mine's expired now."

"Mine's still good," Trenor said aloud, or at least aloud in his dream, though he then regretted giving away that he was awake and listening.

"Christmas has come and gone," the figure said, sweeping one arm dramatically, and he snorted. "It's always a letdown after Christmas, isn't it? It never lives up to what you hoped for. I didn't get anything for my wife. I guess my gift to her is that I'm here, not there. If I was there…well…*ha!* If I was there…at this point…maybe it would be *her* I'd be chewing." He said *chewing* almost wistfully, sensuously. "These foreign girls… It's easier, right? Little brown foreign girls? But let's be honest; it's not just that they're more expendable. They're more beautiful. Well, they are! They know their power, and at the same time they take it for granted, because there's so many of them like that: horribly, cruelly beautiful. My wife…yeah. What can I say? She's a…a big white blob."

"Who are you?" Trenor asked the figure.

"Who?" sighed the shape standing at the mirror. "Am *I?*"

"Tell me your name."

"Name. Right…my name. Call me Bedford," said the figure.

Still lying on his back, as if pinned by sleep paralysis—by some misshapen, not-quite-human form that crouched upon his chest—Trenor saw the murky figure turn its head ever-so-slightly toward him, though it maybe still kept its eyes locked on the dark mirror. A wary tone had crept into its voice. "What are you doing here, in my dream?"

"You're in *my* dream, fucker," Trenor said.

"Oh! Yeah?" chuckled the figure. "Things are *really* getting different now. Now that all the doors are off their hinges, huh?" The man reached up to scratch vigorously under his jaw, on both sides. "*God*, I'm itchy. What is this?"

"Turn around," Trenor commanded, however pinned he might be. "I want to see you."

"I want to see you, too!" the figure exclaimed, seemingly in good humor, and it finally turned away from the mirror. "I guess I need to see who's fucking with my dreams!"

The figure shuffled a few steps, shifting around a little to look down at the mattress laid upon the floor.

"Oh!" Trenor blurted. "Oh God!"

The figure standing at the full-length mirror didn't actually have jet black hair. Rather, its head was entirely encased in a thick, writhing, living mass—like a bondage mask, without eye or mouth holes—of spider-things in dense multitudes.

"Why so damn *itchy?*" the man with the face of spiders complained again, vigorously raking his fingers against where his cheeks would be. In so doing, the creatures swarmed over the backs of his hands.

"Own it!" Trenor hissed. "They're you!"

"Oh yeah?" the man said. "Well, own yourself, buddy! Come over here and you look in the mirror, how 'bout? You look pretty fucked up yourself, Polyphemus."

"Go to hell!"

"*Ah!* Jesus!" The figure dragged its hands down the sides of its face, scooping the seething creatures into both fists. The man looked down at his clenched hands, almost as if he saw what they contained. "*What?*" he cried, though if his mouth gaped in horror, Trenor couldn't see the opening for all those swarming bodies.

He exploded awake, and looking into the darkness all around him, cried out again, "Oh God!"

A few moments later, Thanh was silhouetted in his doorway. "Rick? Are you okay?"

Trenor lay there with his nerves jumping under his skin. Already he'd forgotten most of his dream, besides the image of that thick black mask of tiny, busy demons. He didn't even remember the name "Bedford."

Weirdly, at this moment at the forefront of his memories was the little Tunnel Rat named Castillo. They used Mexican Americans like him and Alvarez because they were small. He remembered Castillo, all too vividly, thrusting a finger at him and joking, "Beware of darkness."

Castillo, who hadn't lived to escape that last tunnel they'd gone down into together. As if he might still be under the earth somewhere, in spirit, to this day...crawling, blind and lost, forever trying to find his way to the surface.

4: DEATH SENTENCE

QUAN HAD GONE OFF ON his motorbike to get them three servings of *pho ga*, chicken noodle soup, for their breakfast, leaving Trenor and Thanh seated alone at the kitchen's glass table. Thanh had asked the older man what he'd been dreaming about last night. Trenor told him, honestly, how he couldn't remember. Just that head entirely composed of the insect-like creatures that he, and apparently he alone, could see.

"I need to know where Long Dien lives," Trenor told him gravely. "You don't know, do you?"

"No. In Saigon somewhere."

"Would Tra Mi have it written down in a book or something, in her room?"

"No...I doubt it, Rick. She probably didn't even know where he lives."

"That girl Hoa...the one who Long Dien hit, for giving you his number. Might she know?"

"Probably, but oh, I don't think she would tell us, after what happened to her last time."

"Well, she might want revenge because of last time. And if we offered her some money..."

"I still think she would be too afraid to help us. She might even tell him we were asking about it, to show him that she's loyal to him."

"Then it looks like we might just have to follow him home. Either from his coffee shop here, or that hair salon in Saigon you told me about. Did you say you know where that is?"

"Yes, I do know. And he spends more time there than at the coffee shop. Following him from the Angel Spa to his home would be easier, too, than following him from Bien Hoa to his home in Saigon."

Trenor nodded, looking down at his reflection in the table's glass. Seeing his patch-eyed face there stirred vague, half-remembered fragments from his dream, as if he looked past his reflection into a stagnant pool, at the bottom of which swam indistinct shapes like black koi fish. If only he could get his hands around one of those elusive shapes, drag it into the light. Something about a mirror? Something about the ruin of his right eye?

"God," he sighed, "I really don't want to take you with me when I talk to him, but without you, he and I can't understand each other." He met Thanh's gaze. "I don't much care what happens to me, anymore. I have no woman waiting for me back in the States. No job, now. No plans…no dreams. But you…you're young. You've never hurt anybody like I have. Like your old man has. You aren't tainted. I don't want to get you fucked…either with some bad guys, or by the police."

"I'm not afraid."

"Oh, I know you're not, my friend. I know you're not. That's the problem." Trenor sipped the iced coffee Quan had made for him before setting out. "At this point, don't you think it might be better to turn this over to the police? Tell them what we've found out, and all our suspicions, and let them interrogate Long Dien?"

"I'm sorry, Rick, but I told you," Thanh said, shaking his head empathically, "the police here are corrupt. Long Dien has more money than you do. He can bribe policemen to find some reason to charge *you* with a crime, or at least get you kicked out of the country. Then they might come after me and my father."

"But if we go see Long Dien, and I have to get rough with him—which I probably would, to get anything valuable out of him—I'm afraid afterwards the same thing will happen to you and your father."

"My father's not afraid of that, either. We only care about justice for Hang Ni." After a moment Thanh added, as if reluctantly, "And Trai Mi."

"You two throwing yourselves into the volcano doesn't work for me," Trenor said. He leaned forward with his arms on the table, and lowered his voice as if someone might be listening in, like that neighborhood police informant "007." "We may never know who, exactly, killed Hang Ni. No matter how I threaten him, or hurt him, Long Dien might not give up the name. And there's a good chance that person's not even in this country anymore. But we can assume that Long Dien set it up—put Hang Ni in that room with some sick john. With Tra Mi's help…but Tra Mi's already paid for that. So let me ask you this." He drew in a long breath. He could hardly believe he was going to say what he was going to say. "The easiest thing to do now might be…might be…" He paused, chewed his upper lip. "Would it satisfy you if we never found out who it was that killed Hang Ni, but we made Long Dien pay for it?"

"Do you mean… Pay for it how, Rick?"

"If I killed him."

"Oh," Thanh said, sitting back in his chair. "Yes…yes, I would feel Hang Ni was avenged if Long Dien died. Even if we're wrong, and Long Dien didn't arrange it, he's a man who deserves to die. But you told my father you wouldn't kill him! If you do that, you could be throwing your own life away. Rick, you don't want to end up in a Vietnamese prison. Believe me…you don't."

"I didn't say I'd be stupid about it. But if I did that, you wouldn't be coming with me. I'd let you help me get close, but you wouldn't be watching it go down."

"Rick...this is too much."

"Is it?" he said. "Thanh, when I came here you asked me how many men I've killed. You asked me here because you *knew* I've killed before. Don't act surprised if it comes to this now. You don't have to put on a big show of morality, man. It's just the two of us."

"It isn't about morality, Rick—it's just about you." Thanh drew in a long breath through his nose, then nodded grimly. "Okay...okay. But first, before you do this, at least try to get a name from him. So I have to be there, to translate."

"Absolutely not. You can't be there. I can't put you at risk like that. Just get me to his house."

"Rick..."

Trenor raised an open palm. "That's the only way it can be, Thanh. Final. You can't be in that room with us."

They heard Quan returning on his motorbike. Trenor picked up his coffee again, as if it were a prop, as if to pretend all he'd been doing while Quan was away was innocently enjoying his beverage. Quan came into the house carrying plastic bags full of broth, meat, leaves and bean sprouts to break into the broth, tiny packets of hoisin and hot sauce.

While Quan combined these components into three good-sized if mismatched bowls set between Thanh and Trenor, the two friends stared at each other across the glass table. Trenor felt sick for what he'd told Thanh he thought he must do. Not because he felt that it was wrong that Long Dien should die. He simply wished that Thanh would have remained uncorrupted, could have gone on into the future without blood on him. Not just blood on his misshapen hands, directly, but blood spattered on him by proximity.

Then again, he supposed that blood had already been spattered on him, indelibly, from the moment Thanh had learned of his little sister's fate.

0: INFESTED

BEDFORD LEANED IN CLOSE TO his hotel room's little bathroom mirror, running a finger through his right eyebrow. It was threaded with white hairs, more than he'd consciously been aware of before. This depressed him, in a fatalistic way. Time, catching up. There was so little time, in the end. He'd hoped for more of that resource in which to...to do whatever it was that people did to fill their life. Perhaps time in which to attain a greater fulfillment than he had heretofore known. If *fulfillment* wasn't just something TV commercials touted to sell products. Products like shiny cars, shiny hair, shiny happiness. But, as time had stretched on, like putty that must eventually snap through strain, his dreams for such fulfillment had proved increasingly unrealistic. Not to mention, increasingly amorphous, unrecognizable even to himself.

Well, this was an unexpected side effect of killing others, wasn't it? Becoming more acutely aware of his own fragile mortality.

He wished he had a double-sided handheld mirror that could magnify what he was seeing. Not that he was seeing anything. Though he'd awakened this morning covered in pinpricks of itchiness, he had as yet not discovered lice in his eyebrows, or in the hair of his head, or in his pubic hair...however little he could see of his pubic hair, beyond the curve of his pallid belly.

Still, he was convinced they were there, as yet undetected, the sly bastards. Under his breath he said, "That dirty little whore. This is her revenge on me. Bugs are a dish best served cold, huh, my dear?"

He showered, shampooed his scalp and crotch vigorously, scrunched his eyes shut and rubbed his eyebrows under the blasting hot water. He dressed in clean clothes, stuffed yesterday's attire down into a plastic basket to be laundered by hotel staff. He summoned them on the phone, and when a woman came to his room he pointed accusingly toward his bed. "Change the sheets, okay?"

The woman nodded obediently, went to the bed, and he watched her strip the pillows and mattress. She was in her thirties, blocky but attractive enough if one was desperate enough, but she didn't trigger his hunger particularly. It was just as well. It was too soon to hop to another hotel.

He went on down to a room off the tiny lobby, where a complimentary breakfast could be ordered. From a limited menu of offerings, which included chicken noodle soup, slices of toast, and fried eggs, Bedford ordered an omelet. It irritated him that the omelet didn't come with toast, but he decided not to make waves. He was a quiet man by nature, in his life had always flown under the radar. He ordered iced coffee as his beverage.

While he ate, despite his shower he still felt a tickle of movement through his eyebrows, through the hair rooted at his forehead. He reached up, itched, but leaned back in his seat as he did so to prevent these pests, if dislodged, from falling into his meal. He'd need some medicated shampoo to deal with these creatures, if such things were available here. He felt strands of his pubic hair being stirred, reached surreptitiously under the table to scratch at his crotch through his khakis. Increasingly, he felt ready to jump out of his skin. Was this what delirium tremens was like?

He fought for control, stubbornly continued eating. As he chewed, he reflected on a dream he had experienced last night.

He'd been standing at a window in a room somewhere, looking through its glass down at the street. There, he'd been watching a stream of Vietnamese schoolgirls as they paraded past along the sidewalk, all of these teenagers dressed in a virginal white *ao dai*. God, the perfection! Could such a thing be surpassed: a schoolgirl in an *ao dai*, clinging to her slender waist, flowing from her narrow hips? The side notches teasing hints of midriff? The sleek spill of long hair, often dyed reddish? Each of them shaped like a candle flame; just as bright, just as ephemeral.

But then, he'd been rudely interrupted by someone behind him, lying in a bed. (A hospital bed, given the grotesque appearance of the speaker when he saw him?) The two of them had talked a bit... About what? He couldn't recall their dream exchange, now. Only, he'd finally given in and turned to look down at this man lying there, and he vaguely recalled seeing that the man—a Caucasian—possessed no right eye. Only a shallow depression of bare flesh, a shadowed hollow.

Polyphemus, he now thought. The cyclops. Had he said that to the dream stranger?

Bedford finished his meal, smiled and nodded politely at the old woman who came to clear his table, got up and contemplated going outside...to do what? Shop? Wander, explore? Visit one of the city's numerous museums, or the zoo? Maybe get some coffee? But he'd already had coffee.

He ended up simply returning to his hotel room, and there in privacy he scratched at himself without restraint. He stripped himself free of his clean clothes, again did his best to examine his pubic hair, head hair, eyebrows.

"Fuck," he whispered, itching hard, feeling through his hairline, around his balls. "*Fuck!* This fucking dirty country! Stupid whore!"

He put on the hotel room's wall-mounted TV—settling on some recent, unfamiliar Hollywood movie on HBO Asia—but he immediately turned away from it and paced naked back and forth from the little entrance hallway to the windows at the room's far end, which looked down into the street. The windows had heavy curtains, glittery metallic gold, which bore a red imprint of full lips where some woman who had stayed here previously had blotted her lipstick. In a flurry of imagination, he pictured several sordid scenes. Money exchanged for flesh. The tears of a frustrated mistress. Before drawing the curtains aside for a better view, Bedford leaned down and pressed his own lips to this red impression.

He saw some Christmas decorations down in the street, already taking on the sad aspect of holiday accoutrements overstaying their welcome, neglected and obsolete, luster fading. Time caught up with him in a jarring rush, as if he'd been sleeping, hibernating, too long. He remembered that Christmas had passed.

He thought, as if in dialogue with himself: *"I didn't get anything for my wife. I guess my gift to her is that I'm here, not there. If I was there…well…ha! If I was there…at this point…maybe it would be* her *I'd be chewing."*

God…*itchy!*

"Fuck, fuck, fuck!" he cried out loud, veering from the window and stomping toward the bathroom.

Bedford's razor rested on the edge of the sink. He first jetted some white foam into his left hand, then he spread this messily across his eyebrows before he took up the razor.

He chuckled as he scraped with bold strokes. "*Yeah*, fuckers! Nowhere to run, nowhere to hide!"

He shaved his eyebrows away entirely, down to the bone ridges. Raw red and shining.

Then, he raked away his pubic hair. It hurt—he wished he had scissors, and might he have called downstairs to borrow a pair?—but he managed it. He shaved his crotch bare. "Like a porn star," he snorted, in pain, trying not to get loud, lest there be a tenant in a room to either side. He'd always disliked seeing men with shaved crotches in porn when he watched it on his PC. Too feminine, like those young men who waxed/shaped their eyebrows. He *despised* that, almost violently so. He could excuse himself, however. His situation was another matter.

But he didn't shave his head bald. That was a bit extreme. He wasn't ready for that.

Not yet.

PART 12: THE ART OF DYING

1: WHITE MAN'S SKULL

TRENOR HAD SLUNG HIMSELF ONTO the motorbike behind Thanh, and rather than hold onto the young man's waist like a lover, he reached both hands behind him to grip the rear of the seat. He felt awkward, being so much larger than Thanh, but knew it was foolish to be concerned about appearances. Hell, there were so many large-bodied tourists in this country, fucking young women, fucking young men. Anonymous and forgettable. Wasn't it just as well he blended in with them? On his head he wore a spare helmet, which felt too small for his white man's skull.

Thanh had found out the closing time of the salon—called the Angel Spa— in Ho Chi Minh City. Quan having made sure their bellies were full first, they set out from Bien Hoa at nine thirty, knowing that the Angel Spa would shut down at half past eleven tonight. As late as that might sound, Thanh assured Trenor that given the neighborhood there were salons that stayed open even later.

Air broke across Trenor's face along the long ride, as if divided across the blade of his nose. This sensation—and the vibration of the machine he straddled, and the concern that his ungainly weight might cause this bike to topple to one side and slide into oblivion—made him feel more weirdly *alive* than he had felt in decades, maybe. Since when he had crawled into tunnels with a flashlight in one hand, a revolver in the other.

Before they got too far, though, Thanh pulled his Honda to a stop in front of a bank in Bien Hoa so that Trenor could extract money from an ATM.

In the USA, Trenor's bank imposed a limit on how much money he could withdraw in a single day. At this ATM, however, he found he could withdraw a certain amount, then this amount again, and again, as he reintroduced his debit card. He took a good chunk out of his savings before they continued on toward Ho Chi Minh City. His meager life savings. All he had to show for providing toilets and chairs too unwelcoming to linger on.

It didn't matter. What was there to save for? His unrealized children's education? Some fantasy retirement, fishing along dappled forest riverbanks? He'd never liked fishing. He'd killed men, but he still hated to see the stare of fish suffocating in dry air. Hell, he'd fished once with a friend at the other's insistence, cast his line and snagged it in a branch, watched his hooked nightcrawler hang there and slowly die and wither in the sun over the next few hours, and it had nagged him with guilt. He even hated remembering it now. Guilt over accidentally killing an earthworm.

Before setting out this evening from the house in Bien Hoa, in a lowered voice Trenor had asked Thanh if Quan owned a gun.

"Oh no, Rick, it's not easy to have a gun in Vietnam now. For my father, especially! Because of his past. Sometimes people *make* their own guns, with plastic tubes. They use—I don't know how to say it. Bottled air? And they shoot small glass balls, like children play with."

"Marbles. Yeah…never mind," Trenor had said to him. He'd felt a black despair that was almost physically nauseating—and again, a surreal disbelief—that he was saying the things he was saying. "What do you have for knives?"

"We have knives," Thanh had confirmed.

2: CLOSING TIME

DIRECTLY ACROSS THE STREET FROM the Angel Spa in Ho Chi Minh City was a little restaurant/pub, its menu presented on a kind of podium on the sidewalk. White tourists in shorts and flip-flops, the men bespectacled and balding and/or white-haired, their wives at least not balding, sat at a few rickety wooden tables out front on the sidewalk. Just inside, behind a wall of glass, were more tables up on an elevated floor. At the back of the shallow room, a staircase gave access to an upper level with more tables on a balcony, and another level was above that, but Trenor chose a table directly behind the wall of glass. They could see the spa across the street just fine from in here. To satisfy the pub's owners, they ordered drinks and a few snacks to nibble on. Thanh had a local soft drink called Sting, while Trenor ordered a Tiger beer, but he nursed it slowly.

This was Bui Vien Street, known to tourists from around the world as Walking Street, where one walked and gawked, hungered and consumed, and it looked to Trenor to be almost entirely composed of bars and restaurants along its garish length.

Trenor had never been here before, and it exceeded anything he had witnessed on R&R in his days as a young soldier. It was an assault on the senses, though he'd be a hypocrite if he said it was actually an unpleasant assault. What man, unless lying even to himself, wouldn't admit to being dazzled by the fantastically colored chaos of lighted signs, the thud of techno music accentuating one's heartbeat and one's stride, the overlapping and tantalizing aromas of food, the ubiquitous display of taut healthy flesh? For young women in miniskirts stood in little packs, or sat on tiny plastic chairs, in front of establishment after establishment, handing out flyers and menus and coaxing men to come inside clubs and massage parlors. He saw a trio of beauties dressed in red and yellow uniforms, with cute little caps, advertising Amstel Beer. Hunger he had long fought to suppress stirred on the floor of his belly like a dumped bucket of eels. He tried to stop noticing all these women. He made himself think of the exploitation, and death, of Hang Ni and Tra Mi. Yes. That helped counteract things a lot.

Just as Thanh had parked their motorbike on the sidewalk, tightly wedged with others in front of a roller shutter a bit further down from the pub, they had been approached by a tired-looking young woman selling souvenirs and such from a tray she carried in front of her that must seem like a part of her body by now. From her, Trenor had directed Thanh to buy a cheap pair of sunglasses with thick frames and extra dark lenses. He pocketed his eye patch, slipped these glasses on instead. He said to Thanh, "I wear my sunglasses at night." The young man didn't catch the reference.

In keeping with his effort to make them go unnoticed in all this bedlam, when they were seated inside the pub Trenor nodded at his friend's hands and said, "Keep your mitts under the table, pal."

Thanh looked down at his hands, resting on his knees. "Huh? Oh...yes. They do look like baseball mitts, yes."

"Oh God, man, that's not what I meant," Trenor said, reaching out to put a hand on his arm. "It's just a saying. It means *hands*, that's all. You know me better than that, Thanh."

The son of his old friend smiled. "I do know you, Rick."

Trenor gazed out through the glass, toward the salon. It was packed between a Western-geared pizza place on its right, and on its left, an art gallery that sold mass-produced paintings, many of them quite impressive from what he could discern of those displayed out front. The salon's face was a wall of glass, too, behind which he saw women either moving or lounging about, all of them wearing identical uniforms of white tube tops and miniskirts overlaid with a flower pattern. He spotted no men in there, from here, besides a few customers reclining far back in chairs, administered to by a number of those sexily attired women. On the sidewalk out front was a sizable artificial Christmas tree, though Christmas had passed now. Wow, it had, hadn't it? Once Christmas had meant something to Trenor. Now, living in solitude in the USA, and as distant from there as he was at this moment, it seemed as alien to him as some Buddhist festival. And his brother in Vancouver, with whom he had originally hoped to spend this Christmas—right now that person seemed to him like some friend he'd met on the internet, but never in person.

The salon closed at eleven thirty. Thanh had asked their waitress about the pub, and been told it would close up at one in the morning. That was good.

As they killed time, Trenor nodded at Thanh's can of Sting soda and said, "Every breath you take, I'll be watching you."

"Hm?" Thanh said, still not getting the references. Trenor shook his head and sipped his Tiger. He looked at his watch. Thanh noticed and asked, "What time is it now, Rick?"

"Five past eleven. Keep your eyes peeled. Uh...that means, keep your eyes open. Don't take me so literally, okay?" Trenor looked out through the glass again, the commotion of lights muted by his sunglasses, and thank God the long-legged bodies of Vietnamese women—not to mention those of tall and athletic young European backpackers in short shorts—shadowed from his view by his lenses, also. Oh, the damned human body and its instincts, each cell of it like some yapping dog on its own straining leash. What good came of it all, except the reproduction of more conglomerations of yapping cells?

"Oh, Rick...look," Thanh said.

Three young women, in those identical outfits, emerged from the salon even as a taxi pulled up out front. They piled in after each other, and the taxi continued on.

"Uh-huh," Trenor said. "Yeah. It's already starting to thin out in there. Let's just hope he's inside, still. For all we know, he left hours ago...or maybe he was somewhere else today. Maybe even back in that coffee place in Bien Hoa. We won't know until they lock up."

Thanh turned to look at the American. Trenor didn't notice this, still staring intently out the window.

Trenor mused, as if talking to himself, "When he comes out—*if* he comes out—it might be hard keeping up with him in all this confusion, whether he's on a bike or in a car. But then again, nobody can move fast in this street. It's mostly pedestrians; wall-to-wall. Because of that, we should be able to keep up. Then, once we're out of this area..." He nodded. He was gazing out into the street through his own reflection, its eye sockets black, a skull-like illusion created by his sunglasses.

Thanh was still staring at him. He realized his own eyes were capped in tears. "Rick." He had to say it again, to get his attention. "Rick."

Trenor heard him at last, looked around. "Yeah?"

"You have your knife?"

"Yeah, of course, the one you gave me." Trenor patted his right leg, a deep pocket of his khakis. "And you have yours?"

"Yes."

"Not that I want you to use it, but it's still a good idea to have it, just in case...whatever." Trenor belatedly caught the look in his eyes. "Are you afraid?"

"Let's go home," Thanh said. "Let's go home, now."

"What? What are you talking about?"

"My sisters are gone. There is no getting them back. All we can do is lose ourselves, too. I pulled you into this, Rick. I curse myself for pulling you into this. I can't let you join my sisters' fate. You're just going to kill yourself. I can't do that to you. I can't let you do that to yourself." The tears, now, broke free and coursed down his face. "We need to go home. To Bien Hoa. And you need to go home...to the USA."

Trenor leaned close to him across their sticky table and whispered, "What the fuck are you saying, man? We didn't come this far to back off now. I understand what you're trying to do...oh, yeah. We can't do anything, it's pointless, so I go home...then you go after Long Dien and whoever else on your own. *No.* No way. We are in this…*I'm* in this. There is no going home, Thanh. Not for me."

"Rick." Thanh half-sobbed his name.

Trenor shot back the last third of his beer, motioned to the waitress with his empty bottle. "Another," he said to her.

Thanh said, "It's over."

"Fuck you, it's over," Trenor hissed through gritted teeth. "It's over when the blood of Long Dien is running through my fucking fingers. I want you and your dad to know that it's *done*. You talk about sharing your sisters' fate? Well, okay, yeah, this *is* our fate, man. This is what we were born to act out. It's why we are *here*, on this street, on this night, right *now*." He jabbed their table with a finger. "This was my real mission in your country, all along. Thanh…you can go home. But I can't go home. Do you understand that?"

Thanh sat up straighter in his chair, and though his face was still slick with tears, a hard look came into his eyes. His upper lip curled when he again spoke. "There's something *you* need to understand, Rick. Something you need to remember. Like I said before…I called you here. This was my idea. This is *my* operation. I began it…and now I'm calling it off." This time it was he who jabbed one of his digits against the table top, unconcerned with who might see his malformed hands. "This is my family. These were my sisters. And this is over."

Though unseen behind his dark glasses, now it was Trenor's left eye that filmed over moistly. He sat quiet for long seconds, at first showing no acknowledgement when the waitress put in front of him the fresh bottle of Tiger he had ordered. Finally, though, he seemed to notice it, picked it up and took a sip. Then he said, "You're a tough little fucker, like your dumbass father. I always knew better than to piss him off, and I guess I'd better not piss you off, either." He took a deeper gulp of beer. "You're right. This was always your operation. You're in command. And I have to respect that."

They sat and drank their drinks in near silence for a while, until activity across the street drew their attention. More of the salon girls leaving, along with a couple of straggler customers. Some of the young women walked off in groups, others seated themselves on the backs of their boyfriends' motorbikes when they arrived. And at last, a car pulled up in front of the salon: a Chinese sedan called a Lifan 520. Trenor didn't know the car's make himself, though, any more than he knew its driver was named Hiep and that Hiep was the young son of one of Long Dien's cousins.

"Are you sure?" Trenor said to Thanh.

"Yes, Rick. Sure."

The salon's lights were extinguished, and the last one out through its glass doors was Long Dien, dressed in a short-sleeved white dress shirt and white trousers. Rather than sit up front in the passenger's seat, he got in back as if Hiep were merely a chauffeur and not family. But first, he held the door open for the last of the salon girls to have exited the Angel Spa.

"Just as well," Trenor said, lifting his beer again, to finish it. "I definitely wouldn't have wanted to have to kill his girl, too."

They heard the sedan's door slam shut, watched it crawl away along Walking Street, which was still thronged even now at eleven thirty, nosing carefully through the massed bodies. After a while, no matter how slowly the vehicle was forced to move, they lost sight of it. Long Dien was gone.

Trenor sighed, set down his empty bottle, and said, "Told you I'm not much of a drinker, but I think I'm going to have a third, if that's all right with you. I'll be going home soon, and I might never have the chance to drink with you again."

Thanh got their waitress' attention and ordered two more Tigers. He explained to Trenor, "I'm not a drinker either, Rick, but I want to drink a beer with you. Like you say, it may be the only beer I ever have with you."

"Sounds good, buddy."

"Of course," Thanh said, "you could always come live here in Vietnam. Think about it. A lot of Vietnamese who live in the USA come here when they retire. It's cheaper to live here."

"Yeah, of course it is. And the food is good. And the ladies are unsurpassed. And the people are friendly. Most of you, anyway." He smiled. "I guess a guy could live like a king here. Though I imagine the government would make a US citizen jump through a shit-ton of hoops to do it."

"Maybe. But there are many expats who live here. Mostly Australians, I think, but Russians too, and others. I personally know of an Italian man who owns a restaurant in Vung Tau, and a Spanish woman who owns a restaurant in Saigon, and there's a French man who owns a café right in Bien Hoa. He's very friendly; we've spoken before. If they can do it…"

"Ha. I'll bear it in mind…I'll bear it in mind. We'll see what happens when I qualify for my social security."

"I'm sorry what I said, when I said this is about my family, Rick," Thanh told him. "You are my family, too."

Trenor nodded. "I'm honored. That's what this was all about, then. I'm happy that I didn't come here for nothing."

"You helped me find Tra Mi. You helped me piece things together, as much as we could do that. And maybe you helped my father value me a little more."

"I hope so, man."

Thanh shook his head. "This was not for nothing."

3: DOUBLE TAP

A WALL SURROUNDED LONG DIEN'S house, the broken bottoms of glass bottles set into cement along its upper edge. In front was a gate of metal bars, and Hiep exited the idling Chinese sedan to go and unlock it. From the car's back seat, Long Dien saw Hiep stand at the gate a moment, confused, before pushing it open on squealing hinges. Then the tall, spiky-haired young man returned to the car and climbed back in. "Guess I forgot to lock it before," he said in Vietnamese.

"It's open?" Long Dien leaned forward in his seat and slapped his cousin's son, but not too roughly, across the back of his head. "Be more careful!"

Hiep grumbled something as he eased the car through the open gate. He shut the motor off, went back to close the gate again while Long Dien slipped from the car and held the door open for the salon girl to slide her bottom across the seat and emerge. She was named Linh, a new hire, and thus his current favorite. She had a third nipple, as fully formed and puffy as the upper two, halfway down her ribcage, and he found this oddly enticing.

Hiep looked at the ground around him for the missing padlock, but he didn't see it, and rather than endure another slap and more demeaning scolding from his boss, he simply pulled the gate shut for now and said nothing. If it didn't turn up, he'd buy a new padlock tomorrow.

He turned to see Long Dien leading Linh into the house, and hastened to catch up to them. He had his own room in his parents' home, but he sometimes slept here when it was more convenient and would do so tonight…though he'd rather it was him, and not Long Dien, who'd be warming a mattress with pretty Linh.

Once Hiep was inside the front room, he slid shut the glass door they had come through. He assumed Long Dien had just switched the light on. Long Dien, in turn, thought Hiep had earlier forgotten to turn the light off.

The front room was a dining room, with a long wooden table as glossy and intricately carved as the facing rows of chairs placed along its length, both table and chairs inset with designs in mother of pearl. A thick sheet of glass protected the top of the table, and the only items resting atop this, Hiep saw, were the front gate's padlock and the long-bladed screwdriver that had been used to force it open.

That was what Hiep focused on. For his part, Long Dien noticed there was a third motorbike parked in here alongside his own two. Bikes were brought in at night to thwart theft. His own bikes were expensive, modern, colorful and clean. Beside them, though, leaned an unfamiliar bike, older and much uglier in aspect. Long Dien didn't know this was a bike the American had borrowed from his maternal uncle, but he knew it portended something bad, and he was already turning toward a curtained doorway as the American slipped into the front room.

"Oh, hey, my friend—*no...no...no!*" Long Dien cried, shooting out a hand as if that might ward him off, banish the American back into the adjoining room's darkness. For he saw that the American held a semiautomatic pistol at the end of his leading arm.

It was young Hiep he shot first, however. One bullet smashed into the narrow space between Hiep's nose and upper lip. The second, fired immediately after the first in a "double tap," tore into his face beside his nose. Before he had even fallen to the floor, Hiep had been remade into a much different and unfamiliar being. On his way down, he bounced off the edge of the dining room table so that he spun and landed hard on that reconfigured face.

Linh had barely opened her mouth to scream, and had begun to lunge for the sliding glass door that would take her back outside, when the American pivoted his handgun her way. She had several feet to cover, his arm only inches. At least she had managed to wheel her body away from him, so that the first bullet to hit her did so in the back of her neck. It emerged, in a flower of unfurled red petals, from the front of her throat. The second projectile of this double tap struck her square in the rear of her skull. She seemed to throw herself across the seat of that grubby incongruous bike. There she remained draped, rump in the air, bare heels risen from her shoes, and her blood pouring noisily to the tiled floor.

Another quick adjustment of the American's arm. A third double tap, just as Long Dien was finishing his "*no...no...no!*"

The initial bullet tore straight through his outthrust hand—into the palm and out the other side, as in some modern-day stigmata—before it lodged itself in the edge of Long Dien's jaw. These wounds wouldn't have killed him, but the next slug passed through the space between the thumb and forefinger of his pierced hand, and drove itself through the bridge of Long Dien's nose. His head snapped backwards, and when he crashed onto the floor the back of his skull smacked against the tiles with a sound that would have made another man's guts clench in horror.

The American had peripherally noticed Kate pushing through the curtain behind him. He had brought her here with him because—though she had witnessed Chen's killing, had in fact lured Chen to his death, and was thus already implicated in his actions—it appeared she required further incentive to never think of betraying him again. If they were to be together, if this were going to be something more serious than he had ever allowed himself before, she must have enough blood on her that they were truly bonded. This purging was their rite of marriage, the dead their witnesses. She might not like it this way, but he would soon remind her that it was better than him emptying the last two bullets in the Black Star's magazine into her head, as he had contemplated doing earlier tonight before setting out to come here.

Looking down at Long Dien's sprawled body—the other two bodies were just incidental—he said to his former associate, "You were stupid and careless, and dangerous to me, my friend. And you were always easily replaced." He began turning toward Kate. He was going to tell her that they should hurry out of here, now, in case someone summoned the police about the gunshots, and in case the police cared enough to respond. He was going to tell her—though maybe later, when they were safely back in his uncle's place—that he was still undecided as to whether he needed to treat that one-eyed American and the freak boy to their own double taps, too.

Having turned, he saw that Kate had plucked from the table the screwdriver that he had used to force open the padlock to the front gate. She had it in her fist and her arm was cocked back beside her head as her body lurched toward him.

"Hey!" he cried.

He wanted to tell Kate that he didn't intend to kill her, too…though in that moment he realized this was what she believed. Believed that because she had sought to betray him, she was no longer anything special—just another loose end to tie up tonight. Another person to punish for violating his personal code.

Despite the Black Star still having those last two bullets in its magazine, he couldn't get the gun centered on her in time. The tip of the screwdriver punched through his right eyeball. The force of her strike, further propelled by her body's forward momentum, spiked the screwdriver's blade all the way through the orb and on through the bone of his eye socket.

He fell backwards to the floor, and she fell atop his body like a wildly passionate lover.

Kate got her left hand onto the butt of the screwdriver, to aid her right hand in grinding the blade deeper. She put the weight of her chest behind the effort. She screamed as she did this, as if her cry too would further impel the blade.

The American tried to turn his head away, to one side or the other, but it was pinned. His mouth stretched wide but the sound that emerged from that unnatural cavern was weak in contrast. Kate saw him attempting to turn the pistol toward her. She took her left hand off the screwdriver, reached over and grasped his wrist. It was easy to restrain it. Just to be safe, however, she rolled to that side, took her right hand off the screwdriver's handle. Anyway, the blade was fully embedded in him now, only the handle protruding from his eyeball as the ruptured sphere seemed to gaze into the clear yellow plastic. She held onto his wrist in both hands now, expecting him to squeeze off a final shot, if only toward that curtained adjoining room. But no further shots proved forthcoming.

Kate finally let go of his arm. No more attempts at turning his head, no more strangled sounds from the gaping mouth. She knew she didn't even have to pry the pistol from his hand. As she scrambled to her feet, she looked down at herself. Of course there was blood on her, but fortunately not as much as there might have been, and it was dark out there in the night.

She felt no regret, gazing down at his body for a stolen moment. She had never really believed him, back at Dai Nam, about wanting to take her to the USA. She'd known that at some point she'd need to escape him. Even then, she'd thought that she might have to escape him in this way.

She extracted his wallet, careful to avoid stepping into pooling blood. Took all the money that was in it. She'd be needing it. She'd be needing to leave Saigon for a while. Well, anyway, her family lived out in the sticks of Chau Doc, near the border with Cambodia. She wouldn't get all the way there tonight, but she'd get there.

Heeding the American's words about the threat of police, as swiftly as possible Kate wheeled his uncle's borrowed bike out of the house via a metal ramp laid across the front steps, and into the courtyard. After opening the barred front gate, she swung herself astride the motorbike, roused its motor, and buzzed out into the street, where the night soon took her into its sheltering folds.

PART 13: AN ENORMOUS DARKNESS

1: THE MIRROR, PART 2

"WHERE DID YOU GO TONIGHT?" Quan asked them when they returned to the house in Bien Hoa. He'd been sitting outside, smoking, when they'd pulled up on Thanh's bike. Obviously he hadn't slept, though it was now in the early hours. At least, Trenor noted, he was sober. He saw Quan kick away a huge cockroach that scuttled too close to his sandaled foot. They came up at night through the cracks between the removable plates that made up the sidewalks around here, so as to give access to water lines. Trenor thought of the insect-things he saw, wondered if they similarly lived in hidden dark passageways within every human being, himself included, waiting for the conditions that called them up into the open air.

He thumped Quan on the shoulder as he walked past him. He was dead tired. "We were drinking beer. You jealous?"

Thanh passed Quan next, and they exchanged looks. Thanh smiled. Quan asked his son no further questions, but Thanh felt that someday soon—probably after their friend had returned to the USA—he would tell his father what had transpired this night. And what hadn't.

After emptying his bladder and brushing his teeth, Trenor went up to Tra Mi's room and soon lay on its mattress in absolute blackness. He was idly wondering what day this was, how many days remained until 2011, if it wasn't already 2011, when sleep caught him unawares, a booby trap he dropped into. A soft pit, but deep.

After a time, he rumpled his face in irritation against an odd green glow that penetrated his left eyelid. He opened his lone eye to see a figure standing in front of the bedroom's full-length mirror. Tra Mi, insecure about her looks, had often stood regarding herself here. This intruding figure, not Tra Mi, was nonetheless familiar, though Trenor couldn't make out its face. Had it been completely naked the last time he'd encountered it in dream? As he had forgotten that earlier dream upon waking, he couldn't be sure. In any case, the figure was naked now, its wide pimpled back and lumpy buttocks pallid in that unearthly illumination—though again, its head lost in shadow.

"Read much?" the figure said to him without looking around.

"Read what?" Trenor replied warily from the mattress. "The Bible? The funny papers?"

"I find my memory's better when I'm asleep," the stranger said. "The conscious mind…it's too cluttered, too distracted." Then he recited, "*It was almost as though I had been killed. Indeed, I could imagine a man suddenly and violently killed would feel very much as I did. One moment, a passion of agonizing existence and fear; the next darkness and stillness, neither light nor life nor sun, moon nor stars, the blank infinite.*" He paused to sigh, as if moved by the words. "*I felt astonished, dumbfounded, and overwhelmed. I seemed to be borne upward into an enormous darkness.*"

"Who said that?"

"Mr. Wells, of course. *First Men in the Moon.*"

"Huh. Saw the movie."

"You did?" The stranger turned then, excited, and his half-step brought his faceless face into the dim fungal glow. His head was completely, thickly layered in an uncountable congregation of scrambling bodies, like spiders or ants but something less terrestrial, less benign. He had no features…only these things, it seemed, to see for him with their accumulated eyes.

This time Trenor didn't cry out in horror at the sight of this mask. Without remembering, he recognized it. A name almost came to him, slippery through his mind's fingers. *Bedlam?*

"You're…itchy," Trenor said. Even he didn't know if that were a memory, or some kind of command.

"Yes! *Yes!*" hissed the faceless man, tensing up his naked body as if he might leap toward the mattress. "It's making me *crazy!* Do you understand? I shaved off my eyebrows. My fucking pubic hair. Today I went to a salon and I had them shave my head bald. I had to tell the bitch ten times to shave my fucking head completely *bald!*" He was almost shouting. "She just didn't get it! But it's still itching! It itches under my skin…under every goddamn inch of my skin! Especially here." He slapped his cheeks with the fingers of both hands. Somehow, none of the spider-things were jarred free to drop to the floor. "They're all over my face! All over *inside* my face!"

"What's your name?"

"I told you before. Last time."

"I don't remember that."

"Me either!" the faceless man cried, in a wild laugh. "Me either, Polyphemus! Hey, did you ever see the movie *Ulysses* with Kirk Douglas? I loved movies like that as a kid…loved them! They stirred my imagination. Real life just doesn't hold up to that stuff, does it? Just doesn't fucking compare. So boring. So empty. *The blank infinite.*"

"You killed Hang Ni."

The faceless man seemed not to hear him now, to speak only to himself. He turned back to the mirror. "After my haircut—ha, well, after I got myself shaved today—I went to an ATM where you can take out money again and again and again. The bank thought it was suspicious activity, though, and they blocked me, so I went to an internet café and had to go online and tell them those were my transactions. Then I took out more money and more money before my wife could notice and block my account or something. It won't last me forever, but it'll last me for a while. It's cheap living here, you know? I'll just have to fly under the radar, right? So they don't know my visa's expired. Can't go back now, can I? Can't ever go back."

"Come see me when I'm awake," Trenor said to him. "Maybe I can help you."

"*Help* me? Oh! Ha! Yes…oh, I'm sure you would! I'm sure you would help me, Polyphemus."

"You're itchy," Trenor said, menacingly. He liked hearing the man say that. He wanted him to say it again. To go on feeling it.

"Oh…my God, yes, it's terrible!" the stranger blurted, leaning in closer to the mirror. "Terrible! Jesus, look at me! I can't even see me! Oh my God…*oh God!*"

He lashed out then, punched the mirror, and it shattered. Heedless of the fact that he'd gashed his knuckles in the process, he pried out a long shard of glass, his fingertips no doubt being sliced in the process. He got this shard free, but somehow—this was, after all, a dream—it now appeared to Trenor the stranger held a good kitchen knife instead. Gripping it in both hands, the faceless man thrust the knife's blade up under the edge of his jaw. Its tip pierced flesh, glided along bone, drove up beneath muscle. Pennies of blood dropped to his bare chest, and the movements of all the creatures smothering his head seemed to double in speed and frenzy. As he cut at his flesh, began flaying a thick strip along his jaw—a strip colonized by those creatures, though the trough exposed beneath was pure red—the stranger let out a long sustained moan, almost like the sound of a man arriving at climax.

Trenor burst awake with a similar moan.

He lay there sucking at the humid air, and expected Thanh to appear in the doorway as he had the night of that earlier nightmare, but he didn't come. Trenor concluded he hadn't cried out as loudly as he had that other time.

Bedlam, he thought. *Bed*…something.

He closed his sole eye again. His dream squirmed elusively away. As if drugged by his weariness, just before submerging back into sleep he returned to wondering what year it was. What year it would be when he awoke.

PART 14: SCARRED

1: A PILGRIMAGE (VIETNAM, 2019)

IN 2019, ON HIS ALMOST annual vacation to Vietnam (he had missed only two years since 2010, mostly due to financial constraints), Trenor had finally given in despite past reluctance and allowed Thanh to take him to see the Cu Chi tunnels. The two of them had invited Quan to come along, too—this had been before Quan passed away from liver cancer—but he had declined, citing his deteriorating health.

So Trenor and Thanh had taken a bus to this remnant of the former network of Viet Cong tunnels, while Thanh's shy, sweet wife Thuy remained home with their two children in Quan's house, where they all lived. Their son, Tuan, was six. Their daughter, Hang, was four. She loved Trenor; would sit on his lap and tease with plucking fingers that she was going to lift his eye patch, but she never did.

At Cu Chi, their gregarious guide—who admitted to having spent time like Quan as a prisoner in a reeducation camp—explained a series of recreated booby traps; not to point out their horrific nature, but to proudly demonstrate one of the ways his people had broken the spirit of the Americans.

The group of which Trenor and Thanh were a part was mostly composed of white people, some from Europe but also including a number of American vets on a tour geared toward such. They had some bitter remarks to make about these variously spiked booby traps. Trenor hadn't interacted with any of them since they'd disembarked from the bus, when one of them, in noticing his eye patch, had asked if he was a vet, too. "Naw," Trenor had told him. "Car crash, when I was a stupid teen."

"You didn't serve?" this man had persisted suspiciously, understanding they were of a similar age.

"Couldn't," Trenor insisted, flipping up his patch to flash that empty cup of skin. "4-F."

When they'd all streamed away from the bus, he'd heard one of the vets recite a remembered chant to the others: "Kill kill, rape and pillage, fuck the women burn the village, we are Rangers one and all, we are Rangers big and tall."

For all he knew, one of these men might be the killer of Hang Ni, having returned to the scene of the crime to gloat over the murder he'd never been apprehended for, as killers liked to do.

Rice wine, called *ruou*, was made on the site and Trenor tried a little cup of this, though Thanh passed. It was rough stuff, a long way from sake, but he'd had it before. Still, it went to his head a bit in the afternoon heat. It made him wish he was back at Quan's air-conditioned house instead of this place, of all places.

There was a firing range here, where one could shoot any number of guns of the various types used in the American War, for a pay-per-bullet price. Thanh asked Trenor if he cared to do this. He said no, so they and the Europeans merely watched the vets go at it. They fired an M-16 and AK-47 at metal targets, whooping at the pings of contact, growing more excited when after a few initial shots the uniformed attendants switched their guns to fully automatic. Trenor noted the guns were chained to posts—lest a veteran suffer a flashback, he joked to Thanh, go into postal mode, and shoot these attendants.

There were two sections of tunnel that visitors could descend into and crawl through: one fifty yards in length, the other a hundred yards. The group was told the tunnels had been widened for foreign physiques, but from having visited the similar tunnels maintained for tourists at Long Phuoc, Thanh assured Trenor they would still be claustrophobically tight. He asked Trenor if he wanted to go down into one of them.

"Absolutely fucking not," Trenor said. His tone was such that Thanh didn't push him at all.

"Going in, buddy?" one of the vets called to him, before starting down a vertical shaft.

"Too old!" Trenor called back, giving an exaggerated shrug. "I'm sixty-nine!"

"So am I, man!" the vet laughed.

"Too afraid of the dark, then!"

He wondered if the ceiling of the tunnels, down there, would be writhing with a solid mass of the spider-things, even after all these years. And if so, if that nest of the creatures was an after-image of the war that would never fade away; just another preserved relic of the tragic museum that was Vietnam.

2: CITY OF THE DEAD (VIETNAM, 2020)

TRENOR HAD WATCHED VIETNAM CHANGE over the years, though admittedly, not to the extent that it had between 1970 and 2010. Where once tattoos would have been considered a sign of low character, by now it seemed every other young person had one. Western food chains were more prevalent, and in the impressive modern malls that had sprung up in Ho Chi Minh City, one might order a Dunkin Donuts coffee then go a cinema upstairs to watch the latest American superhero movie, with Vietnamese subtitles. Thanh had told him that with the easy availability of state-of-the-art smart phones and Wi-Fi, internet cafés had declined in popularity except for gaming. This was one reason he'd quit working at his uncle's place of business.

For this year's trip, to treat Trenor to something different, Thanh and Thuy hired a van and driver and took Trenor and their children up north a hundred and thirty miles, into the mountains, for his first visit to the city of Dalat. With its generally cooler climate and famous waterfalls, it was a popular destination for honeymooners, and Thanh and Thuy had honeymooned there themselves, in fact, eight years ago. Trenor paid for the van, of course. Thanh was doing well running the Bien Hoa coffee shop that Trenor had financed, and shared a small cut of the profits from as a return on his investment, but he was hardly affluent.

In 2012, in an email Thanh had informed Trenor that he'd learned Long Dien's own Bien Hoa coffee shop had been sold to a new owner. And a year before that—after Trenor had already returned to the States—Thanh had informed him in a phone call of what the news media had disclosed about the fate of Long Dien.

Long Dien, a young cousin, and a girlfriend had been found shot to death in his home. Also on the premises was a dead American citizen, a former refugee from Vietnam; a businessman who frequently traveled back to his home country.

The papers and TV channels gave his name, but it meant nothing to either Trenor or Thanh. The murder weapon, a Chinese handgun, was still in this corpse's fist when police arrived. It was believed one of the gunshot victims had managed to stab him to death with a screwdriver before succumbing to their wounds.

At that time, Trenor had said to Thanh, "An American, huh? But he couldn't have been the one who killed Hang Ni. The person we spoke to at the hotel in Vung Tau said the man who rented that room was white. Whoever this guy was, he was just another shady fuck in Long Dien's universe...somebody he pushed too far."

"Can you imagine, Rick," Thanh had said, "what might have happened to us if we had, you know...that night." He was reluctant to speak too plainly about that night over the phone. Who could tell what his government listened in on?

"We did the right thing," Trenor said. "Thank God, right? Or I should say, thanks to you."

*　　*　　*

It was a long drive to Dalat. They stopped once at a restaurant that catered to road travelers such as themselves, their driver eating with them like another family member. Thanh bought Trenor an iced coffee to go, some pastries filled with mung bean for his kids, then it was back on the road.

As they wound their way into higher terrain, he gazed out at towns that lay like water pooled in the bowls between forested blue-gray mountains, which shaded off into increasingly misted layers. He looked upon clouds sliding down mountainsides like slow avalanches of snow.

Trenor had been quiet for most of the ride, dozing on and off, staring out the windshield when he was awake. (With him being the tallest in their party, and out of respect, Thanh had insisted he ride up front.) Affixed to the dashboard, the driver obviously being a Catholic, was an image of Father Truong Buu Diep, a priest who had been executed by the Viet Minh back in the forties. Trenor had been told once, on an earlier vacation, that the priest had refused to disclose the whereabouts of four other priests who were in hiding, even after being tortured. The sacrificed priest's serene face haunted Trenor. Though Quan had been a Buddhist, Trenor found his thoughts returning to his deceased friend, and the cemetery Thanh had taken him to a few days ago. That place, itself, had been a fair distance outside Bien Hoa, in a lonely rural area.

There, Quan's stone sarcophagus stood on a two-tiered platform, shaded under its own stone awning, reminding him a little bit of the aboveground "Cities of the Dead" in New Orleans. At the front corners of the granite base stood two ceramic lions, the paws of each balanced on an orb; a modern-day version of foo dogs. Behind the sarcophagus stood a stone backboard, inset with a plaque bearing Quan's name and the dates of his birth and death, and a photograph of his face. He had been much younger when it was taken. Not as young at the Tunnel Rat Trenor had first met, but it wasn't the wasted man who he had last seen alive a year ago. In any case, here at least Quan looked serene.

Trenor regretted not being able to get to Vietnam in time for the funeral itself, but Thanh had emphatically reassured him about that. Just as Thanh had reassured him for not being able to make it to his wedding to Thuy. Trenor was collecting social security now, but back then he'd been a new hire as an inventory coordinator for an electronics company, and couldn't get enough time off—nor really afford such a trip. Nevertheless, he'd sent Thanh a generous gift of money. The couple had eventually put this toward their coffee shop.

Thanh had backed off to give Trenor some private time speaking quietly to Quan. Trenor had then lighted some joss sticks and planted them in a basin between two vases of flowers at the foot of the sarcophagus.

His left eye brimming, Trenor had next turned toward two graves that had preceded Quan's here. He approached them.

They were a bit more humble than Quan's, not having that stone awning over them, nor foo dogs, but the pink stubs of incense sticks jutted from the basins at the foot of their sarcophagi. Trenor came close to the side of the one nearest to Quan's grave. The face with its bright smile inset into this one's vertical backboard pierced him like a dagger, expertly driven between his ribs and into his heart.

"Your daddy's with you now, baby," Trenor choked, though he wasn't religious and didn't believe what he said at all.

But then he remembered events he had experienced in this country a decade earlier, and wondered if his words were so empty after all. He turned to face the next grave, which was similar to Hang Ni's. This one, however, of course bore an older girl's face.

Though he had never met her in life, he had met Tra Mi after life.

"I hope you're resting okay now," Trenor whispered to her. "I'm sure you didn't mean for things to end the way they did. I'm sure your dad didn't believe that, either. That's why he put you here, beside her."

Trenor had then seen a tiny black creature crawling up the front of the backboard, weaving between the letters of Tra Mi's plaque…as if it meant to add a new message there, with its body.

He had lunged forward and slapped the stone with his palm. Then withdrawn his hand, and looked into it.

Just a squashed ant. Only an ant.

3: CONTACTING SPIRITS

ON THEIR FIRST FULL DAY in Dalat, their party visited Dalat's Flower Park, then drove on to the so-called Clay Tunnel.

"Tunnel?" Trenor had asked suspiciously.

"Oh, I don't know why they call it that," Thanh had reassured him. "It's a park where everything's carved from clay, with many different themes. It's a recent attraction. I hear it's really cool, Rick."

The day after these outings, understanding that the children might become bored and disruptive at a Buddhist temple, Thuy took Tuan and Hang off on their own adventure to the city's zoo. Knowing from previous vacations that Trenor admired Buddhist temples, despite his agnosticism toward all faiths, Thanh promised to take him to perhaps the most beautiful such temple he would ever see.

Trenor found his friend wasn't exaggerating. At the site of the Linh Phuoc Pagoda he entered a state of sustained awe, despite the daunting number of tourists disgorged from buses. Perhaps most dazzling to him was the three-story tall golden statue of the Bodhisattva of compassion, Quan Am, housed in a building tiled in intricate mosaics created from the earthly detritus of broken shards of bottles and pottery. In its grandeur, this structure was a testament to the hopes and delusions of humankind.

There was much else to see here. In another part of the temple complex, Thanh called Trenor's attention to a small room that housed only a worn round table, and explained, "This is the *ban xoay than ky*. It's like the, ah, Ouija board you have in America. See, you put your hands on it, and close your eyes, and spirits will spin the table top to the right or the left."

"And of course, like with the Ouija board, it's really just your own subconscious that's causing you to move it."

"Who can say?" Thanh said, smiling. "Care to try?"

"Nope." Trenor turned away.

They ascended the seven-tiered Da Bao tower, at the top of which was housed a gigantic bell covered in what were essentially sticky notes bearing prayers, which apparently the tolling of the bell vibrated along to the heavens.

They then descended, back to the ground floor, and were preparing to leave the structure when across a wide floor space that displayed fantastically carved wooden banquet tables and benches, Trenor spotted two monstrous statues: a red minotaur-like figure, and another with the head of a horse. He recognized these figures as the guardians of the underworld. Framed between them, behind them, was a dark doorway.

"What's over there?" he asked warily.

"Oh, yes! That goes down into a spooky attraction, like we went to at Dai Nam. Scenes of hell and suffering, to remind people who come here to stay virtuous."

"Thanh," Trenor said, looking around at him, "if you suggest we go in there I swear I'm going to punch you."

*   *   *

Their driver had been napping all this time in his parked van. He roused and drove them from the temple complex. As they meandered through the countryside, Trenor looked out at a scattering of small horses, wandering free, grazing at the sides of the road. Riding horses in Dalat, accompanied by guides in cowboy hats, was popular with tourists.

Thanh was asking him if he wanted to go see something called the "Crazy House." He assured Trenor it would be memorable.

"I think I'm feeling a little overwhelmed, buddy. Can we decompress a bit? Maybe get a coffee?"

"I'm sorry, Rick, of course! We should eat again, too."

Thanh instructed their driver to instead take them to the Dalat Market. "It's famous!" Thanh assured him.

The market proved to be a congestion of vendors hawking fruit and other comestibles, shaded under awnings and umbrellas, facing onto a kind of rotary. They departed from the parked van to explore, and seek out that coffee and something to eat.

They walked close to a vendor selling seafood: fish and crabs, many of these creatures still alive. Eels thrashed so violently in a plastic tub that Trenor expected one of them to flop free to squirm on the pavement. Only steps away was the body of a large rat that had been squashed under a motorbike's wheels. He couldn't believe no one had thought to scoop the thing up and dispose of it.

Thanh told him, "At night this becomes the *cho Am Phu*. That means 'Hell Market.'"

"Why Hell Market?"

He replied, "That's just what we call night markets here. It gets crazy at night. Well, you've seen the night markets in Saigon before."

"Crazy is right. They aren't there, then you blink, and there they are."

"All kinds of street food…and at night it's more about clothing and souvenirs, instead of all this, uh, produce. But you have to be careful, Rick: a lot of people charge insane prices for food and clothing, and they might try to scam you."

"Not to mention beggars, huh?" Trenor said. Though they made their way along the periphery of the densest concentration of wares, and the accompanying activity, they still had to thread between vendors crowding onto the sidewalk. He pointed out to Thanh three children following after a tall, blond European couple, the boys' faces masks of tragedy. When finally the man stopped, scooped out all the Vietnamese change from his pocket and gave it to the lead boy, the child's face altered completely. He looked down into his hand in astonished delight, spun on his heel and dashed away—either afraid the tourist would change his mind and want the money back, or eager to buy some treats. His companions chased after him, and Trenor chuckled.

"It really isn't a good idea to give money to beggars in Vietnam, Rick. I know it's painful to see them, but if you do, in a second you could be surrounded by more of them."

"I know, Thanh, you've told me." They'd encountered them together before, on a number of occasions, mostly outside temples where these unfortunate souls felt visitors would be more inspired to lend them aid. Whenever he'd passed them, Trenor had tried not to see them, but as Thanh said, it wasn't easy. He'd always felt sick for ignoring their appeals.

Thanh stopped abruptly, as if he'd recalled something forgotten, backed up a few steps and pointed them toward a street radiating off the center. "Let's go that way."

"You see something good?" Trenor craned his neck.

"It's as good a direction as any." As they walked that way, Thanh asked, "Have you thought again about possibly coming to live here for good, Rick? You could have my father's room."

"You're going to need that when your kids get bigger, and they want their own rooms."

"We could expand the house; Thuy and I have already talked about that."

Trenor smiled, wagged his head, as they continued pushing on through all the exciting disorder. "I'm seventy now, guy. You know I love it here, but I don't know that I could handle it in more than small doses. This heat gives me headaches…and there're all these tempting beauties around me. I'm too old to have to look at them all the time and groan in frustration." Thanh laughed at this. "But really, there's the mountains of bullshit to slog through to do it. Not to mention, sorry, but the health care is better back home, and I need to be mindful of that."

"I understand. Well, this will always be a second home to you, right?"

"Yes. Yes, it will. I guess that was always meant to be, from the first time I put my boots down here." He added in a more thoughtful tone, "For good or ill."

"My home will always be your home. It's not just me who sees you as family, Rick. Thuy does, too." Thuy spoke very little English, but through her interactions with him, her thoughtfulness toward him, Trenor fully believed Thanh. "She knows that if it wasn't for you, encouraging me and giving me the strength to ask her out, years ago, we wouldn't even be together."

"Aw, come on, you're giving me too much credit."

"No, really, I—"

A woman who had been sitting low to the ground in a miniature plastic chair, in a shaded space between the umbrellas of two vendors, stood up upon seeing their approach and stepped out in front of them, extending a hand. Trenor almost stumbled to a halt, almost recoiled from her. The woman's entire face was profoundly disfigured with scar tissue, giving it the appearance of a crude latex Halloween mask. She might have been mistaken for a victim of an acid attack, but Trenor guessed it was most likely the result of napalm. Trenor thought of that famous photo of children running, screaming, burnt by napalm, their clothing melting away with their skin. That, and the iconic photo of a prisoner having his brains blown out by a Vietnamese general, had outraged the public about the US's involvement in the war. Nowadays, he sometimes reflected, people filmed even worse atrocities on their cell phones and shared them on gore sites, for people to write witty comments about.

Trenor shook his head, said, "I'm sorry." Not as if he were apologizing for not giving the beggar money, but as if he himself had dropped that napalm. He wanted to look away from her, but her eyes were not just pleading; they were hard and demanding, skewering him with guilt. Her life didn't allow her to be soft. She jerked her hand at him insistently.

"Rick," said Thanh, putting a hand on his arm. "Go."

Trenor noticed another arm floating up toward him, to his right. A second person in a low plastic chair. This person didn't stand up like the woman, but in a weirdly distorted voice they said, "*Lam on…giup chung toi!*"

"Jesus," Trenor hissed, staring at this second beggar.

It was a man, wearing filthy shorts and a shirt unbuttoned all the way to show his wiry white chest hair, his skin sun-browned and physique wasted. Like his companion, the scarred woman, he jerked his hand again. He repeated, "*Lam on…giup chung toi!*" "Please…help us!"

This beggar had no face. His entire head was nothing but a seething ball of black spider-things, so thick upon him they buried his features—substituted for his features.

Trenor turned to confront him, ignoring the woman's outthrust arm and fierce glare. "You. Tell me your name."

"Rick," Thanh said, his hand still on his arm. "He doesn't understand you."

"He does," Trenor said. "He's an American."

The seated beggar tilted the tumultuous black ball of his head a little higher.

"What's he look like to you?" Trenor asked his friend. "To me, I'm only seeing those bug-things. His face in nothing but those bugs. His whole head."

Thanh snapped his gaze from Trenor to the beggar.

His friend saw only those creatures he claimed to be able to perceive? As if the beggar's true countenance wasn't terrible enough. The man couldn't enunciate his words well because he had no lips, just a skull's bared yellow teeth in a raw mask of scar tissue. No nose...just slits in its place. Only holes where ears had been. No hair, as if he had not only been shaved but scalped. He looked like an anatomical model, a cadaver who had healed the best he could after partial dissection. At least he still had eyes. Now, rather than being directed at Trenor, they gleamed up at Thanh as if in curiosity.

"Are you Vietnamese?" Thanh asked him in Vietnamese.

The beggar couldn't smile, so why did Thanh have the impression he was smiling?

"I asked you your name," Trenor said. "It's...Bedlam. Something like that. Right?"

"Uh!" the scarred woman said, prodding Trenor's chest with her outstretched claw, as if she sought to divert his attention from her companion. "Uh!"

The seated beggar said a strange word. Without lips, it would have been difficult for anyone other than Trenor to make out. Having switched his gaze back to Trenor, the beggar said, as if in recognition at last, "Polyphemus!" His eyes shimmered, as though with mirth.

"Rick?" Thanh said. "What's going on?"

Trenor started forward along the sidewalk again, brushing past the woman roughly. Thanh had to jolt himself into motion to keep up. Thanh threw a look back over his shoulder. The scarred woman, still standing, had spun and growled a curse after them. The seated beggar had turned his flayed head to watch them hurry away.

"Coffee," Trenor said. "You promised me coffee."

4: FALLING INTO THE SPIDERS' CAVE

THEY FOUND THUY AND THE kids were back from the zoo, relaxing in their hotel room. The children sat on one of the two beds, playing a game on their mother's phone. On the wall-mounted TV, Thuy was watching an episode of the 1986 version of *Tay Du Ky*, the Chinese story *Journey to the West*, dubbed into Vietnamese and extremely popular here. This was episode 21, *Falling Into the Spiders' Cave By Accident*. A row of beautiful women were firing streams of silk from their bejeweled navels, laughing uproariously, while some richly-attired man struggled against the thickening webs.

"What the hell?" Trenor muttered.

Thanh's son, Tuan, looked up from his game and motioned for Trenor to sit down and watch the program, too. He and his sister weren't proficient in English, either, though Thanh was teaching them.

"Not right now, buddy," Trenor told him. They had just come to let Thuy know they were back; then Thanh told her that he and Trenor would be talking in Trenor's own room, next door.

Tuan waved to Trenor on his way out, and Trenor waved back. Tuan's hands, and feet, each possessed only two digits, like mirrored thumbs. The girl Hang's hands and feet were normal.

*   *   *

"What was it with that beggar, Rick? Why did his head look like that to you?" Thanh had told him what the man looked like to him. He'd suggested that the beggar had been disfigured by a fire or napalm, like his female companion.

"I don't think so," Trenor said, pacing the room while Thanh sat in a chair by the window and watched him. "I've dreamed about him, several times...I know I have. Back in 2010. I don't remember much, but I'm getting this image of him cutting his own face off, with a piece of glass or something."

"Why would he do that?"

"Because of the bugs. All those bugs on him."

"He said something to you. What was it?"

"Polyphemus. It's the name of the cyclops—you know, the one-eyed giant in the *Odyssey*. That's what cinched it. I'm sure he called me that in the dreams."

"Rick, you've proved to me you have these…strange gifts of sight. But why would you have dreamed about a beggar in Dalat, ten years ago? Why would we just happen to meet him here, now?"

Trenor stopped pacing to look directly at him. His eye blazed with intensity. "Fate, maybe? Our fates, woven with his? Maybe you have gifts of your own and you just don't know it. Maybe we all do. It was your idea to come to Dalat. It was your idea, all of a sudden, to go down that street…remember?"

"Looking for *coffee*, Rick. Why would my fate be tied to a beggar you dreamed about?"

"Because he's an American. And he's the man who murdered Hang Ni."

For a moment Thanh said nothing. Then, at first, all he could say was, "Rick…"

"I know it, Thanh. I feel it in my fucking core." He thumped his sternum. "I've told you, I've never stopped seeing those bugs. But I've never, *never*, seen anything like this man. He is walking evil, Thanh. It's him." He nodded. "It's him."

"But…if he's American, how could he have lived here all these years?"

"You told me he's got nothing but scars for a face. Could anyone even know he wasn't Vietnamese? He's learned Vietnamese…some, at least. He lives as a beggar. Somewhere along the line, either in Saigon or here, he hooked up with that woman. She helps look out for him. He lives in the shadows."

Thanh absorbed this, and Trenor was quiet for a bit, knowing his friend was working toward saying something. At last Thanh said, "I remember a news story, a few years ago. An old British tourist ran out of money and overstayed his visa. He was living as a beggar in Saigon. But he was out in the open, and he had a face, so the government finally brought him in and arranged a visa for him, and deported him."

"I've heard that after the war, some Americans decided not to go home. They stayed here, out in the sticks…took wives. Guess they were written off as POWs, MIA. This guy here—he's some kind of MIA, to whoever he left back home."

"Rick, are you certain about this?"

"You know me. You've known me all these years. I don't take this lightly. I am deadly serious. If I wasn't sure of it, I wouldn't tell you I was."

"Of course you wouldn't," Thanh said, turning his head to look down into the street. It was overcast in Dalat, threatening rain, which seemed to be the norm for weather here. Finally he looked around again at Trenor. "So, what do we do?"

Trenor wagged his head. "Nothing."

"*Nothing?*"

"I didn't tell you this so you could go cave the guy's head in with a hammer, Thanh. Just…just to let you know. Let you know, I guess, for some closure. Let you know the guy has paid somehow, at least. Clearly, he's lost his mind. He's living in his own hell."

"He should live in *my* hell," Thanh said through bared teeth. "The hell of my choosing!"

"No. Listen to me. You got no dad, now, so I'm taking over." Trenor jutted a finger at him. "You have a beautiful family. You aren't going to fuck that up. And I'm not going to go after him, either."

"He could kill more children! Maybe he already has!"

"With a face like his, no one's going to get close enough to him for that. He's done, man. You told me yourself. He's nothing but scars on bone. His mind is gone. This man is dead already."

"Maybe we could report him."

"We're going on my…whatever, intuition. The 'gift.' We have no evidence. Thanh, like I say…the man is a walking corpse."

Thanh digested all this for several long moments, before finally grunting in assent. "You're right, Rick. You're right. I told you back in Saigon that night, when Long Dien was killed—we need to let it go. We can't let it destroy us, too. These demons have a way of destroying themselves."

"They do, man. Karma, or whatever. They do."

Thanh smiled up at him wanly. "Thank you for telling me, anyway. It's true…it does give me some kind of closure."

Trenor stooped down, opened his room's mini fridge and drew out two 333 beers. "*Ba Ba Ba*," Trenor said, handing one to Thanh. "Let's drink a beer together, like we did that night."

"Okay, Rick," Thanh said, smiling again. He popped his tab, and clinked his can with Trenor's. "Cheers."

"Cheers, brother. Love ya."

"Love you, too, Rick."

0: THE INVISIBLE MAN

BEDFORD AND HIS "*BA XA*"—as he called Hong, though she was not his legal wife—always stayed partly into the night at the Dalat Market, to take advantage of the next wave of shoppers who swarmed to the *cho Am Phu* to buy clothing and souvenirs and kitchen items and whatnot. Their days were long, and hot and dusty, but he was used to it by now; it was all like an unending dream, its sounds a drone, its sensations deadened.

In addition to begging from tourists—come here from other parts of Vietnam and from other countries—he and Hong helped out her niece Le, who sold huge Chinese grapefruit, called *buoi*, heaped in a cart under a weathered umbrella. They helped her set up in the morning, helped her close down come night after the tide changed and the Hell Market swept in. Occasionally, if Le felt ill or had an errand to run, she let Hong handle sales, but she tried to avoid this lest her aunt's appearance discourage business.

Actually, though, Bedford had the impression customers often gave them business *because* of the maimed couple, out of pity. Locals, especially. Le did okay for herself, as these things went. Bedford and Hong lived in a small back bedroom in the house where Le and her husband and three children lived, in a side street not far from the market. Le's children were accustomed to the faces of their aunt and "uncle." The children helped improve Bedford's Vietnamese. They liked to take turns playing schoolteacher, and he would pretend to be a student, and they would laugh at his feigned childish innocence.

Sometimes the youngest girl, a pretty little thing named Trinh, having known him all her life, would climb into his lap, but it made Bedford uneasy and he'd gently lift her away. If she sat upon him too long, he'd begin feeling tickles of itchiness in his scars. He hadn't felt profoundly itchy since the night of transformation. He didn't want to feel that way again.

Tonight, as they did seven days a week, he and Hong left the market and made their way toward home on foot. Le had already gone on ahead of them on her motorbike. As they went, Bedford and Hong never held hands, never joked in a flirtatious way; Hong had a very serious demeanor. Still, she allowed him to make love to her whenever he desired it. It was always in complete darkness, of course. Though they were used to each other's face, bringing them that close together in stark light would be too uncomfortably like confronting themselves in a mirror. Also, without lips, Bedford couldn't kiss her. He relied on fantasy, and memory—as much as he could access his memories, that is—to excite his mind while his body took its pleasure.

He remembered the night of his transformation in broken fragments, like a scene reflected in scattered mirror shards.

He'd earlier that evening bought a bottle of vodka at a convenience store near his hotel. The brand was Men' Vodka. It was so cheap, Bedford joked to himself at the time, they couldn't even afford an "s." He'd been drinking it right from the bottle as he paced his room, until he'd finally passed out on his bed. And dreamed...

He couldn't remember now what the dream had been about, but that man from today—the man with one eye—he'd been in it, hadn't he? *Polyphemus.* But how was that possible? And how had the man recognized him, too?

All he knew was, still drunk, he came awake from the dream in something like a panic. While he'd been asleep and vulnerable, innumerable insects had crawled onto and covered his face. Cockroaches? Bedbugs? Lice? They were burrowing under his skin. Into his meat.

He bolted up from the bed. On the table where he had left the half-empty bottle of vodka rested the good kitchen knife he had bought at the Ben Thanh Market. Frantic and babbling, he picked it up, and looking at his reflection in the black expanse of his hotel room's sliding glass window, he began cutting into, carving away, the parasite-infested flesh.

He must have been screaming. Then he must have lapsed into unconsciousness. He looked up dazedly from where he sat on the floor, his back propped against the wall below the window, saw the hotel counter man and a housekeeper standing over him, the woman with a hand clamped across her lower face and the counter man saying, "*Troi oi! Troi oi! Troi oi!*"

Bedford flopped his head to one side and saw a small red mound beside his hand. Was that...was that a pile of flesh? Weren't those ears, atop it?

He retched hard, once, but held himself back from vomiting. He was afraid the strain of it would stop his heart.

"Doctor," he slurred, finding it hard to annunciate the word for some reason. Blood from his mouth overflowed his chin. He saw the front of his shirt was entirely soaked, sticking to the skin of his chest. The folds in his shorts had collected marshy tributaries of blood. He pretended to take his own pulse, to illustrate his meaning. "Bring a doctor here."

"Police?" the counter man said. "Call police?"

"*No*," Bedford groaned. He found that he was weeping in agony, tears blending with the flowing red. "No police...please. I give you money, understand? No police. Get doctor here. I give you money."

The man and woman lifted him under the arms and got him onto the bed. They then engaged in an agitated conversation. The man was gesturing and apparently ordering the woman to remain with Bedford while he went to call someone. She glanced fearfully back at Bedford and plainly refused. Finally the man gave up and they both fled from the room, leaving him alone and conscious and bleeding onto the pillow and sheet.

Quietly sobbing, Bedford reached a hand up to his face, felt at his nose. He had no nose. "Ohhh *God*," he moaned at this discovery. But his priority now was staying alive, and by lying on his back in this way, blood was running down his throat and he thought he would drown in it. He had to roll onto his side. In a fetal position, he blacked out again.

He surfaced from a deep black pool to find a man leaning over him, cleaning his face with gauze pads soaked in saline solution. He already hurt so badly that he couldn't even tell if this contact made the pain any greater. In and out of consciousness. He came up for air again long enough to feel his face, his head, being wrapped in thick layers of gauze. The wound where his nose had been was packed so that he had to breathe through his mouth only. Elastic bandages were then wound around his head to bind all the gauze in place. The counter man lifted his head from the pillow to help the physician accomplish this.

"Bring me my wallet," Bedford tried to say through the mask of bandages. They didn't understand him. He attempted to sit up to get it himself. "Money," he croaked. "I give you money." He was afraid they would go to the police if he didn't buy their silence immediately.

But the physician pushed him back down onto the bed, with a gentle but firm hand on his chest. "No...no. Money later, okay? You lie down."

He wanted to tell them some story, so they wouldn't know he had done this to himself. He'd been set upon by the pimp of a hooker he'd underpaid. The jealous boyfriend of some girl he'd slept with. But they wouldn't comprehend his lies, and anyway, the counter man would know who had come into the hotel on his watch.

"I need morphine," he wept. He pantomimed an injection in the crook of his arm.

"Okay," said the doctor. "Yes, I do, before." He reached around to retrieve a vial of pills, held it up and and rattled it.

The counter man finally left, perhaps to tend to more mundane business. The physician sat in a chair and watched him with concern and a grim kind of interest. Bedford wanted to smile at him, but he would never be able to smile again. He did manage to say "thank you" sufficiently well that the physician nodded in acknowledgement.

He remained in this hotel for an unknown number of days. The physician returned occasionally to check on him and change his dressings. He gave Bedford antibiotics, but he cut off the morphine, ignoring Bedford's pleas for more. The housekeeper, despite her obvious revulsion, brought him bowls of a thick savory porridge called *chao*, which he drank through a straw. After a while, Bedford could sit up in a chair by the window in his room, even pace his room when he was alone. He tipped the housekeeper nicely. He paid the physician more money each time he came. He gave the counter man a generous sum.

But he was running out. By now, had his wife checked her missing husband's bank account for activity, noted the withdrawals? Blocked him from further access? He forgot how much he might have left. What was he to do when there was nothing?

Eventually, he went outside to find out. First, of course, he tested the waters. Stood out on the sidewalk for a little while, in front of the hotel, before going upstairs again. People passing by would stare openly at him. "What's the matter?" he would laugh in English in his marred voice. "You never met Imhotep before?"

When he could finally take a taxi to an internet café, and go into his online banking, he assessed the gravity of his situation. "Not good," he mumbled to himself. "Not good."

"*Troi oi!*" said a cocky young man who sat down beside him. In Vietnamese, not realizing Bedford was an American, the boy asked, "What happened to you?"

Bedford turned to him and exclaimed, "I'm Claude Rains, my friend! You never saw *The Invisible Man* before?" And he barked a laugh at his own joke.

*   *   *

Begging on the streets of Saigon, he had met Hong. He had been attracted, if that was the word, by the similar devastation of her face. At first she had gruffly tried shooing him away as competition, but he had persisted in sticking close to her—as if stubbornly courting her—until she had come to notice that the two of them seated together on the curb garnered more attention, and hence more money.

They had joined forces, and lived very roughly in Saigon for over a year, before finally Hong had arranged for a niece in Dalat to take them in. Le's husband had begrudgingly driven his car all the way to Saigon to fetch them and bring them to their new home. Le and her husband had plainly resented them at first, but the blighted couple had ultimately proved their worth by helping with Le's sale of *buoi*, and they always turned all their earnings from begging over to Le's husband, knowing that their basic needs would be seen to.

JEFFREY THOMAS

Thank God for their sense of loyalty to their families, Bedford had often thought. For his part, he sometimes remembered he had a wife back in the States, a legal *ba xa*, but he couldn't always recall her face, or her name.

On this narrow back street, more an alley, there were no tourists to gawp at him in horror, or turn their eyes aside in shame for not handing over a few notes. Small groups of people sat out here in tiny plastic chairs, eating, smoking, people who saw this strange couple every night, and some nodded and uttered greetings. Even these people believed he was Vietnamese, though he had admitted to Hong he was not. He hadn't revealed much more about himself, however. She either believed that his wife back home had died many years ago, or she didn't much care. She knew him only in his transformed state. Sometimes, he felt that was all he knew of himself, too.

It was a full moon tonight, and that disc was lustrous. It shone straight ahead in this tight channel between buildings, a beacon leading them home. Bedford tilted his face toward it and thought about all the dead Selenites up there on its surface, in their crumbling ruined cities, killed off by the common cold brought to them by the explorer named Cavor. He wished he could see that movie again. Hong liked fantasy, too, but her tastes ran more toward dubbed Chinese costume dramas like *Journey to the West*, with its adventures of Sun Wukong, the trickster Monkey King. Sometimes Bedford would tease Hong by imitating the cackling laugh of the actor in Sun Wukong's simian makeup. He could almost make her laugh, doing this. Almost. Le's children, of course, would go into hysterics.

A motorbike entered the alley behind them. They walked closer to one side to let it pass by them. They shambled past the open fronts of homes, spied people sitting inside watching TVs in rooms that were more than humble, but cozy in their way. In one home, a family seated on the floor was taking turns singing karaoke into a microphone while reading the lyrics off their little TV. Life didn't get any better than what he was seeing, not really, did it? Bedford reflected that he was probably as happy now—happiness, realistically, simply meaning contentment—as he had ever been in his life.

He decided he wouldn't trouble Hong for sex tonight. She seemed to be trudging along extra slowly, appeared extra tired. Unlike him, her wounds were not just on her face but also on her back and down one arm. Most days they caused her pain, and he was growing more concerned for her as she aged. She was fifty-six now.

"*Ban co met khong?*" he asked, turning his head toward her.

"*Du ma...khung qua,*" she grumbled to him. "Motherfucker...so crazy!" She added in Vietnamese, "I'm tired *every* day!"

Bedford chuckled. Her usual grouchy manner. But tonight, on their thin mattress, if he so much as moaned in rolling over to change position, Hong would groggily ask in her poor English, "*Anh,* you pain? You okay?" And, less than half awake, she'd begin massaging his shoulders.

258

They had only a short way longer to go to get to Le's house. Another motorbike was approaching behind them; again they shifted over to the right to let it pass. The bike slowed to a stop just a bit ahead of them, though, and its rider twisted around in his seat to address them. He wore a scuffed silver helmet and across his nose and mouth, a cloth mask of the type often worn by bike riders to protect them from breathing in exhaust and dust in the streets. This man's face mask had a plaid pattern.

The rider exclaimed in Vietnamese, "Hey, I'm glad I found you! I was looking for you! You left something, back at the market."

"Oh, you have something of ours?" Hong said, stopping before the bike. "What is it?"

The man swung himself off his seat. Watching him, Bedford could swear he'd seen the rider earlier that night, several times in the market. Hadn't he been the one who sat a long time at a little table not very far from their cart piled with its cairn of pomelo, slowly eating some dish he'd bought from a street vendor, his mask at that time pushed down around his neck? Bedford had dismissed the man's frequent glances as being mere curiosity at the condition of their faces. In fact, in his mind he had retorted to the man, "Feast your eyes—glut your soul on my accursed ugliness!" It was a line from the 1925 film *The Phantom of the Opera*. Bedford, movie buff that he was, felt he rather looked like Lon Chaney's Phantom. Well, he was worse than that, really, but...

This was that man, then, wasn't it? The same silver helmet, same plaid face mask? Not that those were unusual items, in this or any other Vietnamese city. But there'd been something funny about that man's hands, hadn't there? Hard to make out from a distance.

"Yes," the masked rider said, answering Hong. "Something you forgot!" He stepped toward them, began reaching into a deep pocket of his loose-fitting trousers to retrieve whatever it was he said he'd found. "Here it is." He closed the distance between them, withdrew the object from his pocket, but it was Bedford he suddenly moved toward instead of Hong. Bedford looked down at the hand that was flashing toward him, as if to check it for abnormalities, but in the splinter of a second he was focused more on what the hand was holding.

It was a good kitchen knife, specifically a paring knife with a four-inch blade, not very long, but the rider punched it into the side of Bedford's neck with such force that it went in all the way to the handle. Bedford grunted, fell back a step, but already the rider was jerking out the blade. Somehow he held onto the knife's handle firmly with his strange hand. The rider stabbed him again, close to the initial wound, again slamming the blade all the way into him.

Hong cried out inarticulately, threw herself at the rider. Bedford wanted to shout to her, warn her not to do so, warn her to flee, but blood was washing down his throat and all he uttered was a spray of red mist. The rider turned toward Hong and slammed her in the sternum with the flat of his free hand. His strange free hand. Thrust back, Hong pinwheeled her arms and fell down hard on her tailbone.

Not too far back down the street, two men and a woman leapt up from the table they'd been sitting at while playing with their smartphones, close to the left wall of the alley. The woman began screaming cries for help. The men began running toward them.

Bedford fell onto his back on the pavement. The rider went down with him, on top of him. He drove his blade into Bedford one last time. Using both of his odd hands, he tugged the knife's handle—the blade still buried in Bedford's neck—to one side with all his strength, as if it were a stuck lever.

Then, before those two neighbors could reach them, the rider scrambled to his feet and rushed to his bike. Clambered astride it, started it, got it surging forward.

Hong reached Bedford before the two neighbors did. One of the men tried chasing the rider down the alley, but the bike picked up speed. At the end of the alley, it turned the corner sharply and was gone.

The other man squatted down near Bedford, but a few feet away as if in respect, giving Hong room to kneel at Bedford's side. His phone still in his hand, the neighbor punched the number for the police.

"*Anh!*" Hong wept, her hands on him, as if she might massage him back to sleep. "*Anh! Em yeu anh! Em yeu anh!*" She told him she loved him. She had never said that before to anyone…had bitter, sullen, scarred Hong.

Bedford wanted to say he loved her, too, something he likewise had never said to anyone with sincerity, and he wanted to smile up at her, but he had no lips, and he died.

5: ACCURSED UGLINESS

THAT MORNING, THE WHOLE FAMILY had walked down the street from the hotel to a nearby restaurant for breakfast: Thanh, Thuy, their two children, and Trenor. It was customary here that people had *pho* for breakfast, and Trenor went with that only because no Western breakfast was represented on this particular menu. He longed for eggs and sausage or bacon, but in the end, he did like *pho*. He broke and scattered herbs into the broth, generously squirted in hoisin and sriracha. As long as he had his iced coffee, all was well.

After they'd eaten they returned to the hotel, and Thanh told Trenor they'd go out and explore more of Dalat later, but for now they should probably rest some more. Trenor had agreed, and so he had returned to his room to nap. In this sultry heat, it was natural to want to nap.

He'd slept, he realized later upon awakening, for hours. It was now well into the afternoon.

Trenor went to Thanh's room, knocked, was admitted inside by his wife. But Thanh wasn't there. The kids sat half-watching cartoons on TV while they also watched a YouTube video on their mom's phone. They were giggling, ignored him.

"Where's your husband?" Trenor asked Thuy.

Thuy made a sad, pouting face, and said, "Girlfriend!"

"Thanh? No...no, sweetie," Trenor told her. "Thanh wouldn't do that to you. He wouldn't cheat on you."

"Girlfriend," Thuy moaned.

"No," Trenor insisted. "No girlfriend."

They waited for Thanh's return, though, for hours. Trenor even returned to his own room, showered, came back and kept Thuy and the kids company. "Hungry? Eat?" Thuy asked him. The children Tuan and Hang watched him expectantly.

"Sure, let's go," Trenor told them, acting jovial. "It's on me."

Thuy was considerate enough that she had their rented driver, who had his own room in the hotel, take them to a restaurant where Trenor could order a hamburger. He did like Vietnamese food, but…God, a *burger*. When he took his first bite into it he moaned, and the children laughed at his orgasmic reaction.

They returned to the hotel and waited. Waited. Thanh's children fell asleep on the bed they shared. Trenor sat in their room, in a chair by the night-black window playing with his iPhone, while Thuy sat on her bed watching HBO with the TV's volume tuned to a murmur. The two didn't talk, didn't really know how to talk, but they waited for the same thing.

Finally, a light rap on the door. Trenor started to get up but Thuy threw herself to her feet and got there first. She opened the door and Thanh stepped in. He glanced toward Trenor, but spoke in Vietnamese to Thuy, apologizing profusely for being gone so long and for not answering his phone when she'd repeatedly tried calling him. Trenor guessed he was also reassuring Thuy he had no girlfriend in this city, had been to no massage parlor.

At last, he leaned around Thuy to say to Trenor, "I'm sorry, Rick. Have you eaten?"

"Yes, no worries, I'm all set. But you had your wife here pretty nervous. Where were you?"

Thanh came further into the room. He was wearing a T-shirt. The denim jacket he'd been wearing over it this morning was gone, but not even Thuy had noticed this. He said, "After what you and I talked about, I needed to be alone for a while. I needed to absorb it."

"I understand."

"So I asked the desk person where I could rent a motorbike, and he let me rent his own. I just drove around to get my head clear. I drove completely around Xuan Huong Lake. I stopped and had something to eat." He shrugged. He came over to sit in another chair near the window, a small table between him and Trenor.

"So…did you get your head clear?"

"Yes. I think I did."

"Good."

"But Rick, if it's okay with you, would you mind if we leave here tomorrow morning? This place is a bad memory for me now. I know that there's so much more I promised to show you…"

"Not at all, Thanh, not at all! I perfectly understand. Whatever you want to do."

"Thanks, Rick. Then I'll have our driver turn us around and take us to Mui Ne. It's a beautiful seaside area, about three hours from here, going south again."

"Sure, sounds great. Thuy and the kids won't mind?"

"They won't mind."

Trenor nodded, looking into the handsome face of his thirty-year-old friend, who had in actuality become a closer friend to him than even his father had been. Trenor felt love for him, as if he were also his adopted son, and he felt a deep stab of sadness as he watched the spider-like creature that was crawling through the hairs of Thanh's right eyebrow.

ABOUT THE AUTHOR

JEFFREY THOMAS IS THE CREATOR of the dark science fiction setting Punktown, in which many of his stories take place. His short story collection *The Unnamed Country* is also inspired by his many visits to Vietnam. His novel *Monstrocity* was a finalist for the Bram Stoker Award, and his novel *Deadstock* a finalist for the John W. Campbell Award.

Thomas' stories have been selected for inclusion in *The Year's Best Horror Stories XXII* (editor, Karl Edward Wagner), *The Year's Best Fantasy and Horror #14* (editors, Ellen Datlow and Terri Windling), and *Year's Best Weird Fiction #1* (editor, Laird Barron).

CPSIA information can be obtained
at www.ICGtesting.com
Printed in the USA
LVHW010323290122
709499LV00002B/178